The Dry Spell

Ryan Loup-Glissant

The Dry Spell

Production copyright FurPlanet Productions © 2023

Text Copyright © Ryan Loup-Glissant 2023

Cover Artwork and illustrations © Slate 2023

Published by FurPlanet Productions
Dallas, Texas
www.FurPlanet.com

Print ISBN 978-1-61450-587-7
Electronic ISBN 978-1-61450-598-3
First Edition Trade Paperback

Table of Contents

The representations of religion within this work are myths to ponder and not truths to live by…unless you need to.

For Kim…far more patient than you needed to be.

Prologue

Six Days Later

Mammals of the law gathered within the North Side Chicago warehouse, checking their claws for dirt and shining badges for the press. The air was heavy with ruddy malted oak and something else that made the teeming creatures nervous.

Illinois Attorney General Brundage held court, thick fur spilling over a too-starched collar as he howled. "Accept this promise. When the scourge of intoxicating liquors have been poured from every den of ill repute, from the wet boardwalks of Atlantic City to San Francisco, only then will God's creatures know the tranquility intended for us," the German shepherd showed vengeful carnivore's teeth. "Until that day, the men and women of this city must be resolute in virtue."

The dog waved a clawed finger airily and a news weasel's flashbulb immortalized it for Chicago's newsstands from the Gold Coast up north to Hammond down south. The raccoon beside the photographer scrawled quickly and chewed tobacco noisily.

Brundage's tail switched behind his checkered trousers. "Last night's violence will see every last one of the mob's feral scofflaws cuffed and caged. Through the hard work of our officers of the law, supported by agents of the Bureau of Internal Revenue assigned to Prohibition enforcement, the good people of Chicago will see justice done, and a better world for our cubs."

The weasel took another photograph as the State Attorney straightened his tie, his white-spatted, black-clawed foot mounting an overturned barrel charred by flames. The speakeasy they'd hauled it from was smoking rubble a mile away, a tragedy that claimed many lives.

Brundage posed proudly above the spoils of war as cameras flashed and glanced back at the line behind him. "Beatie, will you do the honors?"

Towering over the posed line of officers, the Special Agent heading the local office of the Prohibition taskforce scowled around his pipe. The bear's eyes met those of a brown-furred wolf by the door, whose expression begged for anonymity. That lone survivor of the LaSalle massacre kept back from the flashes, but further still from any shadows.

Beatie roved the line of officers instead. "Henderson was first through the door at the Wacker speak and was nearly shot, so I'm going pass it to her."

The mountain lion who came to take the axe had a cold gleam in her eye. Her team fared well enough at Wacker Drive, busting up tables, registers, heads. As for the raid at LaSalle…this charred barrel was its only tribute.

"Now?" she asked the news mammals.

The weasel thumbed-up, the Attorney General nodded. The camera caught the oak splintering.

But not what came after.

There were gasps as an abattoir stink stabbed every nostril. The barrel's cracked lid slipped free, and its contents roiled upon the cement floor, spreading fast.

Henderson saw what was beneath her, dropped the axe and bolted, tail a kite. The throng of reporters fled as sickly corruption chased them. The State's Attorney hollered, soaking his foot in horror as he hopped past the barrel's mouth and slipped to his knees, scampering for escape.

The contents of the barrel oozed forth with a sickening shine and the dirty brown wolf standing alone took a shuddering breath, remembering horrors twisting in the dark and the flames that claimed them.

Head Agent Beatie had retreated to one side of the room, pipe lost. "It's like a window into hell," he breathed.

The wolf said nothing, shutting his eyes tight against the charnel slick spreading forth before opening them to a thud at his feet.

Brundage, the top dog of the law in Chicago, had fainted dead away.

Chapter I

Poured Forth from The Ark

Bucky Cavali sampled the speakeasy's rank air with black fluttering nostrils, turning his slender vulpine head just so. This game was starting to bore him, and the sisters were waiting.

The tilt of his russet head was deliberate, a false tell for the badger fidgeting as Bucky regarded his own cards, a queen of diamonds and two sixes. Three cards up on the table, a third six he'd use, a four that was useless. The ace concerned him.

A soft palm lit across his free hand, velvet fingers teased. The doe's nails were cool as Bucky glanced her way. Celeste was bored too, not bothering to hide it. Too bad.

He glanced up from under the rim of his brown felt bowler. "You lookin' half-hearted friend. You maybe thinkin' of droppin' out?" His Great Lakes accent bit the thick basement air.

The badger's eyes narrowed, and he waved an empty glass. Bottles never left the bar, so the empty glass went away and another with amber glint filled his brown mitt.

Even in weak lamplight, Bucky could see they'd swapped the whiskey for cheaper hooch. The badger was one more sheet to the wind and wouldn't notice.

Bucky would. Nobody tried that shit with him. The speakeasy's crew knew who he was. On Bucky's arm, his doe took a disinterested glance at his cards, hinting nothing. Bucky liked her for that. He dropped another ten dollars.

The badger sourly regarded half his week's mill wages atop the rest and Bucky knew he was already in mourning for what he'd lose. The badger's cards went flat.

"Son of a bitch," the badger rumbled and hoisted himself from his chair.

"Move on, stripe," the fox straightened the ivory tie poking from his high-buttoned, pinstriped vest and showed all his teeth before scooping his winnings delicately as eggs from a farmer's coop. Lips tickled his ear. "We going soon, Bucky? I don't like the smell in here."

Bucky reached back to grab his matching striped coat. "Get us two top shelf from the bar and we'll go. I gotta be somewhere." Bucky watched her white tail bob within the tight folds of her emerald flapper dress as she went to the bar.

With the table cleared, he was gifted with time to think in the din of clinking glasses and hooting laughs. So much to gain if he played all his cards right, and all he had to do was keep Johnny Torrio in the dark for a week longer. Bucky drew a pocket watch from the vest over his white starched shirt. His only truly smart suit would soon be one of many, his pockets about to get flush.

He felt heady just thinking about it. The doe turned back with the barman's ambrosia and Bucky smiled even as Celeste's ears cocked; her attention dragged across the room to where a commotion was turning heads.

Bucky caught it too. His heart stopped. "Pigs."

The speak's door came right off its hinges as brass buttoned bodies hurled through it. A cougar growled loud enough to drop ears flat. "This is a raid!"

Mammals leapt up and chairs fell. Glass broke as the back exit packed with snarling bodies. Bucky shoved grimy cash into his vest pockets as Celeste dropped her drink. Bucky hurried over. "Bar," he growled.

The doorman had fallen asleep at the switch or been bribed, though it didn't really matter to Bucky with a Prohee wolf grasping for his tail's white tip. The wolf huffed as Celeste's hoof cracked his jaw on her own dive over the bar. The back wall had been cleared of contraband, bottles dropped to shatter in a recessed chute below by a marten tender who'd already split. The fox and doe hustled past the swaying curtain after him.

A dark dusty passage ended in a swinging door. Late spring air was crisp on Bucky's whiskers as he pushed through to a soot-bricked back alley and held the door as Celeste leapt past him.

They could still hear cops, barking taunts of contempt as they rounded up those to be damned with fines. The fox and doe ran until they could hear no more.

Two blocks east put them in the shadow of the Chicago loop at Jackson and South Wells. New-smelling steel buckled as a car thundered on the elevated train, sparks raining down on their heads. Celeste winced as she slowed to a walk, delicate fingers massaging her brow for another half block, her toe hooves not making a solitary sound in the fuzzy noise of downtown's night.

"Hold up, doll," Bucky instructed as he regained his breath, digging a case from his pocket and feeling along a smoke's length for quality of roll. "You catch a spark back there?"

Celeste turned, her expression moving from pained to annoyed. "Shouldn't we keep moving?"

"Hey, relax." He snickered. "Weren't for me, your herbie ass would be cramming a paddy with another dozen suckers, hungry carnies mostly."

"My knight in shining armor," her almost imperceptible French accent cleaved sarcasm. "I would have talked my way out of anything worse than a fine."

She hadn't been breathing hard after the two-block sprint from the speak to the grey bulk of the Federal Reserve Building and Bucky was just now getting his own under control. He lit his smoke and it breathed bright. "Might have cost you a bit more." He appraised her from slender ankles to pert bosom. "Good as that tail may talk, it's still smart you stuck with me innit?"

"Sure is, Bucky." The eyes above her grin were cool as she turned away.

Celeste had been referred by Madame Lowry at the Four Deuces with promises the doe was discreet, delicate, all that. Strange that Bucky'd never met her before tonight despite frequenting Johnny Torrio's upper floors often.

He'd show her some fun. He just had to get business out of the way first. He licked a canine. "Come on. I need to make a quick stop on the way back to my place. I won't be two minutes." Bucky beckoned her south past the loop. At an alley's mouth, a squirrel hobo stared into an empty bottle in craggy mitts like President Harding himself was gonna pour it full.

"Spare a nickel, toddy?" a hare croaked from an alley-side gutter, one ear peppered with scars. "I lost my hearing in the Great War."

Bucky was disgusted. "That's bushwa. Wasn't no herbies fightin' the Huns. You only got the vote this year." Bucky glanced at Celeste. "Congratulations incidentally," he added.

"I was a field nurse and…" a coin hit tin. "Thank you."

Bucky glanced back at the doe. She met his gaze balefully, saying nothing. A charitable whore. Didn't that beat all?

He knew full well that poverty wasn't so far off that a shot missed could put him on these streets. Fortunately, he wouldn't be fleeing the cops and the Prohees for much longer. 'Year from now, he'd be paying them off instead.

Two more blocks south into the weaker light led them to row houses. "I knew you had digs that needed work, but this is…" Celeste didn't frown, but she didn't have to.

Bucky tried to keep his hackles from raising his coat. "My place is nicer. There are friends here I need to see."

Bucky led her down a short alley and fished a key from a planter next to the door, opening slowly to minimize the groan. "Stay here. I'll be quick."

The doe said nothing, her eyes fixed on the dark inside.

The smells at this particular door were interesting. Dried juniper berries bled out just under the stink of trash. The air stirred the senses in a way that Bucky could feel, though he couldn't tell if it was the air's taste or the tangible spark of his excitement. Dim lamplight illuminated the filthy kitchen beyond the door where a pot boiled on the stove, diminutive against the battered copper apparatus that glinted in one corner. The sisters were together, waiting.

"You came to see us make dinner, tu et ton ami. Boilin' and bubblin.'" The sister named Grisand drawled in twisty bayou through a yellow grin. She shrugged her polka-dotted housedress and pointed her stubby otter's paw to the kitchen's counter where beef sinew glistened under gas lamplight. "Want some? We gonna add legumes later."

Bucky stepped inside and closed the door on the doe slowly, removing his bowler hat. "Not what I came for, ladies. It's a business call."

"Ahh," Leguna whistled through her slim coyote snout over by the meat, a bloody apron over her night robe. The cleaver was a rusty digit in her paw that thudded on the block as she spoke in rough Georgian. "I tell you, Baliosi, he wunt comin' back fer you. Got hisself a slinky one to play wit' when he's done here." Leguna gazed past the fox with one good eye. Its wooden mate didn't turn, fixed to an eternal distance.

Over by the copper still, there was a rustle as the youngest one rose from the shadows in a brown caftan. A mason jar of semi-clear liquid filled a paw. "You came to see us catch a spirit." The young wolf's eyes were blue as robins' eggs. Only the wart displacing her whiskers on the right side of her muzzle marred a flawless face. She stooped with a weariness that belied her youthful appearance. Her accent, unlike her sister's, was strangely midland. "What else may you steal from our breasts if we're not careful?"

Bucky didn't know what that meant. He shrugged and clapped his paws together. "Come on, girls. I've put a lot up to stake you 'cause word is you're the best shiners in the Midwest." Bucky couldn't remember where he'd heard that, but word circulated far enough that it could only be true. He scuffed his claws on the floorboards, watching where he stepped. "What've you got for me?"

Bucky took the jar from Baliosi, unscrewing it gingerly. The moonshine's smell hammered at the fox's nostrils, giving off hints of its pedigree. Juniper notes of gin overpowered, dashed with lemon peel clouding it just slightly. The contents swirled like something volatile.

"Take you a sip," Leguna said from the stove, wood eye unblinking as her other eye gazed deep into him.

The otter approached and to Bucky's surprise, reached past him. "If you don't like it, we cut in some soda pop or somethin'."

Bucky glanced back and saw that Celeste was in the room with him, not having made a sound. "I told you to wait outside," he growled.

The doe said nothing, gazing into the concoction, which Bucky noticed seemed to stir as though alive with its own glow.

They'd have words later. Right now, he needed an unbiased tongue and does like Celeste getting loose off this stuff could make for frequent customers if things lined up right. "Have a sip, why don't you?"

Celeste glanced from eye to eye, expression guarded. Gingerly she accepted the jar and took a wrinkling sniff before taking a swig of the sisters' gin. Her expression told everybody that it burned all the way down.

"Calm you down, cher?" Grisand soaked the doe with watery eyes. "Or pick you up?"

Celeste gazed back at her, seeming a bit anxious. "It's good. Merci." She blinked, her jaw working around an aftertaste. "What were the herbs I tasted?"

"Juniper. Makes it taste like gin," Baliosi said with a shrug.

Bucky scratched his chin. "Let's just get some oak in that. Soak a couple boards or somethin' makes 'em think it's whiskey. Isn't that what you usually make?"

"That's what you want us to cook," Leguna clicked her tongue, "then that's what we cook."

The doe had seen too much, and Bucky was fuming but had to know for himself. "We should go." He reached for the jar the doe held and she handed it over. Bucky took a long voluminous draw, hammered himself into a swallow, and nearly choked. "Mama, that's strong stuff. Still like the whiskey better."

Lightening crackled from whisker to tail as the drink flooded outward from the fox's tongue. There was a quiet in the air as though everything had stopped.

"Not as strong as the paws about you," Leguna said, her eye closed, wood sentinel blank.

"New paths found through stout new brew," Grisand chuckled, wetness shining her lip.

"And when those paws become jaws, the passage of laws reveal hopes and fears are all true." Baliosi grinned and broke into cutting laughter.

Grisand peered at Celeste thoughtfully. "Careful cher, dis the kind of night for dreams and nightmares to acquaint." She winked at the doe.

The room became warmer as Bucky felt the spirits work at him, fuzzing his senses. Damn, this stuff was good. He could down a whole bottle right now if it wouldn't kill him. Hooked at one sip. Whispers filled his head. Have you tried the sister's elixir? You can only get it at one of Bucky's places up North. Dime a sip, dollar a cup. Leave on a cloud you'll never come down from.

Too many flaskers thought of speaks in volume. More with less was the answer, Bucky knew. "More with less is the future."

"Will you be saying that when the lights go out?" Celeste muttered.

Grisand and Leguna snickered, Baliosi looked amused.

Bucky didn't care, locked in the vault in his head where fortunes grew, and all the suits were mohair and the Rolls Royce that brought him to his uptown penthouse had a sinful waxen glimmer. He'd be the most civilized animal off God's Ark and wax any cop that couldn't take a dollar and walk. His time was coming fast. He could smell it.

They could cut the product with a little water, maybe something fizzy. They'd make a mint with so few bottles to move, pop-up speaks coming and going faster than the pigs and feds could ever hope to catch up. All he needed was muscle.

Leguna punctuated the moment with another drop of the cleaver, parting beef messily and making Bucky jump. "I heard the Prohees have help from outside sources. Informants or somesuch. Lotsa gin joints gettin' rough company," Leguna said conversationally.

"Bastards," Bucky said, riding the numb white joy. "Knocked over a speak' tonight." He stared into the depths of the gin bottle and watched its light sing to him. "Less competition, anyhow. You've agreed to my price per?"

Leguna smiled. "That'll do." She glanced from Bucky to Celeste and narrowed her eyes at the latter. "Hopefully all you transact tonight is successful."

"Probably," Bucky said disinterestedly. "When are you girls moving?"

Baliosi scratched her nails together as though lucre grew like moss underneath them. "Day after tomorrow. We'll be on the move often."

"Soon as you can send the first couple dozen, I'll be ready." Bucky tapped the jar as he handed it back. Baliosi's finger brushed his as she accepted it.

Bucky coughed. "Keep up the quality. I'm not selling your product to the usual riffraff."

"Of course not," Leguna replied, offended.

Grisand licked her jaundiced lips. "Only the best spirits go in our pot." She speared Celeste with another glance. "We know where to find them."

"Have some ready before you ladies leave town, wouldya?"

"Of course. You'll be right pleased."

"Your drinkers much appeased."

"And best you move quick lest your intentions be seized."

Bucky nodded. The sisters were brilliant cooks but the rhyming thing... "Well, alright then."

He left, Celeste quietly followed, her arm in his. They went north up Madison, where Bucky's apartment was on a second-floor walk-up in fired brick the color of his fur.

"So, that is your big plan? That's what's going to make you money?" Celeste muttered.

"And even more of it." Bucky muttered, mind working furiously at how to handle what she'd seen. "Play your cards right, I'll keep you around. We can have all kinds of fun."

Celeste walked through the door to his sparse apartment like she owned the place. Bucky noticed that she kept from showing herself at the window when she crossed to lower the blinds. What, doe couldn't be seen in a place like this?

"Neighbors hear you scheming in here?"

Bucky sighed impatiently. "Nor fucking company, neither. 'Old bat downstairs is deafer than a cracked bell. Look are you gonna—"

"Johnny Torrio know you're doing this? Does he get a cut of your action?"

Bucky felt his blood grow cold and the worries he'd been stewing overcame front and center. She was not supposed to ask questions like that. Any whore should know *never* to ask a question like that. He let a tooth show as he snarled. "Of course, Johnny will get a cut of my action, just like you'll get a cut of my action. The kind of cut that is depends on how quiet you are."

Veggies, the vote notwithstanding, always knew their place or learned it. His father taught him that before kicking him out. Bucky saw himself as ahead of his time, that a rooter could be a cut above if they knew their place and didn't try to get too far above their station. The Ark that saved them from the flood kept the delicates on the lower deck, so the big book said, not that Bucky was actually religious at this point in his life. The carnies ate the body of Christ during the flood while the veggies abstained and became less close to God, so the orthodox went on. Bucky didn't buy that but if it made her more obedient in the sack... "Get that dress off." Bucky didn't ask.

Celeste removed her emerald dress, not artfully like the girls at the Four Deuces where Johnny hosted his best performers, but quickly and efficiently, tossing it on the bed. Her eyes stayed with his the whole time, smile thin as a razor, lips pressed hard together. "You've got a lot of big plans, don't you Bucky?" Her brassiere shed quickly and joined the dress. Underwear laced like sea foam slid down to expose her Venetian figure, white chest from breasts to thighs, faded starlight speckles dotting her oaken pelt. She didn't need to pose for him.

Bucky had his coat, tie and vest off before he knew it, and his shirt was coming undone one button at a time.

"I've got great plans." His white chest rose and fell with his heart quickening.

Celeste glanced him up and down. "I don't know if Johnny would be happy with all of them. Would he, Bucky?"

His hand came up, claws out, and he smacked her hard. She rolled with it, falling naked onto the bed.

"The hell is wrong with you, doe!" He tore his shirt off. "Do you understand that I go to bat for goddam 'rooters every chance I get? I pushed for the veggie vote when my mom and pop said it was sinful, I read veggie papers, hell, I tip yours better than anybody at restaurants. You think those are little things? How'd you think I got the nickname Bucky in the first place?" He wrestled his belt open. "Here's a clue; long ears, first crush. That wasn't easy on my reputation."

Celeste stood again. A cut marred her jaw. It didn't bleed and her smile didn't waver.

Bucky was getting hot. His mouth felt like a slippery thing inside out, nerves dancing at the verge of panic. "I just wanted to have a little fun to celebrate my success, and you stupidly suggest I've said too much and who you're going to say it to. Why would you go and do that?" She'd already covered the window, isolating them both. She wanted him to do things to her, shut her up. Who would be so crazy as to think this was a game?

She caught his eye again and this time he didn't look away.

Black crowded out the whites, then conquered all, eyes going from arresting slits to wide depthless wells.

Celeste's jaw yawned, fangs sliding free with a cold wet glint as a hiss slipped from her throat.

Bucky Cavali's mouth and tongue went slack. In the inky depths of those dark spheres, he saw his reflection, confusion melting into terror.

Faster than a doe could possibly move, she rushed him. His head struck the doorframe behind, stars leaping through his skull. A hungry, breathless mouth found this throat.

The teeth that sunk into him were burning needles. Bucky couldn't scream.

The room rose as he sunk. The floor held him close as the thing called Celeste dragged its fox toward the bed. Bucky Cavali twisted and saw his claws drawing desperate furrows in the floor planks that became shallower and shallower as the veil came down and he let go.

***

Henderson was on the front line. When the door gave way and they hustled in, the cougar's bugle-horn yowl made Crawford Cain's ears flatten. "This is a raid!"

Chaos followed. Drinks shattered, tables overturned. Billy clubs came down on some badger sod who tried to wade through the blue line and a fox and doe leapt the bar, the doe kicking Crawford's lupine partner Charlie in the face, sending the brown wolf's fedora tumbling.

Crawford would have gone after the mooks, but his hands were full with a cat who scratched at his eyes and shouted obscenities to shame whatever tobacco-spitting tug-boat crew had smuggled her hooch down Lake Erie. Crawford shoved her away, muttered a line about ceasing and desisting that went unheard. He grabbed for a ferret who slipped by, claws snagging the throats of two others at the door. Crawford felt the eyes on his back and knew at least a few beat cops had seen the ferret get past. That was on him. With a snarl, Crawford went after him, leaving the heavy air of the speak behind for the fresh air snap of the night outside.

Crawford saw the ferret, tan coat flapping, bound down the street. He wore no hat and Crawford felt his fedora lift off his head. He'd likely never get that back. "Stop! Bureau of Internal Revenue!"

The ferret wasn't stopping. Crawford drew his Colt 1908 from the holster bouncing under his left armpit, regretting it immediately. If the ferret saw the gun he wouldn't stop for breath 'till the Indiana State Line.

The slinky bastard dove left and crossed the empty street, splashing a puddle with one hammering foot. Round a mailbox, Crawford leaned into the wind and followed. He heard a snarl, like the ferret was trying to swear, and hunched as he ran, nearly on all fours like a godless feral.

Crawford followed him down a side street, then right again. The metallic taste of downtown's air dissipated. Row houses split to the gapped teeth of hovelled lots. A service station stunk of gas fumes, a closed fruit stand let out the scent of rot. Despite the ferret's now loping gait, Crawford was gaining.

Twisted wrought iron demarked a border, resolving into a field of stones. The ferret leapt it, coat tearing. Crawford holstered his gun, grabbed metal, and vaulted, crouching low enough upon landing to smell the cemetery's clay. Dates of birth and death were worn low in the shallow moonlight and the ferret was limping for the taller memorials now. He'd sprained something. Crawford's lupine senses were dialed, and his blood was up. He was done chasing this mook. "Bureau of Internal Revenue." He caught his breath as he slowed. "I'm taking you into custody. For violation of the Eighteenth Amendment. Under the Volstead Act. Put your mitts on the nearest tombstone. Don't resist or…"

The ferret stood his whole height. Or tried to. Something was different about the bum who'd slipped past Crawford minutes ago, blocks back. His frame was stooped, limbs distended, claws cruelly pronounced on gnarled fingertips. The jaws that opened and caught the moonlight bore teeth like kitchen knives.

"What the hell is wrong with you," Crawford breathed. And then the ferret's eyes rolled blankly, divorced of awareness.

"Hands on the stone." Crawford's gun was a reassuring weight. The ferret's teeth locked together around a pink tongue that was starting to bleed. The bastard wasn't drunk, Crawford realized. He was something else entirely. "I mean it! You're under arr—"

Fangs wide, the ferret lunged. Claws gripped the wolf's coat and jaws found Crawford's warding left arm, held out ahead of the gun arm in defence. Pain lanced his wrist as teeth pierced his knuckle and palm. Crawford fired, four deafening shots punched the ferret's chest and neck.

The mustelid fell against him, steely fingers clawing rends into his coat, eyes rolling back into his head. Crawford shoved him off. The creature's chest rose and fell three times before it settled.

Crawford dropped to his knees as silence fell. Backup was blocks away, the nearest telephone was anybody's guess. He settled back against the cold of a tombstone and slid to the earth. The semi-automatic came to rest in his lap.

He wrenched his necktie loose, wrapping it around his wrist and palm. Blood soaked it quickly. Taking a moment to confirm he was alone with the dead, Crawford reached into his jacket, deep past the holster and the pocketed badge he hadn't even shown.

"You were just going to get a ticket," he snarled pitifully. The flask was in his good hand and he used his teeth to unscrew it. His gunshot would bring witnesses, so he wouldn't have long to put his nerves back in place. Tipping back, he drew on the whiskey's warmer bite and his heart stopped hammering. He stared into the black June sky, counting the few stars he could see beyond the pale moon.

Truth bit hard. Whatever plagued the weasel, whatever he'd failed to notice back at the speak, Crawford had killed a suspect over a goddam ticket.

Good thing his wife wasn't here to be ashamed of him. She'd had the good sense to stay in Virginia while Crawford went out here to clean himself up.

What would he say to his son? A cold well rose up through Crawford's tail against the tombstone. He could have clubbed the ferret, reasoned with him. Possibilities mounted and fled one by one.

Crawford's partner Charlie caught up with his scent minutes later, nursing a bump on his jaw. Crawford's worry had surrendered to numbness, his stowed flask now drained.

'Good news was one of the beat cops on the raid found Crawford's hat.

***

Donovan Calvert closed his eyes and slid his fingers around the steel ram's head of his cane. The ebb that came from the earth below the car was curious, fading quickly when first the ferret, then the Prohibition agent hurried past. A disturbance to be sure, but not the one he was seeking. Neither escapee nor pursuer paid the rabbit any heed, resting as he was in the passenger salon of his Rolls Royce a few dozen steps from where the speakeasy was being turned over.

The liveried possum in the driver's seat turned back, inquisitive under the oily bill of his chauffeur's cap. "Do you want me to go after them?"

"No." Donovan folded his white-slacked legs, perfectly matched to his ivory-furred feet. His cross-Atlantic Oxford cadence was firm and his long ears folded back in contemplation. He drew a grey handkerchief from his matched jacket. "What we're looking for is still in there, one at least, maybe more. Keep the engine running in case we need to make chase."

Edmond nodded, flexing spotless gloves around the Roll's steering wheel. Donovan knew he wanted to get those hands dirty again. Edmond was always anxious to demonstrate his resourcefulness.

Two officers stood outside the non-descript, below-grade door as the raid proceeded. At one point a window broke, but otherwise, the drama was confined to snarling and cries from within. When dozens of scofflaws wanted to leave and the American constabulary wanted them to stay, things tended to get messy.

Watching the chaos reminded Donovan of school rooms he'd sat in as a young rabbit, absorbing maths, learning Imperial history, and quietly scoffing at the Church of England's take on the word of God. There'd been a mutiny on Noah's Ark in the storm between the ages. A lost battle for control of the wooden refuge saw some animals cast out of knowledge to wallow wordlessly in the new world's mud as ferals, while the chosen were lifted from the burden of original sin to accept knowledge and language as an earned blessing.

Such a metaphorical battle was now waging twenty feet away. Those who sought escape from the confinements of Prohibition were being trammeled by the forces of godly righteousness. He could imagine the windows in the speak breaking as portholes soaked by endless storm. Who the heroes truly were in the greater story was anybody's guess. Truth was, nobody in that whiskey-bathed basement was fighting the right battle. There were vices beyond vices to terrify them all.

Donovan fingered the cane, feeling the ebb, sniffing the essence as his quarry approached.

The first patrons were being led outside, most of them sullen. One cat swore up a storm, already cuffed. A police wagon yawned wide.

Donovan twisted his hands 'round the cane, ears up then down again with sensations he couldn't describe to a layman despite a decade of oratory refinement back in Oxford. "One escaped."

"The ferret, sir?" Edmond tensed to go after them.

"No, someone else." His senses expanded as more drunken louses were dragged outside. "However..."

"Yes?"

"Stop the engine and come with me."

Edmond disembarked and held the door of the Rolls for his master. They moved quickly. The less ceremony the better.

Downtown Chicago's air was thick with animal sweat and traces of blood tinging the wind. No doubt the carnies, of which the police force was almost exclusively comprised, had their teeth wet. Truncheons had been well used.

Police and Prohibition agents read charges, wrote up tickets, sent grumbling lawbreakers on their way with muttered curses, their fun over until they found another covered lantern and gleaned another clever password. So it went.

In the first weeks of the Volstead Act prohibiting alcohol, the detained would all have gone to jail, but cells had swelled beyond capacity. Only those who resisted were brought in now, and the wagons were filling with the wretched and unlucky.

Donovan ignored them. His quarry stood patiently with the smarter crowd who'd surrendered with minimal fuss, intending to take their fines and melt into the night. He approached a brass-buttoned otter brandishing a club. "A word."

The otter barked at those lined up to do so straighter and turned to him. "Certainly, Mister Calvert."

The twenty Edmond had bribed him with was still poking out of the idiot's breast pocket. Donovan didn't trouble himself with it. "That raccoon there, second from the end," the rabbit muttered. "He's known to me. I'll pay for his ticket but would very much like to spare his family the ignominy of his shame tonight. Have him brought to my car."

If the otter smelled something off in that appeal, he didn't care to know more. "As you'd have it, Mister Calvert."

"Don't let him see me." Donovan had already turned away. "He knows I'll be cross."

The otter grinned sharp teeth. "Worried he'll get bit?"

The ribbing at Donovan Calvert's vegetarian species was something he'd learned to absorb in circles such as this one. Carnivore nepotism had likely put the man in that uniform. "Something like that."

Another cop pulled the raccoon out of line. He was confused, large-eyed, small tie poking out of a tweed vest and bulky trousers. Donovan had to admire his comportment as the raccoon traded glances with a mink lass in a flapper who waved goodbye, clearly the raccoon's companion had things gone differently. Lucky girl.

Donovan returned to his car and was situated out of sight when the cops brought the raccoon to Edmond, who doffed his cap and beckoned the raccoon enter.

"Who's in there?" The miscreant was suspicious but didn't bolt with Chicago's finest still present.

Edmond gave nothing away. "A friend."

The raccoon's heightened senses no doubt detected the rabbit, just enough of his smell concealed to keep Donovan's identity tenuous. The black-masked muzzle poked in and fixed Donovan with a squint. The cops wandered away. Edmond was ready.

The raccoon gasped as the dagger found the small of his back, stabbing upward into the lungs, forcing him into the car and down on the floor. Donovan's cane was at his jugular in a moment, pinning the miscreant down. For any mortal, the dagger wound would be fatal, even had the weapon been typical. The victimizer turned victim struggled to move as his teeth drew back and the fangs sprang forth.

"Drive, Edmond, I have him."

The dagger was withdrawn, the raccoon's eyes rolling back in his head from a sear of agony. The blade that Edmond tucked away was bloodless and smoking as though shoved into a fire, the wound through the fabric cauterizing. The car's salon filled with the crisp scent of spent corruption and hide sizzled where the steel cane tip pressed on the raccoon's throat. Donovan smiled thinly as Edmond seated and started the Rolls.

"When the first truncheons drew blood, you were thirsty, no doubt."

The viper's hiss from the raccoon's throat promised death if he rose. Donovan stepped on his head, claws digging at the raccoon's ear. "Your friend was lucky, wasn't she? The mink in the blue flapper? I know you had special plans for her."

Under the cane, his quarry's snarl turned to mewls of pain. The dark pools of his eyes had become supplicant, begging.

Begging for pity.

Donovan's long ears flushed with anger. He knew the creature could smell it, would be thirsting after the wine pulsing through them now. "I know there are many of you in this city, aimless and hungry. How you came to be this way is of little interest. How you'll *come* to be means everything."

The dark eyes rolled to search his, confused.

Donovan sighed. "A law has been passed by the Martyres of the Black Well, far more consequential than any scribble in Washington. You'll come to know my name as its arbiter in Chicago and beyond." The English rabbit smiled flat pitiless teeth as the Rolls took them away. Streetlights flushed and ebbed through the plush cabin. The elevated train beat its steel thunder briefly overhead.

The place his quarry would be taken for education was close by. "I've come to save you from yourself and teach you the ultimate truth. As goes the whiskey still, so the mammal's vein. Make no mistake my friend, this country is now dry."

Chapter 2

Predators at Night, Predators at Dawn

Celeste walked the streets of the South Side alone, every fibre tingling with the life racing through her. The night spoke. Songs of the city carried while the fecundity of creation and decay filled her nostrils from the parks and promenades and burgeoning streets. She weighed nothing, as though the tiniest flex of her ankles could hurl her moonward to gaze back down on the teeming edifices of the city. Chicago was alive and she could feel it.

This would not last long. Celeste was of the flesh again and to a place of the flesh she would go.

She would not go ignored. A dog of German stock out for a night stroll regarded the doe over the firefly of a shortening cigarette and finding no words that were proper, merely tipped his panama hat as he met the unattended doe's stare. He parted his gaze from hers with silent disapproval.

She resisted the urge to laugh at his paternalistic carnivore's disdain, hungry heart on his sleeve, projecting neediness within a presumed sense of innate superiority. Bucky, for all his passing charms had just been one more like this one in the end. She'd almost miss him.

But not quite. Her stolen blood sang as she approached Twenty-two twenty-two South Wabash St, passing the sweet rankness of a cigar shop to drawn shades on the tall window next to a narrow featureless door. Smells and sounds from within were blocked from the casual passer-by, but her heightened sense picked up countless fast beating hearts like tremors through the brick and mortar. Sighs and laughter bled through the cracks. The party was well underway.

Celeste passed the saloon door to the second smaller entrance to the adjoining unit. Three knocks on the oak were met by the parting of a curtain to the dark and a discerning eye. A grey marten in a faded blue suit held the door wide, tobacco gritting his breath. "You are expected."

"Thank you, Van."

Celeste entered the low light of the saloon. Noses twitched over whiskey and gin, dull eyes over cheap suits followed her. The bartender nodded to her, all teeth and no smiles. "Al said to go up."

Nobody ever offered her a drink. She was business to the slobs on the rail and she knew full well where their eyes were roving. "Al or Jonny coming to meet me?"

A spotted glass preoccupied the dog. "I dunno."

Through the curtain and up. Pricier vices were higher. On the next two floors she barely glanced at the roulette wheel and craps tables draining the full pockets of careless marks while Jonny's men waited for somebody to whine just a little too loud. At the fourth-floor vestibule she paused.

Scents loaded the place that spoke of exertion and excitement as pent-up creatures squirmed on long benches, ties loose and eyes needy. Springs creaked and a wall thudded behind them.

This was supposed to be Celeste's place of business as far as most of Johnny's cronies were concerned, with only his right-hand Al the wiser. Celeste's real work for Torrio was a mutual secret since he had other people taking care of any problems he wanted made public. That was just one lesser lie on top of others much more germane to her true nature. No one here knew that secret.

A mink held court in the hall between the rooms, wrapped in a short skirt and dark satin bustier, watching the benches and snapping her fingers under a sleepy hound who was filling a book with figures. "Garret! You clueless ass. Bianca just passed you with a client in hand!"

There was a space before the mutt muttered. "Yeah?"

"She's a vixen. He was a tod. Two foxes! You know we can't have kind with kind."

"Oh right."

"Get in there and split them off! I don't care if you have to fuck him yourself."

Paws thundered down the hall and the mink turned to size Celeste up. "Johnny wants you in room six."

Celeste flicked an ear. "I don't take clients here, Lowry. You know that, Johnny knows that." The mink didn't know *how* Celeste took clients either, to her own benefit.

Lowry showed teeth. "I tolerate your flagrancies because you're obviously one of Johnny's favorites, but he doesn't want you on your back in there. Make sure you close the door. Gertrude pulled duty with a noisy one." Close by bedsprings squeaked harder.

Curious, Celeste took Lowry's direction. The scents of sex exuded from every crack in the plaster as she found the door and pushed it open. Next to a small cot waited a table and a phone.

Even on a blood high, the realization was somewhat infuriating as she picked up the receiver. Goddamn dogs. "What, I have to talk to you by phone from another room in the same damn place?"

The South-side Chicago Outfit's boss sighed, a languid thoughtful speaker by nature who never hurried his words and didn't hurry others. "Celeste. News I take it?"

Best she keep this short. "You were right. A move was being made. I handled it."

There was a grinding of teeth as the old corso dog absorbed that. "Al had a feeling. Stupid fuckin' tod. Anything we need to help your crew with?"

Johnny and Celeste's working relationship went back to New York. He'd always clung to the assumption that Celeste had carnivorous assistance or even guidance. She wore the mask of a doe whore pretty well after all. Like that German shepherd on the street all this city's carnivores wore the same face, were of the same mind.

Their assumptions had their uses. The money was good enough and the absence of questions even better. "You know I have it taken care of."

"Good girl," said as though to one of his bitch nieces due for a treat. "So, you saw the operation?"

Celeste's sated contentment wavered just slightly. She had only the occasional dealings with the Belle sisters and knew not to cross them. However, Bucky had come to work with them was a secret he took to his grave but they kept their discretion about what Celeste really was and she owed them that courtesy in return. "It was...meager. I don't think you'll need to be concerned about them."

"Bucky felt it had enough potential enough to stab me in the back, though, am I right?"

"The merchandise wasn't anything special. Same stuff boiling in tubs all over town. He was going to scale them up."

That was a lie of course. Liquor, like the regular food she could barely taste, gave Celeste little in the way of intoxication, nothing even remotely approaching the explosive rush that an influx of life's crimson elixir provided. She knew well that the sisters offered some brews she didn't ever want to try.

"Just give me an address," Johnny insisted.

A wall shook with impact, a swear in Italian, the client and his pro changes positions. "I'll have to retrace my steps, but I'll get it." She of course knew exactly where the sisters were but would make sure Johnny's people found some empty flat and forget the whole thing.

There was a sound of disappointment on the other end, a show for one or another of his cronies seated in the Four Deuces' top floor office with him, shrugging at the screw-ups of vegetarian deer whores whose meager work was very likely finished by others with fangs.

His next words betrayed the sentiment. "Finishing off bums who step out of line or competition what don't wanna understand the rules may be hard work for a doe on its own, but you could at least pay closer attention to details."

The chide bit, tampering with the elation she'd been enjoying up to that moment. Stupid mobster dogs and their arrogance. He knew full damned well how resourceful Celeste was but admitting that, hell having her in the same room to have that pointed out, was more than the dog would stand. Their relationship in this moment, him in a smoke-filled room and her between caterwauling animals getting off, had never been made clearer.

How quickly he forgot. Her incidental audition for Torrio had come in the dark back in New York six years ago. He'd expected to have his cock sucked but she'd dispatched a rival's assassin with a pistol shot from a range of ten yards, or that's how Torrio recollected the event.

In truth she'd done the deed at zero yards with a paralyzing bite followed with a gunshot to the chest to cover her tracks. Torrio knew he'd found a vegetarian whore who could kill discretely and never thought to suspect any more.

That was how she needed it to stay but that made it no less infuriating. She could drink Johnny dry without a care if she didn't need him just a little more than he needed her. "I'm real sorry Mister Torrio. It won't happen again."

"See that it don't, okay doll?"

"Thanks Johnny."

"Lowry will see to it that you're paid for "entertaining" my ex-employee before he left abruptly for Albuquerque." Albuquerque had many of Johnny's ex-employees and enemies. Must be a nice place. Celeste's found herself musing on how far out she'd have to go to bury Bucky's corpse. "Bye, Johnny."

Italian floated through the line as he ended the call.

Celeste had no warmth to burn her ears, but wished she had. For Johnny's carnicentric old-world way of conducting business, nothing ever changed. France had been over a century ago and introduced Celeste coldly to violence in the name of one presumed natural order supplanting another. Fucking dog carried himself like he was royalty, wouldn't *he* enjoy a meeting with the guillotine?

Heading out, Lowry reluctantly passed a stack of five- and ten-dollar bills. She invited Celeste to grab another client to thicken it, but Celeste declined. Those impatient for relief could go down the street. Johnny Torrio ran more than one bawdy house, after all.

Still annoyed, Celeste kept to shadows on the way back as dawn's first crack was mere hours away, Torrio's disdain biting at her heels.

His money was enough, sometimes. On other days she wanted nothing more than to show him or one of his trigger mutts her real power, make them serve her needs for a change. It was fun to contemplate, seeing the true nature of the world behind the facade they built themselves, with an immortal doe as master.

On the bed, Bucky Cavali's corpse lay where she'd left it, nose chalky and bloodless, whiskers limp, claws still clutching at phantom floorboards. She realized that she hadn't drunk him empty, but the effect was nonetheless the same. "You'd have been fun to play with for a while," she muttered as she gathered bedsheets around the body. "If you could only see through your own pretentious merde."

It was, for Celeste, a night for dreams as well as nightmares to come true.

Bucky Cavali jerked into wakefulness with a laboured gasp that let out no breath at all.

***

Donovan Calvert woke to the first rays of dawn and blinked as his muskrat servant finished drawing the blinds wide. It was, as per instructions, precisely seven in the morning.

His estate on the North Gold Coast had no immediate neighbors, no one to see him throw off the folds of his bedding, stretch naked in sunlight's first kiss and slide out to start his rigorous calisthenics.

One corner window was a baleful eye onto the distant shore of Lake Michigan. Cars motored past one or two horse-drawn carriages up Lakeshore drive just beyond his gate. The other window presided over a small mixed orchard that curled around the south of his mansion to the secluded garden beyond where the morning's most important work was underway.

The caps of Chicago's taller buildings, the Woolworth building and the water tower notable above them, sewed the southern sky with clusters of apartments and more affluent brownstone chimneys approaching. The fingers of new projects rose deeper south still, and it was at these spears of steel that Donovan squinted. A world was pulling itself out of the ground to touch the sky and his own labours were making much of it happen.

With blood pumping, he slipped his robe around tightly muscled shoulders, wandering past trinkets on a fireplace mantle commemorating his many successes in America. A framed certificate from the steelworker's association sat next to a golden plate stamped with citations for charitable work representing Chicago's business sector and a piston flywheel forged of his mill's own steel. The wheel bore the Calvert Steel logo of the rabbit-borne lightning bolt, a spark stolen from the ancient Gods used to light the first forges in some myth he'd been partial to when he founded the company back in Preston, England

Rabbit's gods had been tricksters in the early Celtic myths, always managing to exceed their station. Much like in the real world Calvert navigated, they always earned the most begrudging respect for doing so.

But Donovan Calvert forged his own sparks and let no one forget it.

The knock at his bedroom door was perfunctory. Donovan closed his robe's sash. "Enter."

Edmond Virage entered, last night's chauffeur uniform surrendered for a butler's bow-tied starch. In addition to the possum, Donovan employed four Muskrats, a mongoose and two hares in various capacities. The pecking order was straightforward. All kept to their tasks and informed Edmond for passing on to the master of the house.

The possum had Donovan's attention right away. "Call from downtown?"

"No sir. Nor the mill."

"Concerns in the garden?"

The possum shook his head. "You did mention last week that our benefactors in Cologne intended to check on our progress here."

Donovan felt his heart skip a beat. The people to whom Edmond referred had no commemorations on his wall, no direct association with his growing steel Empire, no family ties. But they were the most significant players in Donovan's trajectory. No words were spoken of the Order of the Martyres of the Black Well beyond the closed doors of his mansion, nor his offices. Donovan took a breath. "Have they sent a telegram?"

"No sir," Edmond took a deep breath. "There was a knock at the door some ten minutes ago. Their representative is in your front foyer with a rather large valise."

Donovan had long cultivated a disposition of eternal readiness for the unexpected and allowed himself no losses of composure before subordinates. That failed him now as grey-tipped white ears fled back on his skull. "What?"

Edmond shifted his feet, his stiff suit seeming to itch. "I should add that she's impatient to see you."

Donovan dressed quickly and was nursing a rising anxiety when he descended the Edwardian-balustraded staircase to the grand hall below. It was empty but for a smattering of furnishings suitable for hosting. The figure pacing back and forth in the space made it feel quite full.

The lioness was light on her feet, long oxblood dress swaying as she stalked, tufted tail lashing. Her thick, short muzzle was fixed between smile and sneer and golden eyes followed the comparatively diminutive rabbit down without a blink.

Though unpracticed in the language, Donovan recognized a muttering of Bavarian German. Of her pacing he heard not a sound. "Good morning."

"My husband told me that you sleep in," she said in clipped English. "I'm surprised to find he was right about something."

They'd never met, but Donovan knew right away who she was and forced a smile to his lips. "I keep late nights. Your husband knows that already having kept those nights himself."

"Christof found you sprightly, if distracted under his tutelage." Evelyn Haften, known more formally in shrinking European circles as Countess Evelyn von Haften, towered over the rabbit by at least a foot or more when their feet were both sunk into the same Egyptian carpet. "You did the best you could of course."

Donovan couldn't resist letting his eyes dart from hers to the art-decked walls and rafters of his estate's front hall. When he'd first steamed to America, he'd brought less than two hundred thousand pounds and the rental agreement for an upscale apartment in New York. The Von Haftens knew as well as any on the Martyre's council how quickly his fortune changed here. "I did indeed."

Her golden eyes narrowed. "Et vos hic servanda ad inceptum tuum redi?"

Donovan sighed.

Evelyn looked disappointed, her expression barely changing. "Tradition is important, Donovan. I need to know that you've not lost your way in this foreign wilderness."

"Ego nihil perdidi. I've lost nothing, not even the Latin."

Her ears perked. Donovan smelled the proximity of Edmond descending to the landing above him. Donovan raised a hand towards a door to the west drawing room. ""I have much to show you, new opportunities in America to aid the cause. Edmond will ensure that we are served refreshments while we talk. Are you staying in Chicago?"

Evelyn's head turned back to the foyer. Leather-bound luggage rested by the rack that bore her tanned coat.

Not a word in advance. Donovan's unease quickened his pulse a bit, but he refused to let it show.

Behind the drawing room's oak walls, staff scurried to prepare an appropriate repast for their carnivorous guest. A servant brought them tea service and vanished with the flick of tail. "The staff have all been deputized as a special trust, all the usual guarantees taken and the unreliable weeded out. I've ensured nothing carry on within these walls that betrays the Martyre's long-term objectives. Or mine."

"Would that be two separate things, Donovan?" The Countess lapped her tea and set it down with distaste before leaning back on the filigree-upholstered bergère chair. "Are there problems with your steel operation?"

"Not in the slightest." Donovan nibbled a shortbread finger, leaning back on his own wing backed Georgian in maroon. "It's all above board. That operation, however, has helped refine…advances in our cause that I look forward to demonstrating." Donovan smiled.

If her interest was piqued, the lioness declined to show it. The flick of her tail was dismissive, even impatient.

The charcuterie board arrived with cold cuts, cheeses, and warm rolls. Donovan left the salami and prosciutto alone and watched the lioness tuck into the meats. The quick lick of her lips and thin smile suggested something in America had at last proved adequate.

One of the rodent valets passed the drawing room dragging Von Haften's luggage and Donovan idly wondered which guest room Edmond would be putting her in. He expected the staff would be on edge around her as her demeanor was off-putting to say the least.

"I have to say that I'm rather put out that I was given no itinerary nor even notice of when you'd be arriving."

"Unexpected eventualities are why you were installed here."

"I wasn't installed here, Countess. I was supported by the inner council of the Martyres for my immigration, but I put myself in this home and expanded my own wealth." Donovan heard the edge in his own voice and immediately regretted being rankled by her. Of all the prominent families forming the inner circle of the Martyres of the Black well, the Von Haftens were the most frustrating to deal with. They'd been a dissenting vote in Donovan's inclusion as the first non-carnivore family in the cause and had kept wary eyes on him from his first days nearly twelve years ago, questioning his fitness, his constitution, his ability to follow through on his tasks. The Austrian lions always kept that old world arrogance about them even as that very world crumbled. He'd only need mention the Great War's outcome to set her off.

When seeking support for his bid to move the cause to America, they'd been among the smattering of members who'd seen it as an assignment he was destined to fail despite having rooted out more blood drinkers in England than any other member during his probation. Much like his successes among the captains of industry here in America, his accomplishments were only begrudged.

He couldn't wait to see her expression in the next ten minutes. The look he traded with Edmond affirmed his man saw things much the same.

Evelyn folded her golden legs. "Oh, you're competent in business Don, certainly. I just don't think you've done enough to warrant such high station in America where the cause is concerned."

"High station? As I recall your husband declared America was a backwater flotsam of refugees. I'd have thought he'd see Illinois as the perfect exile for one such as myself." Donovan smiled, showing as much of his flat teeth as obsequiously as possible. "This little rebel from England is filling its borders quickly with railroads and carriageways and ever taller monuments to progress, all of which started well before it sent its best and finest to fight and die in the trenches of the Great War."

The Countess' sour downturn of ears told him she felt chastened and clearly didn't like it. Good. Let this tart of a pussycat flee back to Europe with her tail between her golden legs, tell her husband of the means by which the rabbit spread their influence to corners of this country nobody had even seen yet.

Two herbie auxiliaries, as the Brits had called them, had served with distinction in that war, contributing in a successful fight to get the vote in America. Donovan doubted that would cross the Countess's feline mind. Only the war's ruination of the Austrian empire and the desolation of most family titles would mean a damn thing to her.

She took a deep breath. "Such a high opinion of yourself. I came here to see if any of that is warranted." She unfolded her legs and sat stiffly, palms to knees.

Enough sparring. "I think you should meet someone." A nod to Edmond sent him away.

"A new business associate?" The lioness ears twitched, seemingly interested for the first time. "Another wife you've taken here?" The subtle implication that the average rabbit took many partners was a common enough slur. How nice of the lioness to hold off so long.

"No. I've not remarried. I've a servant in the cause."

Her gaze pierced the lounge's door gap and Donovan faintly heard curious claws retreating. One of the kitchen staff waiting for refreshment requests no doubt. His ears cocked as other feet approached.

"Not one such as this exists elsewhere," Donovan promised as Edmond opened the drawing room doors and stepped back. A stooped figure entered, an old crone of a squirrel, grey streaks in her reddish fur and arthritic hands clasped together around a wide-brimmed sun hat. A grey matronly robe covered the rest of her. "Hello Sandy," Donovan curtly bowed his head in her direction. "How are you doing this fine day?"

The squirrel smiled. "I am well, Master Calvert. I've seen to our newest guest."

"We can discuss him soon, Sandy, thank you greatly." Donovan slid forward in his chair. "Sandy, this is Countess Evelyn von Haften, a guest from Austria. She is one of my compatriots in the struggle against… temptation."

The diminutive creature's tail twitched as cloudy eyes took the lion in. "I am pleased to meet you, Countess. It's an honor to have another of the Martyres of the Black Well here with us. We've worked so hard to battle the scourge that brings about theft of blood from innocent veins."

The Countess blinked at the small mammal that held her gaze, the squirrel's ear tufts level with the lion's navel. The Countess glanced to Donovan for a clue as to why this rodent stood before her. "We recruit youth for the cause. The fortitude required- "

"Is well observed Countess. I passed those trials myself after all." Donovan favored the Countess with an up and down glance from ear to toe claw. "Tell me, do you keep your reliquary on you? Does it speak to you now?" Donovan reached out and Edmond placed his cane in his white hand. Donovan immediately felt the comforting pull of energies, invisible to all but the innermost senses that told him what he already knew.

The Countess slipped delicate fingers though the folds of her deep maroon dress, flicking a clasp at her thigh and drawing a long dagger in polished steel, straight edged, almost a short sword. Her palm's pad slipped round it's silvery hilt, feeling the same inscrutable eddies from the world that dozens of generations of forged alchemy had accrued.

The rabbit took a deep breath. "The fit and martially practiced are what the Martyres require when taking action against the depraved of vein, but Sandy has fought and beaten the most difficult foe of all."

The Countess's eyes narrowed as they tracked to the squirrel and then widened. "What?"

"Herself," Donovan concluded with a smile.

The Countess leapt from her chair with force enough to topple it. The tray table that bore the remains of breakfast nearly went with it. "You have one of *them* here? In your own house?"

Donovan was between the squirrel and the lion immediately. The squirrel, for her part, didn't react to the upset, meeting the lion's gaze placidly.

"Sandy isn't one of them. Not anymore. She still bears the marks of a life she was drawn into without consent but has no urge to imbibe. Or kill."

"You're foolish enough to believe that?" The Countess's tail lashed. "A Nosfurratu cannot be anything but a killer, a pestilence in flesh. You know this."

"I once presumed the same. But I've made discoveries, Countess, conducted many exploratory ventures in service to the cause. I've learned to fight fire with fire as it were."

The Countess brandished her weapon aggressively, crouched to pounce and stab. "How could you possibly..."

Her words trailed away as Donovan unbuttoned his shirt and vest. Her gaze hardened as he parted his own collar, slid it away, exposing his white shoulders and his ivory inviting neck. "Sandy, if you would please demonstrate to our guest what resolve truly means."

The lioness jaw dropped as the squirrel studied his shoulder, a soft, supple recess of downy furred flesh where his lifeline pulse beckoned like an ambrosial thread. The Countess's eyes darted to Edmond, the possum who'd brought in the squirrel. The possum watched the lion's reaction instead, mild amusement cornering his muzzle.

One arm slid around Donovan's chest to hold him possessively. Donovan kept still as he knew her fangs would be sliding out, nose sampling his scent on the air. Still, he kept himself between the Countess and the squirrel, holding the Countess's gaze with practiced calm.

He felt the squirrel's muzzle hover at his throat, but characteristically felt no breath. Lips brushed his neck just once and the Countess hissed in fury.

The arm around Donovan's chest relinquished its grip and slid away as the squirrel stepped back. Donovan sighed. "Thank you for the demonstration, Ms. Mallory."

"It's a pleasure to prove my commitment to the better path, Mister Calvert."

"If you wouldn't mind providing the Countess and I with some privacy. We have much to discuss. Edmond."

Edmond held the door for the squirrel and Ms. Mallory exited before he closed the doors behind them both with a flourish, leaving Donovan and the Countess alone. Donovan helped himself to cheese from the disturbed breakfast tray.

The Countess slid her weapon home and rearranged her dress in frustration. "What the hell are you doing you root-nibbling moron?"

"To answer your question, I'm exploring news way to handle a problem that won't go away on its own."

"You were sent her to America to find the Nosfurs and *kill* them not make a pet out of one of them. What makes you think you can keep that thing in a docile state?"

"The question you abruptly skipped over, dear Countess, is how did I make her this way in the first place? That took trial and error. There were failed attempts, and certainly more to come. Sandy is a truly special case and unique among her kind. You'll see the next one very shortly."

The lion loomed over him, gaze hard. "I'm doubtful to say the least."

Donovan nodded, crossed to the study's window. Morning sun-soaked tree boughs in milky light. "You're no doubt aware of the Eighteenth Amendment to the Constitution and the Volstead act that enforces it."

"If you're referring to the politics of these States then I am aware enough to be amused. All nonsense. Who cares if peasants who fled Europe soak their troubles? It's all revenue for taxes wasted."

"It may seem that way to you and I. But Anti-Saloon Leaguers and moral activists have been pushing for years against drink as a public scourge. The dram is as dangerous and destructive to their sense of order as the blood-drinking curse has been for us, hence a half century of political and religious struggle, the planks of Noah's Ark soaked in whiskey and blood as the literature has it. The Prohibition against alcohol was seen as impossible here until it wasn't."

"And how would that compare to the drinking of blood by a Nosfur? It's not a habit, but a compulsion driven by their very existence."

"Is it? Has it ever occurred to you that a Nosfur retains its life experiences into the turning specifically because the person they were is still there, merely driven by a compulsion they never asked for? They've no friends, no rest, no safe harbour among mortals save the unlucky few who have been fooled but haven't yet been slaughtered. I do believe the recessed carnivorous urge was cited by your husband as one of the reasons why I wasn't fit to understand the minds of our adversaries in the ancient fight. Do you remember that?"

She met his glance and looked away. "Make your point, Donovan."

"As every mammal who becomes a full-fledged drunkard will in their best moments long for the clarity of sobriety, every blood drinker does indeed yearn to be mammalian again, mortal, able to live among kindred spirits. Eternity only brings the loneliness born un-slakable thirst. It's through this realization that I was able to recruit Sandy."

The lioness paced across the room and back again. "I could use a drink," she said.

Donovan nodded and smiled. "It's after four in the afternoon in Germany now I believe." He stroked his white chin. "Could you stand a brandy?"

She accepted with a nod and Donovan turned to the small bar cart by the window, pouring two snifters of his best Armagnac.

"It's about time I piqued your interest. Come this way."

The brandy globe swirled idly in her clawed fingers as the Countess followed him down the hall behind the grand foyer stairs and past the kitchen. She checked all corners and darkened spaces carefully to see if Mallory was about, and Donovan kept his amusement buttoned up.

The curing of fresh meats from the kitchen fluttered past their noses again. Von Haften made a thoughtful noise as she seemed to forget about the ex-blood drinker for an instant and brought the brandy to her lips. "Is this Cognac?"

"Armagnac." Doors parted to a grand solarium. Lead framed glass windows from hip level to ceiling, or from the Countess' knees to ceiling, opened onto a verdant lush garden. Trellises of vines clutched the house walls round to the back side of the cobbled garage. Trees and hedges framed in the private Eden. A shorn lawn sized for croquet or cricket was demarked by rows of spring flowers mated to small cobble paths that circled round white stone statuary at the garden's corners, a goat bearing grapes, a Sapphic hare bearing a lyre, twin birds dancing into flight from a be-fruited branch and at the last, near the join of sun and shadow, a dais with a stone parchment onto which an inscription in Latin was carved.

That inscription was hidden by the spread-eagled raccoon bound to it, pelt bare except for the modesty of torn trousers.

Donovan watched as the Countess's eyes roved the idyllic scene and came upon the prisoner there. "What is this? Is this a servant who—" Her eyes narrowed as she focussed and saw the blood soaking his muzzle near the tip of his chin. "He's one of them."

"Correct. I'd introduce you but he'll be quite preoccupied. He's been quite a handful since arriving from the speakeasy where we caught him last night."

A door at the garage's back opened and Sandy Mallory emerged, back bent, wide-brimmed hat and dark vestments gathered close. Gloved hands bore a rag and a spouted water jug. Dappled sunlight struck her clothes, but she did not react. "The longer they go un-gorged, the less light damages them. Did you know that?"

"I've never suffered one long enough to know." The Countess drained her glass and set it on a dusty bench. The wicker-furnished solarium where they stood smelled faintly of soil, a greenhouse now employed as an observation lounge.

"That's a pity," Donovan said. "This lesson is a valuable tool in teaching the first principle."

"Which is?"

"Immortality can be hell."

The sunlight was moving across the grass as time ticked by, sipping up the dew and opening flowers. On the dais, the raccoon was struggling to escape as he watched its advance. His fangless mouth opened as he shouted something that Donovan couldn't hear at Sandy, who put down the water can after liberally feeding some dianthus on the garden's outskirts and approached him, glancing back once to the thick paned window where the lion and the rabbit watched.

Words were traded and the Countess made a hiss under her breath. "I can't hear what they're saying."

Donovan perked his ears. "He's asking to be let go and she's telling him she's going to release him forever." He chuckled. "He's cursed her, called her an acorn-stuffed cunt. That's ended that."

The rag stuffed the raccoon's mouth and he thrashed as she tied it behind his neck. Distant neighbors wouldn't hear anything. Only the half dozen or so loyal to Donovan and the cause would catch what was to come.

The squirrel went back to her watering can, gathering her protection against the sun close as morning rays cut over the home's shingles and through branches to strike the raccoon's leg and chest. He thrashed, screamed around the gag, smoke curled up from burned strands of fur.

The Countess was riveted now. "This won't kill it?" Her raised glass indicated the sun.

"No."

She was riveted to the spot. "This is good." She raised the snifter as she watched. "I'll have another."

Chapter 3

Rough Mornings in Chicago

Bucky Cavali sat upright, claws piercing the bedspread beneath. At the bed's foot, Celeste's fangs ached.

She'd finished him, she'd been sure of it, drained the fox well past the point of recovery. She couldn't believe she'd turned him. After a hundred and thirty years with hundreds of meals she had never made another like her. She didn't even know how it was deliberately done.

"What happened?" Bucky muttered in a syrupy drone. His chest fell, then rose again in what would been ragged breathing if he still breathed.

"Bucky," Celeste said, racing through all the options before her.

His eyes fixed on hers, then recognition widened them and he bolted back against the headboard, hand pawing uselessly for the underarm holster he'd shed while alive. "What' you do to me?"

Celeste tried to puzzle through how she could finish the job now. Bucky had crossed the threshold of death in the mortal sense. She'd have to stake him through the heart or tie him down and separate his head from his shoulders, requiring elements of surprise. Dawn had arrived and she was stuck with the unintended fruits of her labour until she figured out what the hell to do.

Her eyes moved to the gun out of his sight and she clutched it, tossing the holster aside. What he didn't know couldn't kill him... "Don't move."

Hands flew out to uselessly ward off a bullet, then upwards when she didn't fire. Celeste got a good lock at the twin dots of crimson on the white of his bare throat, the only blemish on the ruffled fur of his naked torso and arms. His slacks were still on, unbelted.

"Dammit, don't shoot me! I'm sorry I hit you. My Ma raised a gentlemammal, but I lose myself...sometimes." His eyes screwed shut and opened again.

Insincerity had crossed the threshold with him. "I've already forgotten about you hitting me, Bucky."

His ears dropped. "You bit me. I thought you…" He looked down at the gun in confusion.

Self-doubt bought time to calm him down, placate him before she could get close enough to break his neck and stake him. If the fox understood the strength he could wield that would be difficult.

"You did hit me, Bucky, and I hit you back."

A retort on his lips died away, eyes down the barrel of the gun. "I kinda had it coming, didn't I?"

"You did. But I forgive you."

"Doesn't look like it."

"I don't know you won't do it again." More truthful words…

"Why don't I feel right? What did you do to me?" He swallowed. A hand rose to his throat and felt around to where she'd drained him, fingers trembling.

She didn't answer, pondering her next move. Seduction or persuasion was off the table. Even her best efforts couldn't win over the terrified.

Johnny Torrio's sarcastic tongue wagged in her mind; "you could at least pay close attention to the details," but nothing could tell her how to resolve this impasse. She'd finished Bucky Cavali with her bite and yet here he was.

Celeste gazed into Bucky's eyes, recognizing the clenched jaw and low ears of a carnivore trying to look strong when he knew he was terrified.

"You said you liked vegetarians. That's why they called you Bucky, right?"

He blinked. "Yeah."

Time to lower the temperature. "Tell me why you're not a threat Bucky. Why don't need this gun?"

His hands hunted around himself, silently panicking. No thumping heart, no catching breath. "Because you're a great gal," he offered. "And I'm sorry I hurt you."

She tipped the gun away, her gaze softening deliberately. "How do you feel now, Bucky?"

He blinked and gritted his teeth. Honesty broke through turmoil. "I'm scared."

There he was. It was endearing in its own way, seeing him struggle with actual powerlessness. Too few carnivores ever surpassed the illusions afforded by privilege to ever really reflect.

Just maybe she didn't have to kill him.

In another world, another typical night would have passed, another killing, another dig, another month drifting through Bucky and Torrio's world, demurely dodging predatory advances, cultivating the illusion of her diminutive status until Johnny picked up the phone at the Four Deuces with another job for the doe with the knock-out gams. Feed, feel resentment, feed and resent again.

As she met the fox's vulnerable gaze, she realized that she might have turned a page.

Possibilities bloomed. Bucky could be her subordinate, her dependent, her protégé. And if he could learn his place, well, he wasn't half bad looking either.

Doubt tugged at her. An opportunity like this had its challenges. Her last attempt to connect with another of her kind was five years cold now, not a carnivore but still having gone horribly wrong. Celeste had learned not to trust anyone after Sandy.

She would definitely reserve trust in Bucky. And to maintain control she couldn't let the fox know that this had been an accident. She'd have no power over him then.

Somebody would have to be blamed for this situation.

And somebody would have to be a savior.

"I saved you."

His side-long glance, hands still raised, told her that was in doubt.

"I was sent to kill you, but I didn't."

"Not for lack of trying," his sneer showed teeth, but also reluctance to push the matter.

She put on a sympathetic smile with the care of a hat feather. "You're wrong, Bucky. If I wanted you dead, you'd be dead. I had other plans."

"Put down the gun and prove it." He wrapped sinewy arms around the metal of the bedframe behind him, his chest rose and fell to no effect.

She did as asked. The automatic settled into the mattress at his feet. Their eyes met.

"Great," Bucky said. "So, what did you do to me?" His voice wavered as he swallowed.

She needed him calm. "I bit you. And instead of killing you I made you like me."

"A veg—" He bit back the taunt and swallowed, blinking nervously. "I was drunk. There's no way you moved as fast as I thought you did."

There was that niggling doubt, the crutch of presumed 'natural' superiority. The sooner she rescued him from that the better.

"Really?" It was of so little effort that she barely expended it. In an eye blink she was over the bed, straddling him, fist around his neck and slowly pushing his skull against the dull papered plaster. His eyes were wide and glazed. "How?"

"Understand Bucky, I could have killed you last night with the cards in your hand, or in the alley outside that speak. You could have gone cold in any one of this city's gutters at the merest effort and nobody would have known who to blame or thank."

"Who are you?"

Celeste hadn't revealed herself to anyone in decades and there was a satisfaction derived in admission. "I was born in seventeen seventy-five in France. Things were complicated then. I emigrated here after the war."

"The Great one?"

"The Civil one. What matters, Bucky is that I saw potential in you. I decided your death would be a waste, despite the obligations I'd taken."

He couldn't wrap his head about what she'd said and blinked. "Obligations?"

"You stepped out of line. Torrio wanted you dead, I wanted you otherwise."

"Johnny," he muttered, eyes narrowing, then losing focus as he pondered.

"It's not important," she said, realizing from his hard expression that it certainly was to him.

"That bastard, after all the jobs I pulled for him."

Bucky had been a bit-player who held the door for his boss as often as a gun, but clearly esteemed himself higher.

Her grip on his throat had lessened and she tightened it again. There was no breath to steal, and it amused her that he clearly didn't know that.

"I've made sure you don't have to pull jobs for anyone but me, Bucky. And I've given you a new lease on…opportunity. You just have to do what I say and realize that I'm in charge going forward."

She watched truth war with confusion in his dark eyes. His world was torn asunder now. As far as Celeste was concerned it was all for the best.

"I think I need some air," Bucky said.

"You don't. Not ever again."

"What are you talking about?"

"Go ahead, take the deepest breath you can."

He couldn't. His chest arched out like a rooster and back again. "What the hell? I'm not breathing." He puffed his chest, his muzzle gaped. Panic gripped him as the emptiness of his own shell overcame him.

"Let me go."

She didn't.

"Please!"

She released him, slipping from her straddling position off the bed.

He leapt up, clueless to his own speed, and slammed into the dresser across from her, tipping an electric lamp that shattered on his plank floor. He drew air to shout in confusion and pain, but for no other purpose. The realization made his shriek even more despondent and pitiful. He threw open the door and leapt into the hallway.

"Come back, Bucky," Celeste called. Taking a step around the other side of the bed she was stabbed by something sharp and devouring on one arm. She cursed and leapt out of the stray pinprick of sunlight that had made it past the shades and burned her.

Outside the room paws thundered down the stairs fast as a war drum tattoo.

The front door. "Fils de pute." She was out of the room in two strides, down the stairs and at Bucky's back in five more. The door was opened, and morning light fluttered like hungry fire across the vestibule, striking his shoulder and cheek from over a cross-street tenement before she hammered the door shut with a shoulder that cracked the wood. Fire kissed her for just an instant with the flare of a cattle-brand.

Bucky wasn't so lucky. He shrieked where light's barrage bit every pore, every follicle. The sensation, she very well knew, was like tipping into a furnace's heart. He dropped as though shot, back arching in agony, frantically slapping out the burn washing like flames over him that would linger for minutes more.

In the dark of the vestibule, she watched him writhe, jaws parted with nary a sound.

He'd forgotten to try to breathe, Celeste noted proudly, rubbing the stinging flesh under her own pelt. He'd be a quick learner. He'd have to be.

As silence gave way to pitiful whining, she realized that if she was going to end Bucky Cavali once and for all, this would be her best chance.

Instead, she stayed her hand. "There is so much to learn, Bucky. Your gifts come with limitations. Daylight is stolen from you as it is for the dead, but you can be so much more when the sun sets. You just need to listen to me and be patient.

She reached out her hand and saw him fight the urge to scream as his wild dark eyes found hers, canines pushing forth in his panic.

When he found self-possession to endure the pain rather than fight it, his dark vulpine hand crept up and took hers.

***

Crawford didn't want to wake, didn't want to sleep either. Dreams had teeth made of accusations all the way to hell, and so would the waking world. As he rolled out of bed guilt set like cement. He'd killed someone, here in America, not a muddy trench or barbed line in sight.

Why had he taken this job? Was it really all he could do for a living after he and Kamila messily separated and he exiled himself to Illinois? Here as a Federal enforcer, drunkards resisted and sometimes got clubbed, even ones who'd crawled back to America from the same French or German holes Crawford himself had shivered in and suffered to leave.

The world's unfairness was so much easier to be part of when you were just handing out tickets, spouting off snatches of the Volstead Act or the Eighteenth. Perps went home and cursed the pigs from Washington and Fed bastards picking their pockets with enough vigorous indignation to slip out and do it all again the next night. Prohibition drove an animal to drink.

That was the machine that Crawford was a cog in.

Now a bed somewhere was cold and a slab was full and the hypocrisy of the whole thing was just a little too clear in a moment where he desperately wanted a drink.

Turns out you can always hate yourself a little bit more.

He should have dug ditches for a living. In France he'd gotten good at it. But that envelope with cash wouldn't be making its way back to a Virginia farm if he did, and a cub wouldn't be getting new pencils for school. And somebody still holding the last warm spot in his heart would be proven right in believing he didn't care.

Crawford groomed hastily before stumbling to the kitchen. His paltry Federal salary allowed him to share a walk-up apartment with another agent, Charlie Rothscub.

The brown-pelted wolf had lived with him for nearly a year now, sharing Crawford's gripes and pains on the taskforce as his own. He wore a dark red bowtie and his tanned suits were cut neat and form fitting. He always maintained a fastidious air about his appearance. Like Crawford, the slightly shorter wolf was unmarried.

Unlike Crawford, he'd never been so. Confirmed bachelorhood seemed to suit Charlie, and he never seemed to initiate talk about the females of the species, only sharing Crawford's mystification at how bad things could get.

As eggs and bacon danced in grease on the stove, Charlie gave him a baleful muzzle-low glance of sympathy. "You want me to drive?"

"I'm okay," Crawford finished his eggs slowly as Charlie waited. "Let me get my tie on."

Charlie nodded into his coffee, wide nose breathing in steam. He was more than sensitive to Crawford's emotional barriers and knew his partner wasn't talkative right now. Breakfast passed quickly and Charlie went to get himself in order while Crawford cleaned up.

Minutes later, the brown wolf neatly placed on his small-brimmed pork pie and down they went.

Cain drove a grey 1922 Chevrolet '490, half-bought with the few bucks he'd set aside after moving out away from Kamila and his son Lucas. It had eight payments left that would be hell to figure out if he lost his job today. With wind ruffling the fur on his knuckles and cross breezes carrying butcher scents and masonry grit he was able to just stay in the moment.

Sun warmed the bricks of high-climbing buildings as the Chevy chugged downtown. Sleepy creatures of the street milled around clutching newspapers under arms and hats to heads as mid-May winds accosted them. Up high, the L train thundered from elevated perch to perch as they entered Chicago's core.

The office granted for Federal Prohibition enforcement was a small, dingy establishment. Crawford parked out back. The two wolves stalked around to where sun penetrated the Chicago field office of the Bureau of Internal Revenue and struck the oaken bar top, the empty stools and tarnished brass foot rail. Somebody in appropriations had a sense of humor.

The saloon sat empty for months after Prohibition had shut its doors before the government took the property at a steal—what else would anybody call it—and packed it with file cabinets, clerks, and surly agents of the law. Dander, tobacco smoke, and burned coffee choked the air. A ceiling fan lazily twisted to no effect.

At the reception desk a Calico cat straightened suspenders and tutted around a cigarette. "Beatie's waiting." The flat gaze fell on Crawford.

Should he have badge in hand? Crawford realized that leaving here without it was a definite possibility. The Captain didn't particularly dislike him but wouldn't be promoting him. Crawford felt Charlie's hand on his shoulder slide away as Crawford passed coffee slurping records keepers on his way back to Beatie's den. The office was lit by a hooded lamp and bare of decorations save one framed photograph of a matronly bear and the boss's Federal appointment papers, currently askew.

The den's denizen waited. Beatie, short for Agent Ed Bertrand was a Kodiak bear tall as Crawford while still seated. Small eyes judged over a thick nose and arms like L-train girders crossed a barrel chest. His necktie was waffle-iron wide to maintain proportions.

Beatie's elbows creaked the desk as fingers steepled. "I expected a progress call on the raids at Seven AM this morning," he rumbled conversationally. "I hate those calls because I like to be there when the locks break. But my daughter had her school graduation the night before and my wife would be devastated as I would if I weren't there."

Crawford coughed as he took a chair. "Congratulations to your daughter on—"

"You know what I hate worse Agent Cain? What I really don't like?"

Crawford sunk low.

"I hate calls at five am from the chief of police, who in turn got an earlier call from city council, who in turn was woken by a reporter. Everyone down the chain who was taken out of bed couldn't curl back into it because they knew that barring a bombing of the Chicago Tribune press, the whole city is gonna read about how Federal enforcement agents killed a miscreant running from a fine—"

"He attacked me," Crawford raised the hand that was still bandaged. "I didn't want to shoot him."

"You looking for pity? You had a mandate and a club. 'Less he pulls a gun, you don't wax him for what amounted to a drunk and disorderly."

"He was a hell of a lot worse than disorderly." Crawford's words sounded cowardly even to himself.

"I'm supposed to say that to everybody from City Hall and the press calling all damn day?"

They would all want Crawford's head, not that he could blame them. Thigh-flaskers were at each other's territorial throats constantly and the press went all out when innocent bystanders caught lead. The cops and feds were the heroes in ink and the crooks were the crooks, until they weren't.

The writing was on the wall. "I need to atone for this."

Beatie stuffed his pipe with a meaty finger and glanced through his blinds at his receptionist's claws flaying a typewriter. "How're you gonna do that?"

"Anybody speak to his family yet?"

"No. Simon Govic had a wife and son."

Crawford felt his stomach clench. "It's…" He swallowed. "It's my… actions that caused this. I need to be the one to knock."

The match Beatie lit for his pipe flared out unused. He roved eyes up and down the wolf as though seeing him for the first time. "We usually have somebody more…cut out for ringing doorbells with hat in hand. I was gonna send Cirelli."

Marco Cirelli handled matters like this with solemn grace. The silver fox always had a way with people. Crawford took a deep breath. "I need to own up to my mistake. How would you feel if you killed somebody over here, after the war I mean?"

"Depends who," was the flat answer. Beatie's gaze went to the coffee-ringed blotter on his desk. "Speaking to the widow and offering your sincerest apologies is a dicey proposition if you do it wrong. No Fed outfit or police force will take you again if you do. I don't care if she claws your nose off. Contrition and sympathy is all she deserves, no goddam excuses."

Crawford felt a shiver in his whiskers. He could feel his hand itching and he scratched it, feeling a small surge of anger that he couldn't resist. He hadn't wanted to kill anybody, now nor then. But they handed out medals five years ago for murder in France and suspensions or firings here and now. That was just how it worked. "She can cuss me out, spit on me, whatever's appropriate. I'll take the lumps."

"Damn right you will. Then you'll get your mind off it by hitting another speak tonight. I'd administratively put you off, but we need every mammal with a commission on the street."

A grunt dismissed him. Eyes studiously avoided his until he made it to where Charlie was typing up his raid report.

"How'd it go Craw?"

Crawford sighed. "Uncle Sam can't afford to fire me today. I have to go see the widow."

Charlie cocked an ear. "*The* widow?"

"I'll be back before noon."

"I'm going along." Charlie met Crawford's sour muzzle turn. "I'll finish my report later. You'll need me around…after."

"Okay." Crawford said, trying not to think about what was coming. "I'll drive."

He was nervous as they made their way toward where Simon Govic's wallet card said he lived. Five years ago, the war office had dozens of people who did bad news knocks for a living, moving from city to country, lowering muzzles and bringing condolences. He thought of one door he'd never seen, a badger family of a man he'd known getting that knock, opening that letter.

Crawford's flask was empty, unfilled from the bottle behind his bedroom armoire. He could imagine how it would be for a Prohibition agent to show up and confess he'd killed a husband and father for resisting Prohibition arrest with a high-proof Irish kiss under his own nose. '*Sa hard job mam. Whut kinne tell ya.*

"This turn, Craw," Charlie pointed right. Crawford would have missed it otherwise. He was becoming blank stone, emotionless, more than ever the mammal that his wife Kamila wanted to be away from.

He parked before one of Chicago's endless lines of South-side row houses, chimneys puffing from second stories. The dead ferret's place was up scabrously cracked white steps. "Wait here."

"You sure?"

"I am. Let this take as long as it needs to."

Crawford took his fedora off on his way up, then put it back on foolishly. He'd have to take it off when she saw him so she'd understand. Or was that thought just stupid?

Goddamn him. He knocked.

The door opened immediately, and his eyes were drawn down to a tiny ferret kit's half-moon face, nose twitching. They stared at each other. Crawford felt his heart turn to lead.

"It's not Daddy. It's a salesman, Mommy."

She swore something in a Slavic language, maybe Polish. "She wants you to go away. We don't want vacuums or false Bibles," the kit enlightened him.

"I'm not..." Crawford swallowed. "I'm not a salesperson or telling you about...God. Tell your mother I'm an officer with the Bureau of Internal Revenue."

The child's nose was all that moved.

"I handle Prohibition—when people aren't allowed to drink alco—."

An older ferret appeared, checked dress, eyes sallow from lack of sleep. "Is about Simon?" Crawford could detect bitterness in her voice and saw what looked to be the faint purple outlines of darker flesh under the white fur of one eye.

"It is, Ms. Govic. My name is Crawford Cain with the Bureau of Internal Revenue, a Prohibition agent charged with enforcing the Eighteenth Amendment. May I come in to speak with you?"

She sighed and stood back, waving past the cluttered foyer to a small, cramped kitchen with rickety cupboards and tarnished sink. She went to one side of a round yellow table with her son. Crawford kept to the other. She didn't ask him to sit.

"He has fine?" the ferret asked.

"What? I mean, I'm sorry Mrs. Govic."

"He's arrested again? Has to pay fine? We can't afford his fine. He'll have to stay in jail if you want money." There was satisfaction, as though the inevitable had come to pass. Her son looked uncomfortable.

Crawford realized he was still wearing his hat and snatched his fedora off. It bent in his grey-furred thick hands. "I have some bad news, Ms. Govic."

When his eyes met hers, she didn't look away. Her tail thumped the cupboard behind her.

Crawford cleared his throat. "Last night he was detained at an illegal liquor den at the corner of Jackson and Canal St. He resisted arrest and fled. I gave chase and…."

She wasn't afraid, he realized. More like anticipatory, impatient even. Her son's nose and whiskers twitched, button eyes wide and attentive.

"Ms. Govic, he attacked an officer of the law and was shot as a result." Crawford swallowed, his ears getting hot. "It was an accident that took his life."

Right away he felt the sting of guilt. He'd given a coward's passive wording, dissociating action from cause. He took a deep breath, forced himself to say the words. "I was the officer who shot him. His death was unintentional. I'm truly sorry and want to offer my condolences."

The sounds of the city crept into the dead silence of the cramped kitchen.

Govic's wife looked past Crawford, at what he didn't know.

The kit started to sob, and Crawford felt his teeth grind. He'd brought those tears. He'd hollowed out these lives. In the moment he could feel the palpable weight of their futures changed irrevocably. The eyes of Simon Govic's widow, whose name had never been given, were cold. "You did this," she said.

"I'm sorry. Yes, Ms. Govic it was an accident, and I didn't want to hurt your husband much less…." Her son broke away and fled the lupine monster filling his kitchen, flinging the front door wide. Patters of frantic feet faded down the front steps.

Turning to follow him, that's when Crawford saw.

The kitchen cabinet next to the tiny front window was destroyed, its wood panel fractured and splintered. Great gouges of clawed wood poked loose. Shattered crockery glinted within, dust powdered the counter below. When Crawford turned back details he'd ignored leapt out, proof that he had stepped out of himself, at least a little. The table had only one chair left but floor scratches from many, its back bearing fractures. The hanging light fixture had only two of three bulbs, the third broken rather than burned out.

The door to an adjacent room canted, one hinge having roughly parted company.

Crawford's eyes met the widowed ferrets' once again, his throat dry as a furnace and his bit hand on fire. She took a step around the table and even though he knew it was coming he held still. She smacked his jaw hard enough to rattle teeth. The sting hadn't faded before spittle hit his lip. "Leave my house, murdering Prohee pig."

Hat still in hand, Crawford did so.

He was numb when he reached the car. Charlie read him right away. "Did she?"

Crawford's voice croaked. "Somebody busted up half of the house." Crawford remembered the kit fleeing the kitchen in tears. "Daley's has a telephone, right?"

They'd grabbed breakfast there many a time on trips through the South side, great and hearty greasy-spoon bacon sandwiches, and coffee. "It does indeed," the other wolf said.

A crumb of food now should make him puke. But for some reason Crawford was ravenous.

Crawford drove, nearly one handed since the bandage hand smarted now like a bastard. His hairs felt like they were stabbing at him from under the gauze and he was positive Govic had given him an infection. He needed a bite to eat, several in fact, starving even though he was also sick to his stomach with anxiety, which didn't make sense.

First he needed to make a call. It had been two weeks since he'd talked to Kamila and that had been downright perfunctory. He remembered talking about the weather, Lucas 'grades, nothing else of substance passing between them.

He hurried East, summarizing the encounter with the widow for Charlie and only hitting one signal stop. Among the smatter of mammals crossing the street were a young wolf, a grizzled coyote, and a greying otter that drew Crawford's eye. They all had luggage in thick leather cases, but the otter was pushing a wheelbarrow of bent copper tubing and a large jug. Was this a still being transported in broad daylight?

The young wolf with a single wart displacing a whisker seemed to detect Crawford's attention. She turned to wink at him. Behind him the coyote leered his way, one eye askance. The otter huffed, ignoring them. They were across the street and on their way in moments.

Charlie made a noise in his throat. "Bit brazen," he observed.

Crawford kept on to the diner, gaze ahead.

"There are phones at the station, Craw. Beatie is going to be waiting on that report."

"He can wait," Crawford muttered. Twenty minutes later Charlie was ordering two coffees and bacon sandwiches while Crawford closed the diner's phone booth door and put a nickel in. He leaned into the candlestick phone's receiver. "Ay Emm Vee one six two four please."

They could be out, Kamila in the chicken coop or doing errands. He couldn't expect an answer and yet somehow Crawford was certain she'd be there to pick up. Two rings, three. The line connected.

"Yes? Who is calling?" Kamila sounded tired.

"It's me."

There was a long silence. "What can I help you with Crawford?"

"It's just…been a while. How are you and Lucas doing?"

She seemed to be sampling the air, as though scent could travel through the phone line. "Making do. Lucas is schooling well. We had the back fence fixed."

The back fence in Richmond bordered on a tannery where leathers cured. The penetrating oily scent always turned up in sense memory, in the leather that upholstered Crawford's car, the chairs in the office, the gun holstered next to his heart.

Kamila was done talking, facts unembellished.

"I'm proud of him," Crawford said, realizing that with no details given that sounded foolish and insincere. "I'd love to tell him so."

"He's with friends down the road." The weak connection made her voice a whisper and he couldn't tell if she was lying. Is it a lie if you don't deserve the truth?

Simon Govic's widow's expression came unbidden to him, blank but for disgust.

"Kamila, I've been wondering if you and I should…" He broke off, words tripping over uncertainty.

"Should what, Crawford?"

"We should talk this over."

She growled. "What? There were many, many chances to talk this over, Crawford. You didn't want to. You were in your den, or listening to static on the radio or ignoring my son when all he wanted was to know where his Dad was while you sat right there and stared at the newspapers without turning their pages."

"I was figuring things out, Kamila. I'm sorry that I still have trouble putting words to it. I'm sorry for that."

"Sorry that you couldn't snap out of it for us or sorry that you couldn't put a name to it?"

He didn't know which. "Both, Kamila. I had trouble figuring…things out when I came back."

"What things? The war? The war was over. It ended and you never came back."

"That's not true Kamila."

"It isn't? I've seen soldiers come back with burnt faces and hacking coughs and crutches for missing limbs, but it was like *all* of you was amputated. So many times I tried to talk to you about it and you deflected or you turned away or you walked out for hours on end. I realized you would never come back to me, not the real you."

"I had questions about myself, things I couldn't share. I'd lost a friend in that war." The booth had gotten smaller.

"Well, you found another one, didn't you Crawford? It wasn't me. Nor was it your son. I smelled drink on you for half a day, then most hours of it. Drink slept in our bed and you didn't. I lost you and just needed to learn to give you up."

"That's not how it happened!" Crawford's voice rose and his hackles with them. Outside the booth a marten couple dabbed ash off their cigarettes and traded looks before going back to flapjacks. If the whole place could hear him he didn't give a damn. "I didn't want to bring it home to you, Kamila, you or Lucas. You couldn't help me figure out what I couldn't myself."

He remembered olive fatigues under a white stripe of muzzle and muddy walls with a blank sky. He hadn't found himself over there, only confusion between shell bursts. That world was not this one, it could never be.

He was gripping the candlestick of the phone in his injured hand. The pink of the gauze revealed it was bleeding again.

Kamila growled. "That's just it, Crawford. For the past three years we've been stuck with an invisible guest who you didn't want to talk about. It stole our lives. I'm done with it. And you."

"Please Kamila. I don't want to hurt you or Lucas."

"Yet you're doing it right this minute. Sure you don't want a drink?"

"I...look the checks are still coming. I had a little problem, but I've taken care of it."

"They catch you tippling while rounding up other scofflaws? I couldn't believe you'd take a job like that. It was so unlike the Crawford I had a son with and yet so unsurprising all the same."

That cut him deep. "I had a bad arrest last night."

"You beat someone?"

"I...I handled it."

"Handled what? Did you *kill* somebody?"

"I handled it."

"Dammit, Crawford. Just more evasion, locking yourself away. Just tell me that the return address on your checks is correct."

"They are. Why? Did one not arrive? Nothing came back."

"Nothing did, but I won't need them anymore. The coop is doing well and I've found regular buyers for the eggs."

"That's great." He could muster no enthusiasm. "But why are you—?"

"I'm mailing papers. They'll be there in a week."

Crawford gripped the earpiece tighter. "What papers?"

"Read them carefully. The lawyer's office has an address, you can write to them directly."

"What papers, Kamila?"

"Just read them. And don't call again until after you've mailed them back."

"Are they, Kamila I know we need to figure things out for our son but what is this?"

"We don't need a trial separation. We've separated. I've figured out my life and my son's and things are getting better."

The unspoken words leapt out, *without you.*

"No." Crawford said. "Kamila, no. This isn't what you really wa—"

"Time's almost up. Please insert another nickel to resume the call." The operator was too cheerful to have been listening in. Crawford dropped the earpiece and frantically rummaged his coat pockets for change. His empty flask clattered to the floor and he banged his head on the booth bending to scoop it up. He dropped a dime dropped down the telephone's tin throat, lifting the receiver to hear static. Kamila had disconnected.

Rage came unbidden. He grabbed the phone, wrenching it loose enough to cant at an angle and dragged claws down its side, zebra striping dull metal underneath the black paint.

His hands and jaw hurt, as though he'd tried to bite through a car tire. Crawford shoved the booth's door open hard enough to raise every head in the restaurant and stormed past the bus boy. He refused to meet Charlie's eyes, the brown wolf stewarding two steaming coffees and sandwiches. "I'll be back," Crawford growled over his shoulder and hurried into the street.

He knew a place that was unreported, that his outfit hadn't rolled over. One block south, stumbling through foot traffic past a mole's fruit stand. The soda shop was a tidy hole in the wall. Silvery fountain taps lined behind the smart young fox in a paper striped hat. The place had only one other patron this long before lunch. "What can I pour for you good sir? We're well stocked with the fizziest of fares."

"Coca cola."

"Right up sir."

Crawford put a dime down. "More fizz, enough to really giggle."

Eyes met, Crawford's tried not to plead. That would be just pathetic.

"For certain sir." The dime disappeared and the fox looked under his bar with concern. "I'll need a moment to obtain a properly frosted glass."

"Of course."

When the fox returned from the tiny back room a frosted hexagonal glass was palmed so only Crawford could spot three fingers worth of "syrup" at its bottom. The fox filled it from a waiting tap, effervescent bubbles building a foamy head. The concoction was set down and a striped straw proffered.

"Noah drown me, that is a beautiful sight."

The other patron rolled his eyes at the picture show drama over a simple coke and the fox told Crawford to keep his tail on with wide eyes over a smile. "I hope you enjoy, sir."

And Crawford did. One block north his partner was staring at a cooling coffee and sandwiches, wondering where he'd gone. Shame tempered the anger that chased him here and four sucks in he forgot about Kamila's papers on their way, bears who'd can him and widows who damned him. The world attained placid numbness when the straw hunted for the last few bubbles. He was warm all through.

The fox hadn't left his post. "I hope you enjoyed our refreshment sir." The undertone begged him not to do anything untoward. To Crawford's left the polecat patron looked from glass to wolf and then away.

"I'm refreshed," Crawford concluded. "Thank you kindly."

He walked out into sunlight that felt like milk pouring down and a street that was fuzzy at the edges. He'd drank too fast. Fortunately, he had coffee sitting by and some conversation that would provide time to sober up for driving. Charlie was a reliable shoulder to cry on if he needed it.

One block south Crawford resisted the urge to turn around.

An otter weaved the downtown crowd, brass buttoned from navel to neck, cop's hat askew and working a toothpick through flat teeth as webbed toes slapped the pavement purposefully.

Crawford pitched his fedora forward and stepped into the street to study a General Motor's engine bonnet, making thoughtful noises as the cop passed. Crawford glanced back to see the otter enter the soda jerk's establishment and wondered how much of his own scent would hang after a minute.

He was still wondering when the otter emerged moments later, shoving something into his lapel and closing the brass buttons of his authority before melting into the crowd.

Cokes and root beer floats didn't fit into pockets, but payoffs did. No wonder the place never got raided. "Well then."

Crawford was back at Daley's café again ten minutes later. Two steaming coffees and a sandwich waited alone.

Crawford heard a wooden door fold above the din and turned to see Charlie leave the phone booth. "I didn't follow when you huffed out. I had them pour you a new cup."

Charlie lifted his own and sipped it as they sat down, eyeing Crawford coolly. "Was it work?"

"The wife." Soon to be ex-wife, but he wasn't ready to open up about that. "I'm sorry. I needed to get out."

"The car stayed so I didn't worry."

Charlie didn't seem to be trying to smell Crawford's breath so if he suspected anything he was a cool customer. Crawford let the buzz settle to a hum as he sipped his coffee. "Thanks Charlie."

The brown wolf nodded. "I called the office to let Beatie know we'd seen the widow and told him what you told me about the damage to the place. He told me in turn that the medical examiner didn't want to release Govic yet."

The coffee was good. Crawford didn't want to talk about Govic, but it helped him forget Kamila. "Why?"

"There's something abnormal about the weasel that concerned them, said he's, well, feral."

"What, as in can't talk, barks and shits in the woods like God's unchosen or something? Cause he didn't look it to me."

Charlie snickered. "God chose who for what? Regardless, Govic had strange traits. Elongated limbs for loping, thicker jaws, and a curved spine that wouldn't handle standing upright too long." Charlie sipped and sighed. "Did his kid look…strange when you saw him?"

"Kid looked fine. Govic, I couldn't be sure, just wanted to bite my hand off." Crawford's hand itched and he realized he was getting jitters from the caffeine and sugar packed so closely on top of his illicit tipple. He reached under the bandage to feel his flesh getting hot. "This town changes people in all sorts of ways."

CHAPTER 4

PAINFUL TRUTHS, BLISSFUL POSSIBILITIES

Bucky could still smell his own burnt flesh, seared like he'd rolled over a hot stovetop. Beyond the pain there was only nameless hunger. "How long will this burn hurt?"

Celeste grimaced, resting in the kitchen chair across from him. "Hours, perhaps days if the exposure was long. The sun takes forever to kill you, but you'd still be screaming if I hadn't closed that door immediately. You got lucky for the second time today."

The reality of Bucky's situation was setting in, a sickly feeling devoid of a stomach to feel sick with. "Johnny tried to whack me and the only life I have now is indoors? This isn't luck." He rose from his chair and went for the cabinet, extracting a whiskey bottle. He stared at it, not wanting any.

Celeste rose behind him. "You don't have to stay indoors. You just can't be in the sun. Death is much worse don't you think?"

He didn't know.

"The cure for burns is rest. When the night falls again I'll prove that you make up for what you've lost with all that you can do now."

Bucky knew right away what he wanted. "Like whack Torrio? Can I do that?"

"No." Celeste's ears lowered. "I still need him. Take your ego out of this because you're moving on to better things that he won't even live to see. Just keep that in mind. Death is no longer a concern."

It hurt to turn his head, but he did so with a snarl. "Yes, it is. I'm gonna make the old bastard pay."

She rose and stood over him. "No Bucky. Leave it to me and I'll take care of it."

"Goddammit, fine. But I've business to deal with. The sisters already moved their operation. What are they gonna do if I don't meet them?"

Celeste sighed. "They'll move on. You'll be fine without them."

Bucky felt a seething anger at the state of it all. The sensation of knowing he was irrevocably not himself was maddening. "It's my stake. I worked hard for this!"

"You don't even drink alcohol anymore," Celeste chided. "You should accept my gift with gratitude as you'll know better joys over time."

"What fucking gift? I'm a fox with plans, grandi piani con grandi profitti. No way am I throwing in the towel just because I can't handle sun anymore."

"I'll show you things that will astound you, but after you rest. When night falls there will be a new world to see, and I promise you'll become as indifferent to Torrio and the mob racket as you are to baby rattles." She held his gaze. "Learning to let go of unimportant things will help you."

"Okay," Bucky lied, mind aflame. All his doubters walking tall, certain he was flea-food in a ditch, already forgetting him.

Celeste led him back to his bedroom and urged him to lie down. His ceiling was a void above as she lay next to him before closing her eyes. He glanced her way and saw the chest under the green flapper dress she wore didn't rise or fall.

Bucky slipped down towards a deep, dark non-self that wasn't sleep. He resisted, the pain fleeing through his newly reborn nerves feeding indignation. His last conscious thought was a sensation of resolve, that this affliction, or miracle, whatever it was, wouldn't get in the way of his plans.

***

The raccoon now knew the sun wouldn't kill him. Sandy told him this was the first lesson. Daylight was agony, but pain was truth's messenger, the first step in deliverance.

The raccoon's name was Keller, turned less than a decade ago and discarded by whomever turned him. Without a chaperone he had barely enough discipline to sustain himself and was enslaved to the vein. Fortunately, Donovan Calvert had found him before others from his order had. There was no end beyond the end for Nosfur, Sandy believed. Final death was simple oblivion.

Keller could be saved, as Donovan had saved Sandy six years ago. It had been hard at first, the lessons agonizing. But now Sandy had a purpose beyond the cycle of thirst and drink. One day long past she thought her friend Celeste would be the first to follow, but hard lessons had been learned on that day and Sandy knew the doe would never be saved.

Keller moaned as he rolled on the bed inside of Sandy's cottage, hissing when a burnt ear touched the hard wood of the bed-stand. Three hours in direct sun left his flesh in mottled reds and scabbed browns under the shedding pelt. His strength was sapped, his fangs plucked while he was tied down. All Sandy's guests would remain so for as long as clarity took to come.

"I on-ee wen to siii."

"Take your time," Sandy said, careful to rest her red furred hand on the shoulder less burned. He wore no bandages. Infections couldn't harm him, only pain lingered to teach.

The raccoon opened scarred lids and saw her for the briefest moment before closing them again. "I own-ree wa ned to siip her. I naht a kirrer."

When he'd screamed his tongue had burned. Still, Sandy understood. Only wanted to sip. Not a killer. Sandy remembered uttering words like those and would shed tears for him if she had them. Drinkers of blood like drinkers of spirit always consoled themselves with powers of restraint they claimed possession of but never wielded.

"I once thought as you do, Keller. I know you don't wish to be a killer but without our help you'll see no choice. You'll cheat, you'll swindle, you'll murder."

His eyes rolled to the cracked stucco above. Naked beams of wood crossing the ceiling were reinforced with wrought steel installed by Mister Calvert, a beautiful cage indeed.

Sandy took a damp cloth from a porcelain water pan and carefully dabbed the raccoon's forehead. "I was like you, dining on the misery of others, assuming myself a creature of violence by design. I thought this was the way of the world. Mister Calvert revealed that wasn't true."

The memory bidden, Sandy remembered her own struggles against the bindings, the cool brush of fur under her fanged jaw, soothing words from the English rabbit who brought her fury low, blade at her throat but no killing stroke delivered.

She recalled her lessons. "You were taught as a kit, just as I was, that the carnivore is deemed closer to God for his consumption of Christ the carpenter's sacrifice when the chosen were starving after too long on the Ark. His flesh was given with the promise that no flesh from his chosen would follow. As a descendent of herbivores, my kind were said to have rejected the offer." Sandy shrugged. "That's ancient scripture for you, fuzzy on details, sorted on who to blame for the world's ills." She gathered more water, soothed more wounds.

"In the carnivore's eyes this burden against their wants makes them higher regarded in heaven's gaze. But they still sup of feral flank, still find their nourishment. And they still kill one another in wars. Donovan pointed out the bit of hypocrisy in this, but more importantly he revealed something our plight makes very apparent. Do you know what that is, Keller?"

His eyes met her with wordless pleas for relief.

"It means the power of restraint required to live among mortals makes any carnivore's burden pale in comparison, to you or I, bringing you closer to God than anything on two legs upon this earth. You can crawl from the depths of the pit to the doorstep of Heaven itself. Now tell me Keller, whom do you wish to harm?

His grey lids squeezed shut and opened again. "No-bu-ee."

"You understand that you can't live as you've done without causing pain?"

"Yeth."

"Do you wish to be delivered from that pain?"

He nodded, groaning. "Yeth."

Sandy recognized his reluctance. Other Nosfurs had sought to talk their way out of their binds, escape, relapse into their horrors. Sandy had reluctantly turned those over to Donovan's people, and she didn't know where those wretches' ashes were scattered.

She so desperately wished to provide her benefactor with another success, gain Donovan's admiration along with his trust. The rabbit had been such a steady, comforting presence when the pain was greatest, keeping her focused, protected.

She wanted that warm gaze now, that caressing hand on her brow and that gentle promise that salvation could find her. The love Sandy knew Donovan held for her was ever close, despite the ravaged condition her abstinent body had been subjected to. She'd passed Donovan' tests with the same vigor that he himself would show in passing the tests of the lioness sent to grind his designs down. The Lion was of the old world and its old ways, slow to understand.

Loyalty would serve Sandy well and the truth would be apparent, that Donovan and Sandy were meant to be more than master and servant.

She smiled. "You must choose to control your urges, battle temptation and regain yourself as I have. Misery will turn to gratitude. I promise."

"You're eaaa."

"Take your time, Keller, please."

He hissed as the minute movements of his mouth brought pain to the cavities where his fangs had been plucked. Sandy had stood with him, holding his hand as the pliers worked.

He glared through the fog of agony. "You're ollll annn oook ike oouur eaaad. Whaa ii ey ooo too you?"

Old. Looked like she was dead.

A hard nugget of anger grew in the squirrel. "I forgive you Keller. You cannot yet find grace to helps yourself rise above mere pelt-deep concerns. We're children of a cruel world, but we can find our way in a new one."

She thought of how Donovan would delight in her restraint, nod his young head, ears bobbing lightly with that warm smile.

She reached to the hand mirror that she'd kept for watching her own mortal reflection succumb to the ravages of time which immortality had stolen from it. She showed Keller his own face, a pustulous, cracked ruin under patches of sun-singed fur.

The raccoon's eyes widened, and he began to sob.

Sandy took the mirror away, satisfied that another lesson had been taught. "We're far beyond the physical concerns of mortal flesh aren't we Keller?" She wet the rag and returned to soothing his wounds. "I'll help you find that grace," she said sweetly.

Sandy had long fought to control her anger, but if she was to be honest with herself, restraint rarely came right away.

***

The Berghof restaurant delighted Countess Von Haften's nose with the burnt sugary tang of roasted meat. Crisped flesh dripped au jus onto ivory porcelain platters while Roman-styled kylix pooled with ersatz-wine were lapped by fanged mouths. Red hooded lamps cast the Tudor-styled innards of the restaurant in perpetual dusk.

And the cinnamon glaze of sautéed carrots and buttered broccoli wafted from their booth to wrinkle the noses of carnivores downwind.

This amused the Countess, who watched the rabbit consume his roughage. The lioness polished her own fillet off, catching roving appraisals of her that disdained him. The rabbit enjoyed his legumes with gusto and occasionally met beady gazes with a flat toothed grin that owned the world.

"How did you even get in here?" Von Haften dabbed blood from her chin.

His smirk was self-satisfied. "If it has a door, I can get through it. I found out the Berghoff only admitted carnivores shortly after relocating here. I gave myself a year to correct that oversight, managed it in six months."

"You bought your way in," snickered the lioness as she reached under the table. The flask Donovan slipped in was under his coat tail, out of sight from the smart waiters passing by, tight ties shoving hairy chins skyward under their borne platters.

The flask had a tipple left which the Countess added to her shallow stemmed glass before bringing it up to lap at.

Donovan chewed thoughtfully. "Charm goes further than money, but money is the spark. The owner would lose face with peers if they knew a grinder had rescued his business from a zoning dispute that could have shut him down."

Donovan referred to himself as a vegetable grinder with indifference to the slur. He took another bite. "Twice a week I fascinate myself with the discomfort of fanged poshes and prigs who detest my presence." The rabbit met her eyes, challenging her. "I know I don't belong here. What fun would I have if I did?"

The Countess rolled her golden shoulders and laughed. The black dress she'd chosen was oily in the light. "I expected something like that from you."

"Amusing as meat-eater condescension is, I don't come just to cause trouble. This den of starving carnivores is a proving ground for my place in Chicago's society."

"Really?"

"So often I retain great and amiable relations with carnivores behind closed doors, but in public…many melt away, spare the curtest nods and reluctant handshakes. I maintain business with those who can surpass such exclusionist posturing. The rest can fuck right off." Donovan proffered a cigarette case and offered one.

The Countess withdrew an ebony holder stem from her handbag. Donovan slid the rolled tobacco home, then produced a shorter ivory holder for himself. Two flicks of a silver lighter and the Countess puffed her branch to life. They smoked and soaked up the atmosphere.

The Countess broke the silence. "Why do you keep her? The bloodsucker?"

Donovan's ears went back, brushing the golf-leafed oak of the booth. "Honestly, with so many ears drifting our way…"

"If there are Rechtsanwälten," she picked out the English word, "lawyers in here, and I think I smell some, they've heard that term."

Donovan laughed. "Well, if you know anything about loyalty then you understand that one's desire to sublimate the self wholly to a cause is something truly rare. Miss. Mallory has a self-flagellating need to pay for past sins that is astounding."

"Surely a blood sucker," The Countess caught herself and shrugged, "a lawyer is not capable of such self-regard. The hunger is too persuasive in a creature that breaks the natural order of predator and prey in the sight of God."

"And there it is," Donovan tapped his ash into the silver tray set before a lit candle. "The natural order, gatekeeper to your world."

"Some guardians you can't tip your way past, Donovan."

"Some you have to slay I suppose." The rabbit sipped water and the lioness couldn't gather how serious he thought he was.

Loud muttering from the next table drew glances from them both. A pinstripe shirted male cougar with dark vest and bowler hat cocked on his brow glared at Donovan before returning to his plate, snickering to a broad-backed companion of ursine stock.

The Countess would cut the smaller cat to ribbons if he dared give her a look of that sort. She glanced to the rabbit and saw Donovan leaning over in order to see around the bear and catch the cougar's eye. They'd said something his ears caught but hers didn't.

The feline caught Donovan's gaze, near-beer touching his tan lips, blinking in surprise at the rabbit's glare.

"What are you doing?" the Countess asked sourly as Donovan's expression hardened. She could handle the cat if necessary and discourage the ursine from intervening in ways that he'd need to limp off, but she wasn't in the mood. "Ignore them. They won't be impressed by your factory or your money."

"I know what impresses them." Donovan showed his flat teeth.

The cat's jaw dropped, and the bear turned, snubbed nose sampling the air. Four eyes met two for a moment, and then the cat got up.

"What are you doing, Donovan?"

"Demonstrating something, Evelyn."

The lioness took a deep breath. The Council really had sent a Verrückte. "Don't ruin my first night out here. If you're dead, I'll have to go to one of Chicago's horrible hotels".

"I'm building better ones," Donovan smiled with his teeth but kept his eyes hard as the cougar with the bowler stooped over his table. "What do you want?"

The bruiser flared his nostrils, hackles nearly tipping the bowler between his ears. "I don't know why they let some grinder in or how you got on this doll's arm," a smile flashed the Countess's way that she did not reciprocate, then glared back to the rabbit. "but you don't belong in a carnie joint. You and your ears need to hit the bricks."

"I like it here," Donovan said. "Carrion notwithstanding, they prepare the best rice pilaf this side of West Randolf Street. For that I tip better than most reprobates they let in just for having sharper teeth." Donovan dabbed a napkin under his chin and let it drop. "Here is what will occur. You dew-dropping morons shall finish your meal quietly and not glare my way again. Nod if you understand."

Heads had turned at other tables now, switching tails revealing the level of tension rising. At the cougar's table, the bear watched balefully.

For her part, the Countess took another draw from her cigarette. The rabbit was about to get himself hurt and prove what exactly?

Donovan stood his back pointed ears up as if to remind the cougar and all those who surrounded him of his species. "And take that damn hat off in here," Donovan hissed. "It's incredibly rude to the owners of the establishment."

The cat's hackles stood higher. Called to attention for the slight he couldn't leave the cocked bowler in place before those watching, but to remove it at the rabbit's insistence was an unbearable loss of face in present company.

Indecision brought a hiss, then he snatched his hat from his head, claws stabbing the felt. "I want you out, limey rabbit. There's no place for you in an upstanding establishment like this."

Donovan sneered. "I dine where I please with whom I please. I've built parts of this city literally from the ground up and will accomplish more in my slowest year than you will in your whole sorry life." The rabbit thrust a hand into his lapel and withdrew a money clip. Bills counted out quickly but methodically upon the table linen. "Accept no change, Countess. The overworked staff won't be properly compensated by louts like this." He slid from his chair, taking his cane, leaving his top hat on its hook. "I'll return momentarily."

Evelyn glanced at the short stack of twenties and sighed. The rabbit really wanted to do this, as did the cougar who fumed like a stove.

The Countess caught a twinkle in Donovan's eyes, delight from one who knows what the world has in store but is determined to thwart it. She knew the rabbit would hate her intervention. Let Donovan satisfy his ego without an audience.

Donovan pushed past the cougar who followed him, tail low and coiling. The bear who dined with the cougar started to get his own things in order, muttering at being left with the bill again.

A vulpine waiter came to clear away evidence the rabbit was ever there and the money vanished. A weasel followed with a brush, relieving the leather chair of lingering stray hairs in deft strokes.

Evelyn smoked and thought.

***

The sky was dark, dusk glinting the tops of buildings as Donovan pushed through the brassed oak doors into warmer air. His heart was quickening, senses separating smells off the pavement as he crossed West Adams St and paused at an alley's mouth so the cougar could follow without difficulty.

Donovan waited, white suit and fur standing out against the dark trash-spewed maw. Stacked empty wooden crates smelled of moulder. Gravel was rough under his feet.

The cougar came, hanging his hat on a lampstand and rolling up striped sleeves. "You coulda said you were sorry in there, rabbit. I woulda let you walk out. Now you're gonna get a broken jaw and leg too. You can limp to some other joint."

"My business is my business. You don't tell me where I'm to conduct it."

The smattering of pedestrians passing quickened their step to escape. Good.

There were no tricks to be played, no magic, no science. This just might be a fair fight. Donovan let his cane click on the gravel. The cougar didn't see the steel ram's head twist independently of the black wooden shaft.

The cat snickered. "Veggies don't sit with a fine feline like that without expecting to get your eyes served to you."

Donovan breathed slow, set a foot back. "So, claw them you idiot."

The cougar was on him with a yowl, claws slashing for keeps. Donovan dodged right, cane tip nicking the cougar's slacked knee as the larger mammal's left digits struck his shoulder, ripping fabric. They danced apart, the cat off balance and knee smarting.

The cougar shifted weight, tail lashing and flicked a knife up from his pocket, fish-gutting steel dirty in the wan light. Donovan felt a surge of excitement. The cat lunged, blade arcing. Donovan had already set his play, fencing solutions finding sinew's memory. A flick clattered the hollow cane shaft against the brickwork. The freed blade flicked under the cat's swing in a Passato Sotto and an upward jab found flesh.

The cat yowled as the blade bit between rib cage and hip, muscle cut, guts nicked. Nothing fatal, but pain would suggest otherwise. The knife dropped and the cougar hissed as he sunk to his knees.

The fight could have been over, but Donovan knew better. On his knees, nothing was more dangerous than an angry specist.

Murder of a mortal was something he'd never stooped to, nor would he maim the cat with a lost eye or shorn ear. Donavan was coldly decisive.

Thumb aside the blade's steel shaft, Donovan brought the blade under the cougar's muzzle, tracing its contour upwards to his whiskers. With thumb down on the whiskers, Donovan gripped, twisted, and sliced.

The shriek pierced the rabbit's ear drums, likely to heard from blocks away. The cougar went fetal in the thin layer of the alley's muck.

Donovan was to the point. "If I pass by with my companion who's favor you clearly want and find your wounds being licked here in this alley, well that will be your shame, won't it?"

He kicked the cougar's knife down the alley, careful not to touch toe to blade and retrieved his cane which he slid over his rapier's bloodied length.

Re-entering the restaurant, Donovan tossed the bowler on the cat's unfinished meal. The ursine still seated gazed back at the door in confusion. He didn't rise, embarrassed.

The Countess had Donovan's own hat in her lap, thin thread of smoke from her cigarette puffing her only exclamation. They left the Berghoff in silence.

The ride back had Donovan occupying a corner of the salon car as the lioness had to lounge diagonally to avoid brushing the Roll's wood-framed canvas roof. Most of the ride was in awkward reflection.

"The steak there was good," The Countess said.

"I've heard," Donovan muttered indifferently.

"Bit boring near the end," she added.

Edmond steered the car around some dodgy roadwork. Donovan wondered if hitting a deep pothole would bounce the Countess's head through the roof's fabric. The damage would be worth seeing that. "You didn't think I'd win, did you?"

Her shrug boiled his blood. "I wanted to know if your confidence was a fool's impulse. Now I know."

"How often Countess," Donovan tapped his cane on the car's rumbling floor. "How often must I surpass your paltry expectations of me before you, your husband and all the other members of the Martyres finally start seeing my accomplishments as something beyond the overreach of a lesser player. When does the cajoling and undermining of my resourcefulness stop?"

Countess Von Haften showed her teeth, the faintest ring of laughter in her voice. "Why Donovan, you truly *do* care."

The steel ram's head bit into the circulation of Donovan's palm. "I've always cared about the cause, about putting the menace in place before it overruns the world. What…bothers me is your failure to comprehend that the means to achieve this are as within my grasp as anyone's. Can you not at least see the potential of what I've shown you today?"

"A demon as pet does not inspire confidence."

"You've seen the result of an experiment, but you haven't seen the means to maintain the control I've gained." Donovan stamped the floor twice. "To the mill, Edmond."

A look back confirmed his employer was certain. The possum took the next left, towards the city's outskirts.

The Countess sighed. "Where are we going?"

"Someplace illuminating," Donovan replied.

The car passed ever shortening buildings, brick to wood, meagrely lit. Soon enough they followed an industrial side road, dimly lined with shrubbery. The night was ink and crushed gravel terminated in an iron fence with a lone ferret in stiff blues on sentry. Edmond was recognized and the gate opened to admit them.

Once past, small buildings loomed in the shadow of the main factory, squat and ribbed by smokestacks looming behind pools of sodium lit asphalt. Scents of volcanic ignition and cinders penetrated the car.

"Where are we?" The Countess wrinkled at the assault on her nose.

"The future," Donovan replied.

They parked by a corrugated door large enough to disgorge a whale. A grizzled dog pushed the door wider on greased tracks.

Edmond disembarked, opening the Rolls' door with a flourish. Donovan stepped down and held a hand out for the Countess, who slid from the car without help, her expression sour. Their feet pads crunched gravel as they entered.

Tongues of fire emitted from cauldrons borne on raised hoists like the curled knuckles of giants. Troughs stretched below, smoldering with cooling girders, watched over by sweat-mouthed creatures of all species, many shirtless and attentive to sparks spitting from dark machines containing roiling tempests.

"The night shift employs two dozen to maintain the forges. Hundreds work from first whistle at eight in the morning," Donovan led the Countess to a corner away from the spitting forges and the gapes of busy mammals who maintained his broiling enterprise. Naked bulbs illuminated steel stairs rising to gangplanks and a windowed office above. "What I've brought you to see is this way."

The Countess followed, ducking under beams low enough to scrape fur off her brow. Donovan's feet were warm on the steel grating as he brought her up grated stairs and around his office, past tracks dragging hissing cauldrons of molten steel releasing heat that made the air crackle. Towards the forge, where the ladles were poured with fire, steam obscured a gangplank with a closed steel locker. "Only I have the key to this box," Donovan proclaimed as they approached. "Can you guess what's inside?"

"I'm hot, rabbit." The Countess panted hard.

"We'll be quick. You have a knife as your reliquary, same as my cane rapier, blessed in breath with the incantations that make it an extension of your senses and containing the molten veins of iron that bound the coffins of the first anointed kings."

"Who left the Ark for the drying world," The Countess nodded.

"Or evolved in the Darwinian fashion into the first settlements," Donovan shrugged. "One never knows what myths to attach to inexplicable powers, but one can learn power's principle," he worked the key in the lock, "and stretch the perceived limits of that power."

The Countess ignored the heat and stepped forward as Donovan threw the metal doors wide. On three shelves were separate silken cloths, shrivelled from relentless heat. On each cloth lay an assortment of green tinged strips of metal, fractured pieces of iron.

"What is this?"

"Take one and smell." Donovan smiled. "See. Feel."

She did so. And nearly dropped it. "How did you find the nails of the first crypts? These nails held the Ark together as the world drowned, driven in by Noah himself."

"That's one account. Or they're shards of iron with unique properties that science hasn't unravelled but yield powers we've only begun to apply. I won't argue." Donovan gauged her reaction to what he said next. "I found them here in the remains of a settlement that had belonged to coyote tribes pushed off by Americans carving the world westward. It would appear that the European definition of the "first mammals" could do with some revision."

The Countess gritted her teeth. "What are they doing kept in your steel mill? How protected could this find be in a place like this?"

Donovan chuckled despite the sweltering heat. "Kept? Oh, Countess. You don't understand the true potential of these shards yet. Certainly, your dagger and my rapier and your husband's axe-head have been useful to our craft, but I've learned to think a bit bigger. Can you remember the blessing incantation, the words that imbue the reliquaries with their power? How long did they take to recite over our forged weapons when we were ordained into the order?"

"Hours," the Countess breathed.

"Hours to complete the incantations." Donovan closed thin lips over his teeth and cocked his head. "When I stand above this cauldron every few days it takes roughly forty-five minutes." He plucked the shard from her loose, enraptured grasp and threw it over the gangplank into a passing ladle of steel. There was a single hiss, and then it was gone.

The Countess gripped the rails and crouches low as though ready to leap into oblivion after it. "What the hell have you done?"

Donovan wanted to laugh. "I've forged a new future, Evelyn." He closed the locker and secured it as she fumed down upon him. He put up a hand and met her gaze. "Before acting rashly, it's time for you to see what I've accomplished. Come with me."

She swore in German between growls as she glared at the locker containing treasure beyond reckoning and then followed. They retraced their steps, Donovan feeling her eyes bore into him the whole way down.

"You're going to give me that key," the Countess said at last.

"I'm going to give you a bigger gift than that," Donovan said as he moved into the dark and over to a stack of steel girders. He slowly slid his rapier from its cane. Von Haften's own hand was on her dagger, the dresses' hip parted.

"Draw your dagger. Open your senses to it. Feel the nature of the creatures here, no threats, no disturbances. How far do those senses carry,

Countess, ten feet, twenty, your line of sight perhaps or your range of smell?"

"Close enough to know you're the only one I might need to kill tonight," she said firmly. "You've wasted a part of something more precious than anything on this earth."

"No Countess. I put it to its best use. Look." Donovan grabbed a cloth covering and threw it aside. Steel girders lay stacked, flat H joints piled geometrically, bound for their trip to the city. At the cap end, each bore a tiny pressmark of his trademarked rabbit with lightning bolt in hand. Next to that, on a few girders, was a monogrammed spike. What somebody would have taken for a railroad spike, a member of the Martyres would recognise as the monogrammed nail from the Ark used for the crypts of the first kings.

"Do you feel it?" Donovan asked, heart giddy with anticipation.

"Feel what?"

Touch this girder." Donovan reached out and put his hand upon the marked steel. Reluctantly the Countess did the same. All at once Donovan felt the ground hum underneath him, the air crackle, and beyond that, outside to where the deep sky itself breathed upon the beating heart of the world. His senses, and the Countess's were cast outward like the sensitive skin of a creature that spanned the whole of the forge, feeling every breath of the wind, every crawling whisper of the night.

"Now you understand," Donovan said.

The Countess couldn't say a word.

The whole way home she was silent, nothing spoken until the car reached the Gold Coast and Donovan's manor gates parted. Donovan offered his hand as he stepped from the car, and this time she took it. "I must contact the council. I need a secure telegraph line and total privacy."

Not another word was spoken as they entered the house, and he indicated a vestibule in the corner of his room where his morse line was. She locked herself away without a word.

Time passed and Donovan's mood soured from pride to disappointment. What had he honestly expected from the Countess, adulation? Accolades? What had driven him to think a single word of gratitude or acknowledgement of his accomplishment would escape the lioness' lips now that he'd shown her a new world he'd forged out of applied intellect and fearless persistence?

He paced outside his own room, burning a circle in the carpet. He could only imagine the substance of the interchange using undersea cables across the Atlantic to a smoke-filled room where Evelyn's husband would hear of the brilliant discovery that had come to fruition. All under the meager understudy they had exiled to the land of swing dancing and gangsters.

Obviously, Evelyn Von Haften would readily have her husband assume that credit, raise their fortunes within the Martyre's council, cut Donovan just enough slack to glean more of his secrets. Donovan was so glad he hadn't told her everything. Oh God how he was starting to hate her.

The thought hadn't thundered out of the recesses of his soul one moment before the door to his room cracked open. "Donovan. Would you please come here?" It wasn't a demand. Her tone was low and inviting.

His mind clouded, he entered.

Von Haften purred upright on the chaise by a cracked open window, far from the telegraph booth. A breeze caught her scent and cast it Donovan's way. He blinked once, then again.

Her naked flank drank the moon and her bared femininity proudly acquiesced to the chill. Eyes were creamshine slits and her teeth fenced in a tongue that playfully darted. "Come to me."

Donovan came to her.

"Are you all white under those ears?"

He didn't understand the question, then he did, and his ears dropped back to hide a blush. "I…did you speak to your husband?"

She fitted a cigarette into her lacquered holder, shoulders rolling as she leaned back and lit with the lighter Donovan had never taken back at the Berghoff. "No. I informed his secretary that my return is to be delayed, for how long I'm uncertain. Her legs uncrossed and Donovan got a glimpse past the dark pads of her toes and muscular legs to a pink vertical shine. Her tail across the chaise flicked to obscure her, then revealed her once again. Amber eyes followed his necktie downward. "You didn't answer my question, Donovan."

He found his voice, senses cast into a wholly different world from moments ago. His anger had fled. In its place—he watched her bosom rise and fall. "My pelt is white, everywhere," Donovan replied. "Except my ears."

"I don't believe you."

He managed a broken smile at the absurdity of this moment. What had been behind the look on her face when she touched the steel? Had there been something he'd missed when returning from correcting that fool outside the Berghoff?

When she first saw him in the front hall of this very manor?

He was forced to reassess so much but was cottoned-up at that moment. A swell deep down the burning center of his lapine-self insisted that talking was behind them. His dinner jacket was already slipping from his shoulders.

She waited as a natural hunter familiar to stillness. Only her tail tip marked time as she watched buttons part, fabric fall. His coiled muscles bunched under his glassy pelt, malehood rising once freed.

Neither spoke as he left the thicket of clothes, Evelyn ashing out her cigarette. A return tug of breeze brought a single grey flake to rest upon her abdomen where it waited to be smeared into the tawny gold.

Donovan came to the lounge's edge, between the pale knobs of her toes, the inky black of her pads and further still, lips parted to smile as she traced his chest with a finger, up his throat and around his cheek to follow an ear. His own hands explored her shins, then her parted knees.

He leaned in to kiss her, and she stopped him with a shushing finger that slipped up over his brow and began to push downward to where her thighs parted just a bit further. "Burrow for a bit, would you Donovan?" she whispered.

It was subjugatory, demeaning by some standards, but Donovan was only dimly aware of what he was supposed to think. Scent crept upward with mysterious heat, and he was curious at what his tongue could learn.

And teach. The rational seed within him found purchase. He'd make this lion pliant, play her game, perfect his own, see what the morning could bring.

His nose trailed the space between her breasts, supple under his gentle, tracing squeeze and he genuflected as the trail ended at pearlescent shine and the dewspring of a summer to come.

Chapter 5

For Those in Peril

Night air flowed through Bucky's pelt as Celeste led him to the alley behind his apartment. "This is your first lesson," she said. "This skill will save you again and again. Observe."

Outside the gate meager moonlight painted jagged teeth on the alley's picket fence. Beneath all was dark. The doe stepped towards the closest shadow and melted into it completely.

Silence fell. The fox's nose tested the air. Her scent was gone. "Where'd you go?"

The reply had no origin. "Shadows are veils concealing multitudes of mysteries. Now you can see where they begin, and end can't you?"

She was right. A derelict cub's wagon missing two wheels lay against the rickety pine fence. It had previously been something to trip over, but now he could make out its stark outline, the patina of rust dotting its axle. Every detail in the alley was visible now save slivers of darkness deep as gouges in a photograph. From one of these voids Celeste's laughter tinkled. "Here I am."

A hand touched his shoulder and he jumped. "How did you do that?"

"Bind one shadow and you easily bind its neighbor. You can slip the darkness around you to skip from one to another."

"How?" Bucky was skeptical, but the burn from sunlight's morning assault still ached. Doubts were already costly.

"Look to the darkest shadow you can find. Then approach with purpose. There are no doors, just without and within."

"That don't make no sense at all," Bucky replied sourly, finding a space so devoid of light that he couldn't focus.

"Go to it. Enter and bind it. You'll know when it's happened."

Bucky took a step forward, trying not to feel ridiculous as he imagined throwing a black curtain around himself. Had Celeste not disappeared he'd assume she was having a gas at his expense.

He sidled up against that fence and felt in his mind's eye something beyond it, a barrier that wasn't solid, wasn't anything really, yet it was there. He shrugged himself through it with a step that his feet took no part of.

Turning, he saw the alley through gauze, the ruined wagon, scattered trash further on. Night sounds were crystal clear, smells strong. Rust, flaked paint, rank weeds. "To your right," her voice surrounded him. "Come to me. I'm in the shadow next to you."

Bucky moved, and right away felt something off. The veil slipped and loose gravel crunched under a foot.

"You've left your shadow completely. Enter the next one."

He took a useless breath, mortal habits holding strong, and slid back into the void again. Dimmed vision, perfect clarity of scent and sound resumed.

"Now don't walk to the shadow where I am, simply be there. You only need feel the next closest shadow in order to arrive."

The next sliver of perfect black beckoned, and with a nudge it was his shadow instead. Then the next. With glee he sized up the shadow he could feel the doe in and slipped into it like a silk robe. "How are we both in here together?"

"I told you distance doesn't matter." The doe took Bucky's hand in her soft, strong palm. "I'm as near or as far as I need to be."

Bucky felt her palm slide away. In a blink a shadow several feet away released her. "To survive you'll need to practice and understand this skill until it's instinctive. You'll use it often."

They left the alley and practiced. Streetlights were pools of detection to avoid. Doorframes and alleys became intimate friends. Faster and faster, they flitted from shadow to shadow, Bucky narrowly avoiding night porters at first, then deftly avoiding couples departing "dry" cabarets and other venues as the evening progressed. They made their way to the center of town.

A vulpine cop swung a club by the leather loop in white gloved hands, badge and buttons shining on her blue coat. She nodded to patrons exiting restaurants with her nose quivering, plainly checking passing breaths for something that wasn't soda or seltzer. Carnivores nodded politely; vegetarians steered well clear.

"Fucking vixen pig," Bucky muttered.

"Sounds like you're in love," Celeste muttered, amused. "Follow her. Discreetly."

They did, shadow to shadow. A Celtic ditty escaped the cop's lips. A mick fox cop, probably put her own kin in stocks on a regular basis. Getting cocky, Bucky bound a shadow ahead with Celeste close behind. He could smell the vixen strongly, heat of the late spring faded, dander dotting the air off her tail.

The fox cop's throat fur caught the light as she finished a verse and swallowed.

Bucky watched her ivory throat with fascination, like milk pouring down a desert cliff, pure and inviting. He heard life gurgling within her, making him thirsty.

Hid teeth started to hurt.

Celeste slipped into his shadow and her arm slipped round his chest. "Be still," she muttered. "No sound."

Bucky was brought to heel by the prickle of his flesh near the faded fire of his burn. The cop walked on, pushing her cap up with her truncheon, scent hitting Bucky hard enough to make his jaw ache.

The hiss in his ear from Celeste was curt. "No cops. Not here."

The vixen in question stopped, cocked an ear their way and side-eyed the shadows with a squint. Past where they stood two cats trailing cigarette smoke crossed the street. The fox considered them, turned and resumed her beat.

Bucky was on the verge of salivating. His fangs wouldn't retreat. The cop's gait was indolent, confident in a way that reminded him of Johnny Torrio leaving a meet, overcoat worn like a cape.

Whose order put Bucky here on this corner learning the ways of a whole new life after an untimely death? Pity for Johnny, someday.

"When do we eat?" Bucky was now starving. When he slipped from the shadow into a shallower pool of darkness by a closed pharmacy door, he could see the tips of Celeste's own fangs peeking past the rest of her flat teeth.

"Soon," she said. "But self-control is essential. Remember that any-body who disappears has somebody coming looking for them."

"Not everybody though, right?" Bucky sighed bitterly. "We both know that's kinda what you depend on."

"It is," Celeste said unapologetically. "Just remember, I chose a better fate for you."

A better fate. Bucky now had only one person in the whole world to confide in and it was his own assassin. A cold realization hit him. "I'm never gonna get to say goodbye to my mother, am I?"

Celeste was silent for a long time as the honks of evening drivers drift-ed by. "Be grateful you have people left you can't say goodbye to," Celeste finally said. "It's better for those who don't know what we are. The pain of separation passes. You already risked that in your past line of work."

Bucky knew his mother would wonder where he'd gone and worry herself sick for a while. His father would be glad to never see him again, would convince his mother soon enough their son was dead. Bucky would miss the great Italian meals his mother prepared when he dropped by, ground beef sprinkled over penne, offerings to lure him back from the fel-las he'd grown tight with in Johnny's outfit. But he'd maintained *omerta*, his silence. Little good that did him.

His current condition was one man's fault, even if Celeste was the weapon Johnny put into play. "Can we go back to my place?"

"No. Johnny wanted to be notified immediately when you were… removed. He'll send someone to ensure there's no traces for the police. He only trusts the people he has so far, but you know that."

"Yeah." Bucky's grimace was pained around his fangs. The hunger was getting stronger. "Where to then? We supposed to sleep in an alley?"

"Not at all. I have what we need…" Celeste trailed off and Bucky turned to follow her gaze.

Down the street a hunched figure crossed the median from the shad-ow of a pharmacy. The silhouette of a tail large as the person leading it gave the species away as a squirrel. She wore matronly vestments, stooped with age, reddish fur patched in grey. She moved purposely against the stream of night-walking city dwellers.

Celeste stood stock still as the figure stopped, sensed something and turned. The expression on the distant squirrel was unreadable.

"Someone you know?" Bucky asked.

Celeste stood still and Bucky realized she was holding her ground, defiant.

A moment passed before the squirrel left the meager light behind, vanishing in the dark.

***

If there was a secret knock, the doorman had forgotten it. Crawford went hatless and Charlie cocked his to look bohemian. The paisley neck scarf he'd brought completed the affect. A ferret from the bureau named Leslie backed them up, staying at the door. There were seven drinkers, total.

Crawford lifted the needle from the phonograph and Fanny Brice quit singing about how the rich got rich and the poor got children. He held his badge high. "This is exactly what it looks like, so I hope you'll all go to that side of the room without a fuss."

Two hares doing the shimmy tried to break for it. The lady was out the open window in one cotton tail shake, but Charlie caught her company by the foot and held fast. "Evading arrest is a night downtown at best," Charlie called to the rest of the hare outside. "How about you settle the ticket and bygones'll be bygones."

The hare let himself be drawn back in with a grumble before the wolf closed the window. "Skip over there," Charlie said.

"Goddamit!" a voice called from the kitchen where bottles and glasses collected next to loose bills and coins. "You Prohees don't have any big fish to terrorize?" The goat stamped over to where Crawford lowered his badge. "I'm trying to make ends meet!"

Crawford could smell the goat's indignation. The apartment was dilapidated, thread bare furniture and a rickety lean to everything else. Only the phonograph looked new. "You can certainly afford good music with the proceeds of crime," Crawford countered.

"That's borrowed," the goat waved plaintively. "I had to put up a buck in case it gets ruined."

"What if it does?" taunted Leslie from the door. She had a wicked disposition for scofflaws who gave her lip.

"Come on, please! I'm a horn player for God's sake. You Feds emptied the clubs and I barely get work. It's this kinda racket or I have to pawn my brass."

Charlie sighed, wandering over to gather the money. "You writing the slips, Craw?"

He wasn't happy and Crawford knew they both felt the same sour detachment dividing what a mammal felt and what they were expected to do. Grumbling from the handful of partygoers got louder but complaints cut out quick as Leslie drew her gun. "Dewdroppers get in line!" She shouted. "You're all in violation the Eighteenth Amendment as enforced by the Volstead Act. Line up!"

In fear, they cooperated. One by one fines or names were taken and slips given. Lambs and cats and a limping hare melted out of the apartment as Charlie passed the money to Crawford before grabbing the hooch they'd soon dump outside. The last muskrat left kneaded his hands. "Please don't tell my dad about this. He'd hide me good."

"Pay the fine within forty-eight hours and that's a deal," Leslie said indifferently, pointing to the hall with her muzzle. Moments later only the three Prohees and goat tenant remained.

"You're all some pieces of work," the goat had tears in his eyes as he stared at the bottles in Charlie's grasp. "Fed bastards kickin' working mamms right in the teeth. You know that whoever tipped you off most likely works for the mob?"

Charlie met his withering gaze and said nothing. The goat pressed harder. "That's right. Wise guys for the gangs tip you off to little players to kill competition. You're too stupid to know you work for them half the...." The goat ground his teeth together and stared into Charlie's eyes. "Wait a second, I know you."

Charlie blinked and looked from Crawford to Leslie and back again. "No, you don't."

"Yeah. I don't get a lot of gigs anymore, but I *seen* you. Down by tower town where the sailors and whores get trade. Your Missus know where you spend your nights?"

Charlie's hackles jumped. "Listen real careful!"

Crawford stopped counting money and Leslie raised an eyebrow as Charlie snarled. "You slander an officer in the course of their duties and get a trip out that fucking window. We'll see if you enjoy head-butting pavement!"

The goat clammed up, fuming. Charlie turned and marched for the door. "Agent's Cain and Pardor, are we done here?"

"We are," Crawford said, tearing off the final slip. He watched Charlie adjust his hat straight enough to balance a marble and step out past Leslie, who gave a questioning look to the brown wolf's back.

"Do the honors?" She asked Cain.

First offence warnings. "Yeah."

The wolf was left with the goat and the goat put spittle next to Crawford's foot. "Suppose you're gonna tell my landlord. Have her kick me out before my rent's even late, right?"

Crawford looked the place over, nose working as he caught a scent over by the long-worn sofa. One cushion was bent and one was perfectly straight. "You shoulda had somebody sitting here when strangers came in," Crawford said apologetically as he lifted the cushion and exposed one more bottle stuffed between bent springs. If the label was authentic, it was decent stuff.

The goat's face practically caved in, destitution making a grave inside him. "Take it," he muttered miserably.

Charlie and Leslie were now down the hall. Before he could change his mind, Crawford tucked the bottle under one arm and clutched the dollars in his pocket. Bringing out the stack, he broke off two fives and a few ones. The ten would have to go, as would most of the rest. "Quickly," he said with a hand outstretched, and the goat snatched it. "Wherever you do this next, get somebody who checks passwords. Make sure it's *not here*."

"You're not a total bastard," the goat muttered, studying the money in his hand like a ticket to faintest hope.

Crawford pulled the cork. His hand hurt like hell as he took a swallow. Fire brushed his gums and throat. "No. It's quite likely I'm going to drown in hell." Crawford handed the bottle back and left, bandaged hand itching again.

Leslie was down the hall, Charlie a little further on. Nobody said a word as they returned to Crawford's car.

"He give you any lip?" Agent Pardor asked from the passenger seat. Charlie had taken back seat without a word.

"He understands how things are," Crawford fished for his keys.

"What is that?" Leslie turned her muzzle up so her ears could better hear the sad roll of a horn drifting down on them. All three held still as notes softened the night.

"Old naval dirge," Charlie said with a sigh. "For those in peril on the sea."

***

"Someone you know?" Bucky asked.

Celeste watched Sandy Mallory move on, shoulders stooped with seventy plus years of mortal age. The Irish squirrel was infirm, perhaps even dying, but knowing how she became that way made Sandy more dangerous than any of her kind. "It doesn't matter. Make sure to stay away from her. We need to bind shadows all the way to my home. Mind what you've learned and check to ensure we aren't followed."

"Who's going to follow us?" The fox was confused.

Celeste knew they had to move. "If we're careful enough, no one."

Bucky did as told. With increasing confidence, he bound shadows down Michigan Avenue like a leaf in a breeze.

They passed through less-populated areas, closed shops, and gas parlors, chattering basement speaks and gambling dens buzzing with life. Celeste's place was much like Bucky's own, but an end lot on a row with higher fences for privacy and three floors all to herself.

Inside was a picture of cleanliness. Most of the rooms were empty with windows boarded over. The main floor had a covered sofa and a table for a telephone. The bed upstairs was tidily made with a single depression in the springs of a doe in repose, day after day.

"You could open a great speak' here," Bucky sniffed at the sparsely furnished parlour and the dark vacant kitchen beyond.

"And be closed down in a week by Volsteaders leaving me homeless." Celeste chided patiently.

The fox's tail swished. "Anything to drink?"

Celeste knew that the next lesson would be hard. Better to get things over with. "I have wine in a cupboard by the stove."

Bucky wandered into the kitchen and rummaged, seemingly unaware of how dark it was and how much his night vision had improved.

"We'll need to feed," Celeste said. She was only slightly hungry from making a meal of him, but he had to be ravenous.

He appeared with a bottle of chianti and two glasses. "Wine would go well with it, yeah?"

He was about to find out. "Dinner's on the second floor. Make sure you only take a live one."

Confused, but curious, Bucky followed her up. They passed a disused study sparsely shelved with English language books and a dusty lavatory to a closed room with the faint sounds of scratching at its walls.

Inside the doorway was a short wall of lumber to keep the creatures from slipping out. Excremental and urinary scents dirtied the air.

About a dozen feral rats darted around the room, naked and aimless, what the religious referred to as God's unchosen, the Darwinists as unevolved. The largest rat was the size of a lunch pail.

The doe watched the fox as he watched rats dart, collide and hiss. "Swig that wine you're holding," she said above the thin screeches.

He sourly regarded the menagerie for a moment longer before setting the glasses on a rickety hall table, pulling the cork and pouring one for himself. He gave Celeste a questioning look.

"None for me. Please try it." The label indicated it was a 1909 Chateaux Margaux, a vintage that would dance on the average mortal's palate. He took a sip, worked it his mouth. Shock lowered his whiskers. "This is…it's tap water." He looked into the glass, swirled it, drank again. "I'm drinking nothing!"

"That which used to sustain us no longer does, Bucky." She stepped forward and bent to grab one of the rats. The dumb creature squirmed and snarled in her hand but couldn't get its head around to bite her. "Close the door."

The fox elbowed it shut, still in shock. Celeste had gleaned somewhere that Bucky was second generation Italian, his parents having steamed across the Atlantic. Personally, Bucky was a pure and unapologetic sybarite who no doubt loved the culinary bounty of his ancestry. Having his whole world reduced to textures was likely terrifying. A crueller pedagogue would tease this moment out, let him ponder eternity without zest or flavor.

Celeste wouldn't do that. She held the snuffling rodent up under Bucky's quivering nose. "All the vitality that life can bring starts with the vein and ends there. For us, there is only one path to nourishment." Her fangs sprouted as she brought the creature to her own nose. "Some sources are better than others, but all can provide us with what we need."

She bit the rat around the spinal column, and it hissed and bucked. Bucky flinched.

Celeste held the fox's gaze as she drank. The rat's limbs went stiff and then slack as its breathing slowed. She allowed the life to flow, copper and hot, swallowing once then twice before relinquishing her jaws. Bucky's eyes had lost their color and gained depth, black pools of hunger. "You know what to do. Remember the cop downtown. Go slowly, it'll be warm for a while."

He took the twitching rodent in one hand, sniffing it, revulsion losing its war quickly. He bit and drank without a second thought and Celeste dimly recalled that collision of disgust and urgent desire that marked her own first time. "Finish it all. You'll know when you have."

Blood quickly taken brought the headiness of a stiff drink and she saw it in his eyes. The wine of life dribbled from the corner of his mouth as he released the empty carcass. It bounced off the floor between his feet with a hollow thud, miniscule drops of blood speckling one foot.

Celeste watched the fox come back to himself, his gaze finding focus. His perception was already heightened, but now he would feel the vitality in the world around him. "Drink the wine again. Feel what's different."

Bucky lifted the vintage again and drank once more. The smile that crept to his lips revealed that flavor had returned. The wine was complex, currents and oak under the copper that would still be basting his tongue. The vintage was one of Celeste's own favorites in the small doses her condition allowed.

Glass empty, the fox licked his shrinking fangs. "A Montulpulcino would have gone better."

Celeste gave him a withering look. "With a rat pairing, that's not the boast you think it is."

"I could have gone with beef."

Celeste laughed. "Cows marched in here would raise eyebrows from the neighbors."

Bucky smiled and grabbed the bottle. "Let me have another."

"Not too much. Food and drink don't sustain you and you can only digest very small amounts without getting sick. When the blood is spent and potency lost the mortal processes of our bodies grind to a halt again, taste, aging, everything. Don't have a bellyful of food when that happens."

"Aging? Don't we...age?"

One truth opened the door to deeper ones. "With the senses brought to life, we do for a short while, but our candles burn slowly during that time. At the rate most of us consume we'll barely age a week or two in a year, provided we stay fed. Stop feeding long enough and the mortal processes will slowly return, not enough to enjoy taste and other sensual states, but enough to age the body again in slow decay."

"You're saying I'm..."

Celeste shook her head. "Not exactly. This isn't forever, but it very nearly will be if you feed at a pace of moderation, neither over-indulging nor starving." She held his gaze to ensure he understood. "Life will be longer than you've ever conceived possible, Bucky. I have aged mere months since I turned nearly one-hundred and thirty years ago."

Buck swayed slightly, setting the glass down. "I need..." he trailed off, lost in himself, the implications hitting hard.

The fact of long life, decades becoming centuries becoming eons, was difficult to accept. Mammalian philosophy had no concept of time as an indefinite accumulation of experiences. Life was a race from one moment to another down a short mortal corridor with an impassible end. Celeste herself had seen empires end, some abruptly, some slowly crumbling in her century and a half of life, only twenty of them mortal.

Bucky would need to learn to stand apart from the march of time, to avoid rumination of life without end. Celeste saw he was trying to breathe again, air pulled in and pushed out uselessly. He went for the bottle, pulled the cork to pour himself another glass, his gaze unfixed.

Celeste snatched the glass from his hand and set it down before grabbing him by the shoulders. Speckles of wine joined speckles of blood at his feet. "You need..." Celeste said, feeling his heart thud through her touch, blood making him fully live now. "To stay present with me Bucky. When the blood flows, so do you. So do we. Living in the moment is the only way to hold back madness. I've seen that happen. You must let go of so much that you assume you can't."

Bucky looked at her but didn't see her. With truth, blood, and wine mixing freely he was lost in confusion. "How do I do that?"

When bringing someone like Bucky back to the moment the simplest ways were best. She pulled him close and kissed him.

Breathless, there was only the softness of lip on lip, wet by the trace drops of vine and vein. His body immediately nestled into her larger ungulate frame. He was speechless when they parted.

"My room," she said, and he was in tow as though chained, urges aligning with the spark inside him. Standing by the bed, she fanned that spark to life with the fingering of his shirt buttons. These were the very same steps that had been interrupted when a mortal fox with mortal ambitions had threatened to kill her. That Bucky Cavali had to be cast off and forgotten.

Once again clothes were shed. He was frantic as a school kit, she was patient, keeping her eyes locked on his. Her own blood high brought heat to the erogenous join of body and mind, but she could keep her lust leashed where needed. Her kind survived on restraint. She had to teach the fox to learn the same. "Do you like to be rough?"

His heart was pounding again, not for long, but flush with life as he backed her into a corner. "You know I do."

His old self wasn't cast of yet. That required her help. "Do you want to be or need to be?"

He gave an idiot's hungry grin, tongue slipping out as his lips curled in a cruel tease. "I'll show you and you tell me." He kissed her again, his muzzle forcing its way against hers. His dark finger pads were on her bare breasts, claws digging. Celeste felt pain, but didn't react to that violation directly, instead leaning into that copper-lined kiss, her own hands slipping down his russet sides to his waist. His cock was already pressing against the inside of her thighs.

She found his scrotum with one hand and his cock with the other. Deftly, she twisted.

He screeched a register higher than she'd ever heard him speak and his claws released her chest to try and wrench her hands free. Celeste's grip was of pure steel, with Bucky's own malehood as the weakest link in the chain between them. He hissed and stamped one foot.

Celeste was unsmiling. "You showed me that you like it rough." She pressed her chest against his and pushed his back to the wall. "So, which is it, Bucky? Rough or gentle?"

He whined and tipped his head back, shuddering.

She kept his balls but released his cock to grab him by the throat before he could push her away. "It's a very important question I asked before Bucky. Do you want it to be rough or do you need it to be? Because if you don't need this to be rough then we can have fun a different way." Her grip on both throat and testicles eased off a bit, one thumb stroking his undercarriage.

He found his voice. "That hurt."

She felt his slowing heart as she purred like a cat into his ear. "You hurt me, your choice to make. You can't hurt me in any way that I can't hurt you. You can pleasure me in most of the ways I can pleasure you." She released his throat and coaxed his muzzle up so their gazes met again. "See? We can find enjoyment in letting go of certain specist assumptions. The first is that you're ever going to dominate me, Bucky. We can play at control. We can even play at pain." She flicked his cock with a forefinger and thumb, then rubbed its length to coax it again.

He flinched. "I'll..." his throat was dry.

"Yes?"

"I'll be good." He was embarrassed, his tail through his own legs, brushing her shins. He was growing hard all the same. "I want to play nice with you. I really do, Celeste."

Celeste smiled. Lesson learned. "I would certainly like that. Rough gets tiresome quickly, doesn't it?"

He nodded and she stepped away, hands gently gliding along his manhood to reel him to the bed. "Let's kiss each other's wounds better. Wouldn't that be nice?"

He was silently agreeable as she told him with a downward glance to go first. He bowed and cautiously kissed her breasts with lips and tongue, delicately working around each spot he'd been rough with, his malehood a leash in her hand. No doubt he knew that if he bit her, she'd return the favor, so he was careful.

He'd learn to like it and she'd reward him for that. Hurts soothed, she delicately lay Bucky on the bed and took his cock in her mouth, smiling as he hissed around her ministrations to what she'd harmed. Each hiss was more delighted than pained and the fox rolled his hips with the doe's slides.

What Bucky didn't yet know about himself wouldn't bother him. Brought to orgasm, nothing material issued. She swallowed around his loin's empty shudder, leaving him with the illusion of mortal potency. He wouldn't learn he was beyond that till he was ready.

They lay naked as heat faded, sex and mortality cooling, the blood's work done. Hunger would find them again in time.

"How do you feel?" Celeste asked.

"Better," Bucky said. His tail flicked to brush her shin. "I needed that."

"We both did," Celeste assured him. "There's a mess to clean before we sleep."

He propped himself on his elbows, squinting. "Oh, did I get any—"

"I refer to the dead rat downstairs." She smiled sweetly. "Would you please take care of that for me?"

They were both still for a moment, Bucky's attention drifted. "You know where I'd be tonight if you hadn't bit me?"

"No Bucky. In bed with a different vegetable eater? Or a carnivore?"

"I'd be getting a big shipment off a boat that Johnny has coming in; Canadian whiskey."

"So, grunt work for your old boss."

Bucky's sighed. "I've been removed and it's all going on like I never was."

For fucks sake. She had to be patient with him. "And in short time you'll be going on while they are no longer here, so forget them. You can be so much more than a bit player in the liquor racket."

"I was no bit player."

There was threat in his growl and Celeste sat up straight. "Get your head together. They don't matter. Now in the basement is a furnace, useless for keeping us warm but excellent for disposing of small unwanted things."

She let him think and he blinked. "The rat."

"Yes. Once that's done, there's kibble in the closet. Throw some into the rat room. Go now and if you're quick I'll help soothe you to rest when you return."

Bucky stood and crossed to the door, still naked. "The world needs rats, don't it?"

Celeste had her ears open to all the sounds in her house as Bucky collected the feral corpse and the rusty furnace door far below opened and closed. When he lifted the receiver of the phone on her main floor and whispered to the operator she sighed and shook her head.

CHAPTER 6

COPS, CADS, SCHEMERS, AND SOLDIERS

Charlie's bleary words snapped Crawford awake. "We've got to work."

Memory came in cold from ignorant bliss where there were no killings, divorces, or itching wounds. It took a moment for Charlie's words to penetrate. A speak was going to roll over, even though they weren't on call tonight.

"What?"

"Anonymous tip half an hour ago, big enough that Beatie cancelled two raids. He wants everybody hightailing it to Kinzie and North State. A big liquor shipment is coming in."

Crawford thankfully lay turned away from Charlie. Whiskey burned on his breath. "Okay, give me a minute."

Crawford collected himself and hurried to the icebox while Charlie loaded his Bureau issued .38 Smith and Wesson. There was fish in the ice box, one wrapped chicken leg and a fruit Crawford suspected was a tiny green apple that had shrivelled to leather. That would have the strongest scent and disgusting as it looked was, he needed that. Grimacing, he took a bite.

The thick shell broke and juice squirted thick upon his mouth and tongue, gagging him with a sour stab. The globe was a lime.

He hissed as acidic citrus attacked gums made raw by pain in his jaw. "Chawree, gawd."

The other wolf blinked and recoiled, nose snorting against the evidence. "Did you just bite straight into a lime? You think you have scurvy?"

"Thought it waahhs, ah, appal."

Charlie looked away, embarrassed for him. "I'll get you haddock at the diner when this raid is over, Craw. My treat. Let's go."

With dignity in tatters, Crawford followed. The escort from the office had already left and Charlie wasn't surprised when asked to drive. Charlie obliged, muttering complaints about how the office wouldn't install a phone for them but was fine sending blurry-eyed couriers. "We cross the water at Indiana and meet up at Dearborn and Michigan. That's where we're staging."

Crawford nodded. As the whiskey's grip faded, he didn't like the sensations he was getting. He ached in places he didn't know existed, bruises deep within. He checked his 1908's safety before pulling back the slide to confirm a .380 was chambered.

Charlie hung a quick right and bounced the curb, the road's demarcation barely visible in the weak streetlight.

Crawford swallowed. "Waking me up's gonna make us late isn't it?"

Charlie shook his head. "Raid's at one ay emm. It's only twelve fifty-something."

"Lucky us." The Chevy mounted the trussed swing bridge over Little Calumet River, just north of the Chicago waterway fork to the Lake, wheels clacking as it crossed. Buildings got taller as the Near North side loomed on their left where Gold Coast swanks held court beyond smaller tenements and mixed businesses. No doubt a sizable percentage of whatever was being unloaded in the shadow of Chicago's richest neighborhood would be pouring down wealthy gullets.

Charlie halted in the shadow of a small brick lot with cars boxing in cops and Beatie's core Prohibition unit. Heads turned, then turned back to the officers holding court after Charlie waved.

Crawford tipped his fedora low so his bloodshot eyes wouldn't be seen. The lime on his breath wouldn't be questioned.

"Good of you to join us," said Beatie, small eyes glinting under the rim of his homburg. "To review, Henderson, you're first on the front door, Keller your team covers through the alley."

A cougar cop and an ocelot in a trench coat each nodded, flanked by feds and cops looking antsy. Beatie had the local police and the Federal team integrating well, Crawford observed, grateful that he wasn't going to be on the team in cuffs very soon.

Beatie pointed at Charlie. "Agent Rothscub and Cain, you secure the docks from the East, check any boats you see docked, order a heave to of any marine craft on the channel that isn't. We've a boat blocking the River mouth, but only one so best you stop 'em here."

I'll swim out and catch any schooners with my very jaws sir, Crawford thought sardonically but nodded instead.

"You'll have a police detail with you, let me see if I get the names right, Rutherfurrd, Lockley and…Tulley?"

"Tooley sir," an otter in blue replied in working-clash Irish draught. "Rutherfurrd, Lockley and I can hold the dock if need be. The miscreant's'll be stampin for the alleys."

Crawford knew he'd seen the cop somewhere but couldn't place him.

Beatie shook his head. "We've enough bodies on the exits and I don't want them jumping boats for a lift up shore."

The otter's whiskers jumbled in silent disagreement. He was clearly one of those cops who didn't like playing with feds. "Sir," Tooley muttered.

A ferret slunk around the corner in plain clothes and approached Beatie. "Coast's clear, no lookouts." It was agent Pardor again, inconspicuous as always until she needed to be otherwise.

Beatie lifted his homburg and scratched the pelt between his cookie ears. "Remember that these scofflaws loading crates are foot-soldiers of Johnny Torrio, taking delivery from the Detroit Purple Gang. Most will be armed so you shoot resisters without hesitation. Anybody have any questions?" Every head shook.

"Not a peep till Henderson puts foot to wood and calls the warrant. Get moving."

The cougar's tail lashed behind her buttoned blues. "Stay low and keep close." She led her team away. Keller, the trench-coated ocelot snapped fingers to get the second into action.

Crawford and Charlie led the remainder, three cops backing Charlie and himself. They rounded the south side, following the river behind darkened buildings, keeping low. The wind blew west, sending the stink of the channel up their advancing noses, but Crawford was grateful for that. Nobody moving boxes off the boats would catch the scent of lupines, mustelids, felines and the tiniest hint of lime. Downwind was peachy.

Scent told tales. Wet pine crates, motor oil, damp pelts. In the dark behind the warehouse, shapes toiled and muttered. An ember burned, dropping to the sands for a foot to extinguish.

Crawford's team padded across docks and shoreline sand, ducking low behind a pile of kindling.

They didn't wait long. Wood splintered somewhere close and Henderson shouted. "This is a raid!"

Gunshots rang out. Calm dissociation spread through Crawford ahead of the adrenaline. Most brave people weren't really brave, he'd learned in France. They simply didn't respond to fear until it was too late to do otherwise. What came next settled how stupid a move that was.

On the dock, some were smart, some weren't. A pug with a hat flatter than his face unslung a revolver and hurried to the loading gate while the rest either dropped crates or hustled for the boat, biting off swears.

"While you've a Lucifer to light your fag, smile boys that's the style," Crawford muttered from a song he'd heard overseas. The 1908 weighted in his hand like a cold promise. He drew a breath.

Charlie beat him to it. "Stop there! Bureau of Internal Revenue!"

A fool drew iron, shooting wide and loose. Crawford and at least two cops put the hare down, gasping as he died.

Gunfire echoed inside the warehouse over yowls and screams. Whiskey scent spread like a kiss as merchandise shattered. Crawford's party hustled from cover to cover, Charlie at Crawford's side, close enough to hear him pant. One of Torrio's black wolves yipped as he took one low and center, rolled and started crawling away. Water splashed as somebody dived.

The three cops peeled off, moving on the boat. Charlie was potting at boxes hiding one perp whose ears kept poking up.

"The cops are taking the boat, let's pincher the warehouse," Crawford growled.

Scofflaws hightailed it, ironically with tails curled low. Two dock muscle were dead, one more leaving a long red trail as he crawled away, gut shot and soon to meet judgement. Only the ears-up canine shot back, clipping off a few before dropping again. Charlie flanked left while Crawford inched right as the canine's gun clicked twice. After a moment's hesitation a semi-auto bounced on the ground between the wolves.

"Ya fuckas gat me," came a New England drawl. Claws stabbed the air.

In the warehouse, gunfire trailed off under orders shouted for surrender. Over at the boat gunshots were still popping. The dock was on an

L-curve over the water obscured by other crates. Muzzle flashes tinted a sail.

"Charlie cuff em, and then get to the boat."

"Careful Craw." Charlie warned and nodded his revolver nodded downward. "Grab mud." The disarmed dog looked sourly into the dirt and Charlie wasn't having it. "You wore your Sunday best to a felony that's your problem."

Charlie had the dog in hand, so Crawford hurried on. As he approached the crates and reloaded he heard the Irish otter shouting between shots. "Go get 'em Lockley! I'll cover you."

Feet pounded wood. Crawford passed one of the cops, crouched and tail tucked. Blood speckled the marten's injured shoulder.

An Irish affected voice shouted something authoritative. A single gunshot rang out.

"Stay put, we'll get you looked after." Crawford told the marten before leaning out, gun up. The otter cop was crouched before a wooden gangplank that tumbled into the river as a skiff's motor chugged it away. The boat's skipper, a Canadian moose chomping a cigarillo, leaned into the wheel's sharp turn.

Crawford fired, missing the moose with the first shot and cracking an antler with the second. The moose bellowed curses in French as he ducked, hands spinning the wheel.

"It's too late!" came a shout to his left. The otter raised a hand to ward off more shots, his own gun smoking.

Crawford turned back to the ship chugging away. On the deck Crawford saw a body just beyond the gangplank egress, facedown over flotsam. In his heighted state of awareness Crawford realized it was the cat in Chicago police blues, Lockley.

A bloody hole spread across his back as the boat chugged away.

Crawford's breathing slowed as he turned to Tooley. The otter cop thumbed the gun's hammer home, and it was then that the wolf recognized him.

Crawford had been drunk, distraught at his ruined marriage and his slap by Govic's widow, and then he'd hurried out of that soda jerk establishment.

Cokes and root beer floats didn't fit into pockets, but payoffs sure did. The otter swallowed. "I ran out of bullets and, well, they had gas cans under tarps up there. If you'd hit that…"

"I didn't see any tarps."

"Heat of the moment, we all miss things," the Otter muttered quickly.

Crawford felt his limbs ache again as the implications set in. "We do, don't we."

Tooley holstered his gun, took his hat off and faced the channel. "There goes a hero," the Otter said, crocodile tears already finding his cheeks.

Crawford said nothing, staring at the space the Otter had filled long after the bastard walked past him. Rage was cold inside cowardly silence.

The ache in his limbs grew in quiet, burgeoning agony.

***

The Countess hissed her pleasure into Donovan's ear as he came. They traded cryptic smiles and he rolled away on mussed, musked sheets.

Donovan slipped the cigarette case from his bed stand and a golden arm straddled him, playing with the fur of his chest. "I'll have one."

They lit and smoked and watched the iris of dawn clear Donovan's treetops through the open window. The rabbit laughed. "What would happen if I went to Austria and called your husband a Hahnrei to his face?

The Countess took a long drag, thinking on it. "You'd die. And you'd be wrong. My husband is not what you English call a cuckold. You interest me and I play with the things I like."

"Things."

"You're no different. You're loath to admit that you were curious about me from the moment I arrived."

"Was I?" Donovan could voice his doubts, but he was already reconsidering them. Evelyn had dripped contempt from the moment they'd met and yet here he was, enjoying the post-coital heat rising off her.

He didn't want to think about motives in this moment, but he'd been long stripped of sentimentality by capricious actors in his life. The Countess was just curious, and playing, as she said. Maybe that was it.

She smoked some more. "That was enjoyable." She pushed back the covers, allowing the light breeze coming in collect the rest of her spent heat. "Are the creatures here?"

Donovan raised a brow and then realized who she meant. "No. Mallory sequesters in a house just down the lane, watched of course but not too intrusively. Her new charge is with her."

"The raccoon." The Countess smiled thinly. "Or what used to be."

"Yes. She'll be helping him understand the nature of his predicament and guiding his recovery."

Evelyn dabbed her cigarette in her bedside tray. "You actually believe she can do this?"

Donovan nodded. "She will break him down and restore him as I did with her. She's very astute with receptive pupils, Countess. Apart from this task she's already an evening studies teacher at a school for wayward children called Noah's Plank, administered by an associate of mine."

Evelyn nearly dropped her cigarette. "You have that creature dealing with children?"

"It helps her remember who she was. For her advanced age, she's a simple creature at heart. I've noticed a great affection for me and my aims." Donovan smiled as he ran a sly finger down the lioness' chest and round one breast. "Well, once we came to our understanding."

The Countess ignored his touch. "You're so certain that will work that you don't keep an eye on her yourself?"

Donovan smiled. He'd been wondering when to reveal the next detail in his plans and this was a natural opportunity. He rose naked and crossed to his armoire, lifting an object from the top drawer. "I had her cottage built to afford the appearance of privacy, partly of wood…" he bore the locket in his palm, silver chain dangling, "and I provided the steel for its frame. I would surmise it's the sturdiest building in the whole of the Gold Coast."

Donovan returned to the bed and slipped in next to the lioness. She studied the locket curiously. "Would her photo be in that locket?"

"No. It's sealed with something important. You can guess." He passed it to the Countess and she turned the smooth object in her hands. The scent of power made her show teeth. "It's more of the crypt shards, Another reliquary?"

"A focused one, trace steel bound to girders I showed you that hold up repaired portions of the L-train in downtown Chicago, bolster the floors and ceilings of several commercial warehouses east of here, and that form the frame of Sandy Mallory's little house." Donovan pointed to a wall. "It's in that direction, not a quarter mile, walled in by wrought iron, hedges, fragrant flowers planted to conceal unpleasant scents and keep sounds from travelling. With the locket in your hand can you focus, see it in your head?"

The Countess gasped. As she did so the chain of the locket slid down between her breasts.

Donovan pushed back the lingering tickle of carnality and kept his eyes locked on hers as they closed and rolled under the lids, questing and exploring.

"I feel her," the Countess said. "And the raccoon in pain, hungry and furious."

"Tuned senses can collect much more than mere proximity of a Nosfur from the fingers of my net. I've already—" the door was wrapped by urgent knuckles. "Yes?"

The door opened a crack and a possum's muzzle poked in. "Sir, your eight o'clock call with Superintendent Leicester."

Donovan glanced to the Countess, who was enraptured by this new extension to her senses. "Patch it through to the phone in here Edmond. And let the kitchen know we'll be down in an hour."

"Sir."

Donovan rose again, taking time to stretch through the crackle of electricity that was the afterglow of sex. He took the candlestick phone over to the armchair, not bothering to dress and crossed his legs against the sun's intrusion with the telephone resting on his white furred knee. "Dick Leicester, how are you this fine morning?"

The basset hound was curt. "Well enough, Donovan. I hope I didn't wake you."

Donovan laughed "No, I'm always working. Thank you for taking time this morning with your busy schedule. Congratulations on your increased poll numbers. I was disappointed that your bid for city Alderman hit a snag with this needed runoff election. Glad the district attorney's investigation into, what was it, non-carnie voter suppression finally ended. Not your fault of course but my, what a bad look for the city. Mayor Thompson must be incensed."

The basset sighed. "The results of April weren't contested by a long shot but Thompson will agree to anything if he can keep his job a little longer."

"Delays notwithstanding, I want you to succeed, Dick. From what I understand, you need to wrap up the labor vote. Your liberal-leaning friends are grateful for your unerring support of the vegetarian public, but the unions aren't behind your bid I'm told. You need them to close the gap."

There was vexed silence from Leicester's end of the line. "You can't help that, Donnie. You may get sympathy with those long ears of yours but you aren't exactly unionist's best friend."

Donovan sighed and uncrossed his legs. Morning breeze tickled his genitalia so he folded them the other way. "I'm not the steel union's darling, but you could be. Let me explain."

Silence was acquiescence.

"My advisors tell me that I need to downsize to maintain projections for this year. That's unfortunate because it means I'd have to let go over two hundred workers, half of whom live in the ward you're running for as Alderman."

The phone clattered as the dog fumbled it. "Why would you fire workers in my ward? My opponent has fingered you as a businessman I'm affiliated with! I get the vegetarian vote through that connection and now you're going to kill my chances with labour. How does that help me?"

No guile at all for this canine hothead. "No, Dick, nobody is going to be fired. What's going to happen is a day after I make that announcement, immediately before the runoff election mind you, I'm going to announce to friends with direct lines to the press that an impassioned phone call from you stayed my greedy hand and I won't discharge one solitary soul. The board of shareholders won't like that, but you're a convincing dog."

Donovan heard a tail striking leather at locomotive speed. "Yes, that's brilliant."

Donovan knew it was. "I'm going to help you out, Dick. And when you're sworn in as Alderman, I'm going to help get you engaged with the city's planning board where you can wield considerable influence. We both know the Union Train Station project in your ward has gone over budget with structural issues and I'm willing to help complete its construction at a price only a fool would consider profitable." The basset hound drew breath but Donovan cut him off. "It doesn't matter how I know. You think the elements threating to ruin all that beautiful masonry installed and nobody would find out why? These ears hear everything."

Across the room, the Countess gazed at him as she set the locket down, taking in what he said, absorbing all the implications. Donovan smiled. "Dick, I already have bids in to supply construction of the Tribune Company Broadcast tower and the Chicago Board of Trade are drawing up plans for a new structure on the old one's current site. I want those projects. When heading the planning commission, that's your end of things."

Leicester sighed. "You've certainly thought things through and one hand is indeed ready to wash the other. I'm going to send you a nice vegetable basket."

"What I've asked for is enough but go ahead and send sirloins too." Donovan locked eyes with the Countess. "I'll have entertaining to do."

He ended the call and the rabbit joined the lion, carrying the phone with him. She took a deep breath. "So, you're going to install reliquary steel all over Chicago to create a Nosfur…detector?"

"Yes," Donovan replied, "within three years."

"And you're sure you can secure the election that will give you the influence to put all this in motion?"

"No," Donovan replied. "That's why I'm putting an insurance policy together with some influential acquaintances." He lifted the receiver. "Operator connect me with exchange double-you, eye, tee, two, four, three, seven, thank you."

A tired voice at Ma Bell tried to be chipper. "A moment sir."

As the line rang, the Countess rose. "Have your possum take me on a short errand after breakfast."

"Where are you going?" Donovan asked.

"Nowhere important. I'll return in an hour or two."

Donovan had no time to ask additional questions. There was already breathing on the line. A voice in spindly Creole sighed. "Why you call when yer distracted by company?"

"Hello there. Do you have a minute?"

Cold laughter drifted through. "Minutes have the sourest flavor when all you seek is cashing favors…"

Donovan sighed. "Long ago I paid your price. It's time to keep a promise."

***

"Rest is important, Bucky. Close your eyes, empty your mind. When the sun descends, you'll have more to learn."

With the onset of morning, Bucky felt increasing exhaustion. His body had slowed again and he wondered what was happening out in the world where things moved at the speed of life. "Do you get newspapers?"

"I do. But only after dawn. Despite complaints to the Tribune, they say it won't fit into the mail slot. You'd have to cover yourself in bedsheets like a moving picture ghost just to grab it without pure agony."

Bucky clutched the blankets below them. "Mind if I borrow these? We don't need them to…rest or whatever we do."

Closed doe eyes opened and narrowed. "You that anxious to find out if your citizen's tip did its work?"

Bucky couldn't feel colder but he could feel numb. "What?"

"You made two local exchange calls with my telephone. One was asking when you could meet and demanding to know what other commitment they'd taken on election night. The second was to the local Prohibition bureau to provide a hot tip."

Caught out, Bucky felt embarrassed. "So? You doin' this to me doesn't end things already happening. If I gotta play behind the scenes, I'll still play."

"Even if that revenge tip was anonymous and caused the Chicago Outfit grief you've tipped somebody else off that you're still alive. Who was that Bucky?"

"None of your business," Bucky's ire rose. Celeste really thought her bite put an end all his plans. Who cared if the hags knew he was alive? They talked to nobody. "Nothin's getting back to Johnny, less you told him who I was working with when you whacked me."

Celeste groaned. "Merde. You called the Sisters. Damn you Bucky, they have their hands in things you should avoid. You need to forget them."

"What they have is a great pot-still whiskey recipe that's gonna have mooks beating down my door. They're useful to me."

Celeste sat up. "No, Bucky. *You* were useful to *them*. I just don't know why. Were I not playing whore for you on the night we met I wouldn't have drunk what they gave me. There are things they brew that I recognize that—look it doesn't matter. That deal is off."

Bucky felt the pit in his stomach turn hot. Who did this doe think she was? "I can't just back out, even if I don't love the hooch anymore. There's money to be made."

"I'm making it for both of us."

Bucky was off the bed and stalking. "From the guy who had me whacked? From *you*? Teach me all you want but no herbie makes *my* daily bread."

"And there it is, typical carnivorous inferiority. You have no idea what is truly important."

"So, tell me Celeste. What's important?"

"Survival first of all. We have more enemies than just the sun. Survival means a solitary existence—"

"You haven't always been a solitary dame though, have you? The way you looked at that squirrel we saw while doing the bit with the shadows... is she like us?"

"She's nothing like us anymore. And she's even more dangerous than the sisters."

"She looked like an old broad, older even then them."

"She certainly does." Celeste settled back on the bed. "She knows dangerous people you should avoid at all costs."

Keep away from the Sisters. Keep away from others like them. Everything the doe said kept him in this darkest of dark. "Maybe I'm not all about...being in fear."

"Her friends will gladly change your mind," Celeste bitterly told the ceiling.

"Seems you know everybody I oughta run from," Bucky said to the same stucco.

Celeste's next words were in his ear. "Running would have been wise. Isn't that obvious yet?"

They were quiet for a moment. Bucky felt tired. The dark within the dark was dragging sense away and he had to yield. "Celeste?"

"Yes."

"I gotta get clean clothes tomorrow night. These have gone a couple day now and, uh, my sense of smell hasn't exactly gone away if you know what I mean."

"Mine either Bucky. We'll deal with that. Now rest. Let your mind go blank."

He closed one eye, then the other with a sigh. Questions frustrated Bucky as he fought the dark the whole way down.

***

The department was in shock that morning and Crawford twisted in his own private hell. The day passed in agonies big and small and the drinks he stole didn't relieve either pains in his body or pangs to his conscience, merely twisting them into knots.

He desperately needed a doctor and rang one before banging out his report. A receptionist booked him for an appointment in a week.

With no immediate assignments and unable to sleep, he'd dropped Charlie off before heading to the medical examiner's office in the antiseptic halls of St. Luke's hospital, trying not to think of Tooley on that dock the prior night, unable to accept what he'd seen but unable to dismiss it.

The report placed in Crawford's hand made no sense. "Can I take this home?"

The raccoon nodded behind iceberg thick spectacles as he looked up from the corpse he was sewing shut. "Please return it intact."

An hour later, Crawford settled in his kitchen and took the bottle from its hiding place behind his dresser as Charlie's snore was heard from under his bedroom door. There were two photographs in the report that Crawford held up to the light, a rare inclusion as photography cost the medical examiner's office money they were short on.

What was in them made him nearly spill his drink. Simon Govic, mouth wide in death, had abnormally sharp and elongated teeth and his folded arms crossed like boat oars over his stitched-shut chest.

He hadn't had arms that freakishly long when Crawford had confronted him, nor teeth that large, which would have bit his hand clean off. Crawford read the full report as the dusk turned to night, then again by the light of a moon that was nearly full. A complete list of attributes leaped out. Elongated forelimbs, powerful jaws, pronounced claws, fingers thick enough to stand the rigors of four limbed loping. In short, a specimen out of a museum.

Another hour passed as Crawford replayed that confrontation again. Bite. Shot. Calming swig, Charlie arriving. A kitchen with a cupboard reduced to matchsticks and a widow who owed him no answers.

He was swigging straight from the bottle now. Give me strength Hermitage rye, he thought.

He refilled the flask that he'd rubbed with baking soda to dim the smell before corking the bottle. Crawford knew what he'd seen, a ferret with some abnormalities he'd barely made out in the dark, yet photographs didn't lie. Crawford put his hands over his muzzle, the ache in his limbs like a million small fires all throughout his body.

Fuck if God's furies hadn't followed him back from France. His hands gripped the milled wooden table edge as he fought for self-control. The wave of pain passed.

When he let go, claw gouges bit the varnished surface and Crawford stared at them for a long time before rising to get ready for the raid debrief. He woke Charlie with a knock on the brown wolf's bedroom door and they went in.

***

Dusk pierced the half-drawn shades of Noah's Plank School for Wayward Cubs, painting the wood-paneled classroom in shades of rose. Sandy Mallory watched the cubs with interest from behind dark glasses, keeping out of the sun's rays. The little ones worked their brushes clumsily, paint smearing the wooden feral votives that students down the hall had carved, wooden animals for the communion walk to the Ark-rendered alter at St. Patrick's Church uptown. A young fawn stuck his tongue out in supreme concentration as he made dark stripes on the white surface of an equine he'd decided to make a zebra. Next to him, Lucinda the calm-eyed capybara from Brazil, gently worked lavender across the belly of the sheep she'd chosen after sorting the wooden options carefully.

Across the table from them, a grey-haired goat kid ignored the bare wooded ram on his desk and instead turned a tin soldier in faded union blues in his hand, studying a feline muzzle that could have been a cougar or lion or any other tan-furred cat. He made popping noises as though the ramrod straight gun pointed skyward in the soldier's hands fired at some avian menace above.

"Samson, why aren't you painting your ram?" Sandy asked.

The goat kid glanced in her direction then back at the wooden creature standing forlorn on his desk next to shared pots of paint from which other cubs drew dollops for their creatures.

He muttered a reply she didn't hear.

"What was that dear?"

"I don't want to paint animals for the Ark," the kid replied in a moaning Scottish brogue. "Other kids say it's all bunk to keep us in guilt."

Sandy regarded a slat of sunlight crawling across the school-room floor. The children's smell filled her nostrils whenever she looked away from them, bright peaty down tinged with the dirt of play on their young pelts and rough-hewn clothes. She could hear the pulses of their hearts, brimming with the distracted vigor of their young lives, calling to her in every quiet moment. But she was strong. Resolute.

"Guilt helps us defeat temptation, Samson. It's the path to our place in God's Kingdom. Don't you want your soul to sail the path to heaven?"

The goat's slitted eyes wouldn't meet hers, instead gazed into the pinprick black dots on the stern face of the tin lion. "My last foster said our place in heaven is less than others because of things that aren't true. Nobody ate the flesh of Christ the navigator and that's something carnivores say to make us feel like we deserve to be less special than they are."

Sandy saw the other two children look up, then at her, brushes paused above wooden charges. Sandy knew doubt festered fast and couldn't help applying the child's wandering impressions to her own past, sybarite and murderous. It was the very path she now sought to save Keller from back at her cottage.

It had taken months for the fangs Donovan had plucked to grow back and remain unused. The way ahead didn't need fangs, not for the confined Nosfur raccoon, nor these precocious children.

"Temptations exist that carnivores resist to remain in God's light, temptations you children needn't bear. But that doesn't make you less special. Anyone who says so is a liar. And our lot is now a better one. We now have the vote in who gets to be mayor, and congressman and everything up to being president of these United States."

"But Ms. Mallory, my foster Dad wanted to fight in the war and they told him he didn't have the stomach to be anything other than a cook or a doctor's helper. It was a violent horrible war that hurt lots of people and sent mammals home with no arms and missing faces and—"

"Samson, you'll scare the other children." Of the two others, Victor the fawn looked uncomfortable and Lucinda the capybara appeared merely curious, such a cheeky girl she was.

"Ms. Mallory why are carnivores made better than us for not letting tem-pation," he struggled around the word, "temp-ta-tion make them kill anymore, when they are thought to be better by the leaders who have wars *because* they can kill better. I don't understand."

Sandy took a deep breath as she heard distant footfalls on the staircase down the hall, two larger bodies ascending. She perked her ears under her shawl, certain the children wouldn't notice. "You'll understand when you're older," was all she could say to Samson.

With the talents from her receding curse Sandy heard the approaching mammals speaking long before their voices would carry to anyone in the classroom. "The room where she ministers the orphans is here to the left, vegetarian orphans with problems taking more conventional instruction." It was Superintendent Richard Leicester, the school's master of instructional values and administrator. A mutter of disinterested acknowledgement came from someone with softer footfalls than him. Leicester kept on. "My mother always declared too many vegetables made one a vegetable, but with proper instruction even these louts can be made to benefit society. For that we have mister Calvert's generous donations to thank."

The voice that answered was accented in aloof Austrian. "Donovan is an enthusiastic rabbit when you get him engaged."

The door to the classroom opened and a brown pelted basset hound trudged in, ears hanging down his tweed to mid chest like second and third neckties to match the brown one between.

Towering over him was Donovan Calvert's guest, Countess Von Haften. Sandy's eyes met the lion's unkind gaze.

Minding witnesses old and young, the squirrel looked away first.

"This is one of our special classes for very special children. Please meet Victor, Samson and Lucinda." Of the three Lucinda pushed her chair back and sleepily rose.

"Boys, manners please," Sandy chided. The goat kid and fawn pushed their chairs noisily back and stood, looking at no direction in particular.

"Children," The Countess said flatly.

"Be seated," The Superintendent said. "This," he indicated the squirrel who rose creakily to her feet, "Is Sandy Mallory. Donovan Calvert recommended her as a supply teacher for late afternoon and evening instruction."

The Countess wandered the periphery of the room, regarding simple math on the chalkboard as well as the metal globe crookedly resting on a cabinet. She stopped in a square of sunlight. "Bit overdressed, aren't you Ms. Mallory?"

"I have a condition," Sandy replied, her Irish accent making her retort especially clipped.

The Countess looked down as her bare ankles and feet caught the light in her golden fur. "Pity, such a beautiful May day."

The basset hound turned his quivering nose from squirrel to lioness. "Have you ladies met?"

"Once," the Countess replied dismissively. "I did take interest in those unique talents of yours."

"Thank you, Countess," Mallory replied evenly. "I would say the same but we never did discuss what you do."

"Someday..." The Countess turned to the children. "Have you cubs and kids been taught by Sandy long? Sorry, Ms. Mallory." She looked at the fawn. "Well, have you?"

The fawn swallowed and looked down at his wooden animal, clearly uncomfortable with meeting the lioness' gaze. The clear act of intimidation made Sandy battle a sting of anger.

"She's been teaching me since last summer," Samson spoke up and met the lion's gaze, also intimidated by her but hardening his jaw to be brave.

The Countess smiled, but deliberately showed little of her teeth. Not as cruel as she could be, Sandy took note, but no kind soul either.

The lioness nostrils gathered scent. "Has she been a good teacher?"

Leicester spoke up. "Ms. Mallory has been a fine and reliable instructor for the more distracted children. Our faculty have remarked upon her immaculate patience." He flashed Sandy a toothy smile.

The Countess ignored him, studying the goat who studied her in return. "I see you like soldiers."

The kid nodded.

"Have you ever wanted to be a fighter for an important cause?"

Despite years of practiced reserve, the look in the Countess's eyes was more than Sandy could bear. She stepped towards them. "If you don't mind these children—"

"Yes," Samson said, his small ears twitching, the tin soldier turning in his hands. "I want to be a soldier just like my Dad wanted to be a soldier. I know I'd be great." His stammering ended abruptly when he noticed Ms. Mallory's concern and the Superintendent's disapproval.

The basset hound laughed. "This is why more refined attention is required." He ruffled the capybara's head fur and ignored her obvious discomfort. "The second you take your eye off them they get the worst ideas."

The Countess gave him a withering glance. "I'd think self-sacrifice is the most difficult virtue to instill. There's evil in this world, right under that nose of yours. You'd help us fight evil, right little goat?"

Samson set his toy soldier down next to his unpainted wooden ram, as though the Union-blued cat escorted the animal up the ramp to Noah's Ark itself. "Yes."

The Countess regarded Sandy again, smiling with all her teeth. The squirrel's heart would have beat faster were it engorged with the essences she'd renounced. Her preternatural nose, far more powerful than the Superintendent's could smell the traces of alcohol on the lion's lips.

And the traces of rabbit sweat as well. Recognition came quickly and realization flooded in behind it. Donovan, her master and benefactor had been intimate with this…harlot.

Truth cut Sandy deep where she didn't know she could feel as implications set in. All the sacrifices that Sandy had made, the pain she bore constantly in perfect, chaste silence for the greatest of causes, and when Donovan finally had love to give...

A numb horror settled on her as Sandy fought to retain control. "Samson, like all these children. will be soldiers in the fight against the scourge of liquor, and all the other licentious vices that tempt the flesh." She fought to keep her fangs from sprouting. "That is forthright enough, is it not?"

The lioness narrowed her gaze and the Superintendent shifted his feet, aware he was missing something inexplicable between them.

The Countess' smile thinned. "Why Sandy, so much potential in these children and you confine them to mere supporting roles in the temperance movement. What greatness could ever come of that?" She turned to the Superintendent and shrugged. "I guess they have their place in things."

Leicester smiled uncomfortably. The Countess turned back to Samson. "I for one think you have a great purpose ahead. Never let anyone tell you otherwise."

With that Countess Von Haften turned and left.

Superintendent Leicester stared in confusion at her departing back before clearing his throat. "Well then, please tidy this room, Sandy. As you know I am running for political office and a photographer from the Tribune will be visiting this class shortly. As the rest of the school will be closing early for the local elections, I'll want photographs with the students and yourself, an upstanding member of the vegetarian community who works with disadvantaged children under our care."

The squirrel met his gaze evenly. "Of course, Superintendent. I'll have the place in proper order with the children's help."

"All and good, Ms. Mallory." Without another word the basset hound followed the departed lioness, leaving the door ajar.

Sandy heard distant footfalls receding, the basset hound seeking a delicate way to ask what just happened and the lioness declining to reply.

When Sandy collected herself, cold pangs of sorrow kept mutely within, she turned back to see the children reluctantly painting their animals for the Ark again, including Samson.

As the feline soldier stood guarding the paint pots, the goat kid painted his wooden ram in faded blue, attention fixed on spilling no drops.

CHAPTER 7

LATE DAY MEALS

Crawford realized he might be dying. His limbs ached when they bent, when picking anything up or scuffing a claw on the pavement. His heartbeat like a marathon underway and his innards below felt perforated by hot iron ore. His claws stung like he'd fingered electrical sockets and his jaw seemed clocked by a prizefighter in the third round. Pains left abruptly to return in waves, and he started running through the possibilities.

Was it Lupus? No, no under pelt rashes anywhere even though he'd nearly gotten naked to check in the small office rest room. Rheumatoid arthritis? Didn't occur this quickly, symptoms took much longer to develop.

What truly confounded him was that his pain didn't weaken him by a long shot. To the contrary, he was a bundle of nervous energy, as thought he could bare-claw scale the nearest building or race on foot to Lake Michigan and swim it to Canada. He'd try either if the agonies would abate for more than a couple goddam minutes.

For now, he needed professional help and didn't know if he'd make it to his appointment next week.

Was he on death's door? Should he call Kamila one last time? In his mind's eye he remembered his estranged son Lucas tumbling out of brambles behind their house six, seven years back, right side of his face festooned with burrs that Crawford spent an hour picking off, trying not to laugh until Kamila met his eyes and he couldn't hold it in anymore. Moments in his life where he was happy came in snatches like leaves on the wind. All of that before conscription, before France, before experiences he still couldn't put words to. Then back to America where he couldn't say the things he didn't know how to say, all those cold shoulders and long silences.

Against that backdrop his current mistakes stood in relief. One day after accidentally killing a suspect Crawford had inadvertently covered up for a bad cop, not just a badge on the take but someone who'd murdered one his own cohort in cold blood.

Crawford knew what he couldn't prove. But he still knew it.

The saloon turned Prohibition Office was tomblike in the evening light as the debrief concluded with a short prayer for Officer Lockley. Despite the large take from John Torrio, fiercely denied as ringleader by the felons in lockup, there was no taste of victory on anyone's tongues. A cop was dead, his body gone.

Caps remained off, smokes left unlit and the Irish contingent of which Lockley had been a part hugged one another, blinked back tears and muttered of a dry wake for a stand-up cat as they drifted away from the debriefing.

Cirelli, the grey-haired fox who'd have visited Govic's widow had Crawford not assumed the duty had a hard but distant stare, having already visited a small stoop just outside the city where a widow and two cubs cried. He'd be handling collections for Lockley's family.

Tooley, the otter remained till last. He mourned with everyone, patted Cirelli's shoulder, wrung his hat, shed tears amply, and spooled comforting words.

And Crawford had said nothing, no body to show, no smoking gun to offer up. Only his knowledge of Tooley's exit from the malt shop had a chance of pinning something on him, and Cain had frequented that place himself. His only testimony against the otter was tainted by his own tipple there. The jerk on the taps wouldn't say a damn word that did the otter any harm, only the wolf who ratted out his own watering spot.

Cowardly lupine bastard, Crawford knew he'd see that slumped cat cop face down on boats off the shores of his nightmares for years.

Leaving, Crawford found cover by his car in which to steal a couple swallows from his flask. Times like these help one find themselves, a friend had said back then. "Bullshit," Crawford said as he got behind the wheel and tossed his next comment over his shoulder to an empty back seat. "Times like these help one get lost. Just like they did back then." The last word choked off as a wave of pain passed through, limbs to tail, like his own car had driven over him.

Dark as his current circumstances were Crawford hadn't forgotten May of nineteen eighteen at the Marne crossing, nor the Bellau Wood where screams had been choked by mud and gas. Crawford could never hope to. With a start he realized that his engagement against the Huns in hell had been five years and two days ago.

And here in the now he'd spent that very anniversary rolling over a gin joint, getting bit and killing an impossible ferret named Simon Govic.

The irony of it hurt to contemplate. Five years since he'd taken lives, met the most unlikely of friends and seen the briefest hint of a self he'd never known existed.

But that hadn't been real, not really. The war was another world. "I've fucking cocked it up, Reggie," He glanced in his car mirror, expecting to see a shadow slumping in the back seats, caked with mud and burning with disappointment. "I haven't changed things. Kamila was smart to get rid of—"

The back door of the field office opened, and Crawford thrust the flask away, fishing for smokes. Tobacco buried everything. He was fumbling for his lighter when he caught the thick-bodied otter in blue move past him, cap low as he lit his own smoke.

Crawford could smell it was officer Tooley. The otter's tail slapped pavement rhythmically ever other step.

Crawford bit his cigarette in half as he passed. The payout at the soda shop could be accepted as the desperate move of an underpaid public servant slipping from grace. Crawford himself had been tempted though never succumbed. Taking the mob's money, even a little bit, was the first step on a path that could only end at the worst of places. And for Tooley it had.

There was a grind and a chitter as the otter's Ford came to life and shuddered back out of its spot. Crawford's breath was catching ragged and his heart beating fast as he turned the key and primed his car to a quick coughing start.

He kept back as he followed, Tooley's dark silhouette through the Ford's back windowpane puffing smoke as he headed south.

The sun was getting low again, and it was late in the day, seven or eight pm.

Where was he following the otter to? Crawford stalked carefully, maintaining distance. If he followed the otter back to his house, what then? Would he tell any pups Tooley had that their father had made two orphans across town? Would he ask his wife if the money from his vice paid for the fish and mussels on their table?

Crawford weaved the car slightly, whiskey and anxiety burning his nerves. He shouldn't be driving like this but kept rolling.

A right took him into familiar territory. Washington Park crept by on the right and buildings thinned out on the left where the University sprawled. They ended abruptly to more store-fronted buildings and the soda shop passed by where Crawford had first crossed the otter cop's path with bubbles in his gullet and his head.

A couple blocks further Tooley pulled over, parking in front of Daley's where Crawford's best and worst memories in this city mingled, divorce calls and sizzling bacon, careerist misery and fresh brewed coffee.

Crawford didn't stop. As Tooley settled under the steel trestle of the Cottage Grove elevated train, Crawford turned the next corner and parked behind an empty ice wagon. Crawford left his hat in the car, keeping low to keep out of sight from anyone in the diner. He found himself next to Tooley's Ford, engine still pinging from the May heat.

Inside the diner, two window-side booths down from where Charlie and himself had washed down laps of coffee just a day ago, Dooley took a seat, unfolding a ratty newspaper flat before the mastiff across from him who smoothed down an expensive suit. A shape under the paper was slid the dog's way. Bills disappeared into the mastiff's vest.

Crawford crouched low enough that he was almost on all fours and his aches were lessened in that position. He was hungry and nearly salivating. Strangely, under the melange of steaks and fried eggs, crisp-fried chicken and tobacco and buttered hot rolls he could smell mammalian fur and hot breath whenever the diner's door opened again.

Making a move, he hurried past the window, hands shoved in pockets, clawed feet flat on the pavement. In motion he could hear the pair perfectly for a moment.

"—Me to do when the tip was anonymous, and I had it twenty mins before we arrived. How was I supposed to pass that on?" Dooley was nearly stuttering with fear.

"By whatever fucking means you have, Dooley. Shoot your pistol in the air, I dunno. Johnny's out nine thou—" The faded reply was unsympathetic.

Two windows down from their booth, a brick abutment provided cover. Crawford stopped with his back against the wall. It was late in the evening, traffic was sparse, so he wasn't too obtrusive. Inside silverware tinkled and the feathery hush of conversations carried.

With his ear cocked just so, he could make words out. A drab discursion about curtains drifted from the table closest to his vantage and a cub of lapine persuasion squealed about French fries at a table further on. He worked to pick apart sounds the way one would pick apart crowding scents, unravelling pieces to create the patterns of individual voices.

Fortunately for him, the mastiff grilling Tooley was very distinctive in his Brooklyn-Italian mix and didn't seem to care who heard him. "If the Prohees had taken the boat our whole operation woulda been cut loose by our friends upriver so you did good. Johnny'll remember that. Anybody wise?"

The otter's voice was harder to make out and Crawford nearly missed the Otter replying with two names, or rather two species.

One of them was a wolf.

Crawford had seen too much. By the sounds of things, he had to go.

To cover himself, the otter was discussing taking two officers out of commission, one of them a Bureau of Internal Revenue agent. Crawford would never get the divorce papers sent to him, never see his estranged son again, never get the chance to somehow reconcile with the woman who hated him like a rotted fang.

The sun was out of sight and streetlamps competed with moon glint in the window as it became clear. Crawford was a loose end in this crooked cop's side game, nothing more.

"Do what you need to," the mastiff responded. "I'm not getting involved and Johnny isn't either. Don't say a word, just drink your soda and listen. When it's handled you get back to us. You don't do drops, no rounds, you don't...shut up I wasn't done talking."

"Come on Al, I have debts..."

Crawford could hear no more. He turned away with a seething fury and his deep breath hurt like hell itself. His claws dug at the brick wall and limbs nearly buckled as pain tore his nerves with a razor's cruelty.

Right here, he was dying. Tooley didn't need to do a thing.

But Crawford did. With whatever time he had left.

Stumbling at first, then crouching, Crawford made his way back towards Tooley's Ford, ignoring the passing raccoon that swerved to avoid him. A glance back at Daley's saw otter and mastiff rising, the latter trading reluctant words with the hard-eyed dog.

Tooley's night was going to get worse. Crawford made it to Tooley's Ford and gripped the front driver's white walled tire, intending to use if for leverage to open the engine bonnet cover and twist something loose.

His claws actually punctured it. A hiss of air escaped and he plucked his aching hand away, staring at the elongated claws that ended each digit. This was not his hand. He didn't have the strength to do this.

Ignoring the rush of stale air, he let go and stepped back, his spine starting to spasm. He pitched forward, landing on his knees. A glance around showed the immediate area empty.

The bell rang as the Daley Diner's front door pushed out into the street. Feeling knives up his legs, Crawford crouched and hurried around the car, then to the alley by the diner as the otter came around. Through the pounding of his heart and head, Crawford heard him swear at the sight of his tire. With a fast waddle, the otter came round the back of the car to his spare, squinting left and right. The streetlamps and moon above hid more than they revealed.

The otter went for the spare tire strap and then froze. If someone wanted him to stay here, the crooked cop would do anything but.

From his vantage, Crawford saw the otter work out a direction to go, and then headed west under the elevated line along East Sixty-third. There was a precinct four blocks down, Crawford knew it too.

Leaning, almost crawling, Crawford followed, grabbing meager cover whenever Tooley glanced back. A peek into the diner showed the mastiff was gone and Crawford couldn't smell him. Instead, his nostrils were crowded by the iron of the L, the ozone of sparks as a car shot by overhead, oil on the pavement and the sheen of anxiety that wafted off the otter's worrying hide.

And Crawford was getting excited, heat building with the pain even though he had no plan. Confront Tooley? Shoot him?

He couldn't think clearly. His coat wasn't fitting right. He wrestled it off, balled it and tossed it by an abandoned crate before loosening his tie to let it fall like shed skin. Heat built inside him and he had to get the useless things covering him away. Buttons bounced on the pavement as he tore away his shirt. Palms flat on the sidewalk felt cool slickness in a way his desensitized feet had long forgotten and when the otter finally turned and saw what was behind him, the squeak he released was joyous.

"You haaaave deeeehhts," wheezed a mouth that wasn't Crawford Cain's anymore. Sense evaporated as the full merciless moon cleared a low building, painting stalker and quarry.

The otter ran. The hunter followed, kicking whatever tried to shackle its legs away. Down a dark canyon of masonry, the otter tripped as something sliver in his hand popped fire and heat into shattering stone.

The hunter was upon him. Fur, flesh and warm wet copper and fear song. Wine was a fountain, white cracks of flavor, gristle tickled jaw and gullet. Squealing gurgles were delightful as teeth unwrapped sinuous mysteries.

The moon smiled down on its freshly sated son.

***

Donovan was anxious as they passed a darkened polling station where patriotic bunting hung red, white and blue from lamppost to lamppost. Even for municipal elections Chicago disdained subtlety. Word of downsizing at the plant had been circulated and news would follow in the morning that Leicester had stayed his hand, but that was academic at this point. Donovan had other worries. "Tell me again what she said to you, precisely."

In the Rolls' driver's seat, Edmond's whiskers twitched nervously. "She said she needed to complete some errands and had me drive her downtown. It was upon leaving the car that I saw she had a red book."

The red book Edmond referred to but hadn't recognized at the time was the very book Donovan had frantically searched his office for after the Countess left. It had all his contacts in America, both political and business related. Of those, half a dozen were right in this city. "Did you think to ask her what the book was, Edmond?"

"No sir," the possum replied defensively, eyes down under his cap. "Nothing seemed amiss until she fetched another car where I left her and raced off. I tried to follow but," the possum redirected his attention to an intersection he'd nearly run against a white gloved officer's whistle. "I'm sorry sir."

Cold dread settled. Donovan had harboured doubts before last night but had instead followed his stiff Shillelagh and stupidly concluded their roll in the hay meant they could trust each other. How could he be so predictable a rabbit as that?

"Have you called the mill?"

"We have men guarding the catwalk. As of last call she hasn't visited."

If the shards were safe, then one possibility remained. Donovan knew Ms. Mallory wasn't at her cottage. With the locket provided by Donovan, the Countess knew that as well. Her antipathy for Sandy had been made plain.

The squirrel in question was done teaching for the evening and Noah's Plank school would be closed by now. Donovan had telephoned its Superintendent to provide a progress update on Donovan's action with the workers and found that Leicester had not driven home yet.

"If Sandy hasn't walked her usual route home then perhaps she hasn't left the school."

"Shall I drive back there?"

Donovan searched the concrete caverns of night beyond the Rolls' windows. "How are we on petrol?"

"Low sir."

"Visit the nearest fill station and find a telephone to call the house. If the Countess returned then we—" A whisper of power tugged him, channeled through the locket against his fur. Releasing his cane, Donovan hastily unbuttoned his top shirt buttons and wrapped his right hand around it.

He'd hoped it was Ms. Mallory returning home, but the pull was elsewhere. A thread leading south to one of the girders reinforcing the elevated line near the University. It throbbed like a tooth touched with a shock of ice.

The presence had awakened it was off kilter, distorted.

"We have to go south."

"The nearest gas station is west of here."

"Do we have enough to get to Cottage Grove station on East Sixty Third?"

Edmond knew where all the iron elements in Donovan's network were and clicked with the implications immediately. "That and then some sir."

"Quickly, Edmond. The passage is fresh." The invisible ebb pulled, and Donovan closed his eyes, trying to discern its makeup. Was it a recently infected Nosfur or an old killer wandering for prey? Something was definitely amiss with this contact.

He was grateful once again for the circumstances that had granted him the bid to upgrade the elevated transit lines of the Chicago Edison Utility. The trains radiating from the core of Chicago made a perfect web of detection for Nosfurs, each link repaired with the spike monogrammed steel imbued with the essence of a melted shard.

If Donovan backed his consciousness out as far as possible from the place and time he occupied he could discern the sum total rather than the singular digit of his senses, obtaining glimpses into the overall eddies of unnatural miasma darting through his city. Such had drawn him to the speak two nights ago as it did now. "Faster Edmond."

The car hurtled through the night, the pull as familiar as an ocean current's rushing under a transatlantic hull. The contact refined as they approached and passed the unremarkable iron beam in the light of an old diner. "It's not what I expected," Donovan said, a chill running through him.

"Sir?"

"Stop here. Now!"

The possum pulled over abruptly and Donovan didn't wait, hurling the carriage door open and leaping to the street. "See what that is," Donovan pointed his drawn rapier to a balled-up bundle behind a dirty crate and hurried ahead. He drank the sense of something unfamiliar, not the corruption of natural order he'd grown so accustomed to hunting but something that bitterly distilled it, burning mortal essence away like weak tallow. His rapier sang in his hand.

In an alley where his nose burned, and his gorge rose all his questions were answered.

***

Celeste didn't dream when the day stole consciousness away, knowing only oblivion. In the brief states between them she could sense changes in the world she would rise to. She could sense danger close by and could sense absences too. Before her eyes opened, she knew that Bucky was gone.

There was an indentation where the fox had been, meaning he'd either staved off unconsciousness until the setting sun released him from this house or had somehow arisen before her. Celeste heard the chittering of the rodents downstairs but nothing else. Her nose caught no freshy spilt blood. Bucky hadn't fed before he'd gone, meaning he'd been in a hurry.

The how of it all was unimportant now. What mattered was why.

Revenge on Torrio? Sending a Prohee raid down on his operation might not have sated the vindictive fox, but would he have been stupid enough to go after his former boss? He'd barely begun learning the tricks he'd need to survive.

In all her years taking down prey of all species she'd never turned anyone, but between her failed bite and this strange accumulation of stamina there was something unusual about Bucky Cavali. And it wasn't just his willful stupidity.

Celeste rose and changed into something form fitting enough to avoid snags but loose enough to move fast, better to bind shadows completely out of mortal sight as she searched him out. Bucky was single-minded but he wasn't a total fool. He'd have to kill a lot of his former associates before killing Torrio, which meant the fox would have gone to observe and plan. His last words came back as he'd slowly settled in the prior dawn. "Can I get some clean clothes tomorrow night?"

Tough to stalk when wearing a day's worth of your own post-death musk.

Night shopping was out of the question. He'd gone back home. Celeste darted to the main floor and found that the door was unlocked. Her late edition newspaper had already been brought in. On it was fox scent and the front page had been taken.

The phone rang at that moment and she was snatching it up in the empty study it rang again. "Yes."

"Mon cher," Madame Lowry said with a silky whisper, "Johnny called. He has a friend who needs special attention."

Dammit, she didn't have time for this. "Tonight?"

"This week, a guest from out of town."

Celeste had to go. "I'll get the particulars from Johnny later and ensure you get your cut."

"Will you finally be entertaining a client at the Deuces?"

She'd want a bigger cut for renting a room. "No but thank you so much for offering."

The reply was flat as a razor kissed tire. "Anytime."

Celeste ended the call and made the distance to Bucky's flat in under an hour, effortlessly avoiding the evening traffic on the core's outskirts.

Circling around behind the yard behind Bucky's place where she had so recently taught him to bind shadows, Celeste took a good look to confirm no watchers before rapidly scaling the building with her thick ungulate limbs and hooves in the manner of a cliff scaling goat. She let herself in through a bedroom window and immediately smelled blood.

Doors and drawers were flung open, and closets ransacked. She found Bucky's prior duds, dapper on their night in the speak, discarded in a damp pile. The blood smell beckoned her to the kitchenette, where the cupboard under the sink wasn't fully closed.

A wolf was stuffed inside, a former enforcer of Torrio's based on the ragdoll neck and lifeless eyes. Celeste had seen him in line to get his rocks off at the Deuce's once.

The twin rivulets of blood down his collar told her Bucky had been clumsy, fed messily. He'd drank nearly all the wolf had.

Dammit, his first full blood high and Celeste wasn't there to guide him through. Had the bastard even donned new clothes before heading out on his next errand? The presence of mind with which he'd stowed the body out of sight suggested he'd not crested immediately.

By now he'd be in the maelstrom of stars and drunk with a boundless sense of power, inhibitions completely gone.

She had to warn Torrio. Or at the very least get close enough to keep him safe till near dawn. Bucky didn't have a phone. Her own place was in the opposite direction and to top everything off there was now a corpse to hastily bury.

She'd have to hide the dead wolf later, covering up the smell for now. Under the sink were a series of cleaner chemicals that she could spread around to bury the bloody stink. She gathered a small pile onto all but bare wooden table and noticed the only object already resting on it was balled up newsprint.

Celeste unfurled the Chicago Tribune's front page, taken from her own paper on the stoop at home when Bucky fled. There was news of a raid above the fold, a daring takedown by Prohibition officers and cops fighting the wet devil scofflaws of the mob. Celeste could imagine that Bucky would revel in the chaos he'd likely caused.

But what lay below the hot sheet's fold was even more interesting. The picture was badly developed and even harder to make out with the torn paper but the Superintendent of a finishing school for wayward children grinned thick teeth under sad basset eyes at the photographer. Cubs and kits in silhouette could be made out behind him, their attention focused on a section of the photo torn right out, a now headless figure in a thick head to toe shawl.

Behind the decapitated minder, drooping in shadow but still prominent, the tail of a squirrel.

No.

Celeste lay the paper flat, erasing all its creases and smearing its ink. The teacher's photograph had been hastily but deliberately liberated from the rest of the paper.

Bucky Cavali was carrying the image of Sandy Mallory in his pocket.

It shouldn't have made sense but of course it did. The only chaperone the confused fox had to this world was that same doe who had stolen his former life. Keeping him under her wing was a much easier proposition when he had no clue how many others of their kind were lurking in this city much less anywhere at all. Celeste only knew of half dozen like herself and stayed apart from them, but Sandy was still the most dangerous.

Now she had to anticipate Bucky's next move. If the fox went for Torrio, he'd ruin her cover, successful in killing the old bastard or not.

And if he sought out Sandy Mallory, Bucky would learn all of his vulnerabilities in the hardest way possible.

Work would help her decide. Celeste was a quick digger and had no time to spare. Arms under the limp wolf, she dragged the poor son of a bitch to the window over the yard, checking to ensure the coast was clear before the push. Carrying him through bound shadows back to her place wouldn't take too long, pity he couldn't just be buried right here. The wet crack of bones as the lupine hit dirt ensured that staying dead would be a blessing.

***

The world was a song that Bucky Cavali wanted to dance to. The wolf Torrio sent to ransack his place hadn't got a shot off before the fox had him. Hunger did the rest. Like sex, no instructions were required.

No words could describe what followed.

To call the meal that woke his every sense fine wine was to compare the best Sangiovese to creek water. In moments he was alive again, all nerves firing with bliss as the mook Johnny sent went to the dark. As the pelted sack hit the floor, Bucky was already ascending to the heavens.

Being dead or alive in this way was fucking amazing. No doubt about it.

He stuffed the remains of his meal away and hurried out again, wondering how little gas could torch the place on his return.

First…

He'd first seen the squirrel in the vicinity of the lake. While he didn't know her destination then, he now knew where she spent some of her time, existing amongst the living, holding who knew how many secrets. No wonder Celeste didn't want him near her.

Bucky couldn't sort his feelings out about the doe. She'd killed him, unmade and made him anew. This high upon highs that burned inside as he bound the shadows and drank in the sensual delights of the city's mere closeness had come from her intervention in what was supposed to be his curtain call to the world, but what had this cost him?

His mother was lost to him, his small gang of friends in Torrio's crew too. He hadn't signed any agreement for that.

And he couldn't even begin to accept was that he was the doe's inferior in this new experience. He resented being forced to trust only his hired killer for the way through this. It might very well be that his charms and magnetism were the only reason he wasn't feeding worms. Who knew how long that would keep him in whatever good graces the murderous doe had?

Bucky took the crumpled paper from his jacket and studied the cameo-sized fragment of newsprint, committing the squirrel's crooked features to memory. She was old, wizened and yet tucked in the photo behind some hound dog who filled the Tribune's broadsheet with some political blow-hard bullshit. The old squirrel who Celeste hated so much, possibly older than the city itself if Celeste's own declared age was true, would have a fresh perspective on a world he was new to and could teach him all the things he yearned to know.

The school mentioned in the paper was close, out on the north-west outskirts of the city, Bucktown it seemed, a squat squallored brick of learning that sourly resembled the juvenile halls and jails of his youth. With his nose primed along with all his senses, smells crowded as he crossed the weed-ruled field across from old warehouses and factories.

Chalk and fruit rot and young dead fur cloyed the air. He kept to shadow listening carefully. He could sense them through a high cracked window, the mists of tiny breaths, the quick taps of flush hearts. The school had a dormitory for detained youth. Stinging rulers on his black pads from cold-eyed nuns leapt into memory and he hated the place immediately.

At the entrance to the school, where the main doors were locked, scents of recent passages mingled from many species. Tobacco burn buried a few of them, but what he could pick apart, yes, there was a squirrel.

The trace had a mothball quality that was inoffensive if slightly rank. He followed it as it meandered to the grounds gate and left heading south for the city proper past where factories vanished and rickety homes sprout-ed like mushrooms, rusty cars sparsely dotted at gutterside.

From shadow to shadow, Bucky sampled and followed. The traces become stronger as more affluent small manors and well-to-do apartments banished other smells and gathered slow disapproval about him. Bucky Cavali was never meant to live in places like this, not the Bucky that died two days ago, anyhow.

Better connections meant better plans. Bucky's path followed the looming north branch of the Chicago River and soon enough he saw a squirrel's silhouette slowly crossing the West Cortland St. Bridge into Sheffield and the Gold Coast beyond.

She was alone and unafraid.

Bucky hurried after the bobbing tail, reaching the steel span bridge's edge as his quarry passed beyond it. There were few shadows to bind here, so he flitted across the barren bridge quickly, keeping low, body pressed up against the steel stanchion's he passed. Halfway across his hand brushed a section of steel railing that was new and shiny and as yet unpainted.

Something seized him, as though the organs in his body were clutched by invisible claws. He gagged at a sensation that was pain and nauseous pressure all in one, pitching forward on his hands and knees. Bucky stared at his black-furred fingers for a solid few seconds of agony before feeling the pain abate as he slowly dragged himself forward.

A few moments later the pain receded. Bucky stopped, urged to pant but with presence of mind to know his breathing was useless. He reached questing fingers back behind himself and felt a throb in the proximity of the shiny new section of rail he'd touched a moment ago. "Goddamn, what is that?"

He pondered turning back but the scent of the squirrel was fading into the mist. If he lost her trail, he might not get it back.

He tailed after, nose low, his blood high painting details into every space that wasn't a shadow. He saw her again two blocks West, heading for the coast again.

It was now or never. He bound another shadow, flitted to the next, closer and closer until just a few yards away the geriatric squirrel's tail stiffened skyward.

She turned his way, directly to him, and stared into the shadow by the closed butcher shop that he'd bound to. This close, Bucky could tell she was at least a foot shorter than he even if she were standing straight, so unlike Celeste who had several inches of height on the fox.

"Come no closer," a reedy Irish voice warned, promising consequences.

"No problem," Bucky cocked his hat, the discomfort from the bridge having fled. He let the shadow go, cocked his head and studied the stooped squirrel up and down as she did him, her nose wriggling as it worked. Her gaze darkened as she peered into his eyes. "You're turned."

Bucky didn't know what that meant so he shrugged. "I'm charmed."

"I smell blood on your teeth."

The disgust in her voice was confusing. "Well, I didn't spill any so give me credit."

She pulled her lips back and her yellowing teeth gleamed. "I thought I sensed you last night, skulking out there by the water. Who turned you to this misery and sent you to follow me?"

132

Bucky could laugh. "Nobody sent me, and the last thing I'm in is misery. This is the best I've ever felt in fact. I wanted to find you so I could talk about whatever this.... life really is, ask you questions I couldn't ask my friend."

The nose worked again, the squirrel's eyes shutting tight before opening with a hard resolve. "Celeste. You're of her, aren't you?"

That accusation made him hot. "I'm not of anybody. She ain't my mother."

"But she sent you."

Bucky remembered that Celeste and the squirrel were acquainted, but still didn't know how. This had been a great idea when he was high on blood in his old kitchen an hour ago. "Nobody sent me. I wanted to meet you and Celeste didn't want that. I needed to talk to you about—"

"I won't speak with you if you're a slave to the vein as she is. I can see in your eyes that you killed an innocent tonight."

"That mook I finished off was picking my place clean. And what the hell does slave to the vein mean? You're like me ain't ya?"

"I was you. Corrupted and drowning in the same liquid curse. I was saved from it."

Her words sounded familiar, and Bucky caught on quick. "What, you an Anti-Saloon Leaguer for blood drinkers? This is rich. You know how many people I killed since I was fifteen, squirrely? I never wanted to, but now for the first time I can make use of whoever comes at me. The snack you're mourning was gonna kill me. How do you feel about that?"

The squirrel's tail twitched, and she crouched, ready to leap. "I feel you're being used and with the blood tainting your soul you have no idea. You may yet be saved—."

"Saved? Are you playing with me? Chicago is kill or get killed. How can you be what I am and not know that?" Disappointment chilled him. Celeste was right about her, not that he would ever say as much. "Celeste was wrong. If you were ever any big deal you sure aren't now."

"You're a confused slave to your wants, but I've become more powerful serving a greater plan and my..." she faltered a moment. "—friend who brought me back from the brink." She froze, gazing past Bucky's shoulder.

Bucky felt the same disturbance and turned back to the bridge. In the distance a sleek vehicle rumbled. The silhouette of its driver winked a lick of flame that cracked the air.

The squirrel grew a hole in her chest and fell to her knees, tail in a spasm. Bucky dropped and rolled away as another gunshot cracked. The butcher shop's window spider-webbed behind him, suspended ham shank swinging as though punched by a boxer.

An engine roared as the low-cut beast of a car hurtled towards them. Bucky glanced the squirrel's way. Dull surprise crept over her face as she tried to haul herself up. For a moment it seemed as though the car was going to run her down on the open sidewalk.

But brakes hissed the car to a stop a dozen yards away and a lithe form leaped over the driver's door to land soundlessly on the pavement.

Squirrel and fox regarded one another for a moment. Bucky was a split second from running for it.

But to where? Back to Celeste? Who'd turned and kept him like a curiosity, who held real death over him?

If the old crone squirrel was lost, so would go his only chance to escape the doe.

Time to take chances. The flush of blood burning within thrilled him. He could smell the oily pelt of a lioness, hot with anger as he was.

Steel dragged from leather, slithering death in a whisper. The lioness had turned to him first. Her bared teeth were wicked. "I knew this parasite kept company with other vermin."

Her accent was thick, unmistakable. Bucky winked, "The Huns just invaded."

A blade gathered light in one of the lion's hands while a long gun dangled in the other. "Time to see hell," she promised with delight.

Bucky lunged, but not at her. The squirrel was three quarters his size and he scooped her up neatly, her ruined chest against his. He rushed the dark of an alley at a speed that surprised even him, feeling traces of the pain that plagued him minutes ago as he tried to set her down gently. Behind him, masonry from an alley wall exploded.

Bucky realized the burn was coming from the squirrel. Whatever was in that girder on the bridge was in her bullet. "Can you move?"

The squirrel couldn't answer. She sputtered anguished Gaelic curses that Bucky couldn't understand.

At the mouth of the alley meager light framed the lion's silhouette. "You lied to Donovan, but you can't lie to me! The company you keep proves what's in that black heart of yours."

The squirrel hissed back. "He's not my…" her words trailed off in a near wail of pain as the lioness advanced.

***

Edmond moved the car far from the scene. Artifacts textile and otherwise arrayed in front of Donovan on the floor of his car. "I felt this the other night at the speak," the rabbit muttered. "I just didn't realize."

"The Nosfur presence overpowered it?" Edmond wondered.

"Had to have been more than one for that to happen. These essences don't typically outshine one another." He turned over the badge of the Federal Bureau of Internal Revenue and the full moon's light made it shine. This bauble of authority had been far from the mess and bloodless. "At least we know the point of transmission." He placed the scent without even having to read the attached identification. "Lupine. This is disastrous."

Edmond didn't want to ask the next question. "Do I need to clean up the…"

"No. The clothes are enough. The Otter will be found tomorrow, and the city will be scoured for a feral murderer, probably blamed on vengeful mobsters in liquor or prostitution. Chicago's press is nothing if not inventive." Donovan read the identification's details. "We will make acquaintance when the time is right. For now, we need to find the Countess."

He took hold of the locket around his neck and reached out. "Sandy hasn't come home yet. She should—"

A flare of contact brushed by one of his markers to the west of her abode, either the elevated train steps at Armitage station or the West Courtland bridge a mere quarter mile away. He concentrated. The sense was a mere blip and he know Sandy's route home. "Head north toward Sandy's cottage. Quickly but discreetly."

Edmond snapped to it, grateful he wouldn't be collecting otter innards. They were passing the University again when the locket touched Donovan's senses once more. A second contact, stronger, hot and vital.

Recently fed.

Donovan wasn't concerned about the Countess anymore. "Edmond."

"Sir."

"Sod discretion. Bring me there fast as you can."

Chapter 8

Invitations

Doubt and anguish smothered Sandy as her nose recalled that smell on the lion's fur.

How had it come to this? Sandy devoted years to accepting her new life and grace in swearing off blood's consumption to earn Donovan's trust. Years of willpower had sown fate's cruel hand upon her body. Hair greyed, fingers gnarled, decades of stolen youth lost.

But her heart had stayed pure. She'd trusted Donovan implicitly.

All the pains of her new path had been accepted with the sure sense that she'd earned a blessed life, finding strength and purpose in service to the Martyres of the Black Well. Devotion to Donovan's cause had washed away her sins and his affection in the wake of brutal discipline had given her strength to resist the pangs of temptation.

All for his confidence. And just maybe, after so long, his love.

Then the lioness came, the golden pelted monster decked in old world hatred brought scandalous lies and prosecutorial attacks, all while gorging on the sybarite luxuries of the drinker, the slanderer.

The faithless slut.

Sandy had presumed the lioness was one more test, one last mountain to climb in commitment to the cause. How wrong she'd been proven in the space of a single day and the whiff of a faithless stink.

What betrayal she'd felt, smelling Donovan's carnal scent upon the Countess while serving in the school children's domain where Sandy could not utter one syllable of reprobation. Hours had passed as Sandy remained, teaching the orphans maths, pains knotting deep within. Fury broke like a fever and she had imagined Von Haften's violent death dozens of times before heading to her lonely home.

Past the bridge over Chicago's North Branch River, she was stopped in her furious tracks. The dapper-dressed vulpine who followed stank of recent kill, a fever dream from hell.

Sandy recoiled in disgust at confrontation with her dark reflection, her worst impulses manifest in flesh. She confronted him in his shamelessness and for the briefest moment her exalted charge as one of the Martyre's willing disciples reasserted itself in righteousness.

The wee cunt lioness popped round to make sure that didn't last.

The bullet that pierced Sandy's flesh burned like the sun itself. Sandy had learned to avoid touching Donovan's markers. So long purified of blood, pain only came from direct contact and Sandy's devotion was proven by residing in a home-made of that which caused the blood-fed Nosfur to feel agony's wrath.

Forced within her body, that same steel burned like hell.

The lion who'd lain with the rabbit Sandy gave her devotion to had come to kill her with the very tools Donovan promised would keep her safe.

The urge to beg the lioness for understanding touched her lips only once, to scream that she didn't know the Nosfur fox or what horrors he'd perpetuated, to assure her restrained devotion.

This desire fled in an instant as the vulpine Nosfur hoisted her with preternatural strength and hurried Sandy to the safety of shadows.

The lioness followed, lashing her tail, weapons brandished. "You lied to Donovan but you can't lie to me! The company you keep proves what's in that black heart of yours."

"He's not my..." Sandy's hiss broke off as the bullet leeching her strength shifted in her shoulder, gouging her with fire.

The lion hissed. "Donovan will be glad to be rid of you. Despite your pretense at obedience my soft-headed rabbit knew this experiment was a failure. I've shown him that."

Despair drowned all else. Every kind word, every approving gesture lost its warmth, culled back to the first weeks of bindings, pulled fangs and the burning of sunlight, purifications to make Sandy subservient, weak, and desperate for approval.

Hoping for mercy, trust, and love.

"Would this Donnie be happy to be rid of me?" Through fangs the fox's Midwest Italian interruption was pure spite. He was in the alley with Sandy but didn't acknowledge that he was trapped.

The lioness crouched and twisted the blade she bore. "I certainly will," she replied.

"Fuck you then." From his hip the fox fired two shots from a pistol, one catching the lioness' side. Von Haften's scream pierced the alley, and she scrambled back, dropping the long gun and scraping her blade on pavement as she rolled away. The fox fired again, shattering brick.

The fox's ears went back, then up. "She was surprised I'd shoot back?" he asked incredulously.

"Run," Sandy spat through pain. Strength fled as dark became grey and she realized these moments were the last she'd ever know.

Why? She'd done everything Donovan asked of her. Now a sordid existence that started in Ireland seventy years ago was to finish on Chicago's Northern bricks. A gift of life, a curse of death, a wasted climb to salvation. Wasted! Sandy Mallory felt the wind in her fur and the beating of harmless, soothing moonlight upon her face. Tar stink revealed the fox had brought her to a rooftop.

"Be right back," he said with blood-hot vulpine breath and left Sandy alone to face cold stars above. Time passed meaninglessly and she wondered when she'd slip away.

Something was dragged to her side, quivering. Her nose was turned to a dirty pelt. The fox's voice was oily in her ear. "Drink. The lion's wounded but she's still coming."

Sandy felt fangs ache at the stink of flesh.

The scent was vital, drawing her like lightening to ground, every instinct commanding her to feed, to persist. *I'm going to lapse*, she realized. *I'm going to lose all I fought for, all I promised.*

In her mind's eye she saw a lion's nakedness entwined with a white rabbit's and realized she may already be forgotten, her relentless devotion a spent convenience.

She'd been betrayed before meeting Donovan, both by those who knew her nature and those who did not. Spite fired within her.

To hell with them all.

Sandy's fangs sunk into a neck already bleeding and drew her first living draught in six years.

Stars exploded within and the pain numbed almost immediately.

Head clearing, Sandy knew she'd found an old friend. It had laid low her enemies in Dundalk and led her cross the ocean to a new world of discoveries and delights both familiar and alien. Without thought she drank of the throat offered until her new fangs scraped bone.

From prone to fetal to on her knees, a vigor battled pain and she plucked at the shoulder the lioness' bullet had torn through. Fire raced within that she'd long consigned to memory. The muscle was already engorging itself around the bullet, setting to heal and seal the burning steel inside. Time was too short to hold back so she plunged her claws deep, biting back cries as she hunted, found the bullet wedged within and tore it free, burning her slender fingers.

The fox caught the tossed slug, gasping as he juggled the object from hand to hand and then away before blowing on his palms as though they'd brushed a hissing stovetop.

Sandy knew pain again, but she also knew truth. The fox was close, tail swinging with the fresh infusion of life in his veins. "That looks like it hurts. A lot," he whispered, so close their whiskers almost touched. "Goldie-pelt is on her way up. I only got a flesh wound on her. We've gotta hop."

The squirrel met the fox's dark eyes. "Sandy. My name is Sandy."

"Bucky." He glanced to the nearest ledge. "Who the hell is she?"

"One of the Martyres of…It doesn't matter." Sandy let those worthless words die on her flush lips. As the blood high flowed, years in congenial captivity fell into pitiful perspective. "Who is this?" Sandy glanced over to the corpse splayed next to her. The pelt within the rough clothes was curly and she couldn't guess the species.

"Some bum passed out. It don't matter, does it?"

She couldn't answer. It hit her all at once as the colors of the night filled in and the stars shined brighter. She'd taken a life for the first time in years. "My God."

The fox's eyes trailed to her shoulder and widened. "You healing already?"

Sandy's tail twitched. "Of course I am."

His ears perked to metal creaking that they both heard.

Sandy fought for focus. "If it's the lion, you can get her when she peeks over. I'll call out to distract her."

"I gotta better idea," Bucky cut in. "Her car's down there and I gotta say…I have a thing for Alfa's."

"Alfas?"

"Romeos. Distract her and I'll bring our ride around. Get ready to leap off there." He pointed to a roof edge. "Can you do that?"

Her wound would hurt when she landed. Pain was transitory. "We're faster on foot," Sandy caught herself. Of course the Countess could follow them if the means were left to her. "Never mind. Go take her motor car."

Bucky hurried off as trouble arrived. Ears flat, the lioness poked her head up and leapt, landing mere feet from the dead mammal Sandy and Bucky had supped on. She favored one side and Sandy smelled fresh blood from where the fox had clipped her.

"A penitent Prohibitionist is it?" the Countess hissed. "You could not fool me."

Sandy showed her fangs. "I know you never had real belief in a true cause. It was all a game to toy with me."

"There is a cause, squirrel," The blade was wicked in Von Haften's fist. "You'll feel it dragged from sex to nose when you drown in that blood you've stolen." Her ears rose at the same sound that Sandy heard. A rumbling engine struggled through one gear before finding the next. Tires squealed and the fox's holler drifted upward.

Sandy scrabbled and leapt with the limber spring of her species, amplified greatly by her preternatural state. The swing of a blade removed tail fur as the other hand clutched at her garments. A shrug of Sandy's shoulders left her vestments of chastity behind, leaving only knickers as she dug into the opposite building's high wall, then lower still on the building she'd leapt from, then down to the dark passenger seat of the roadster the fox had stolen. Fire flared in her shoulder but she ignored it.

A jerk of acceleration and they were off, Austrian curses fading under the engine's roar.

Every fibre of Sandy's being was aflame, her shoulder a blaze with the rush of blood within. In the space of three blocks, the discipline Sandy honed in years as Donovan's slave helped her center herself. The blood high dampened pain, elevating a mortal sense of release.

They headed south to rising lights and rushing city life, clinks of glasses in a thousand scofflaw cellars and darts of raucous laughter drifting from mezzanines where whiskey and wine flowed, down further to swinging brass and horns that urged hot bodies onto pool hall floors and tenement rows and spread joy and humor and sensual heat. The windy city breathed in and out with forbidden life.

Sandy Mallory felt the wind over her body and the engine's buzz purr up through her. She'd not felt this way in years and memories of excursions with Celeste flooded back, experiences she now realised she sorely missed. She turned to study her new friend. "Sorry we got off on the wrong foot."

The fox rose a coy eyebrow that Sandy found cute.

"As I'm free for the foreseeable future, we should get acquainted. Take me somewhere for a drink," she suggested.

Bucky drove and offered a Player's Nay Cut from a beaten pack that the red squirrel accepted. They let burning tobacco do nothing at all but take them back to simpler times. "I'm actually looking for a place of my own where we can do just that," his teeth gleamed. "I'll be inviting new friends."

Sandy closed her eyes and let the wind rush by. A horn swore as they narrowly missed colliding with another car. "Bring your enemies too if you want," she sighed. With two of her own enemies in mind her fangs sprouted fully and shamelessly at long last.

***

Bucky hadn't gone to Torrio. Celeste confirmed he was all right with a phone call to the Four Deuces. Bucky was most certainly after Sandy, who had to be done teaching and now returning to the gilded cage the rabbit steel magnate kept for her. Celeste's path had never crossed Donovan Calvert's directly, nor Sandy's since they'd fallen out, but Celeste knew Sandy had told him about her before the rabbit's operation relocated them from New York.

Needless to say, that move had complicated things. Celeste kept sequestered, catching rare whispers of Nosfurs who had vanished. There was no direct evidence that Donovan Calvert was responsible but Celeste knew the rabbit was dangerous and kept as apart from them as her work for the Chicago outfit allowed.

The doe would never forgive Sandy for betrayal of a friendship that had brought them to America together, acquaintances that became much more before Sandy disappeared for months and then tried to lure Celeste into a trap.

The squirrel could hate herself all she wanted, but to betray those who sought to help them in a world that wanted both of them snuffed out... Celeste had changed her address no less than three times in the last six years in the city where she'd grown roots with Torrio's circle, always ready to drop everything and flee for her very survival if Sandy came for her.

Now thanks to Bucky Celeste might have to relocate yet again, escape to another state if not Canada or Mexico. Establishing herself elsewhere with her particular skill set would be difficult to say the least or she'd have done it years ago.

And Bucky would squeal if put to the rabbit's screws.

Where to find him? Sandy had a Tudor-styled cottage close to the steel magnate's Gold Coast mansion, but Bucky wouldn't know unless he followed her there as Celeste had done once. Sandy was on a tight leash and the place where she'd sequestered herself emanated with a miasma of such incredible discomfort that Celeste was loathe to approach its white picket gate.

If Bucky wasn't a fool, he'd feel it and run.

If Bucky wasn't a fool...

Celeste bound shadows as she moved north, coming to the end of the block where the white picket boundary of Sandy Mallory's abode loomed.

A car idled on the curb with a Rolls Royce hood emblem. A possum fidgeted behind the wheel. Celeste drew close enough to feel the familiar ache of discomfort that haunted the lot, but no further. She'd felt that same discomfort recently, out on the town, couldn't recall where in that moment.

Focussing, Celeste watched from her shadow as the cottage's terracotta door opened, expelling a well-dressed rabbit in a homburg and three-piece suit.

The possum opened the rear salon and the rabbit settled within. His voice drifted, one ear visible through the Roll's rear window square.

"She's not here. Keller hasn't seen her in hours and was unsurprisingly reluctant to speak to me."

Celeste knew that name. She'd spotted the Nosfur at the speak-easy the night she was working Bucky over. As discomforting as the house was from here, she could only imagine what horrors lay inside if the raccoon was a prisoner.

The rabbit sighed. "Sandy or Von Haften could be at the house. Once there I'll need you to telephone your friend at the Tribune regarding that alley off Cottage Grove. Remember to stress that it looked like a mob hit."

"Is anybody going to believe that?" The possum sounded incredulous.

"The press will. Let's head back to the house and hope that—" The rabbit ceased abruptly, and Celeste saw his ears go erect as he fumbled for something.

The car rocked as he spun around and glared through the narrow square of the Rolls Rear window.

Directly at Celeste.

No. She was bound to a shadow. A mortal couldn't see her.

The rabbit held her gaze and muttered low enough that she could just barely hear; "We've company, not Sandy. It's right there. Get us around and hurry back a block. Now!"

Tires squealed as the Rolls thundered around, clipping a curb. Celeste glimpsed steel being drawn in the rear carriage where the rabbit braced against the turn. Every fibre in her being told her she was in danger.

The doe broke cover and raced through past Roll's lights, crossing the street and leaping a hedge into a manicured neighbor's lot. The door flung open and the rabbit leapt that same hedge, speed impressive even for a lapine.

Celeste fought the impulse to bind another shadow. She didn't know how he sensed her but ambushes were impossible. The stone wall fencing the lawn's garden was tall, but she could hurdle it effortlessly. Six bounds covered ground, ripping a croquet hoop from its mooring. Thick fingers found purchase, —

A thud showered mortar chips on her shoulders. The blade with a cane's ram-headed handle wobbled in a crack above, blocking her path. A wave of nausea washed over Celeste and her hooved feet scrabbled to keep her on the wall.

"You've felt that before, haven't you?" The rabbit's British accent was clipped as he regained his breath. "Discomforts in places you've tread? I know you've been in my city for some time. Sandy's told me much about you, Celeste."

Celeste twisted and let the rabbit see fangs. If he had a second weapon it wasn't brandished. "I've been here far longer than you, petit lapin so I'd say it's my city."

He smiled bucked teeth. "Yet it's my influence spreading here, fortunately for you Celeste. There's so much harm that I can save you from."

"I've heard this nonsense before." The nausea was becoming pain, follicles needling within her pelt, sinews starting to saw against bones.

The rabbit took a step forward. "Sandy brought you an offer that you declined and I'll extend again. You needn't be destroyed like so many others. You only need help to surrender your vices."

Celeste knew what he meant, having seen glimpses of Sandy in the intervening years, stooping, greying, steps heavier as she faded into decay.

If the rabbit got her back to that picturesque little cottage of horrors the end would come long or short but it would come. Bucky may already be doomed, she realized.

"I offer release from your afflictions. Come Celeste, just to talk." The rabbit gestured across the lawn to where his car's door yawned. "I invite you in."

The pain was tiring her quickly. The way forward was plain so she took it.

She grabbed the blade by the handle and it burned enough to draw a scream as it came loose. A spin and a flick and the rabbit leaped sideways, homburg spilling from his white skull as his weapon pierced the lawn.

Celeste hauled herself over with her uninjured hand and into the copse of trees beyond. She dashed through the orchard to the city, no lungs to burst, driven by fear. She was halfway into the downtown core's meager shadows before she finally slowed her pace, wounded hand throbbing.

Bucky was out there, so was the squirrel and now Donovan Calvert.

Celeste now had a single clue to follow.

Calvert had mentioned an alley off Cottage Grove, a small enough part of South Chicago that she could canvas quickly. Her attire was torn, but not enough to merit questions if she slipped from shadow. Taking the alleys, she found a feral rat that she dispatched to get her strength back. The burn from the blade was already retreating.

An hour later she bound shadows through the Cottage Grove station area. A slight twinge of discomfort from the station was enough to keep her from approaching too closely. Murmurs in the night became whispers, mammals gathering at an alley's mouth. In the flash of a newsmammal's camera bulb Celeste saw brass-buttoned officers pushing back press, handkerchiefs blocking countless noses and retching maws. A crosswind brought the scent before a white plank-panelled ford somberly blocked a dark alley ahead.

Celeste knew from the stench that things had gotten more complicated.

***

Back at Donovan Calvert's mansion a primly dressed mongoose sweated profusely as the Countess screamed in Austrian. He couldn't understand a word as she tore off strip after strip of soiled clothing in the main foyer until she was down to unmentionables and the mongoose studiously put his muzzle down, examining swirls in the Carrera marble under her dirty feet. Only the last accented curses in English came through. "No taxi to summon? No constables? Are they all turning over basements for their stupid liquor amendment? Is all of America as idiotic as Chicago?" An avalanche of Germanic swears folded the mongoose's ears shut as he gathered soiled bloody clothes. The lioness stalked away, knife bound to a bare hip and tail lashing the statues flanking Master Calvert's grand staircase. "Send up a drink. Whiskey, brandy I don't care!" she called down.

The mongoose smartly turned towards the study, then remembered the soiled fabrics in his arms and turned on a heel to the servant's hall laundry service. Two steps later he remembered Master Calvert's urgent demand to be telephoned at Mallory's cottage if the Countess or Ms. Mallory arrived. The attendant turned smartly once again and collided with a snoutfull of hot feline belly fur. The Countess glared down at him. "Donovan had a home build for the bloodsucker squirrel. Give me a key."

***

The night was magic. So was she. The purloined Alfa Romeo prowled Chicago's outskirts, wind whipping symphonies of scents through their fur. Bucky noticed that she'd lost nearly ten years in an hour. Her grey was fading, dark eyes reflecting the majesties of the city. Bucky had felt powerful since waking from the bite that didn't kill him, but now he felt free.

The squirrel was equally drunk on the life in her veins, gawking at the world flitting by as though for the first time. An hour ago, she'd treated him like the most hideous thing alive. Now, following a quick quiet smash and grab to steal a dark red flapper dress for some modesty, well, now was all that mattered.

Bucky had made a friend on the other side of death. Bees' knees. He had questions aplenty but they could wait.

The Italian roadster was a thirsty beast, growling at Fords, Chevys and Packards it darted past. They stopped for gas. Bucky went to pay, realized he had no money and took the marten night attendant behind his own desk, he was full after ten swallows but forced down twelve.

Sandy, such a beautiful name for a red Irish squirrel, was lost in thought outside, staring straight ahead. Bucky emptied the register of lettuce. It wouldn't do to be broke on their first date, he thought through a thick red haze.

"All paid up," he said outside and started the Alfa.

Sandy sighed. "I gave everything to Calvert, and what was it all for?" She laughed at nothing in particular as they rolled off the lot. "I want to drive. I'm sure I remember how."

Bucky almost argued, but joy's flow quelled that impulse. He could always put her in her place later if that was needed. He pulled over again. "Where you gonna take us?"

Sandy crossed to the driver's side and got the car rolling with a jerk. "I want…" she shivered. "I need to dance. It's been years."

Bucky tasted red on his teeth and licked them clean. "I know just the place."

Twenty minutes later they were on the south side. Sticky air was filled with juniper, thyme, lavender, a thousand scents to throw off the noses of pigs who'd ruin the fun unravelling down stairwells and past wooden doors where ragtime bands brassily chased claws across stone cellar floors.

"One night," Sandy was saying to herself in that charming Irish lilt as whiskies filled their hands. "It took one night to turn so much around."

Bucky's arm was around the squirrel already and she didn't mind. "This town is like that," he smiled again. "So many possibilities. We could go far, you and me."

"In what way?" She was curious but not suspicious, her grin soft.

"I have plans."

She raised an eyebrow and Bucky noticed the grey and white had bled away completely. The lines around her eyes had retreated further. "Do tell."

"Friends of mine and I have plans to go into business. They just have a little side gig to wrap up." He sipped whiskey and shrugged. "You have a place you're living now?"

Sandy wrinkled her nose and shrugged her healing shoulder. "I suppose not."

Bucky ran through the possibilities he'd already scoped out before that fateful night with Celeste. "I have to square things away with some former associates before moving ahead."

Bucky watched Sandy's tongue dart over those thick squirrel front teeth and was conscious of how attractive he was finding her now that she'd receded to late middle age. "I have things I need to settle," she said.

"I can help." Bucky didn't know how, or even with what, but that feeling of incredible power surging through him had a potency that lit sparks.

"Only if you can help me escape. He'll come after me."

"That lion was a dame."

"I meant somebody else."

"Oh. A certain somebody's coming after me too. You've met Celeste, right?"

"We were close once," Sandy was momentarily lost in herself. "I suppose I owe her..." She looked into her empty glass. "This still does nothing for me," she observed. "I thought the long break from the vein might change that but there's only ever the vein."

Bucky looked at his own glass, tipped it back, swirled it around his muzzle and swallowed. He gazed back to the bar where a limited selection of hooch beckoned before turning back to the noisy, swinging, hot and musky crowd. He took a sniff. "Lots of great vintages in here," he muttered as he watched the dancers in fascination. "We find the right people and we can corner a new market."

"What do you mean?"

"We'll talk later," Bucky set his empty glass down as the band picked up off a snare drum's thunder.

Feet pounded the earth and animals whooped. "Let's dance."

Chapter 9

Dead Otters and Misplaced Cars

Crawford needed a drink and to throw up.

The second came first. The tub's porcelain was damp as he lay on his left side. When he retched it echoed all around. He slithered on his stomach, genitals coldly confirming he was naked and most of what he threw up went down the drain. Some bounced back on his neck and muzzle fur.

In a panic he pushed himself back, limbs rubber, feet kicking through the reddish slop he'd expelled.

Everything was red. His bare chest, forearms and thighs were crusted with ichor as though he'd toiled naked in a slaughterhouse.

He panicked, gorge rising again. He almost slipped face first into the horror gurgling away. Fingers clutched clumsily at both taps, freezing then scalding under his raw knees. His head pounded as he tried to put all that came before together. He'd tailed the Tooley to Daley's restaurant. And then....

He grabbed handfuls of water to slap at himself, brushed at the crimson stains in his fur. Panic crested as he was momentarily unsure whose bathroom this was, then saw the familiar crack on the mirror over the sink. Fumbling for the drain plug, he started filling the tub, seeing evidence coalesce. He'd crossed half of Chicago to his shared apartment with Charlie, covered in blood with every stitch of clothing gone, none of which was on this bathroom floor.

Were bloody clothes in his bedroom, on the kitchen floor?

Was something else?

He made to slip from the tub to check, then settled back into the soup. He could only track more mess back into the apartment, provide even more evidence of disaster. He needed to get clean fast, so he clutched the fur soap powder and set to work.

The frosted window next to the toilet gleamed with the nectar of first light. Hours had passed. He scrubbed harder, feeling aches return to his limbs, ragged heart beating harder and teeth raw. He remembered skulking outside the diner, the otter placating the gangster who pulled his strings, the scents of burned steaks, coffee.

The L-train thundered, whipped up newspapers, coat-doffing heat. Shirt and pants following.

Jesus boat-crafting fuck, what had he done?

His tongue dragged back and forth, stress reaction for want of a tipple. It caught something sharp wedged next to a fang. Crawford used his claws to work it out.

A fragment of bone gleamed wet in his fingers.

He wretched again, stomach now empty and scrubbed in panic. The taste of death was in the back of his throat and he knew.

The sun had left the small window behind when Crawford rose dripping from the tub and pulled the chain to let the horror drain away. The solid bits left behind made him sick to his empty stomach and he used a cloth to gather the mess up, ball it and slip it out the cracked window to the narrow alley below. Hopefully vermin would drag it away.

Soaked fur to damp took another twenty minutes. He stole some of Charlie's scented talcum to bury butchery's scents and gazed at the civilized looking lupine in the mirror. He muttered the truth out loud. "You ate Tooley. You sick feral bastard."

The reflection was surprised.

The hall was empty, so was his bedroom. No blood on the floor. He hurried to the bedroom, dressed himself over damp fur, got a tie Windsored after three tries. "I'm going to drown in hell."

Was he? There was no bright side but he dumbfoundly scrabbled for one anyway. Even if he'd gone feral last night, he'd killed a cop who murdered another cop. Was there a worse scourge to decency on earth?

He had to put himself together, learn what had actually happened. A cold pit rose inside as he realized that nothing he'd left the office with was here. No clothes, no coat, no car key, no badge, no gun.

He threw on slacks in his room, hurried back to the hall and into the kitchen where the wolf froze like a caught cub.

Charlie sat at the table, dress shirt half-buttoned, his expression bleary and blank. An empty plate sat before him, a second setting with cold eggs and congealed bacon across. He said not a word.

Soberly, it occurred to Crawford to wonder how many of his fears had been spoken aloud. "Charlie," he said. "Good morning."

"Feeling better?" the brown wolf asked. "I cleaned up the blood."

Crawford's innards plunged deep enough to mine for coal. "What?"

"You left footprints from the door to the bathroom. The door was locked but you said you were fine. Did you cut yourself?"

Crawford had never bled in front of Charlie before. Even if he had, he'd never personally distinguished one mammal's blood from another's the same way he could recognize pelts. Hopefully Charlie couldn't either. "Cut my foot. Only hurts a little."

"I smell otter."

Charlie's nose *was* better. Shit. "Do you?"

"Did you...meet somebody last night?

Crawford couldn't piece the question together. "I don't follow."

Charlie sighed. "You look terrible. And I know why, Crawford. Let's just clear the air."

"Okay." Crawford realized he was still standing in the kitchen's vestibule with a still tail, the very picture of guilt. He approached, dragged a chair back noisily and sat.

"I know some of what you're going through." Charlie sounded sympathetic.

"Oh yeah?"

Charlie set Crawford's whiskey bottle on the table. "This fell out from behind your dresser when I checked your room to see if you'd returned. When I found the bathroom door locked and you told me to go away, I got wise."

Crawford didn't remember speaking to Charlie.

"It's not illegal to own whiskey from before the Eighteenth came into effect, we both know that, but we raided the warehouse where this was taken. Two crates went missing."

Goddammit. "I only took the one bottle. I needed it."

"I know. I've known for a while because I've seen the flask, smelled your breath past the mint or...apples." Charlie sat back. "Killing Simon

Govic hit hard. Taking a life, even accidentally...you've been buttoned up about it ever since visiting his widow, that's just...you." The wan smile was pained. "But I know you're carrying more weight than just that."

How could the whole world in and out of this apartment be so silent? "What do you know, Charlie?"

"I'm sorry Crawford. It had no name and was slipped under the door." Charlie nodded his muzzle towards the counter and Crawford turned to see a long envelope. He wracked his mind for a moment to guess what was inside, and then he did.

Charlie's hands opened in supplication. "I'm here for you, Craw, you know that's no joke." Charlie wet his lips. "I know you've wanted to patch things up with your wife and..." Charlie drummed his claws nervously, "she's losing a good wolf."

Crawford had doubted those papers would come. Deep down he'd just refused to accept it.

He leaned over and drew the envelope off the counter, withdrew the papers and let conditions and demands settle next to his cold breakfast. Lucas' name appeared several times, but all else was a blur. "I've done bad things, Charlie."

"What, this?" He lifted the bottle and set it down. "You didn't want to kill anyone, this is nothing, and if you needed relief, or companionship, that's okay too. Nobody gets to tell you to be alone."

His hand reached for Crawford's but slipped back just shy of touching and he sat back, sympathy in the kind eyes over his muzzle. "I...find my comfort in a different part of town than you do but we find it just the same. And I'd..."

Crawford read something of weight in what trailed off and their eyes only met for a second.

Charlie looked away first. "It'll be okay. Give yourself time to figure it all out. You're due that."

Crawford took deep breaths, in through the jaws, out through the nose. "Thank you, Charlie. You're a true friend."

"I'm glad to be that, Crawford." Charlie nodded at Crawford's plate. "You should eat if you can. We need to get to the office."

Crawford picked up the fork, uncertain why he found himself hungry so soon after...but maybe that was a good thing. Charlie rose and went to the window while Crawford bolted down bacon and eggs, negotiating with his gorge to keep it there.

Charlie frowned as he scanned the street below. "Where's the car?"

An hour later, with the vehicle confirmed by Crawford as somewhere south of the loop and the otter prostitute theory of Charlie's neither confirmed nor denied, they left for the office.

Crawford ran through scenarios. Nobody would ask to see his badge or gun or ask why he wore an off-season coat unless somebody found what he'd lost. He could obtain another gun since the 1908 was his own rather than requisitioned, but the badge worried him. If things happened as his frazzled mind rudely constructed them and his badge was with that corpse then he was truly fucked and muzzled.

Could he play clueless as to when his badge had been lost? Maybe he'd dropped it at the warehouse raid and hadn't noticed.

As the elevated train took them into town, they passed deco facades of buildings, parks teeming with scruffy cubs playing filthy and happy and tried not to think of his son Lucas. Had his son any say in this divorce? Did he miss his father or, like Kamila, was he glad he was gone? Crawford forced himself to keep that out of his mind now lest he start weeping on the L-train. Reliably buttoned-up Crawford; always a box to put his emotions in.

Scenery passed. A few stations later they came upon a cemetery between apartments which reminded Crawford of the one where he'd been bitten and the train ground to a halt to let on passengers.

That graveyard bite started whatever was afflicting him now. The photos of Simon Govic's corpse, the confused medical examiner's notes, none of that was coincidence, he felt it with cold certainly.

Charlie leaned over from his isle seat. "What the hell are they doing?"

"What?" Crawford's eyes darted from stone to tree to stone, and then he saw them. Three crouched figures, a wolf, an otter, and a coyote, the latter two stooped with age, prayed around one grave with eyes closed. Then as one they raised wine bottles, splashing a stone masthead cross in crimson. Several other stones in the yard had dark stains.

"What a weird thing to do with booze," Charlie said. "Should we go down there?"

"No," Crawford said, transfixed. "They aren't imbibing it and it'll dry before the ink on a vandalism charge does."

The trio shuffled to the next stone and started again. A mangy cat approached, hat literally in hand, miming for a sip. The coyote barked something that made the cat scamper away and they resumed.

"Weren't they the one's pushing that wheelbarrow of still parts on Tuesday?" Charlie mused.

As though on cue, they stopped chanting and the wolf turned and looked up at the still train car, seemingly directly at Crawford, petite face serene. The train started rolling again as she winked him. A chill ran like a cold breath down his back.

The two Prohee wolves were nonplussed as the train pulled away. "This town..." Charlie started to say and neither could say more.

The office was somber when they arrived, like yesterday, but now a shock had taken hold, the taste of fear unmistakable. At the back of the room, outside his office, Beatie stood, hat in one hand and a clutched paper in the other.

A broadsheet on a nearby desk was messily spread open, and Crawford turned it back to the front.

Above the photograph of an alley mouth blocked by an ambulance, the headline blared: VICIOUS GANGLAND REPRISAL TO WAREHOUSE RAID SEES POLICEMAN SLAIN. Underneath, the subhead was no less subdued: Chief of police and Mayor Demand State resources to combat Lawless Menace.

Crawford quickly hurried through the lead and first three paragraphs. Brutal murder, unspeakable horror, details guarded to protect the family. Identity of the slain was not verified but expert noses verified the species as otter.

The paper fell from Crawford's hand and settled to the floorboards. Charlie was at his shoulder. "What the hell happened?"

A pat at Crawford's other shoulder startled him. It was Ned, one of the tomcats on Beatie's unit. "Can you believe it," he muttered through a hiss. "Feral mobster bastards."

Charlie's ears perked up. "Beatie wants us."

They crowded into the bear's office and Crawford smelled musk pushing to the rafters. He couldn't help noticing that in confined spaces minute smells were now easier to separate from one another. Bear sweat, pipe tobacco, ink, pelt oil, gun oil. It was disorienting and Crawford forced himself to focus.

"This information is confidential," Beatie said. "Only a handful of officers on the police force know because cooler heads need to prevail until we get more information. Officer Tooley, who participated in the North side warehouse raid with us, was killed in a violent fashion consistent with a feral attack." He puffed angrily. "And I'm not talking rats."

"My God," Charlie doffed his hat and clutched it tight.

"Our God," Beatie puffed his pipe. "Certainly not this monster's. We don't yet know what species of mammal did this."

"We're sure it was a feral attack?" Crawford felt small and naïve even asking.

"As sure as I live and breath," Beatie rumbled. "While the police work that case, we're set to ramp up our operations in order to strangle the mob's reach. Torrio's outfit has clearly decided it's war."

Charlie set his hat down. "Could it have been O'Banion? The Irish would love to frame up the Italians for this. We don't even know who gave that anonymous call on the warehouse."

Beatie shrugged. "I wish whomever tipped us off had given a name but they're in the wind."

Crawford tried to clear his head but could still see the gore he'd washed down his drain not two hours ago. Getting his doctor's appointment moved up in order to figure out what he had and if he was a danger to anyone was going to be tough when he couldn't be honest about the symptoms. His limbs were aching again and a headache was rounding that out.

He tried to remember exactly what information he'd given the receptionist when he called. Did they write down that he was feeling angry? That he'd been bitten?

Did the doctors know something about his condition based on symptoms alone that would make today's news seem familiar to them? It was an insane, paranoid thought, but what if his call had flagged something?

"Crawford are you with us? I asked if you want a cigarette," Beatie's eyes were hard.

Crawford smelled the Rothmans that Beatie offered before he saw them. He nodded, thinking hard about things doctor's assistants wrote that triggered inquiries, like they'd done a few years back for the Spanish flu when morons refused to mask up and they were tracing contacts.

How many of doctor's calls were monitored now that the flu was under control?

Had they even stopped doing that?

It hit him as the smoke slipped into his fingers and the lick of flame raised to his lips. "Records."

"What?"

"Records." He nearly blew the flame out, then puffed his smoke to life instead. "A circular went around three months ago about how Ma Bell was helping the bureau by writing down information pertaining to alcohol informants just like they did contact tracing for the Spanish flu. Remember?"

Beatie frowned. "I remember."

"Record keeping was sloppy and only kept if the caller mentioned it to the operator. Plus, too many pranksters. The wheels might have been too slow to stop the reporting though. Have we checked to see if the informant might have said something to the connecting operator to trigger making notations? We'd have a source number."

"We were so over the moon on the raid that we didn't even think to check that," Beatie said. "Glad your head's on straight Crawford. Get on it."

"Thanks chief," Crawford nodded. It was time to lose himself in work. He had nothing else.

***

Edmond Virage was angry. Donovan knew this was usually so regardless of the carefully coifed implacability his servant studiously applied. When the possum entered his study that veneer had slipped and the blood dripping from his nose suggested why.

Donovan held up a hand up to forestall the tirade until his telephone call was finished. The possum's tail twisted and writhed as the rest of him remained stock still.

On the phone, Laguna Belle was making less sense than usual. "We delivered forteh-two. Aimed for fifteh but couldn't find 'em fresh enough."

Donovan frowned. "What does fresh mean? Young voters? I need about fifty to close the margins in both those districts for Leicester to win."

"This isn't our first dance, Donnie. Y'only need forty and they all gonna fill the right dot. A victory will be shortly clinched,"

"And destiny's hooks are slowly winched," floated in the voice of a young wolf near the phone.

There was a space of crackling silence that followed. "And?" Donovan snapped.

Laguna sighed. "Grisand has the last paht, but she's in the privy now."

Donovan closed his eyes. "For God's sake."

"Your hound'll get elected. If you don't mind, we gotta meet a fox friend bout a job we have brewin.'"

"Wonderful." a shadow filled the study door behind Edmond that resolved into a lioness in black slip licking blood off the back of her broad golden hand. "I must go."

"We know," the two sisters on the line said at once. Baliosi coughed. "You sound wrung out, Don. Want we come over and pour you a drink?"

Donovan hung the phone up on their laughter, his heart skipping a beat.

Rabbit and Lion traded glares as the possum trailed his dignity back behind Donovan's desk.

"A quick stop in town, you said. Back in an hour you said," Donovan spat. "On top of my appointments book missing, I found one of my servants locked in a closet."

"I did borrow your book." The Countess hefted it in her unbloodied hand. "...but your pet demanded I wait. I reminded him of his place."

"My people know their place, but you fail to understand you're a guest here, Countess. You've had me racing all night around Chicago trying to find you."

"And why should you be concerned about what I do? Your precious business is the Martyre's business. You keep no secrets from us and despite your innovations in Nosfur detection you have already earned my suspicions with your pet monster."

She entered the study and set the red book on Donovan's desk before taking the plush chair across from him. Something in the way she lowered herself gave Donovan pause. "You seem to be walking rather stiffy. Are you hurt?"

"No. Have you seen your squirrel of late, Donovan? She's not at the cottage where your servant so kindly directed me to. Only the pathetic creature you didn't destroy."

Donovan felt the temperature dropping. Evelyn was holding something back and toying with him. "She frequently goes to ground in order to find new candidates."

The smile she gave was chilling. "And you trust her implicitly, do you?"

Donovan knew he couldn't tell her the truth about Sandy. To admit she had never returned last night would cost much more than face with her. He could only hope that Evelyn hadn't felt this town's most recent preternatural denizen with the pendant he'd given her. She was already wont to presume he couldn't control affairs here. "Yes. She's earned that trust. Drink?"

She smiled, then looked to Edmond as though he were lint drifting past Donovan's shoulder. "Brandy for me."

Donovan nodded and Edmond stormed out without a word, leaving the rabbit and lion alone. "Did you manage to see some of Chicago?" Donovan asked, keeping his long ears back.

"Some parts you haven't I would suspect. How goes your election rigging?"

"We should have enough votes to get my man in."

"The School Superintendent with political dreams. I took the liberty of meeting him to tour the school as a potential benefactor. He was without a doubt the most boring, self-absorbed canine I've ever met," she said indifferently.

Donovan took a deep breath. Her thorough monitoring of his plans wasn't the least bit comforting. "When he's installed, our work will go forward at considerable speed."

The lion looked impatient for her drink but nodded. "Donovan, I regret I misplaced something of my own yesterday." The drink was set down next to her and she ignored both it and the possum whose tail lashed furiously as he vanished. "I need you to provide me with a new car."

Donovan let his ears drop. "Are you serious?"

"Yes. And most certainly not that lupine-stinking Chevrolet you've parked outside. I have standards."

***

Celeste sat in her empty home as the sun rose to trap her there, the long night having ended in defeat. Bucky was gone and the stir of emotions within her ensured she wouldn't rest, even as sun began to bleed around the seals of her soon to be abandoned home.

She hated him for his idiocy, fearing for him at the same time. If Sandy had brought him to the rabbit, well Celeste could only imagine he'd be dead in the truest sense. She greatly doubted that whatever charming tortures turned Sandy against her own nature would work on a hedonist like Bucky Cavali.

If he got wise and backed off then getting a handle on his true powers might convince him to go after Torrio. In that case Celeste would be out of a job, either fired or having no employer to pay her.

Even worse possibilities occurred to her. If he exposed himself, killed carelessly, released their secret out into a photographic, radio-wave ridden world, well, who knows what it would do to the very fabric of society.

Survived exposure to her kind had long been written off to madness, tricks of the eye, or nightmares from the bottoms of bottles. Try as Celeste did to keep her mind on the fox who'd gone to ground, she couldn't keep the smell from that alley out of her mind, the one that Calvert had spoken to his footman about in such stressed terms. She knew the deeds down that dark corridor were care of something unnatural.

If only the dog who'd brought her daily paper would set it on her doorstep rather than simply throw the thing so it bounced halfway back down the steps, she'd be able to get news without needing three days to heal from bathing in fire. "When I move again, expense be damned, I need to buy a radio."

She started to ruminate yet again on how Bucky had ruined her life when she heard the creak of her front steps. There was the slightest sound that touched Celeste's ears along with it, the panting of someone of canine stock.

Was it a salesman? She crept down her staircase half-way, hooves soundless and crouched to listen.

Sounds outside resolved themselves into two pairs of feet, one retreating back down the steps while the other crept across her front porch. Salesmen didn't come in pairs, nor did census takers.

The breathing at her door was ragged. There was a knock, not too hard but firm. Celeste said nothing.

Another knock, and Celeste crept down a step closer. The voice was gravelled with what sounded like exhaustion. "Hello? Sir or Mam, anybody home?"

Celeste caught the hint of a scent. Not quite canine, less musky than Bucky who didn't shed after death. A little closer and she could get a better idea before he gave up and left.

All sound stopped abruptly as the person on the other side of the door froze. A second of silence was broken as the front door's handle turned. Celeste knew she'd locked it.

When the handle kept turning and the door pressed in with the lock's housing fractured like butter, Celeste barely got out a bleat of surprise. A ray of light fell across one leg and burned like a brand of fire.

Celeste leaped to shadow as the door swung open, filled by a long-coated grey lupine silhouette, surprise on his own face at the door handle in his claws. The acrid scent hit the doe right away, unnatural as her own, heady, tinged with tobacco, whisky, and traces of blood.

Her fangs were out and her eyes went dark as the wolf stepped into her abode. Her hiss drew his hackles straight up.

CHAPTER 10

DARKENED DOORS

"Take a look round back, see if you see another entrance."

"Shouldn't we both be here for the knock?" Charlie's expression was dubious under his pork pie.

"Naw, I have a feeling." Crawford couldn't explain it any better than that. The place was somehow tidy yet derelict, the porch spotless with every curtain not just drawn but actually tied from frame to frame, to keep the inside invisible from out. The look was unsettling.

Then came the scent.

Ever since waking from the stupor that morning, Crawford's lupine senses had gone wildfire. He smelled cigarettes in passing glove boxes, hooch in passing coats. Masons hammered a block away and Crawford caught the lyrics of the Ma Rainey they sang.

And now...Crawford's nose caught a scent that was somehow bereft of all sound. Cervine but not cervine. No sweat, no breath, just...essence.

The knock wasn't answered. "Hello? Sir or Mam or you home?"

No answer but he sensed a presence. Instinct screamed that something was wrong on the other side of that door.

Caution and procedure thrown to the wind, Crawford grabbed the handle and twisted it

before he even knew what he was doing. To his bewilderment the knob broke off in his hand.

The door flew open. In weak shadows a brown furred deer retreated from the light. She was speckled where her blouse and flapper-length skirt ended, the dress in black, the blouse in maroon.

As she retreated, she hissed in pain and Crawford's hackles instinctively shot up. A hand dived inside his coat for the badge he forgot he didn't have as he stepped forward into the foyer. "Mam I'm sorry to intrude are you all..."

Crawford's words died away as her jaw parted in the dim light of the darkened hall and sprouted fangs.

"Oh, fuck me."

In the space of a blink, slender, impossibly strong cervine fingers clutched his lapel and bodily pulled the wolf into darkness. His body fractured wall-papered plaster. As he crumpled low, a kicked hoof slammed the door shut again, casting them both into black.

Crawford's eyes adapted fast, registering the base of a staircase and a living room nearly bereft of furniture, before the slender deer hauled him up again like a garden root.

Singed fur was burning, not his own. Crawford fumbled for his thirty-eight only to have it knocked from his hand to skitter deeper into the house. He realized only one of the deer's arms had hauled him up.

A slap to his muzzle landed like a haymaker. Crawford gasped at stars. "What are you?" Crawford grimaced around the blood coppering his mouth.

The doe twisted, bodily throwing him into the living room. He struck a draped couch and rolled onto his forelimbs, blood dripping through his jaws. She, he could smell for certain the deer was female, advanced with impossibly long fangs gleaming.

"You're not welcome here," her teeth mashed her words into pure hostility.

"You dragged me in," Crawford growled.

Taking two more steps, she clutched the white bedsheet covering the long-neglected couch and snapped her wrist. The undulating cloth hurled dust into Crawford's face. He gagged, squeezing his eyes shut.

A blink later, she'd dragged him up again like a rag dog, shoving him against the wall next to a solitary table where a candlestick telephone wobbled and nearly spilled its receiver.

The cold vice around his throat wound tight. "I didn't come to fiiggh..." Increased pressure stole breath away.

The doe wasn't out of breath at all. Dark irises had grown enormous, windows to an endless night. "Why did you come? Who sent you?"

Crawford felt the pressure would increase until his neck snapped. Desperation pumped blood hard with no upward path to his brain, and when the change began he didn't even feel it.

His arms around hers began to lengthen, claws thickening and expanding to wicked white thorns. They closed tight, piercing the doe's forearm as his foot's expanding claws scrabbled for purchase.

He could feel his throat expanding within her grip, the muzzle and teeth above gaining proportion.

The realization that his body wasn't his, that he was becoming something else, brought a cold torrent of fear.

A memory flashed of officer Tooley, terror on the Otter's face as his gun fired impotently into brick and Crawford's fangs sunk into the slick red confectionary of his shoulder.

As claws dug into arms and the unnatural doe's strength wavered, Crawford felt inexplicable excitement flutter in his belly, like the urge to play. He started to fade from himself and battled for focus, aware the empty room would be drenched in irredeemable carrion horror if he awoke here again at all. The couch was in relief in his vision, as was the small table.

The phone. Why had he knocked on this door?

To kill? He wasn't hungry. He'd not come to play.

He'd come to investigate. To find out why she'd informed on Johnny Torrio. He held that nugget of thought as implications collided with urges.

If Crawford Cain killed here, he'd have a blood-soaked mistake he couldn't hide from Charlie.

Unless Charlie himself became…

Panic sobered him, became a talisman. He couldn't let Charlie see this. He couldn't hurt Charlie *with* this.

Distorted limbs forcing the unnatural doe's arms apart were foreign things he had to command. One hard shove sent the doe reeling. Her hand extended backward effortlessly preventing a plaster-splintering collision with the opposite wall.

"Enough!" Crawford shouted through a mouth that made his words a bark. "I didn't come to fiighhht."

The doe didn't seem remotely frightened by him. She crouched for a rush. "Then why are you darkening my door?"

Crawford fought to get his breathing under control, mouth finding its own strings like a freed puppet. He concentrated on speaking. "A tip came from a phone…here…" keeping the facts straight was hard, even more so with wicked teeth slowly receding. "The call was about a warehouse supplying speakeasy liquor."

What was the rest? "It belonged to John Torrio."

The doe didn't drop her guard but didn't lunge again. Her wicked scimitar smile confirmed she could manage whatever was afflicting her better than Crawford could. He wiped away drool dangling from his chin with a hand that was regaining normal scale.

The doe pushed herself from the wall and Crawford saw a distressed handprint an inch deep. He knew that hand should be broken.

She said a name and shook her head in disappointment.

Crawford took a deep breath. "Who's Lucky?"

"Somebody whom I wish I could forget. He's gone. I didn't phone you."

Crawford took deep breaths, wary that the doe, if she was a doe, could strike at any moment. He reached into his coat.

"If you're going to draw another gun, you'll be dead before you do."

Crawford found a business card and withdrew it slowly. "I promise I brought no trouble. Your Lucky friend called to provide a tip that aided in many arrests."

"You're a policeman?" She said this with incredulity and derision as she snapped the card from his hand and took a step back.

"No. I'm an agent with the Federal Bureau of Internal Revenue working in Prohibition enforcement."

"This trade card says you sell Chevrolets, Mr. Walter Privens."

Old coat, dammit. He wavered as the inner monster fully receded, restored muzzle raw from the abuse. "I don't have the right card with me now. Just take my word that a call came from this number informing of a liquor distribution ring the night before last. I wanted to speak with that caller."

"I'm not him."

"Do you have a roommate? A…husband?"

The look was sour as a lemon gone bad. "No. And I don't believe you. I strongly doubt the Federal Government is employing weres, even in ignorance."

Crawford didn't care if he looked confused. "What the hell is 'weres?'"

Her ears went low. "I suppose you haven't guessed what I am either?" The question dripped sarcasm.

Crawford's ears pulled back. "French?"

She moved in a blur. Crawford was against the couch, then on the floor in a creaking clatter of pelt, upholstery and wood. Wind left his lungs as her elbow found his ribs and fangs were hot and wet against his cheek.

***

Crawford knocked up front as Charlie went round. Much as he wanted to be there when Crawford knocked two wolves on someone's stoop might be intimidating to whomever opened the door. Plus, they needed to ensure nobody slipped out back when Crawford rang. Anonymous tippers chose anonymity for a reason.

Charlie circled the house quickly to the fenced yard with a single gate. It swung into a space that had been extensively tilled but undeveloped, as though the homeowner dug a garden they hadn't got round to planting. There was a smell that he couldn't quite place.

The back of the house had one door off a wooden step with windows boarded up in tight planked rows. Windows on the second floor were also blocked.

Maybe it was full of hooch stills and the tip was to eliminate competition.

Charlie slipped the cigarette pack from his jacket, scuffing a clod of loose dirt with a claw. Thoughts intruded on the stillness. Crawford was under a hell of a lot of strain and they'd need to have a long talk at some point. He'd respected his pack-mate's family life and the pains of its unravelling while Charlie delicately managed his own affairs. Secrets kept from one so close to a pack-mate were problematic but occasionally necessary.

Despite harboring the suspicion that Crawford himself had tendencies that were unconventional, Charlie had to be professional, keep demure and find friends north around tower-town on the nights where he "worked late." With relief obtained through the right friend, Charlie attained calm, and thus way Crawford's hips and tail swished when he was on the move became just part of the scenery, nothing to get excited about.

Charlie regarded the door that might fly open at any second and decided he could tackle somebody with a butt in his mouth. He queued a smoke, struck a match and puffed it bright. Long as the government didn't confiscate his Rothmans with yet another amendment, he could keep it together.

A minute passed and Charlie's ears perked. Was that a slam?

"Hullo friend," came a voice at his shoulder. Charlie's cigarette sparked as it tumbled down his mohair jacket. The stooped coyote in the dark brown housedress at his shoulder waggled grey whiskers and smiled brown teeth. One eye went his way, the other downward. "Strange place to find a gentleman callah, not to knock, not to hollah." She said in honeyed Georgian.

She had to be quiet as death to approach through the gate ten feet away.

"Beg pardon mam?"

"Wolf invested, double-breasted in deeds that leave his kind detested." The elderly otter with the creole accent at his elbow raised the Rothman Charlie dropped and took a drag. "Wanna say hi Baliosi?"

The younger black wolf seated on the fence's edge had to be light as a bird. "I'm not his type. He can't love in a world with hate so ripe."

Charlie's ears went flat "Who are you people? Do you live here?"

"None live here but one persists," said the otter.

"Lonely, angry, grasps at mists," added the coyote.

Baliosi's gaze fell to recently overturned dirt. "The hard lived stature of true nature leaves a heart that still resists."

The otter and coyote followed her glance to mound of earth.

"Another one?" asked the wolf?

The other two traded glances and nodded. "Couldn't hurt," the otter muttered around the pilfered cigarette.

The wolf on the fence produced a dusty bottle and Charlie's head cleared. "You three were in the graveyard this morning, pouring wine on stones. Why the hell—"

"Can't you hear that?" The coyote asked. Charlie realized that one eye didn't line with the other because one of them was painted, slugged wood. "Your friend is in a ruckus."

"In a what?" Charlie did hear something from the house. A thud, a slam, a fracturing of plaster. Goddammit.

He turned and threw himself at the back door. It was bolted shut like a bank vault and he bounced off like a rubber ball to land claws over ass. "I'm coming Craw!" He rolled from a crouch and bolted past the three woman who converged on the mound of disturbed soil.

Undefinable mutterings that tugged from the earth itself filled the yard behind Charlie as the Sisters closed ranks.

A cork popped.

***

The were's thrown body shifted the couch. If he started another change Celeste would have to kill him fast.

She rushed him, ready to open his artery as soon as she could clutch that scruffy throat, but he stumbled back from the couch, an elbow breaking one window. A deadly shaft of light speared a spot on her floor.

The wolf spoke through a sprouting deadly chain of ivory, starting to drool as the change renewed. "I don't wannnt thiiii." He closed his eyes, took deep breaths. If Celeste could get around the light, she could take him.

His roving elbow broke more window, fattened paw gripping for purchase. More light flooded through broken glass. Celeste kept no mirrors in her home so luckily there was nothing to bounce the rays around. Still, the wolf would soon tear a hole in the home itself.

He slid to the floor, taking ragged gasps with extreme effort. His teeth receded for a second time and his muzzle became less distended.

Despite herself, Celeste was fascinated. She'd only encountered a were once before her flight to America. Two other passengers had ended that fateful night-time carriage trip as corpses in the Rhone. Till that scent triggered her memory from her porch, she'd assumed that crossing the ocean had left one threat behind.

Now she was trapped. The sunlight breaking through betrayed a cloudless sky. Fighting him might tear her fragile shelter apart, or at the very least bring more attention in the form of onlookers, policeman, and soon enough cultish rabbits with burning rapiers.

For both their sakes, she realized she had to calm the wolf down. "I'm sorry I harmed you."

That sounded as convincing to her own ears as Bucky's pretentions to vegetarian suffrage but she forged ahead. "Take deep breaths." She caught his glazed eye and mimed the working of lungs under her bosom like a fainting stage actor. Looking ridiculous didn't matter.

The wolf nearly doubled over as something shifted painfully. Then he caught her gaze with his grey flinty eyes as his mouth regained speech. "I'm a Prohibition agent. I didn't come to arrest you." A few more breaths helped him collect himself. "Point in fact..." he teetered to his feet and steadied himself over the back of her couch, "If you have whisky somewhere I'll be grateful for a sip." The wolf studied his forelimbs, flexing a paw back into a clawed hand.

Celeste was about to respond when a thud at the front door made her jump.

"Craw, what's going on in there? You okay?"

The wolf and doe regarded one another warily before the wolf cleared his throat. "We're all good, Charlie. I'm, uh, talking with the homeowner."

"I heard a...ruckus." The other voice, another lupine by its timbre, sounded out of breath.

"I knocked over some furniture accidentally. You know the kind of day I'm having." The look on the grey wolf's face spoke pitiful things words couldn't begin to convey and Celeste intuited that the were's secret was his own. That would be leverage in the right situation.

"Can I...come in too?"

If that door flew open again, Celeste would have to flee upstairs to stay unburnt. "I would rather you wouldn't," she called out. "I am not comfortable with strange wolves within my home but will speak with your partner. Alone."

"Crawford?" The other wolf sounded disappointed.

"Won't be long, Charlie."

Porch-boards creaked. "It's hot out here," the wolf muttered, assuming himself out of earshot. From the were's expression he heard his partner just as clearly.

Celeste waited for the wolf to gather his thoughts. "Sorry about your door, that was an accident." He glanced to the holes in the walls and swallowed. "Once again, I'm here about an anonymous liquor tip. That's all. I don't know what the hell a "were" is."

Celeste realized that this wolf might help her find Bucky, clueless as he clearly was about other matters. "I had a house guest, someone who borrowed my phone after I showed him some charity."

"Charity. Okay. Can you tell about him? Species? Name?"

"Fox. His name was Antony and he only stayed one night. I know nothing else that you would find useful as he gave no forwarding address."

The following silence was uncomfortably long. "What are you?" He finally settled on asking.

She cocked her ear. "I know what you are, Walter."

"My name isn't Walter."

"It's Craw?"

"Short for Crawford." He rubbed his chin as he glanced across the room to where his gun lay.

Celeste stepped between wolf and weapon. "You can reclaim that in a moment. Do you want to know what I know about you? You have questions that no one else in this city can answer for you and you'll need answers before you cause serious damage."

"I have some sense of what kind of damage I can do." He didn't seem proud to know that.

"Wait here." She returned from the kitchen with wine and a glass. "Take this," she studiously avoided the sunbeam's reach as she passed them both over. Diffidently, the wolf uncorked the dark bottle and sniffed at its contents. He clearly wasn't a wine drinker but poured a glass anyway. "Thanks."

Celeste let him have a drink before spooling out her reasoning. "I'm sure you know that had we kept fighting, you wouldn't have been able to control yourself past a certain point. Had your partner entered to investigate...you wouldn't have one."

He listened soberly as he sipped to get otherwise. "What can you tell me?"

"Too much to reveal right now. Your partner is impatient. The less time he waits the less of a lie you'll need. I'll come to you tonight after dark, maybe near your offices."

The wolf sighed. "There's a city election going on now and there will be a function we have to go to at City Hall hosted by Mayor Thompson. He might not be Mayor by then."

"I see. Did you spot a newspaper on my stoop when you came to knock?"

"I think so."

"Can you please toss it back in here when you leave? I have an...aversion to going outside."

"That somehow connected with you having the strength of a bull moose?"

"Let's add that to the list of things we should discuss."

"Long list," he muttered and rose, moving over to get his gun. She watched as he checked its safety catch and slipped it away in his coat. "I have to ask, do you know why your fox friend would call us? You suspect he had bad connections? Maybe he visited you to hide away from some of them."

"I can't know his motives and I regret that I don't know where he is now." She studiously kept disdain from her voice. "Let's pick a place to speak after your...function."

The wolf met her side-eye and finished the wine in his glass. "Dannovey's coffee shop on West Washington. Say...nine in the evening and I won't darken your door here again."

"I know that place. Hopefully you can get away in a timely fashion."

"I can get away. Sorry about your doorknob and...the rest of it." The wolf set the empty glass next to the telephone and gingerly slipped through the front door, closing its furnace of light behind him. A moment later it opened a crack and Celeste's rolled Tribune bounced against the wall before that light closed off completely.

That was it. A lost vulpine Nosfur and now a lupine were had both filled her vestibule in the space of a few nights. All her things would soon be packed to leave this house and its many liabilities for good.

Chapter 11

Plans Within Plans

The Duesenberg purring under Countess Von Haften was adequate. She missed the Alfa Romeo she'd had shipped to America, a gift from one of the inner-council's affiliates in Italy. It infuriated her that Nosfur parasites had pilfered it and she wouldn't mind getting it messy when it was eventually reclaimed. For now, she had other priorities.

The office discreetly leased weeks before her arrival waited uptown. Its only contents were a modestly stocked bar and a single desk-mounted telegraph machine whose exchange terminated four thousand miles away.

The relay was in England, which in turn would be communicated by telephone with the rest of the council. She was late for check-in but didn't much care. This assignment was hers and therefore proceeded on her schedule. Preparing Morse in English took a few minutes before she tapped away:

[Verified D's contacts. Stop. Feral in employ confirmed consort with other vulpine Feral. Donovan unaware. Will contend. Stop.]

Feral was the shorthand for Nosfurs used in cables. Talk of eradication wouldn't seem suspicious if intercepted. Von Haften winced as she leaned to open the desk and withdraw the bottle within. The wound from the bullet graze reminded her just how dangerous the local vermin she'd kill could be.

The telegraph buzzed its longs and shorts moments later. [Is metal formula secure. Stop. Have D's business contacts been traced. Stop]

While waiting for the telegraph to finish the Countess poured herself a drink. [Yes to all. Stop]

Time passed as those on the council deliberated.

[Steel needed for shipping. Prevent action authorized. Stop]

She knew they'd want Donovan's steel shipped back to England, and from there to France, Austria and Italy for metallurgical testing and implementation. Donovan's discoveries were certainly genius as far as the council was concerned but his intended application disgusted the council no less than Evelyn.

To ensure it would be redirected they had to prevent its further usage here. That meant severing ties to local business while she got Donovan refocussed on the Martyre's true task of eradication.

She drank and then asked the question. [Preventions preferred. Stop]

What would they choose? Assassination? Bribery? She frowned at the prospect that they might want her to fuck the school hound running for office and blackmail him. That wasn't going to happen. Donovan, while deluded was at least entertaining and she was sickened by the more lecherous members of the council presuming that solutions to their problems lay between Evelyn's legs. Sad that her husband was one of them, the dirty cuckold.

There were so many other ways to disrupt Donovan's plans without causing him direct harm and she was resourceful enough for all of them.

She was relieved when the reply came back. [Authorized removal. Stop.]

Then the next part caught her breath. [Begin public vermin exposure, the council is decided seven to four. Stop.]

Public exposure! The implications of that directive made the air itself electric. The Martyres had long weighed the merits and perils of exposing Nosfurs to the world, always in consideration of public panic and overreaction. Such a truth could have burned Europe to the ground, but isolated across the Ocean in an upstart nation that was expendable...

She had a candidate, but getting them ready... [Feral available has no tools to implement removal. Stop.]

[Be resourceful. Facilitate. Stop.]

Facilitate. She knew what that meant and let the prospect settle. The raccoon waited, but somebody needed to get close to the target, kill him... and be found with him. The prospect was both exciting and terrifying. She drank and ran her tongue over her fangs as a plan came together.

They sent more. [Can election be prevented. Stop]

She typed back. [Best to proceed. Will provide more exposure for next steps if candidate elected prior to removal. Stop]

Sun would fall shortly and she'd have to move quickly. The far Western world was about to change forever at her guiding hand. How Donovan was going to get enough votes to get his Superintendent elected Alderman really wouldn't matter in the end.

***

The day waned and ballot boxes for both Mayor and dozens of Alderman's posts filled quickly. Mister Slavison shuffled through the marvels of the world, horseless carriages having taken Chicago by storm and buildings sprouting tall enough to kiss the blue sky. Incredible!

In line to vote that all important vote, Johnathan glanced down the tail of a comely mink lass who turned his way every so often, sniffing the air before moving quickly ahead.

Johnathan realized his comportment was off somewhat and was slightly embarrassed, but how could a mammal be blamed for failing to mind cleanliness when voting that all important vote? Exercising the franchise was important.

At the front he croaked his name and accepted a voting card from a bored clerk who barely glanced up under Johnathan's downturned hat brim. Johnathan stepped into the nice wooden booth while the cat boy passing cards wrinkled his nose and clutched at the throat above his bow tie before ducking round a corner to be loudly sick.

Okay, maybe cleanliness had been a little more important than he'd expected but wasn't it grand having the opportunity to vote for the most qualified candidate for Alderman that Chicago had ever seen? With creaking joints, he put pen to paper and selected Richard Leicester for Alderman of ward twenty-four.

Dirty claws left smudges around the margins as he folded his card and fed the slot.

Johnathan Slavison left the booth with an inner glow and an outer chill. It was getting late.

The night was ushered under a dusk peach sky like a dame's petticoat. He remembered someone he'd once known, fair furred, bright of smile.

174

A civet dame walked the path ahead intersecting the way back to his rest. Johnathan Slavison pushed back the shawl protecting his slipping pelt and lifted the spider-squirmed hat upon his head.

The civet caught his eye and she screamed, darting across the road against the worried honk of beetle-roofed horseless carriages chugging down the thoroughfare.

Johnathan Slavison turned dejectedly to a closed store window, catching his reflection in dying light. With a deliberate mash of white naked fingers, he shoved his dangling lower jaw back home and slipped the frayed pelt back over the bone of his muzzle. A bug jigged from the empty socket of one eye and found a different home through his gumless lips.

Perdition take it, hygiene was kinda pointless at this juncture. Johnathan was very tired.

Two blocks later he slipped through wrought iron and found his soiled bed. His neighbor was settling in before his own stone with dates that started and ended.

"Who'd you vote for?" his neighbor asked, milky sunken eyes teeming with worms as he slipped low. "I was so flummoxed seeing that herbies got the vote, I almost turned round."

Funny, now Jonathan couldn't even remember. "Does it matter? We'll wind up with somebody who just told the better lie."

Laughter took his jaw out again, and they settled in mirth. Johnathan Slavison settled into his sturdy box and methodically brought cold welcome dirt down around himself.

***

"You saw Freddy doin' what?" Johnny Torrio cocked an ear. The corso-dog hated things that didn't make sense even by this city's standards.

Al's mastiff features fell. "I dunno what to tell you Johnny, I saw him in a line and could only get so close. Freddy's clothes were throat to cuffs in dirt like he'd been rolling in it all day and his neck was kinked all weird. And the smell, Johnny, I coulda vomited. I said what are you doing? He says, I'm voting for the best Alderman candidate this city's ever had. He said it like it was the proudest thing he'd ever done. Cops were walking the line so I had to split."

Johnny blinked. "Alderman? We want Bill Thompson back as Mayor but how many Aldermen did we even pocket? I thought we sent Freddy over to check out Bucky's place, make sure he didn't have a still running after the doe whacked him."

"We did, Johnny. It made no sense. I went back in half-an-hour but the line had gone inside and Freddy was gone. He's always been reliable and wouldn't fuck around on a thing like this. It was like he was there but not there."

Johnny swigged back some middle-shelf whisky, best left after the last shipment turned over. The Deuces saloon two floors down was all but dry. "Drunk?"

"Naw, somethin' else."

Johnny looked at the heavens past the stucco. "I can't handle all this bullshit Al. With this cop killing the papers have us framed up for it's like the walls are closing in. We can't be losing enforcers to civic shit."

"Word came back on that cop."

Johnny didn't want to hear it but wanted to hear it. "Yeah."

"My guy Tooley was turned into pie filling for Moses' sake. Some feral-gone bastard actually *ate* him. West Side gang doesn't do that shit, Dean O'Bannion's outfit neither."

"I wouldn't put anything past that Irish-setter fuck if it would hobble us. This detente is a fuckin' joke over there and we both know it. The dock raid was just inside our territory. Fucken' mick might of called it in himself."

"I'm on it, Johnny. That said, if small-timers are lifting our trucks at one end of town and snitches for the Irish are calling cops at the other, we need to shuffle supply lines again. Somebody opened their fat mouth and I can't close it till I find it."

"I know you'll handle it Al, so handle it. O'Banion can wait, the snitch is what's important." Johnny sighed. "I'm going up. Ensure I'm not disturbed."

"Want some company sent?"

"Naw. An hour of peace is all I need. You know what to do."

Johnny went up. The top floor office of the Four Deuces was tidy, non-descript. No traces lingered of the vices below. Putting an ear to any grate, Johnny could hear horny johns gasp past the finish line a floor down and cries as the roulette wheel slowed a floor below that. Cumming or going with empty pockets, Johnny made money off those sounds. Herbs in the ductwork kept the more distracting smells at bay.

The light was kept low and the shades drawn on his windows. He hated the summer heat on its way but didn't want a silhouette shown to Wabash Avenue when he peeked out for several calibers of reasons.

So, it brought a general sense of unease when he picked up the bottle on his desk and pondered the open window with drapes blowing in and out like quiet breath.

There was no fire escape outside, ensuring nobody surprised him by climbing up, and nobody could see him through the drapes. More than likely Al or one of the other boys had thought it stuffy and decided to move air through the room.

But caution followed every other step since his youthful days and found his hackles now.

Something wasn't right.

"I didn't want to rob you of alone time Johnny," said a voice over his shoulder. "But you tried to rob me of all of mine so we're almost even."

Johnny let the bottle wobble on the desk. His jacket was open and he knew he could work the holster clasp fast.

"You won't need it. I promise." By his tone, Bucky was indifferent to whether the old corso tried for his gun.

Johnny's mouth was dry. Fear wouldn't serve him, only the firm hand his people were used to. "You stepped out on me Bucky. You knew it was dishonest by how you buried your tracks." Johnny turned and was surprised to see the fox in a new suit, tie impeccably straight despite the way he perched atop the wooden filing cabinet that Johnny made sure held nothing incriminating.

The fox was unarmed. Johnny growled. "I gave you the same shot I gave Al and Marco and Freddy and what did you do?"

A shrug. "Seriously Johnny, I'd of cut you in. I just needed to see if I could get off the ground first. It was a new product you'd of liked."

"Not if you didn't bring it to me first. Word I got back was you were making moves in my back yard. I can't keep the Irish in line if my guys are stepping out."

He could see the fox's eyes, but not their whites. Bucky's eyes were dark as beetle shells and Jonny realized with a chill he had no idea what was going on in them. Bucky smiled and his canine teeth were different, like he couldn't entirely close his mouth. "Who'd word get back through, Johnny? Did the doe you sent to kill me give you a full report? I had great plans and it hurt my feelings that you didn't take me aside to have a word." The fox's tail hung still down the side of the cabinet and curled to rest in his lap. "That hurts me a lot Johnny."

A bullet through the head would hurt more. Celeste failed him as the doe broad inevitably had to. Unless... "The doe make a deal with you to keep you around?"

The fox looked at the stucco above and frowned. "Changes of heart are complicated. Let's just say we have things to work out."

That told Johnny nothing. He didn't know how but he was getting the impression the fox wasn't armed, and his scent couldn't pick anybody else up. The room was out of darker corners. "So what stops me from finishing the job she started?" Johnny asked.

"A proposition. It starts with an apology." The fox slipped light as paper to the floor. "I'm sorry I stepped out of line Johnny. That was a mistake I won't make again."

"And the part where I make sure you don't get a chance to?"

"I'm opening a place. It won't be in your territory, won't complete with your business or deal in the same product."

"Whore joint?"

Bucky laughed. "Something a very tiny contingent of Chicago's thirsty need, something that I can bring in without smuggling if chosen correctly and that nobody will miss."

"What are you the sphinx with these fucking riddles now?"

"My supply line."

"What?"

"The product I was working on, you can have ninety percent of it, a dozen cases a month of the best home-made shine ever served, no charge as a peace offering. I won't need it for my...venture. If you get a dime a finger now, you can charge a quarter for what I'm providing."

"And?"

"And I will take care of problems you have that some of your current associates can't. You still have a beef with Dean O'Bannion's crew, right? That treaty leaving some doubts for you?"

"Every treaty leaves doubts. So what?"

"I'm gonna take care of people you want taken care of. Frankie Yale can't whack everybody you're unhappy with because some will turn out Irish and then you'll have a war. Celeste obviously can't take care of the rest. I'm gonna whittle down Dean's crew a bit at a time and nobody will know why he's losing fellas. They're just gonna drift away bit by bit, leaving him alone. Also, those small gangs nibbling at your toes with upstart speaks and truck-jackings…you want that handled, don't you Johnny?"

Johnny was still quick at his age. His gun was in his hand in a breath. "This is bullshit. I don't believe a word and I'm sending Celeste the carpet cleaning bill when I—"

He didn't blink, but Bucky moved in the space of one. The gun twisted in Johnny's hand and before he could even cry out, the magazine was falling free and the slide drawn back to chuck the chambered round.

The fox smiled. "You don't have to believe me Johnny. Burden of proof's on me and that's my fault."

Johnny set the gun down slowly, hand smarting. "You've got blood on your shirt."

"I always did Johnny. Isn't that why you liked me? Work was dirty but I never complained. I like it even more now."

Johnny blinked again, wondering if he'd blacked out momentarily. The fox was at his shoulder, one arm round him heavy but cold.

Bucky's mouth whispered without scent or breath. "I always respected you Johnny but you never really saw my potential. Al's your favorite, I get that. So let me get back into your good graces. You don't need to trust me with money or secrets. You have enemies." The fox's voice dropped to a level that was hungry, almost seductive. "I just want names. And much less time than you think it's gonna take."

Johnny felt a chill. One pig-stick through the ribs or a quick glide across the throat and he'd be washing out on the carpet. He'd been stupid to let Bucky get this close.

But the voice in Johnny's ear soothed and the vulpine's comradely grip was reassuring. Those dark eyes returned to warm copper, coins of promise above the white slit of his muzzle. Teeth gleamed in a smile.

Johnny wasn't afraid. In fact, he found himself interested. Weren't the mammals who made mistakes and learned from them the most valuable people? "I'll try this out with you kid." He brought an authoritative growl to his voice but felt strangely relaxed. "Just don't step out of line again, okay?"

"Okay!" Bucky said brightly. "We've got a deal. All I need is a name to start with."

Johnny struggled to remember the O'Bannion thug who'd shot their driver on the road down from Milwaukee. The scrappy cub, God rest his soul, was on his third drive for The Outfit when they got him. He'd given a cursory description in the hospital before bleeding out.

Flowers and a fat stack of cash went to his wailing mother. The description went down the line. The murdering weasel's face had a name now and Johnny gave that name to Bucky then and there. "Want a drink before you go kid?"

The fox slipped his arm away but the muzzle hovered at Torrio's shoulder. "You've no idea how badly, Johnny." The fox showed teeth and hid them again. "My friend and I need to prepare."

A potent breath of wind parted the office window drapes. In the near distance the old corso dog saw a moon-painted shape, russet fur, dark linen, the twitch of an ample tail. Then the curtain settled again.

He'd think nothing of it until hours later, when the fog of implications became recollection of events and a chill up his spine brought realization missing in that moment. There were no buildings out that window, just four stories of emptiness to the cobbled street of Wabash below.

He turned to pour a drink. "So, when will I know it's been done?"

The empty room gave no answer.

***

"How badly does it hurt?"

The whisper from the dark of Sandy Mallory's cottage seemed from the feverish depths of Keller's wide-awake hell. He hurt, his burns scabbing too slowly, his body parched. The nausea and pain of this place ebbed and attacked. He croaked a question. "Are you real?"

"Am I real?" The lioness slipped into the moonlight's slit, eyes aflame. "Was my sister real? My brother? Were any of my great pride whom your kind slunk in and murdered in the night?"

"Who are you?" Keller winced around where his fangs had been plucked. He smelled alcohol. And some of her blood. The thirst hurt.

The lioness ignored the question. "Was my mother real whom your kind tainted over a long day while we thought she battled a fever? Was my father real who had to end her existence while I watched?"

"I didn't... hurt you."

"Of course not. You live in America, where vermin run rampant, not in my country where those charged with ending your scourge fulfill their oaths, who took me in and gave my pain shape, purpose, power."

"I'm sorry..."

"That you were stopped. Only for that. You can smell where the bullet grazed me and lick the air for a feast. I see it."

The lioness crossed through the moonlight and sat in the chair where Sandy had whispered platitudes not a night ago. "With this foolishness Donovan has nurtured you would have played the Irish squirrel's game, living fat on his wealth while lulling him to sleep, all the while you slither in the dark and steal life from the innocent."

This was a test. Keller was sure of it. "I can't...bite. Sandy said I can become—"

"But even without the fangs, you can drink." A knife slid free and the lioness let it gleam in that tiny path of moonlight for the raccoon to see.

"You'll kill me." It wasn't a question. In Keller's relentless pain, it wasn't feared either.

"No."

"No?"

"This house of cards Donovan has built must come down if he's to see how stupid he's been. I intend to show him the error of his ways. To do that, you will do the only thing you are capable of."

Keller swallowed a ruined throat. "What will I do?"

"You will drink."

***

Crawford had a shot of meeting the doe at Dannovey's coffee shop, but nine would be a tough call.

Strangely he had no injuries to speak of from fighting with...whatever Celeste was. Sores mingled with other aches he was getting used to and he'd made sure to square away his story with Charlie before ringing the office and promising a full report of the visit tomorrow. A reclusive home-owner had a guest who used their phone for reasons not divulged and was distrustful of the visitors her lodgers brought back, hence a scuffle in her living room that Crawford patched up by proving he was not a masher or invading pervert. Simple. Tidy. If the department sent anyone else, she'd rough them up too and Crawford's story would square with anybody who didn't die.

That was one matter. There was still his badge and car to worry about. If Crawford could concoct a story for his missing badge he'd probably be in the clear. If whispers from the hospital were true, Tooley's medical examiner hadn't found anything incriminating any species in particular. Crawford's Chevy was down in the vicinity of Daley's and he just needed time to get there alone and pick it up with his spare key. The likelihood that somebody found his missing one and matched it to his car among so many was quite unlikely. Charlie wasn't complaining about taking the "L" or getting taxis and he didn't want to humiliate his martially aggrieved partner. Forgetting one's car was a problem usually found at the bottom of a bottle.

Humiliation notwithstanding, just maybe Crawford would get through this.

Crawford's formal suit was stiff as a parachute in the wind and his tie wanted to strangle his thick lupine neck. As fashionably late and he and Charlie were—the golden wolf having coifed like he was meeting English Royals—the whole affair was annoyingly in very early stages.

Near-beer and de-alcoholised wine circulated, muttered conversation stayed muted, press mammal's noses roved low and high, taking stock of the law rubbing shoulders with the city's elite.

Half the city's business sector was here and every ranking cop on handheld court in white gloves and tasseled shoulders.

Opening remarks came care of Attorney General Brundage, fiery commentary that was authoritarian in all the way the Anti-Saloon Leaguers, clergy and men from Washington tended to like. They were soldiers against evil and would man the battlements against the hordes of gangsters and killers. Metaphors were tortured aplenty.

The speech moved into solemn territory. Six officers had died in the line of duty in Chicago in the past year, including Lockley and Tooley in the last few days. Speeches wound down as Chicago's finest and the Bureau's local office team sat and the meat was brought out. Crawford had the chicken and Charlie the duck.

Talk in earshot was jovial despite the circumstances. "This near-beer ain't too bad," Beatie remarked at the suds climbing his glass one table over.

"Almost worth kicking the kitchen door down to secure the register, eh?" Beatie's elbow mate was Attorney General Brundage himself. Laughter around him was perfunctory.

The feline Mayor William Hale Thompson gave a short update about votes being tallied at that very moment for election of the next city hall. Little did that matter to Crawford. Whoever had city hall tomorrow, Crawford would still have his problems. And a doe who could throw him like his own Fedora would have all his answers, providing he made it in time.

Crawford had to hit the head. He asked Charlie to let him know if anything important happened while he was up and the sad smile in return asked if he was kidding.

Crawford went, feeling telltale itches he didn't like, and he was checking the distance to exits he might need, when he collided with another guest.

"Excuse me." He muttered as the smaller mammal nearly bounced off him. Small cold eyes met his, and the white-suited possum with snap-neat bow tie revealed a flash of teeth. There was a small dot of pink near his nose. Crawford's own sniffer picked out a trace of blood.

"My mistake friend. I'm not trying to run you over."

"Of course not," the possum's tone made such a stupid prospect amusing. He dripped with that perfect blend of accommodation and condescension that well do to maintained for riff raff. "My patron knows you don't want to hurt anyone. He'll be waiting for you down the hall, past the lavatory in a smoking room he's had set aside. A placard will declare it off limits, but not for you."

That caught Crawford off guard. "Your...patron?"

"He's quite grateful for the chance to meet you. He has something of yours, agent Crawford Cain of the Bureau of Internal Revenue." Without another word the possum slipped round him, tail brushing Crawford's leg in passing.

Crawford thought on those words the entire time he relieved himself, searching his distorted reflection in the lavatory tile. Anyone carving a private space at City Hall like a slice of cake on its busiest night had to be somebody important. After washing up Crawford pondered returning to the hall where voices and applause drifted out.

He went to the smoking room with the "off limits" placard instead, slipping around it to find the door unlocked. Inside a mahogany walled study, the possum stood by a white rabbit seated comfortably in pinstripes kneading a ram-headed cane. The rabbit's grey-tinted ears were erect as he studied the wolf with interest.

Another leather-bound chair waited next to the small sitting table bearing two crystal glasses. Between them lay Crawford's badge.

The rabbit smiled thick teeth. "Please have a seat Mr. Cain. We need to talk."

***

Samson woke in his bed in the dormitory of the Noah's Plank school. A slightly sweet taste drifted over his tongue and nostrils and the soft embrace of silk settled over his muzzle. He heard soft snores of his dormitory mates and glimpsed cold moonlight through the opened window.

He couldn't place the shadow that stood over him. "Ms. Mallory," Samson's mind swam through molasses. "Is that you?"

Consciousness fled as quickly as it came and with it two whispered, sad words. "Little soldier."

Samson woke again with a bitter taste on his tongue. He was thirsty, so thirsty, and dust shifted underneath him. He was numb but brought into focus with the feel of two sharp pricks and the heat of breath on his neck. Someone stalked away to spit. "Quickly," said that same feminine voice, devoid of emotion. "Get back your strength."

Samson smelled corruption. Vicelike fingers closed around his shoulders and the goat kid struggled against rubber limbs as a scabrous face loomed, nose working, tongue panting. The raccoon had no breath. Its eyes black wells of pitiless want.

The kid bleated weakly as lips slid around his throat and shoulder, revulsion and fear overcoming him. Weakness overtook him as his hoof beat the floor, echoing endlessly in a void. Only the faces of his school mates, warm and sullen and lost in the world as he was formed in his mind's eye as Samson's heart slowed.

Darkness fell in mercy.

Chapter 12

Under Peaceful Conditions

The phone rang as Celeste rose at the final wink of day. Johnny wanted to see her and wouldn't say why. She lied that she'd be there that evening.

Time was short. She had her next rental prospects already picked out from the paper, got lucky on the first call. Of course, she could pay first and last. She'd be out of here with time enough to meet the wolf.

Packing up her things took no time at all. She went to the cage room and methodically fed on each of the captive feral rats, draining them in turn before bringing them to the furnace in the basement. The air stank when the phone above rang once more.

Her two packed suitcases would not weigh her down. If it was Torrio again she'd keep it short and if it was Bucky…well that would be a surprise indeed.

She lifted the telephone's earpiece and waited.

"Please don't hang up," Sandy Mallory said.

Celeste said nothing, her senses perked for the tiniest scent or sound beyond her walls.

"I know I'm the last person you would want to speak with, but I have to see you," the red Irish squirrel said reluctantly. "I've…reconsidered my path in life."

"Ran out of people to betray?" Celeste asked coldly. She wanted to grab her bags and rush out, but Sandy had gotten her exchange somehow and she needed to know where.

Sandy collected her thoughts. "I owe you an apology, Celeste. I've made mistakes."

That was galling. "Is that so? What precisely brought you this new-found regret? Was it when you disappeared in New York after a decade together? Was it when you betrayed my trust to lure me to your English lapine friend? Or were they one and the same?"

"I was not myself. I know I can't expect you to forgive me. Not yet, Celeste"

"You can never expect that, Sandy. After what I gave and what you took…what do you want?"

"To meet you."

"You really have to assume I'm stupid."

A moment of fidgeting left a crackle on the line. "I've left Donovan Calvert."

Celeste took the phone away from her ear, listened, smelled. Nocturnal city sounds crept in through the cracks as the night thickened, car tires crushing distant gravel and smells of countless badly tended cookstoves for late evening meals. "I don't believe for a second that he let you walk out even if you decided to do so."

"It wasn't that simple."

"Was it as simple as trying to draw me into whatever prison you were twisted in? I've seen you, Sandy. You've barely the skill to hide yourself anymore. You're fading away to nothing. What influence does that to you and then lets you go?"

"I was…I was rescued from a bad mistake. I made a new friend."

"What new friend could that be?" The phone went momentarily silent. Celeste felt a chill as she suspected the answer.

"Hi," Bucky said brightly. "Friends are so important when you've got questions that don't have answers, you know what I mean, doll?"

The voice was like a slap. "Dammit, Bucky. Where are you? What happened?"

"Wouldn't you like to know? I've been making friends, Celeste. Sandy knows others just like us and we've good things in the works that were already coming before you came into my life." The fox paused for an unneeded breath. "And ended it."

"Bucky whatever Sandy has told you, you can't trust her. We were more than friends for ten years and she tried to sell me out to mortals who think we're animals to be kept like…" Celeste realized that Bucky had set the earpiece down to shut her up and could hear him asking Sandy something about a lion. Sandy answered glumly that the problem involved a rabbit.

A lion? "Bucky what happened?"

There was a scratch as claws scooped the receiver up again. "I knew you were holding out on me Celeste. I hit the road and found a path back to my dreams. Sandy's gonna help me."

"Bucky, I returned to your place and brought that wolf back here to bury. You need to understand that if Johnny learns you're alive—"

"Johnny and I are back in business," the fox said flatly. "I have his blessing care of some new skills that you were never gonna teach me. If you're trying to warn me, I'll return the favor. He knows you didn't do what you were paid for."

Celeste's grip tightened on the telephone till it cracked. That was it, the very worst had happened. Bucky Cavali had carelessly destroyed all she'd built. "You bastard. You stinking vulpine *carnivore bastard*. You were marked for death, and I *spared* you. Despite any doubts I had I *spared you*." Her erupted fangs made her curse a hiss.

Even with all her caution, all her knowledge, a matter of sentiment had ruined her. She'd dared to not be lonely after so long and now had been betrayed. Again.

There was no time for the weight of it settle. If Torrio found out where she lived…

There was a long silence before the fox spoke again. The hurt in his tone enraged her to an extent Celeste hadn't felt in years. "You've no right to be sore at the fox you tried to cage like a bird. Despite how hurt that makes me feel I want you involved in our new gig. Sandy wants peace and so do I. We need to stick together, Celeste. That lion and…I guess there's a rabbit too, they're bad news."

The cluelessness of that statement left her dumbstruck. Maybe Sandy was playing him. Maybe he'd wake the next day chained in some sunny place where they'd shove hot pokers up his ass and tear his fangs out. Rage was ever imaginative.

At the distant end the phone passed from one claw to another. When Sandy came back Celeste noticed what she'd missed before in her distracted desire to drop the call and flee. The Irish squirrel's voice was lighter, musical…young.

She'd fed again. "We have something wonderful to show you, you and so many others we're bringing together to celebrate our newfound freedom. We want you to be our honored guest."

Celeste didn't know what to say. Rage and grief warred. Maybe the favor Bucky had paid her needed to be returned. "Where?" she asked.

Bucky came back. "Barber shop midtown on Michigan, Siegfried's Silvershears, tomorrow night. You can hear us out."

"Why not tonight?" Celeste wondered aloud. Suspicion was now and forever her only friend.

"We're doing…preda, uh, preparations tonight."

There was a lilting giggle from Sandy on the call's edge. Celeste remembered how Bucky tried to get his dick in Celeste every other moment they'd been together. The thought that these two might be happy together actually hurt to contemplate.

"Turns out so am I."

"So, you'll be there?" Bucky asked.

"Wait and see," Celeste broke the call and started undoing the catch of her valise to unplug the phone and wedge it inside amongst her unmentionables.

But the idea of the two people who'd betrayed her in succession whittled into her mind, cuddling, kissing, going further.

The phone was splinters minutes later and the loss of control for those few brief moments brought relief. An hour later, her luggage was moved to the Congress Hotel for a night before she headed uptown to see if a wolf liked coffee.

***

Crawford would have liked a drink. The shallow glasses between him and the rabbit were empty, and Crawford ignored his dry throat.

The possum traded one cryptic glance with the rabbit before stepping outside and closing the door.

"Thank you for speaking with me." The rabbit's British accent was polite yet unaccommodating, as though this conversion was a favor to Crawford, not to him.

"Don't mention it," Crawford said. The chair leather was cold.

"Your name is Crawford Ellis Cain, currently enforcing the Volstead Act for the Federal Bureau of Internal Revenue."

The badge said as much. Crawford kept quiet.

"You were briefly a policeman for the Virginian Police Force, finding it much to your dislike, and prior to that you were a soldier serving in the 2nd Infantry Division against the German, Austrian advance in the Saissons and Rheim near the end of the war. No injuries, but you lost compatriots—"

"Who are you?" Crawford was fast growing uncomfortable.

"Somebody who needs to confirm several things." The tone was of someone unaccustomed to interruption. "You're married but separated from your wife Kamila who lives in Virginia with your son Lucas."

"How is my life any of your goddamn business?" Crawford reached forward and snatched up his badge wallet. He felt from its thickness that the business cards he kept were still in the wallet. The tiniest flash of dark green confirmed the few dollars he'd kept in there were still present.

The rabbit met the wolf's glare. "You made it my business when you left a considerable mess for me to deal with." The rabbit opened his own jacket and flashed the butt of a gun tucked in a familiar holster. "Getting all traces of you off the otter you disagreed with was no simple task. But I can assure you that nothing remains in that West Woodlawn alley leading to a knock on your door by your colleagues currently enjoying their poultry."

Crawford felt his nape fur crawl. "What exactly do you think happened?"

The jacket closed over the gun and the rabbit reached into the other lapel, withdrawing a flask. "I can promise that the contents of this flask were in my personal possession prior to January seventeenth of nineteen twenty and that I have not sought to sell its like to any third parties. I wouldn't want to break the law as there are certainly consequences for breaking laws, aren't there?"

Crawford kept his mouth closed and nodded. He'd play the game. "Again, why did you have my badge, Mister…?"

The rabbit poured whiskey, good stuff by oak's touch on Crawford's nose, into both glasses. "Donovan Calvert."

"I've heard the name," Crawford said, trying to sound indifferent. Truthfully, he'd heard or read the name in several places.

"Everybody's heard my name," Calvert snickered. "But tonight, I'm not important, Mr. Cain. We have a municipal election underway, a crime spree brought on by organized criminal elements, and problems that exceed even those. Don't we?"

Whiskey bobbed in the glass before him. Crawford kept his claws on the chair's arm rest. "What you mean?"

"The otter. You know what happened."

Crawford wished his Panama wasn't hanging in the coat room. It could hide his hackles. "I've heard rumors—"

"You killed him, Mr. Cain. You physically regressed into a primal, primitive state and ate him."

"No." Crawford swallowed.

"There's no need to jump to denials my lupine friend. As I said, the sequestering of misplaced sundries has you in the clear." He shifted the shoulder over Crawford's gun. "Shouldn't you have a drink?"

Crawford wanted it, badly. He wanted answers more. "If you're so sure I killed officer Tooley," he swallowed to ease down the bullshit he needed to shovel, "a decorated officer who helped us in battles against the mob—"

"And my liaison who passed on tips regarding speakeasy raids," Calvert interrupted with a reflective nod. "Thanks to him I was able to see one such establishment turned over not a few days ago. You were there I recall."

Crawford had a flash of the street onto which he'd chased Simon Govic, damp concrete, waxy lamp-light and the flank of a dark Rolls parked beyond the two paddy wagons. "I do."

Calvert cocked his ear. "You were saying…"

"If you're sure I…ate Tooley, why aren't you afraid I'll do it right now?"

"There are symptoms of your condition to herald the change. At this juncture in this place, you are more scared than angry, a state you've not been in for a few days— "

"I've been in a lot of states in the past few days. "

"I know. I was brought the divorce filing just an hour ago."

The glass was in Crawford's hand, and he tipped it back without a second thought. Warm smooth fire.

"Waste to drink a twenty-year scotch like a thimble of moonshine."

"I'll sip the next one. If we're going to stay cordial, you'll leave my marriage by the wayside, my long-eared friend." Crawford let the growl offer its own promise.

Donovan was nonplussed. "You're going to tear the upholstery off that chair, Mister Cain. Please mind where you are and what nobody else needs to know."

"What do I need to know? Let's start there. Because I don't remember killing a cop, much less anything else."

"You would have woken up somewhere with plenty of evidence. Let me ease the tension here," he poured Crawford another finger of scotch, "by informing you right off the cuff that I am not looking to blackmail, threaten, or berate you. I know that Tooley was bent and worked for criminals."

Admitting nothing while letting the rabbit talk seemed smart. "Oh?"

"He reported many speak raids in advance to his mob contacts."

"A bastard if that's true," Crawford said.

"And no longer a problem."

"You've lost a liaison though."

"One of many." No emotion in those words.

Of course, the silver-spooned fucker would say that. "Really proud of how little you need people."

"Back to the matter at hand," the rabbit's ears switched to the side and back. "I know things that can help you. And I want to help you."

Crawford took a deep breath, feeling the scotch work. "Drop the other spat already. Assuming you know anything about any condition, what do you want from me?"

"I want you to do what you've been doing. Root out corruption that your existing systems of law and justice can't cope with or even face."

"You want somebody eating corrupt cops?" Crawford didn't snicker but wanted to.

"No. Nor mobsters, though I'm certain there are plenty of well-deserving in Chicago alone. What you need to understand Mister Cain is that I wasn't at that speak to see scofflaws pay tickets, or witness law enforcement's enthusiasm for property damage. Nor handle the affliction that Simon Govic passed on to you before you put him out of ever deepening misery." Donovan drank the rest of his whiskey with a flourish and poured himself a fresh dram.

"My present mandate is to deal with a far worse scourge that inflicts all the violence you manage at your very worst but as a matter of course, slave to appetites that make the most shameless alcoholics skulking the gutters and bowels of this town seem innocent by comparison. Mister Cain, I seek to rescue those in the grip of eternal bloodlust itself."

Crawford didn't know what to say. "That's frightening."

"There are creatures of the night whose path you've likely crossed with as open a gesture as a tipped hat or as subtle a sense as a dark shadow drifting by, a dark presence at your back without breath threatening to all of natural order."

"I heard that verbatim at the last union-busting speech."

The rabbit looked disappointed. "I'm being serious."

"About working people demanding better pay? Or a foot on the rail at the end of a long day, or—"

"The Nosfurratu."

Crawford dug into his coat for his Luckies. Claws around one, he brought it to his lips and held the pack out while the other fished for his lighter.

Donovan waved a hand dismissively, lifted the lapel that didn't hide Crawford's gun and removed a silver cigarette case, preferring something impeccably hand rolled. He drew a nickeled lighter and flame bobbed under his smoke.

Crawford realized his lighter was mislaid and sighed audibly. Donovan raised a brow in return and held the flame out. Crawford brought his own smoke to life with a few puffs.

"Thanks. What's a Noss fratoo?"

"They've had many names over many centuries throughout history, running rampant in the wakes of plagues or wars, picking off the weak and defenceless who wouldn't be missed in service of a need that enslaves them. They drink the blood of the living to sustain themselves and in so doing spread their disease amongst a very small number of their victims."

Crawford absorbed this. A week ago, he'd have thought the rabbit a kook. Now… "So, they don't drink from already dead people?"

"No more than you'd choose to eat gravel-strewn carrion killed by an automobile. Warm blood sustains them Mister Cain because they themselves are not alive in any sense that you or I would fully understand."

"Are you saying you're not an expert."

"When it comes to Nosfur, few are. I represent a, well let's just say it's an exclusive club that knows quite a great deal about them."

"I'm in a club too. As a government employee who's been to a lot of seedy places why haven't I ever heard of or seen one of these…Nosfurratus."

"For the same reason chickens don't suspect foul play upon those removed from the coop. These killers learn to be careful, covering their tracks well."

The question that leapt to mind was worrisome, but Crawford had to ask. "Am I turning into…"

"No, you're afflicted by something else entirely Mister Cain. You, in point of fact, can barely cover your tracks at all."

Crawford felt his hackles reaching for the sky. "So why are we talking about these Nosfur things when we should be talking about what I am becoming? I'm concerned about what may have happened last night and shouldn't it concern you too? If I get really upset—"

The blade was drawn and pointing at Crawford's heart in a mere second, but not close enough to touch. The thin steel hovered a foot or so away as the Rabbit didn't leave his chair. In his left hand, the black handle of a cane rested without a head.

Donovan smiled around the cigarette in his flat teeth. "I can handle more than you assume Mister Cain. Touch it."

"What?"

"Touch the blade."

"Why?"

"To satisfy my curiosity."

On those words the door to the smoking room opened and the possum re-entered, ignoring completely the blade pointed by the rabbit into the wolf's chest. He stepped over and leaned into the rabbit's ear to whisper something he tried to keep private but which Crawford heard as clearly as though he'd shouted. "They've just now called it for Leicester. He'll read his acceptance speech in the next twenty minutes after a dozen new Aldermen."

"That's excellent news. Carry on."

The possum carried on out.

Crawford flicked ash out into the cigarette stand to his right. "Friend of yours?"

"Acquaintance. Please, if you would…"

Crawford reached up with the same hand. The hot metal he touched nearly caused him to fumble his Luckie. "It's hot. What's in the cane?"

Donovan lowered his weapon. "Interesting. Were you a Nosfur your hand would have burned to blistering. If memory serves there would need to be more silver in the mix."

The smoke nearly slipped free as Crawford's muzzle curled into a growl. "Are you saying you thought my hand would outright catch on fire and didn't tell me?"

"Of course not. Think nothing of it." Donovan slid the sword back into the cane. "Let me get right to it. We need each other. I need help in getting America's Nosfur problem under control and you need help managing the change that is coursing through your veins at this moment."

Crawford reached back and smoothed his hackles as he took another few puffs. He needed to stay calm. "You're saying you want me to kill these things for you."

"No. As chained as the Nosfur currently are to their afflictions, I, contrary to many of my compatriots, think they can be brought back from the errant path of consumption and be rescued from their addiction."

"Alright. You're gonna bring them back to God like an Anti-Saloon leaguer for blood drinkers. How does that involve me?"

"With your considerable background, you would be a competent investigator whose badge provides access to resources I cannot wield without exposing my hand in various affairs. A person of great importance to me is missing; an Irish Squirrel, red furred, relatively old, named Sandy Mallory. I need her found and returned to me as she is an integral part of my work here." Donovan took one last puff of his smoke and jammed it out on his own chair's cigar stand. "She is much endeared to me."

"Mistress? Lover?"

Donovan seemed amused. "Nothing of the sort, but she is very much like family. We've…grown together in a quest to forge a path out of the darkness for her kind. You see Mister Cain, Sandy is reformed Nosfur."

"Reformed. This affliction of hers can be cured?"

"Not cured, Mister Cain, but managed through correction and reinforced willpower. Sandy is my very best pupil, proof that addictions of the vein can be conquered. You must find her and bring her back to me, but only at night. Her affliction makes exposure to sun light dangerous. You must be mindful of that at all times." The rabbit smoothed the tops of his ears where the white fur turned slightly grey.

Exposure to sunlight. Everything that happened earlier in the day clicked and Crawford realized he was holding secrets of his own. Did Donovan know of the doe who used wolf bodies to destroy homes? "In exchange?"

Donovan fondled his cane. "I'll not only ensure no one finds out about your cleaning law enforcement's house of corruption in a culinary fashion, I'll also help you manage that which you'll soon face." The rabbit looked the wolf square in the eye with appraising eyes. "I know you visited Govic's widow and what you found there. Without my help all your fears will come true."

Crawford could see the splintered cabinet in Govic's row house. Cold fingers ran down his neck and his tail went static next to him as he imagined Charlie wakening once more to utter horror over his bed.

This was the second time promises of help had been dangled in front of him and no less compelling. "Do you think your squirrel friend is being held against her will?"

"Doubtful," Donovan took a deep breath. "But I must find her. To that end I've collected a file for you—"

"Hold on. You already know I have an affliction that makes discretion a challenge, yet rather than get a private investigator at what would be peanuts in cost to you, you choose me. You're anticipating I'm going to get into a fight, aren't you?"

"The possibility exists, yes."

"These Nosfurs, are they very strong?"

Donovan nodded curtly. "Avoid conflict where you can. But if you must…"

There it was then. "I knew it. I'm just dumb muscle for the state so who else to send against creatures who can throw people across rooms and—"

Donovan's ears cocked and Crawford stopped talking. Silence passed as Crawford got himself under control.

Donovan sighed. "Are you distressed at the idea of working for a vegetable eater? Is that a demotion in your eyes?"

"That's not it at all. I'm no specist."

"No?"

"No. Doesn't matter to me what goes on your dinner plate. I hate working for the rich, Mister Calvert." Crawford could feel his hackles standing again, but this wasn't fury. Disgust was more like it. "Your type starts wars, build empires off other mammals' backs, and people like me are just means to an end. You have it in your little file exactly why I quit the Police Force in Virginia?"

"I assumed it was beneath your talents."

"It was because with the pay so bad, the only extra work held out to the brass was strike breaking. People like you paying for clubs to come down on working joes and janes who needed a bit more to take home to their cubs."

"And threatened the productivity of greater mammals to achieve that."

"Greater mammals. Fangs on you and you'd be unbelievably insufferable, wouldn't you?"

That nicked a nerve. The smile didn't go away but the rabbit's eyes hardened. "And yet look what it is that you do now, Mister Cain. Siphoning one of the last expressions of relief from suffering salary earners around you. You think the Eighteenth Amendment is as moronic as I do and thwart it yourself. That started long before you were bitten, didn't it? Care to tell me what I'm missing?"

Crawford said nothing, teeth grinding hard enough to hurt. He'd looked inward during the war and found he was a stranger to himself in so many ways. He'd found no one to open up to upon returning, not his wife or son, not his partner here. So, he'd lost himself in work he hated enough to stay preoccupied.

Calvert took the silence as acquiescence. "The fact is my lupine friend, under peaceful conditions warlike mammals set upon themselves. You're living proof if I've ever seen it."

"That some rabbit British aphorism?"

Donovan sighed. "Nietzsche was a wolf. You hate what you do no less for being good at it, but you need not be a tool of the state without real purpose. All you need to do is trust me. Can you do that Mister Cain?"

Donovan removed his jacket and then slipped away the holster and Crawford's Colt 1908 with it. He dangled it like a treat for a good feral.

Crawford's ears burned as took it and slipped his own jacket off. "Not to put too fine a point on it but can you be trusted if your best people are running away from you?"

"Sandy did not run Mister Cain. She is the most loyal companion I've ever cultivated, and loss of resolve and purpose is not the culprit. I'm well aware that your new…condition provides you with impeccable senses that will prove valuable. Can you find her for me?" The rabbit pointed at a coat rack that Crawford had passed upon walking in. The wolf turned to see the trench coat he'd been wearing before killing Tooley, freshly laundered.

"Your car is just outside the West exit and the keys in that pocket."

Crawford sighed as the weapon he'd brought back from the war found itself back at his bosom. "I supposed that regardless of my answer you're going to say I owe you."

***

Sandy Mallory gazed into her reflection in the bathtub's surface, disturbed and resolved again as drips from coiled copper came one after the other, the still's liquid heartbeat. She was beautiful again, the same russet maiden whose last sunset had been so many decades ago, a stranger she was afraid to know again.

She'd been led astray. No, she'd been freed. Who had freed her, who had chained her? High on the elixir of life she couldn't sort truth from lie. The malted meal of corn and rye and the yeast that broke them down cloyed her heightened senses. Packed in with the stinks of creation in the clay-walled basement, the scents of coppery potency from the three sisters that crowded round was overpowering.

"Under red coats bleed red doubts."

"Flowing pulse of urging shouts."

"Remorse brings tears too late to shed,"

"For past given life once gladly dead."

Over by the crates, Bucky Cavali swept his tail as he laughed. "No remorse here, sisters. I'm happy with the change in arrangements. Just make sure Torrio knows I got my cut when his mamm' come's by." He turned a bottle around, watching spirits dance within.

Baliosi caught Sandy's gaze as she glanced up and the wolf winked at her. "We've no doubts."

Sandy swallowed and shook her head. A hand on her shoulder brought her eye to wooden eye with the coyote Laguna. "All secrets are kept here." The coyote's black-toothed smile was oddly comforting. "We won't rock your Ark."

The sister released her friendly grip on Sandy's shoulder as Bucky turned, bottle in hand. "I figure a case of this will last us, what a month?"

Sandy realized he was talking to her and thought back on the plans already discussed. "Sure Bucky. A case will do us just fine."

The joyous abandon that Sandy felt at getting out from under Donovan's thumb had been a precious breath of mortal air after departing the Four Deuces. The handsome fox had whispered wonderful plans to her as they huddled on a nearby rooftop, the new contract deeded in mob-honor promises simultaneously airtight as God's laws yet fragile enough to break with one bullet. Such was the short, fraught life of the Chicago made mammal.

Sandy thought, for not the first or last time, of the children at Noah's Plank school who would never see her again or recognize her if they did.

Only Donovan plotting in his mansion would put face to name and know she'd abandoned all he stood for. She had to be content with that, no, proud. The fawning, suffering servant had seen through him at last. This was the proper way forward, a re-acquaintance with her true self.

Upon leaving the sisters to their work at their new still in the dilapidated fringe of the city, the squirrel and fox headed for an abandoned barn in the country Bucky knew of. They found a high loft above the stolen Alfa Romeo and fumbled one another's clothes away. Bucky's hands did all the talking and Sandy heard her own words in his touch. "I'll help you find a grace of your own." It wasn't until Bucky's empty orgasm made a keen through the hay that she remembered who she'd spoken those words to and why. The weight of what she'd done even with the best of intentions made her shudder in his arms.

If he noticed, Bucky misunderstood and kissed her deeply. "I'll have a palace for my new Queen soon," he promised giddily. "Pearls and satin and the best of everything." Daybreak in the old barn would be dangerous but exhilarating, sun beating ancient planks inches from their heads in long-abandoned rafters. In the time till that first light, they'd make their plans.

By early the next evening, the rental agreement Bucky had paid for weeks ago with his living hand would be ratified by a dead one, passed on by the bachelor badger landlord who would be floating out to the lake, lifeblood flooding through Buck's and Sandy's veins. "It'll all be ours, Red," Bucky said affectionately. "The bar and the back room and our special place upstairs, the dream, real. How many more like us do you know?"

Sandy had been puzzled by that question, but not worried. "Bucky, we can't have enough for every Nosfur in Illinois. How many enemies does your old boss have?"

With Bucky's lack of an answer came the first doubts.

***

Crawford had much to think about and little time to decide. Dinner finished quickly as press herded in. The city's newly minted Mayor and Aldermen started arriving in as ward numbers were called on a radio turned all the way up. At least one table was pounded, and a mink stalked out, proving at least one incumbent had been unseated.

Judging by the smiles of the well-to-do assembled to hob-nob between the last fiery speech and the crème brute dessert course there were going to be high placed people in well-lined pockets before the last vote was even called.

Crawford remembered the parting words by which Donovan Calvert tried to get the wolf on his side. "We don't have to like each other, Mister Cain, but you need me as much as I need you. We both are smaller players in a higher cause." He'd given Crawford an exchange number and requested a decision by midday. That was about fourteen hours away by one of the many ornate clocks in the main hall. For now, he had another appointment to keep.

"Did you try this? It's pretty good," Charlie had caramel and coffee on his breath.

Crawford sniffed. "Are they bringing that to us or do we—" He saw the line to the dessert table and realized that barely picking at his chicken had left him hungry despite the pain in his jaw. Was it coming again? "You know what, no desert for me. I have to get going soon."

"The last speech comes after this. They expect to wrap up around nine or so." Charlie looked concerned. "You need to go somewhere quiet and talk? You were gone most of the way though dinner. I don't know if it was that knock that went bad or…all the rest but I'm here for you, you know that." The golden fur around his mouth made his wan smile shine and Crawford immediately felt bad about the piling mountain of secrets he hid behind.

He wanted to go back to their apartment and tell Charlie everything, from the bite all the way up until the divorce papers landed on their shared doorstep. Perhaps even things going back further that he couldn't figure out. Charlie's ears stood slender; his head cocked in a way Crawford found familiar. With Donovan's expensive whiskey coursing through him Crawford felt the other wolf's closeness in a tangible sense. So long together, so little divulged. But what to say.

"I'd like to talk," Crawford muttered. "But tonight, I have to be somewhere."

A series of small bells rang, cutlery tapping china. Guests who were up and mingling returned to their seats. Crawford knew it was now or never and wondered if he'd need the gun he now wore where he was going. "Take the car home Charlie, it's outside the west exit. I'll ring a cab. I'm sorry I can't stay."

"You got your car from down by Daley's just now?" Charlie was guardedly suspicious.

Crawford didn't know what else to say. "Yeah."

Up on the dais, Illinois Attorney General Brundage shook Beatie's hand, and the bear stood back as the German shepherd straightened his tie for the umpteenth time that night.

Charlie looked at the key in his hand sourly. "I'm worried about you," he said, not meeting Crawford's eye. The lie didn't add up. They both knew it.

"I'll be fine, and I meant what I said. We'll talk. I promise. Thanks for being there for me Charlie."

Charlie nodded wordlessly, then buttoned up whatever emotions he guarded and smiled in the general direction of the dais.

Crawford beelined for the exit, blinking at press flashbulbs in the corner of his eyes.

Brundage's booming howl followed him out. "On this night where we turn a new page at City Hall, we must be ever mindful of the threats our public servants face, forces of graft and corruption drip like poison from the criminal stills of Chicago!"

Crawford turned back only once as Brundage fired up his audience with warnings of dark forces attacking the purity of stalwart Carnivores and impressionable, upstanding vegetarians. Donovan Calvert was sitting up with the other captains of city industry, long ear perked with amusement as he pushed roughage around his plate.

CHAPTER 13

ALWAYS GET A SECOND OPINION

Crawford arrived at Dannovey's Coffee Shop just before nine, soft light glazing the wooden booths. He ordered a cup of joe and waited.

She arrived shortly wearing a dark, form fitting getup with a cloche hat to suggest a somber, reserved ensemble. Black gloves slipped to her elbows and matched black leggings travelled hoof to skirt. "You look nice." Crawford said.

"There is a small but definitive difference between dressing to make tails wag and dressing formally."

"What's that?" Crawford realized his panama was still on and transferred it to the booth's hook.

Her nose wrinkled as she smiled, which Crawford found fetching. "Less pelt shown."

Crawford nodded. "I guess I should thank you for coming after we threw each other around."

"Not my first time." She raised a finger. The beaver who trundled over looked short on sleep. "Tea, please," Her voice poured like honey.

"Mam." His flat tail fanned them in parting.

"Was the paper I tossed a good read?"

The doe cocked her head, then remembered. "It had what I needed."

"The Cardinals win?"

"I believe so. Are you dancing around questions until you figure out how to ask them and worried you can't be charming enough until you do?"

"You got me. Smoke?"

"No but go right ahead." Her tea arrived and was ignored.

Crawford lit a Lucky, sending smoke upward with a tip of his muzzle. "I need to know what...this mess is I'm in. Good place to start."

"You were bitten very recently."

"How do you know?"

"You're not prepared for changes. Had you known you were on the cusp you wouldn't have been at that house."

"You mean your house."

She lifted the cup and sniffed it. "Not anymore. You won't find me there again and shouldn't go back."

Crawford shifted to avoid pinching his tail. "Not a sentimental sort."

"No." She sipped with a grimace.

"Bad tea?"

"It's fine, not my drink of choice."

"I guess we couldn't meet in a speak."

"You've scotch on your breath so I would assume avoidance is only a matter of professional appearances." She set the tea down. "Fortunately, that's common enough amongst buttons that you shouldn't feel bad."

"I'm not a policeman," Crawford said.

Celeste smiled without humor. "Fine. Let's talk about what you really are. Being a were means that you regress to a primitive, feral state during lunar cycles. Deep within every mammal is the seed of their first progenitors from before history, lying dormant. No longer dormant for you."

"But why? I know about rabies and measles but what's in a bite that turns me into some kind of goddamn…cave wolf." Crawford's voice sharpened and he forced his voice low. "Is this the right place for this conversation?"

The doe cocked an ear. "Knowing the consequences of making a scene makes this the perfect place for this conversation. We already made note of that."

Crawford sat straight and linked his fingers, looking down to see if bemusement would make his claws get longer. "I'm sorry if I'm a bit sharp. I'm not as accustomed to what I am as what, well, whatever you are."

"I'm a doe."

They traded baleful looks.

She sighed. "There are reasons why I only go out at night."

Crawford cocked an ear. "I've heard rumors."

"I'm not a ghoul or demon if that's what—"

"How about a Nosfurratu?"

He enjoyed catching her surprised, even if she immediately buried it. "Where did you hear a word like that?"

"Wouldn't you like to know?"

"Honesty depends on information going both ways."

"I understand, I just…" His ears went back as he realized how stupid the thought he'd had was.

"Just what?"

Crawford sighed wistfully. "My wife loved lording over what she knew that I didn't and hates when I…anyway you reminded me of her for a second."

"Charming. Again, where'd you hear that term? Somebody at your bureau with a hobby?"

"I heard it from a rich eccentric who told me he has all the answers but refuses to divulge much unless I help him find someone."

"You've definitely piqued my interest."

"Peak mine. What is this bite doing to me? I haven't done anything that I'm ashamed of yet but I have had a couple periods where I've gotten confused."

"And you are extremely worried you've done things you're ashamed of which is why you denied that before I asked. Possibly something horrifying. I do read my papers."

Crawford's muzzle hung open a moment and his blood chilled.

"I'm not asking you to admit or deny. I know what urges you're contending with and how dangerous you worry you are. I know I went through those fears for the first twenty years after my…change."

Crawford collected himself. "So, you have the desire to…"

"I don't have your specific predilections, but I need sustenance that is very rarely provided voluntarily."

"Really?" Donovan Calvert's warning came back. Slave to horrible appetites. The rabbit appealed to a prosecutorial zeal Crawford didn't succumb to, but he'd felt the rabbit's sincerity. "Is that sustenance…blood?"

Her suspicious glare gave him pause. "Learn that from your eccentric friend?"

"Yes. You said you'd had difficulty handling things for the first twenty years. Without being too forward, you seem very young. Twenties, thirties at the oldest."

Celeste smirked. "So unflattering."

"Government work saps charisma, I'm told. How old are you, really?"

She reluctantly sipped the tea and set it down. "I'm old enough to have potentially met your great, great, great grandfather, had I left France for England or Austria or wherever your people roamed."

"How do you know I'm not a French Wolf, ancestrally I mean?"

"I can always tell."

Crawford couldn't be sure if she was joking. "Over a hundred years then?"

"Just a shade under a hundred and fifty."

"Oh." Crawford tried to put that in perspective and couldn't. "Is that going to happen to me?"

Her eyes gave it away, sympathetic but detached. "That's doubtful. The only one like you I ever met didn't live long. The end was…inevitable."

There it was. Crawford felt cold, but in a familiar disconnected way. He saw his wife and cub in his mind's eye and wondered if that would be easier for them. The sense memory of an alley painted with otter woke him to the realization that it most likely would. "I need to control this. There has to be a way."

Celeste sat back, avoiding his eyes. "I can sympathize with how you're feeling even If that doesn't help you."

Desperation made the shop colder. "You just said you had a lust for… you have needs that you figured out how to manage. Why can't I do that?"

Celeste lowered her slender ears. "Your voice is carrying. It takes a lot to lose myself to my needs. Reason comes more easily to what I am and more difficult for what you're becoming."

"How's that work? Even if you only take part of…what's there to consume, that's the same damn thing."

"Actually, it's not. You're approaching your basic nature as an animal while I am a step in the opposite direction, not alive in any sense known by nature. I have command of rationality that the change takes from you."

"What if I can get it back? I mean, what kind of notes were people like me keeping when this started happening to them?"

"None that I'm aware of."

"Okay, so I'll write stuff down."

"And eat it, or your note taker if you have one."

"Can't you help me through this? I mean, it's a lot to ask but you can stop me if I lose control, right?"

"There's more to that than you think. As fascinating as this idea is, I am in dangers you don't know of. My kind is actively hunted by those who know what we are."

Crawford hadn't even thought of that. "You're hunted? Or *we're* hunted?"

"Those who hunt my kind despise me than they would you." Celeste sighed. "Give me one of your cigarettes. I need to keep up appearances."

Confused, Crawford gave her a Lucky and lit it with a shaky match. She inhaled and exhaled quickly, not a trace of coughing.

"Do you smoke often?"

"I use these lungs for talking and nothing else."

"Alright."

"As I was saying, I am hunted as a dire threat, while you are seen as a dangerous and rare curiosity to those who know of us."

"Please explain that."

"As someone with experience in mammalian depravities as I'm sure you are, you have seen that violence is perpetuated by the stronger against those perceived as weaker. Under rare circumstances, my kind can make others into Nosfurs. Most often, the chosen prey are those convenient to subdue. And so are those who are changed."

"You're saying that more vegetarians are fed on so more vegetarians become what you are?"

"It's rare that it happens at all but yes. And Nosfur vegetarians are seen as the worst threat by those in the know with power."

"Why is that?"

"What I am confounds the presumed natural order established in most religious or social hierarchies. It's why as volatile as you are they would pity you while putting you down while they would kill me with glee. I'm not the meek creature society demands of me and am therefore the more ungodly creature."

Crawford thought on that. "I wouldn't look at what either of us do as Godly."

"No?" Celeste held his gaze. "Violence isn't a lupine's birthright? You should read some history, especially since your occupation perpetuates the worst of it."

Crawford's ears went blush-hot. "You mean Prohibition? Some heads do get clobbered in enforcement of the Eighteenth amendment but that's not what I want. I hate that part of it."

"The badge stays in your pocket."

"I took that job to save a marriage."

"It didn't work. There's no ring there."

Of course there wasn't. He tried to remember when he'd removed it, his bedroom at home, near the alley where Tooley was killed? He'd certainly had it when Kamila told him the papers were coming. He'd turned it on his finger then. "That's my business."

Celeste's Lucky's ash fell in her tea. "Very well," she whispered. "If you want help then you need to help me trust you. Where did you hear about my kind? What was this person's name?"

If she were to walk out, Crawford would have no choice but to trust the rabbit. He didn't want to. "Donovan Calvert. He's a rich rabbit, owns a…"

"Steel company," She sat back, ears low. Crawford saw she didn't care for that name. "He's not someone who you want to associate with regardless of how much he pays you. Does he know what you are?"

Crawford scratched his scalp and it hurt. His pelt felt like it wanted to leave his head. "Yes. He knows about my involvement with last night."

"So, he has a Prohee were' in his pocket."

Crawford chuffed. "It's not like that. He's interested in your kind, wants my help in finding one of you. I kinda owe him."

The beaver returned with coffee and topped Crawford off before trudging away. Crawford watched the doe consider.

"I will help you try to manage your problem," Celeste said reluctantly. "But I'll need your help in return."

Crawford's ears went forward.

"Two things," Celeste said. "Firstly, you will tell Donovan nothing about meeting me."

"That goes without saying."

"Second, I need your resources to find someone, a fox who recently became like me. He's a low-level player in Johnny Torrio's gang named Bucky Cavali."

Crawford sighed. "Calvert already wants me looking for an Irish Squirrel. Why not."

The doe's ears and slim brows shot up.

Crawford cocked his head. "That caffeine start to work, or do you know—"

"Sandy Mallory?" The doe's eyes were cold again. "Why yes, I do. If you find her, you'll find Bucky too."

"Really, she's with your fox?"

She nodded, visibly agitated.

Crawford cleared his throat. "Who the hell names a Fox *Bucky?*"

***

Von Haften parked Donovan's Duesenberg and took deep breaths to settle her nerves. She'd need a brandy, maybe something stronger. Old memories had returned with teeth, her sister's last agonies, the pains of an innocent, and she'd willfully accepted the task that resurrected them, saw it through, no turning back.

For a great and noble purpose, certainly. Regardless…She broke into a sob that she forced into a growl. She'd have to confront Donovan soon, get him repentant, compliant.

"Then you can do the talking," she muttered to the shape under the tarp on the seat next to hers. "I'll be busy ensuring you don't go to hell alone."

Would she…? No. The cause was just. She had to keep that in focus.

For now, she needed relief. Brandy waited inside Donovan's absurd little mansion. She'd get his men distracted with pointless investigations and have the raccoon's disappearance explained, hopefully get her mind to another place with use of his natural proclivities before she returned the next evening to where her new weapon waited.

She took a deep breath and wrestled the large, wrapped shape and small satchel from the car. What did the Americans like to say? Showtime.

Minutes later, Evelyn dumped the wrapped form out on Donovan's study rug as the rabbit looked on pensively. "Does this look familiar Don?"

Donovan rose from his wing-backed chair to study the crumpled form. The modestly dressed grey furred corpse was unidentifiable for one key reason. "Those I maintain relationships with have heads."

Evelyn raised the burlap clutched to her side. The head that spilled out bounced on the already ruined rug. Scarred flesh and singed fur made Keller the raccoon immediately recognizable.

"You killed a tied-down defenseless man in recovery?" Donovan scoffed.

Her teeth flashed. "He was not tied to anything Donovan. Nor was he *recovering*. He'd escaped your little prison some time ago."

"I don't believe you," Donovan glanced at his pet possum Edmond. The blank expression on his henchman's face confirmed his surprise.

"Do you wonder what he was found doing when supposedly tied to his bed, administered by another monster of his own ilk with only the smallest degree of supervision from you?" Evelyn spat on the raccoon's corpse.

Donovan stood up. "Where did you find him?"

Evelyn smiled. Time to make Donovan's puppets dance. "I'd be glad to tell you."

***

Crawford's night ended without incident. Celeste took his office number and promised they'd meet again after handling something. The advice she'd parted on was unexpected. "Drinking won't necessarily work if it gets your ire up. Otherwise…" She imparted an anecdotal example of canine monks who ran a Bavarian brewery. Rumor had that one of them lasted several years while livestock went missing for miles. Crawford skeptically asked how reliable the story was and Celeste said that rumors were truth's small change.

Tip in hand, Crawford found a speak, had a couple under the lowest of profiles, walked for a bit before getting a cab home balanced by booze and caffeine.

Charlie hadn't waited up. Crawford heard the wolf's genteel snore from under his bedroom door.

He read the divorce papers slowly. The settlement offer seemed fair. Crawford took the savings, they took the house and chicken coop. Kamila didn't want him to fight, just let her and her son, *his* son, go.

Could it end this way? Crawford could close his eyes and remember times spent with his son gazing into a clear blue sky cut by waves in wispy clouds. His son had asked if oceans looked as blue as this and Crawford promised to take him the coast someday. Less than a year later, he waved goodbye from the ocean in fatigues heading for France.

Would a signature ensure their ways part? On the verge of sobbing and wondering if he had the strength to put pen to paper, Crawford's misery flooded in drink.

One swish of ink and the worst would be behind him. But his pen wasn't in his night table, not on his windowsill, not in or on his dresser. Nor on the bed where his cheek fur brushed against a cold soft pillow and settled in.

Sounds from the kitchen made him blink and light smeared through the window above him.

He'd slept in. No time for a shower or even a body combing.

He found a semi-presentable change of clothes and trudged to the kitchen. The window was open. He could smell it had recently rained, the same clouds hiding the moon made the sun a runny egg.

"Morning," Charlie said without emotion. "We're running behind again. Better bolt breakfast down."

Even cold, bacon did the trick on the back of lukewarm coffee. The Chevrolet's key turned ten minutes later. "Sorry I left early last night. Had to meet someone."

Charlie glanced at him then tipped his pork-pie hat lower as he changed the subject. "Chief sent us on our way last night with notice that we'd have new field work in the next day or so. We're getting our budget raised. Deever wants a full-on war against the mob."

Crawford had realized he'd need to bring a pen home from the office to sign those papers for Kamila and failed to catch that. "Say it again Charlie."

"The new Mayor said we're gonna fight the mob," Charlie said without enthusiasm. "More moolah from Washington to go all in."

"Beatie must be glowing."

"Like a new bride."

Crawford had to laugh. The image of his boss in a dress lingered as he drove and smelled whatever cologne Charlie was wearing fill the car.

As Crawford steered the Chevrolet through the city he felt the weight of silence between the questions Charlie didn't ask and the answers Crawford didn't want to give.

The office buzzed when they went in. The mourning for Tooley was behind and war against the mob ahead. A couple speak raids a day didn't stand out, but several over several days put the lawless on their claws.

A meaty hand landed on Crawford's shoulder as he pulled out his desk chair and Beatie's massive muzzle was in Crawford's ear. "I'm told two calls came for you, same guy said he had a tip you'd want to hear." The exchange number was scrawled in paper.

Beatie wandered off. If he'd noticed Crawford leave the party early last night, he didn't care. Crawford went to the front office phone. The voice on the other end when connected was familiar. "Take down this address. Arrive in one hour."

"How about two?" Crawford asked the possum who'd brought him to Calvert last night.

"One if you want Donovan's time. He has commitments."

"Don't we all?" Crawford put on his hat. "Chasing down a lead," he told Charlie as the latter gathered a paperwork mound of mammals disputing tickets who'd be shaken for information in return. Chasing down a lead wasn't technically lying but that didn't make him feel better.

An hour later a weasel waved his Chevrolet past the foundry gates. Stinks of oil and vulcanized metal assaulted his nose with stenches he'd have to bathe out later. Shirtless, leather suspendered mammals wandered in and out of the mill where fire winked hungrily from cages of molten hell.

Crawford parked the car far enough away that heat wouldn't soften his tires and left hat and coat behind. His shirt, slacks and four-buttoned vest were tight around his fur as Calvert's waiting possum guided him to a door left of the mill's entrance.

A spinning fan cooled the immediate space to a tolerable level within. Steel steps bore Crawford up.

A catwalk was sweat-warm under Crawford's claws, high enough to gaze at trundling ladles of liquid fire pouring into moulds below. Crawford couldn't see clearly through the steam but thought he glimpsed a white furred, shirtless creature, broad chest heaving, mouth opening and closing in whispered monologue with arm raised high.

The possum ushered Crawford into an elevated office, window to the outside revealing the weed-like rise of Chicago in the distance and inner windows fogged with steam, revealing little. A heavy wooden desk was flanked by three chairs. A lamp in one corner tried to compensate for the outside light's deficiencies and a file cabinet was crowned by a crystal decanter set.

The possum poured from the decanter and set the drink on the desk and left without another word.

Crawford took the drink to the window. And sipped. Honeyed smoke rolled on his tongue when the door opened and a blast of heat followed the rabbit in. "Please take a seat," Donovan said, closing the last two buttons on his shirt.

Crawford sat. "This is good," he wagged the glass.

The rabbit shrugged. "Of course. Have you considered my offer?"

"Yes. I have to ask, based on what you know about my condition, is this helping or do I need to worry I'm going to lose myself?" He waved the glass.

Donovan cocked an ear. "That hinders your change, yes, but too much and you'll lose yourself in other ways."

Crawford gave a blank look. "You don't say."

Donovan smiled. "We all need to cope with existential fears and guilts that our feral cousins escape. Such a disappointment to see America supress the simplest remedy against the pains of being a mammal of mind, especially in a world where far more dangerous proclivities abound."

"I should quit the bureau and come work for you instead."

"I'd counter with staying working with your bureau but also, and more expediently, working for me as well. I can make that lucrative."

"I'm not looking for a bigger paycheque from you."

Donovan took the chair on his side of the desk, leather cracked by the heat. "Beyond managing your new affliction, what do you want?"

A small headache was getting more prominent, and Crawford felt his lungs hurt. Latent pain from his condition? No, he hadn't felt this before now. The ache of oncoming change and these pains were distinctly different. "I want things I can't have. You poked enough wounds to know that."

"Perhaps you can." The rabbit took a deep breath. "You've already demonstrated you dislike Prohibition work. An Irish acquaintance of mine would be grateful for your other skills. How good is your nose, Mister Cain?"

Crawford's chest felt each dull thud of his heart. "I can make out more than I used to. The possum is still close by. You've got bears downstairs doing most of the sweating and I know you've got more cigarettes in your desk."

"Excellent. There's a warehouse on Chicago's West side in where I'm told a raccoon and our aforementioned red squirrel were encountered."

"Who else?" Crawford finished his drink, rose to help himself to another. The headache was abating a bit.

"Else?"

"They didn't encounter themselves."

"Yes, of course. You may scent lion on the air."

"He work for you too?"

Calvert sighed as he drew paper and fountain pen from his desk's drawer. "She does not. I'd rather you avoid her. She plays loose with information and can't be trusted. This information was vetted independently."

There was a story there. Crawford read the address, knowing the area, mixed residences, empty lots, a few struggling businesses. There was a fire station and a school too. "This lead shouldn't take long."

"Just be reminded that when found you can't bring Ms. Mallory back during the day. She has an unnatural aversion to sunlight."

"I know all—" Crawford could kick himself. He cleared his throat. "I had a relative who suffered from something sun related. Was it a bite that made her that way?" Crawford looked at the empty glass he didn't remember draining and decided not to fill it a third time. "Like me?"

"Not quite. Weres never intentionally seek to propagate their own."

"So, what was Simon Govic going to make me?"

The rabbit's ears cocked in a way that humored him for a fool. "Dinner."

Crawford decided it was time to go. "Will Ms. Mallory come voluntarily if I drop your name?"

"Yes. Tell her my garden is looking worse for wear. That will amuse her."

"Quaint. I feel compelled to ask, what are you trying to accomplish by curing her? No offense but I read about your recent labour dispute, and you're not thought of in certain press as the charitable type."

Donovan rose, crossed the room and poured himself a drink, tugging at his collar "I'll give you the short of it now that we're becoming friends. As you know I came up in a world that didn't want me in its upper ranks, obstructing my successes in business and attainment of key social positions both back in England and here in America. I succeeded despite having teeth that ground instead of pierced. Much as I was hated for it, no one could stop me."

"Congratulations but that didn't answer my question."

"I am not curing, Sandy, I am helping her manage fate's cruel hand. The world would see her crushed as an aberration, but I want her to conquer her affliction, achieve greater things. As more and more of the Nosfurratu are rescued from these appetites, a better world can be made for them. By me." He quickly glanced to the inner window as steel poured a lance into the dark, steam obscuring everything. "I will provide them purpose."

"How many have you rescued? Besides Sandy herself?" Crawford asked.

Donovan's eyes fixed on the steel. "Take that scotch. It won't stop your affliction in its tracks but will curtail it. Find Sandy Mallory and bring her home."

Crawford took the decanter, content that he'd gotten a free clinical second opinion. It was cut crystal, probably worth enough to buy a new suit if he was inclined to hawk it.

Donovan caught his eye. "You'll find a new addition at the home you share with your partner in the next day or so that will make both of your jobs considerably easier. Call it a bonus."

"My department keeps careful eye out for graft, so…"

"It will be the result of a contest you've won, all above board. Trust me."

Crawford sighed. The possum was by the door ready to escort him down, but Crawford felt the instinctual need to wander his way out. "Gonna take the other stairs." He walked around the rabbit's desk and ignored the quizzical raise of Donovan's ears. "I know the way out."

Through the other door, heat hit Crawford hard, bringing him to panting. Mammals of his type weren't comfortable here, which was why the majority he could see were naked to the waist, well back from the forges and operating the cauldron's pulleys with slick sinewy limbs. Crawford descended quickly, feeling faint. His headache had increased with pounding force as his walkway traversed a tall stack of steel girders awaiting transfer out.

As he took the final flight of steps down, he glanced outward to see a spouted cauldron pour flaming steel into a mould down in the dim light.

Beyond that mould, as though floating, a single girder of steel trundled away from its companions, a ton of rigid metal impossibly borne on a single bent bare back with fur thinned by age and exertion. The figure vanished from sight into the dark.

Crawford was behind his car's wheel minutes later, blinking to account for what he couldn't have actually seen as he started the Chevrolet and made for the exit gate in a fog of confusion.

Chapter 14

Entrepreneurial Moves

Night came. The fox and squirrel hit the ground running. Sandy had shown Bucky so much that Celeste hadn't; the means to coax others to trust with the glint of persuasion and how to become infinitesimal enough in body to carry oneself on a breeze or move at great speed. Bucky had already instinctively begun mastering that skill.

They parked the dead Landlord's Packard next to the thwarted Lioness' Alfa in the garage behind their new digs. They'd need the Packard's back seat to collect supplies, "Until we can get something better" Bucky reasoned. "I know where to hawk the Packard for cash."

The case of liquor obtained from the Sisters went behind the bar, and space was made for hoists behind a door they concealed.

A short while later they went upstairs to the private room where a desk, rickety chair and lone mattress awaited. "This is certainly better than a barn," Sandy said approvingly. "Why so few bottles for the speak? Mortal guests will empty those bottles in mere hours, even if some get sorted out." She'd spent every waking moment pondering the implications of what was to come.

Could she do this? So many of the orphans Sandy had taught for the past two years had been made so by drunkards who abandoned them or gangsters whose indiscriminate bullets had torn families asunder. Such horror and loneliness with no end in sight.

She certainly couldn't teach her students anymore but could certainly right wrongs done to them.

Therefore, this wasn't just a business, it was retribution.

"The bottles won't be a problem." Bucky answered, gazing through dirt smudged windowpanes. His moonlit hand touched her arm, slid round down the slip on her back. Where he'd found another dress that fit her,

Sandy didn't know, but she'd been grateful. She'd left loneliness behind at last.

A muzzle crept over her shoulder and his whiskers tickled her cheek. Sandy settled into his touch. "Our kind feed from ferals when we need to, tame or wild as we find them. That matters if we're serving our sort," Sandy said as Bucky explored her ears with his nose and lips.

"Tame or wild, as we find 'em," he replied into her neck.

The fox wordlessly and methodically undressed her. Sandy's hands crept back to return the favor. Short work later had him in her hand and his own hands roving from pert breast to recesses the dark couldn't hide. "We need to be at Siegfried's in an hour." Bucky checked a wristwatch taken from the dispatched landlord. "That's enough time."

Bucky's tongue searched for clues to Sandy Mallory's more immediate wants. Soon enough her questions were forgotten under the cold nickel eye of the moon.

***

Celeste's lodgings at the Congress Plaza Hotel required concocting a story for the front desk regarding a husband whose train was late. That addressed assumptions that the doe was travelling alone, which was untoward for fairer species, or using the room for illicit rendezvous, which would have the vice cops sniffing for blood. Celeste drew the shades as dawn approached and spent her recuperative time under covers, concealed from ears to hooves.

Oblivion passed quickly and she rose with dusk to hurry down to the lobby telephones. Arrangements were made to have keys to her new place left under the matt and paperwork she'd sign put through the mail slot. She checked out of the Congress promising her husband was meeting her elsewhere.

An hour after dark she reached her new two-story rental, barren as the place she'd abandoned. She stood within its dark stillness and listened to the ghosts she'd brought with her, to every place she'd ever been. Their hopes and regrets, like their names were laid to rest in crypts under Paris, crypts within herself.

Putting her meager things down, she desired the noise of life to get her centered. Lucky for her, and Bucky especially, the speak they'd meet at was a very public place.

Her precarious position with Torrio prevented her from wandering the night openly as was her want, possibly the worst damage Bucky had inflicted through his selfishness. She left her things in her new sitting room and from there bound shadow after shadow, taking alleys and side streets.

She found the speak without difficulty. It was hidden within a modestly sized barber shop with sweating white tiles and smelling of barbicide and fur oils. Hanging partitions guarded stations where naked pelts were coifed and clipped during daylight hours. Among partitions that the lone hyena escort wordlessly guided her through, Celeste heard the ministrations of one mammal on another, no barber implements involved.

It only made sense that a speakeasy hidden on the back of a barber shop wouldn't restrain itself to one vice. Nothing made prostitution more at home than sequestered compartments where one was already administered to with clothes removed. Torrio had pros working many such places. They in turn enticed many hungry souls to full-fledged whorehouses under his care like Madame Lowry's floor in the 'Deuces.

A final curtain parted against sighs and grunts, narrow stairs descended into heat and racket. Mammals crowded, breath heavy, feet light to ragtime rolling on stage where marten, possum and goat jammed with horns and drums. Celeste waded through dancers, drinkers and flirters to the bar, senses alert. There she saw them, arm in arm, the fox in pinstripes and the squirrel in a flapper. She registered the change immediately.

Sandy was young again, young as the first time Celeste had seen her sixteen years ago at the Dublin docks. The squirrel had indeed partaken of the vein.

The fox Sandy leaned into seemed indifferent to their surroundings and the drink in his hand. He studied the crowd, searching in that assuredly predatory manner he'd brought to the poker table just days ago at another speak.

Celeste thought him rakish and overconfident then. Now she wanted to bury a hatchet in his head.

When his eyes met hers, he knew how she felt.

He nudged Sandy and his muzzle told her where to look. They watched Celeste approach.

"Hi Celeste," Bucky said.

"Buzz off."

Bucky's languidly waving tail stilled.

"You and I are going to settle this. Don't think we won't. And you—" Celeste pointed her nose at Sandy. "You look healthier. Would your rabbit friend be happy about that?"

Sandy showed a bit of fang. "I told you, I'm no longer…working with him."

"This part of that reconsidered path in life?"

"It is."

"And all for the better!" Bucky squeezed Sandy with one arm and raised his glass. Whiskey sloshed. "We've got things to show you, Celeste. You wouldn't believe—"

"Bucky," Celeste said. "I don't want to hear your voice or see you. I want to break each bottle behind that bar inside your jaws and make you eat the shards. Let Sandy and I speak."

Shock settled on the fox like a cold bucket of water. Then anger set in, dragging lips back from teeth. He released Sandy, took his fedora from the bar and stalked into the crowd.

"You're not going to get this one," Celeste hissed, grateful the music prevented any but Sandy from hearing. "Bucky is an ignorant fool whom I made a mistake with, but Donovan won't turn him like he did you. If this is some sort of ruse, it won't work."

Sandy was younger, stronger, but diminutive as though unsure of the power she'd regained. She flicked her tail. "No ruses, Celeste. Look at me. Donovan only ever allowed me to partake once during all my years with him, only because I took the juniper and drank to the half."

"What the hell does that mean?" Celeste frowned.

"I'd had limited success with older Nosfurs. Donovan had me try with a volunteer he had me freshly turn to see if younger Nosfurs could be weaned more easily. It failed."

Something in Sandy's words didn't make sense, but the implication left was chilling. "He's an utter bastard."

Sandy stepped towards Celeste, hands clasped to demonstrate supplication. "I didn't see Donovan that way. You have to understand I'd carried so much guilt for the things I'd done, even if just to survive. He fed that sorrow as he did things to me, told me I was an unclean creature who could be saved. He helped me save myself, or that's what I believed. I thought for years that he had my best interests at heart. He did not. Not mine, nor any of the others I either drew to the cause or failed to. I've made a right mess of everything."

Celeste lowered her ears, unconvinced. "If that's real guilt I hope you feel it for a long time. You knew from experience what he had in store for me."

"I was brought to believe I was saving you. I know now what a betrayal that was." Sandy looked away, unable to meet the doe's eyes any longer. Celeste kept mind of all the pulses crowding close and absorbed Sandy's words with all the calm she could muster. They were close enough to embrace, or to grapple.

Sandy's eyes cautiously meet hers. "But I found joy again, Celeste. I've found a way to satisfy my needs without fear that I'll taint or harm the innocent."

The hopeful gleam in the squirrel's eye was, Celeste had to admit, pleasantly naïve. Even after all they'd been through... "Telling ourselves that is a false comfort. Even rats only last so long."

"Bucky helped me find a way. That's what we want to show you."

Celeste glanced around. The fox was out of sight, stalking darker corners, perhaps bounding shadows. "Show me what? Sandy what are you two doing here?"

Sandy perked up. "We've found a way to get what we want from only those who deserve to give it to us, just as you have."

"Those who deserve..."

"It's a violent city. I believed that before Donovan and I'm certain now."

"Yeah, we're gonna take from those who deserve it. And make a killing at the bank too," Bucky was in Celeste's other ear, his tongue flicking out to caress the fuzz on its edge.

Celeste spun around, gripping the fox by the throat. She had one good squeeze that made the fox cough instinctively before he escaped her slender finger's thick nails. A couple nearby patrons glanced their way. A dog laughed. Getting manhandled by a vegetarian was socially demeaning for any carnivore, even if the doe was his size or better.

Bucky clutched for dignity. "Hells bells, Celeste, you need a sense of humor. You're just jealous because Sandy taught me how to move quiet as a breath. You never taught me that."

"You left. And you're proving that you weren't going to learn a thing you didn't want to. What are you two doing?"

Sandy put a hand on Celeste's arm. Celeste hadn't felt the squirrel's touch in so long that she couldn't untangle the feelings it stirred. She didn't quite want to break every finger in Sandy's hand, didn't want to respond with a touch of her own. She was frozen in indecision.

The touch was delicate. "We're making a place for us. You, Bucky, I… and others."

"What kind of place?"

Bucky had an empty glass in his hand. "Come see us when we're up and running. We're already stocking the best vintages right here."

Celeste followed his gaze to fast-footed dancers, shot-glass slingers, and carousers rubbing shoulders. "Did you say stalking or stocking?"

Bucky raised a brow. "You just said the same word twice. Don't matter. Tomorrow night, a little place we've set up at Madison and Lasalle, just look for an oily plaid rag above a dark door. I'm sorry you gotta go now."

"Why does she need to leave so soon?" Sandy's hand slid from Celeste's arm.

Bucky set his glass on the bar and scuffed the wooden floor with a claw. "This is one of Torrio's places. They know she's here."

He wouldn't meet Celeste's gaze. "You know that because you told them."

He gave a wan smile. "Course not, but we couldn't have a scene, right? It's for the best."

Celeste let just a bit of fang slip and tasted the smallest bit of that fear he'd never admit he had. "I've got more to teach you, Bucky. Soon." She put her own hand on Sandy's. "Walk me to the door, quickly."

The squirrel reluctantly followed as they left Bucky behind and weaved through the dancers.

At the barber shop's curtain Celeste saw the hyena approaching, teeth-clenching black bear in tow, sleeves already rolled.

"You said a few minutes ago that Donovan made you take the juniper and drink to the half. What does that phrase mean? In a hundred and thirty years since turning I've never heard it."

Sandy was momentarily confused. "It's in the archives Donovan collected from the Martyres of the Black Well. That's the order he's part of."

The hyena and bear were close. "Quicky, Sandy."

Sandy's whiskers twitched. "Juniper herb imbibed along with the half-drunk body laid in repose is how one of us deliberately turns another to be like us. The seed combined with our essence suppresses the rigor that kills."

Celeste didn't know what to say. "I didn't know that." Of course, she'd never wanted to turn another so she'd never sought such information out.

She took leave without another word and the bear followed with purpose.

A block later the black bear rolled on the sidewalk, honking curses to God through the gushing blood of his nose.

A block after that, past the streetlight's reach, a shadow took its guest in silence.

***

The day dragged and Crawford's affliction gained ground. Churns in his guts, aches in his limbs, teeth wanting to wiggle out of his head. He was assigned to map speak locations in the last week to discern patterns for where they'd set up shop next, canvas witnesses and shake them down for tips. The only notable informant was a druggist who Crawford quickly figured was no civic-minded citizen but rather someone wanting competition eliminated. The old hare sold liquor prescriptions now undersold by a popup speak two doors down. The hare got wise to the note-scribbling wolf figuring him out and offered both aspirin and a litre of prescription whiskey to ease Crawford's obvious discomfort.

Shouldn't he accept as a hardworking public servant who recognized the real scofflaws and miscreants darkening this city's doors? No, he actually couldn't. The discussion ended awkwardly.

As the day wore down, Crawford finally found opportunity to insert Don Calvert's request into the flow of his own duties, leaving the office to scramble for the address the rabbit provided.

Sitting in his car, Crawford stretched in order to relieve his aches and realized his time away from the condition he fought was borrowed. He was staring at his clawed hands, contemplating whether he should spend the night far outside of the city where nothing horrible could happen when his door opened, and the Chevrolet's springs groaned on the passenger side. Beatie blew smoke on Crawford's dash. "You left last night's shindig a bit early. A team photograph is going in the paper without you."

Crawford made himself seem regretful. "I wasn't feeling well."

The bear moved the pipe to his other cheek. "That business with Tooley was hard for everybody," Beatie said assuredly. "I don't know how I would have coped if it were one of mine. We'll get the sick cannibal bastards, don't you worry. I've faith in all of you."

"Thank you sir."

"City's going straight to hell. Gang wars, murdered cops, even graves disturbed. Caretaker found a corpse outside of a mausoleum last night. Somebody sneaked a recently deceased skunk's body out while it was still unlocked, did devil knows what with it and dropped it outside later when the crypt was locked by the caretaker on rounds. Put a voter's ribbon in its hand. Whatever's in the gutrot the speaks are moving is driving people mad."

It hurt to talk so Crawford just nodded, wishing to God for another drink. Silence lingered uncomfortably.

"I know you've been through a lot after Govic. The city financially settled with the widow. I just hope you put that behind you soon as you can. Going to them with hat in hand took stern teeth. Too few agents take that kind of responsibility, especially for something they couldn't prevent. Don't become a recluse from the team for a waste of meat like Govic."

Smoke was fogging the car but Crawford felt clarity in pain. "What if he wasn't a waste of meat? What if I am part of the problem that drives people into those basements? The world is already beating people down…"

Beatie ground his pipe in a circle. "You know the feral bastards were up against, Crawford. I know that Govic hit his wife. I saw the bruises on her when she collected the city's check."

Crawford was taken aback. "I don't know that he—"

"He beat her, Crawford. Probably hurt that kit too. That a mammal you sympathize with? The law is the law, and we can't question our purpose in enforcing it as we must. Don't ever doubt how horrible this world would be without us."

Crawford's pain-mudded mind rolled that over. *We've taken away the freedom to seek relief from the pains we make worse. We've made the world criminals are thriving in and throw a few dollars at our messes when we overstep, or worse, when we become the very thing we claim to despise. Like Tooley did.*

Crawford didn't speak a word, feeling teeth ache on the verge of sprouting something far beyond words.

Only the response to those tortured thoughts came out loud. He didn't think of Govic, but rather Tooley. "I can clean up some mistakes. I've already done it once."

Beatie blew more smoke, flooding the Chevrolet. "That's the spirit, Crawford. Anytime you want to talk, my office is open. Get home and get some rest."

Crawford nodded stiffly. The car lurched again and Beatie froze. "What's this?" he asked with one foot on the side rail, peering over the seat. "Did you log this yet?"

Crawford turned and saw the crystal decanter he'd taken from Donovan's office.

"Even one illegal bottle is worth the effort. I'll take this and you can log it tomorrow," Beatie said helpfully. His long reach transferred the scotch under his arm. "Good work, agent Cain."

Christ the fucking Navigator in a leaky dinghy. Crawford ground his teeth. "Thank you, sir." The scotch left, taking the bear with it.

Crawford took a couple breaths. It was coming. He'd drank in small doses of scotch through the day but foolishly hadn't transferred any to his flask, which had just a swallow of whiskey.

Rank stinks of trash invaded from distant alleys and suspension rattled cars a block away. He wanted to crouch, sniff ground, find blood on the wind. He couldn't find a sympathetic ear now unless he went to Charlie and told him everything, but reason was unkind. Charlie would think him insane, unless he stayed around to see what afflicted Crawford happen again. Then Charlie might be dead.

He had a job to do. Focus would keep him aware, keep him from harming himself or others. That and a sip to clear his head.

His flask's last swallow of whiskey washed aspirin down. He started the car and rolled out.

The dusk drive was blurry, and Crawford cornered with a bit too much throttle at one point, bouncing a tire on one curb. A cop directing traffic flagged him and Crawford slowed, fumbling in his pocket after easing the throttle and flashing his badge. The cop laughed, shrugged blue-wooled shoulders and waved the wolf on with a wag. Prohees were close enough to cops to get the wink and nod. Most of the time.

Crawford's destination was at the outskirts of the Northwest part of town. He scouted the path in his headlamps for a telephone, spotting a booth in the shadow of a gas bar a block from where he'd stop.

He parked outside a large lot, saw the signs and understood Donovan Calvert's reluctance to send one of his own people here.

The building was a warehouse for United States Steel, one of Calvert's biggest competitors. Strange place for the last sighting of an elderly Irish squirrel.

The fence had a gate that parted just wide enough to slip through. Guard duty seemed absent but he had his excuses prepared if caught snooping. Liquor caches could be anywhere, and he could falsify a warrant in the event that he needed to prove a tip-off. Others on the department had done it before.

He gathered scents, finding little to sort through. The only light came from streetlamps outside the compound and the place looked abandoned. The warehouse itself was across a gravel lot with fractured machine parts strewn around, quality control rejects maybe. Tire furrows revealed where cars had come through.

The warehouse' loading door was cracked open, revealing a slit of dark. There were no smells of forges here, but his mind's eye recalled sparks raining down around silhouettes back at Calvert steel, ghosts of one steel mill invading another.

Inside skeletal racks stretched empty under high broken windows. He pulled scents apart. Stale dander lingered with fresh traces of effluvia that his nose sorted into recognizable species. Strongest was the corrupted miasma of flesh, scabbed and rank. It wasn't squirrel but rather weasel, or maybe raccoon. Blood had been shed.

He crouched and found that going to all fours was easier. The soiled floor surrendered traces of exertion from at least three species; feline, ungulate, and the creature who had been badly wounded. Claws stirred the warehouse floor's dirt; trace sweat, turned earth from scuffling. He spread in eccentric circles nosing back to one rack where he found a small item left behind.

Thick and clumsy claws collected a trinket, feeling strange contours before shoving it into his coat.

There was no trace of the Irish squirrel here, but he found where blood had soaked the earth. He couldn't trace which of the three species he'd detected spilled it. Best guess, it was likely the wounded creature. Scents parted as he roved outward again, the ungulate scent rubbed on a south side exit door propped an inch by a masonry fragment.

He peered out across the wide field where the lot terminated and checked lights on the close horizon. He saw tenements as well as a larger, wider building far off, a sign half buried by tall shrubbery that caught the barest sliver of moon. He made out the top line: NOAH'S PLANK.

A billboard sharing that horizon had a sophisticated otter lighting up a Player's Navy Cut cigarette. Crawford scanned the horizon as he made his way round, losing the ungulate scent. Back at the fence, he wandered past his car down the street on foot to the gas bar, swollen paw drawing out the metal totem in his pocket.

He glanced at the toy soldier in his palm and decided. In the light of the gas bar sign he entered the booth, fished out a nickel, gave the operator an exchange that he'd only used a few times, twice now this week.

Two rings later, tight panting breath on the line. "Hello?" Lucas's reedy voice was assertive, like cub's voices are when projecting the self-assuredness of grown-ups. "Who is calling?"

Crawford took a breath, couldn't find the right words, took another breath.

"Who is calling please?" Lucas asked again.

"It's me, Lucas. It's your father." The words almost put him out of breath.

"Dad?" Lucas jostled the phone's receiver. "Are you, are you coming home?"

Christ on a wet plank he didn't even know. "I…I'm sorry that I haven't been back to see you, Lucas. I've been working hard to…I just want to make sure I take care of you and there's lots of work for me to do here in Chicago."

"Mom says you aren't coming home." Not an accusation, but plaintive. Had Kamila told Lucas that what was to pass was Crawford's decision? That *he'd* decided to divorce *her?* Swollen knuckles ached around a receiver that was harder and harder to hold. She would never be that cruel. She just didn't know how to tell him anymore than Crawford did.

"I'm not. Not now." Silence was unbearably heavy. "Your mother and I, we have to work things out."

"I can get her Dad, if you want to talk—"

"No, you don't need to get her. I want to talk to you right now. Listen, I do love you son. I haven't been good at showing you that in all the time since I came back from France but…"

Lucas didn't fill the space that Crawford trailed into and he heard a heart on the point of fracture in the breathing through the phone. "Lucas your dad had things happen while he was in the war that were… confusing and I…I can't explain everything. Not yet."

He couldn't explain it to Kamila either. Time hadn't given him clarity. A ghost of memory stood outside the booth and fogged the window with disappointment.

"We don't want you to feel sad," Crawford said uselessly. "You're a good cub and don't deserve to be sad."

"When will you come home?" Lucas clipped his small words to make them demands, try to hide that he was crying. "Nothing here smells like you anymore."

The words were on Crawford's lips; *I want to come home right now.* "I'm sorry," he said instead. "I'm sorry that I haven't been the father you deserve. And you deserve better." His vision was starting to blur.

Tears were too late. He knew that much. He also knew why it was getting harder to talk. It was starting. "Lucas, tell your mother I called and that…I'll settle things. Tell her that."

"Settle things?" Lucas was confused and his voice wavered.

Crawford held up and studied the lead soldier in the Union blue jacket from the warehouse, bent musket skyward. Its muzzle was worn down to anonymity and Crawford couldn't tell what species it was supposed to represent.

"I'm sending some mail," Crawford said, his words thick, mouth losing power of speech. He was out of time. "I have to go."

"Dad?"

"I love you." Lucas' father hung up. He didn't curse or cry or scream. Another nickel, the operator took his exchange.

Donovan was on the line with him several hard wheezes later. The booth was smaller and somewhere a cub was confused and crying. Another day, another hurt.

"Yes," the rabbit said impatiently.

Crawford nearly hung up the phone but he wanted the spying, interrogating bastard out of his affairs. Misery bled into anger and Crawford spat his report out. "I don't have the squirreh, but I found some-ing yere, a toy solyer."

"What did you find, Mister Cain?"

"A oy solyer." The world was turning grey and red at once.

There was a moment as Donovan Calvert considered. "Moon's out. You're turning," the rabbit observed dryly. "You have minutes at most. Is your car there?"

Crawford turned back up the dark road, his spine being danced on by jackknives. "It ih neah."

"I'll take that for a yes. Get your coat, gun, badge and anything you found into the car, then lock it and place the key under the door flap. I'll obtain your exchange from the operator and send Edmond to collect it and yourself if possible. Move quickly."

"Mooh weah?" He thrust the toy into his pocket.

"Away from people. We don't want another incident. They're expensive to hide."

Behind the warehouse was a tall grassy field. Crawford wondered what things smelled like in there, if they were his if he marked them.

"Hang up and go. No more questions."

Crawford dropped the receiver, elevated hearing picking out the dings of the gas pump and questions Donovan put to the operator through the dangling earpiece. Claws furrowed the ground as he bound on all fours back to the Chevrolet.

He struggled out of his coat and slipped his holster from his expanding shoulders, flinging them hard enough to crack the car's opposite window. His badge was a shiny thing that slipped out to the floor. Where were the keys again? Keys?

His clothes were tight and itched and they came off, some buttons undone, the rest torn. The shiny ring of metal teeth fell and were kicked under the car as useless fabric fell away. The night breeze teased his flanks, loins and belly. The vaguest impression urged him to slam the metal den shut-*his* den!- and he pissed on a wheel and rubbed his flank on it before bounding under the white eye of the moon to the scent of grass and thistles. He howled against faceless cares as nature crowded. Small creeping things that were tasty and slow began to flee.

***

Charlie was tired but giddy, nose working dozens of scents that mingled in the cottage basement. A dress sashayed past his slacks and a slender white glove brushed his jacket's collar before playing with the petal of his bow tie. The husky tossed a rouge lipped kiss back at the brown wolf as Charlie's gaze followed curling tail and curves down to pads softly spreading on the heat-slicked floor. The paramour winked. Charlie followed.

It had taken some doing to get here but was worth it. At the northeast side by the old Chicago water tower he met friends who knew the words and signals. Tonight, orchids gained entry, or their scent at the very least, which Charlie rubbed on his bowtie at a florist while waiting for the daisies he would give away. The deep breath taken of his throat by the dachshund on the door was his passport and he left the flower for his "date" at the bar where he bought just one drink.

And then prowled for the next half hour, courting friends new and old in the secret joys they guarded. "I've seen you here before," the husky said when he joined her at the bar, voice an octave low enough to get his heart moving.

Charlie's short, brimmed pork pie settled on the bar. "Sorry I took too long to say hello."

"Buy us a drink?"

Charlie knew the caramel suit he wore, and the layered scents would help separate him from the mess that was his day job, but he played careful regardless. He couldn't recklessly mix the proclivities he was paid to suppress. "I'll buy you one." He did.

Her tongue worked the cherry dabbed in the brandy without ever extracting it. "Your kind of cute, like an enlisted sailor lost on land. Strapping but unsteady," she teased with a wink.

"Those blue eyes look ready to take me out to sea. Maybe I'm steadier than you think."

She extricated the cherry, rolled it front to back and swallowed before leaning in so his nose could pick out orchid over the musk. "They've got a Libby Holman record on upstairs. You can show me how steady you are."

"Sounds splendid," Charlie drank the husky's scent in and leaned in till their bodies touched through fabric. Under the husky's dress, a cock pressed hard against his thigh. Charlie held his sigh. "Lead the way."

His date rose and Charlie picked up his hat to follow. A grip on his arm stopped him. "Hi Charlie," said a reedy voice.

The wolf glanced back and it took a moment to recognize the squat tabby who had him. He felt his ears flush and turned back to the Husky. "I'll be right behind you. Just saying hi to somebody real quick."

The husky looked past him and chuffed. "Well, don't keep me waiting." Hips and tail stirred as slender padded feet ascended the stairs and Charlie had to shift his stance to keep his arousal hidden. He turned slowly and beckoned the tabby to a dark corner. He had to be sure. "Are you…"

"Not a word, Charles. Loose lips get up to dangerous things in here." The smile on the tabby's face was wide, yet guarded, as it should be. Louie Pederson was a police officer even less likely to turn up here than any cop or Federal agent whom Charlie ever crossed paths with.

"Are you here alone?" Charlie glanced around, heart hammering, searching the sea of gaiety for others who looked out of place.

"But of course I am," the cat's brows rose. "Where else do upstanding men in search of fun find themselves after such a harrowing week?" Charlie caught his scent and recognized the orchid's fragrance dotting his tie, his carefully coifed fur and the thin white cigarette holder that he set between his lips as he lit a smoke alight.

Charlie could have pinched himself. Louie wasn't just a cop, he was the son of a prominent member of the Committee of Fourteen, an off-shoot of the Anti-Saloon League who pushed for the onset of Prohibition. While the ASL attacked the vice of drinking, the Committee of Fourteen prosecuted prostitution and moral deviancy with merciless religious zeal. Charlie avoided making friends with members of Louie's circle for good reason. While no money changed hands for companionship in places like this, relations that were "unnatural" would ruin a mammal behind badge or public office.

An ingénue of mustelid persuasion passed and gazed at them both, long lashed over a fan. Louie smiled warmly and Charlie sheepishly. They waited till the crowd took her back. "I…" Charlie fought to keep from stammering, "I'm quite surprised to find you here."

The cat shrugged. "Our trade by day is indeed quite rough."

Charlie wanted to laugh. The anxiety that he felt building began to level off. Officer Pederson, decorated son of one of the country's most virulent enemies of sexual expression, was himself in the market. The wolf had so long explored his predilections alone, and one of those whom he was determined to hide from turned out to be a comrade. The knowledge almost made him giddy despite the sheer hypocrisy of the whole thing. "How long have you…been a horticultural lad?"

Louie shrugged. "About an hour. We've been keeping a close eye on the comings and goings of all the friends we're going to make here," his hands danced and claws came out and retracted.

Charlie didn't have a glass to raise but would have saluted. The singular whiskey he'd treated himself to was flowing and he was feeling looser. He didn't want the husky waiting but was too enamoured with his new fellow traveller to push away too fast. The cat hadn't ever been his type, even without his presumed antagonism, but a newly kindred spirit had an attraction all its own. "I guess when you only get a day a week."

The cat raised a brow. "One day a week? My friend we've been to three this week alone."

Louie was indeed a busy mammal. "We?"

Louie leaned in. "Of course 'we.' I've got a man on the door, and another by the bar. You won't see them, they're well embedded."

"Embedded?" Charlie immediately felt the stirrings of something amiss. Louie kept smiling, his teeth gleaming and his eyes alight with nothing carnal in any sense Charlie recognized. Officer Pederson leaned in so only Charlie could hear. "Team's outside. I see you've kept close to the register. You'll be moving on that first I expect. I just wish I'd been told you were here for a knock tonight. Fucking faggots are gonna get sixty days in workhouse for the citations we'll log tonight." Pitiless sadism lurked deep within that smile.

Charlie felt his mask clasp on faster than his heart could cave. When the cat's hot breath left his ear Charlie was all business, fear and loathing locked within the shell he'd crafted over years.

Officer Pederson's gaze connected with another across the room and passed a curt nod.

Charlie knew right away that he'd have time to save very few. "Word is there's more cash flow upstairs. Give me about a minute to get into position." The enthusiasm he had to project made him feel sick.

"Be quick," Pederson told him.

Charlie made his way up the stairs quickly, angry for all the quiet tender connections around him that would soon be torn asunder. The husky was waiting, drink refreshed, two cherries this time. Charlie led him to a curtained off area where they were alone, scoping out the distance to windows and remembering the path to the street.

"You keep a lady waiting at your peril but when you're cute enough to—"

"There's a place to buy drinks up here, right?"

"Well, you can buy me the next one but if you need—"

Charlie kissed him on the lips and broke off fast. "Shut up. We're about to get raided. I'm dead serious. You need to get that window there, lean outside to smoke this cigarette. Soon as you hear a commotion, you leap out and I pretend to chase you."

The husky's brows rose and the soft affect of femininity dropped. "How do you know that buster? My God, I have friends down there."

"I recognized two vice cops trading the nod. There's no time, I'm sorry."

"Can we go back to your place?"

The knowledge that Crawford would likely be there poured cold water on things. Charlie's answer was almost a sulk. "No. We have to move."

They had the night air on both their muzzles and smokes in their lips, sharing space with a goat and a lemur trading soft compliments in silken French, when the door broke in below. "Go!" Charlie, urged. With reflexes honed from countless nights like this, three bodies were down the ladder in seconds, more following.

Charlie turned, pulled his hat low and rushed through the perked revelers to reach behind the bar and shout at the bartender. "Grab the cash and run." He hurried back to the window, lie prepared. A celebrant had grabbed stacks of cash. He'd given chase only to lose them.

By the time he himself was at street level, four more had escaped and others above were being hauled back in. Charlie melted into the night.

An hour later, heartbroken and night thwarted he mounted the stairs to his and Crawford's apartment. His key was dejectedly raised to enter the lock of the apartment when the door opened and a muskrat marched out, toolbox in hand. "Congratulations to Mister Crawford Cain on his raffle win. The telephone is now installed. Please enjoy on behalf of the Bell Telephonics Company." The muskrat descended past him and marched out the front foyer into the night.

Charlie blinked away confusion and went in. Nothing was out of place, but the small table next to the living room chair now had a candlestick telephone with cord running back to a wall outlet. He approached it and lifted the receiver to hear the hum of electric life.

Down below an engine chugged a car away. Charlie set the receiver down, dejected. "Who installs a telephone at eleven o'clock at night?"

He made certain the front door was locked and added yet another question to the endless list he had for his partner before running the bath.

Chapter 15

It's Just Politics

"Congratulations, Alderman of ward forty-three, Richard Leicester. The education system will miss you but the city planning committee will be glad to have you." Donovan twisted the telephone's cord, weighing excitement against worry.

Richard laughed. "Lots of projects to get rolling. There are blueprints at city hall I suppose you'll need to see. Mayor Deever is all out for progress to take the public eye off crime in Chicago. I'll get word in his ear to push ahead with Union station and the canal. Many maintenance contracts will need supplying."

"I'll gladly provide, Dick. Hopefully your transition from the demands of education to the morass that is city hall goes smoothly."

"You have no idea how glad I am to hang up the ruler. Keeping goddam miscreants in line was a never-ending chore. I can't wait to put it behind me."

"Before you pack your things away, I must ask if you've seen Sandy?"

"Oh, her. No, she never came this evening. Is she ill?"

Donovan's anxious foot hammered the floor. "I'm not sure. Please leave word with your replacement to keep an eye out for her."

"The school doesn't have one yet. I pulled a minder off night watch which proved disastrous as one of the kids ran away last night. I hope they'll keep Sandy on but it's hard to recommend someone who disappears without word and leaves us short-handed."

Too few of Donovan's own people and the wolf Prohee only stretched so far. Making her disappearance into anything public would be disastrous. "So do I. She has family concerns that are somewhat private. Should you see her…."

"Of course, Donnie. The little buggers missed her."

"On other matters, please set a meeting for next week. I'd like to speak to the planning committee when it's assembled, as a concerned voter of course."

"We'll keep a chair warm."

Donovan ended the call as Edmond slipped in, eyes down. Donovan knew that he wouldn't like what he was to hear.

"The Countess lost our tail. Between her, Ms. Mallory, and Cain we are spread quite thin."

Edmond meant it. He was very rarely one to admit the limits of his own resourcefulness. "Any other news?" Donovan muttered through his teeth.

"Still no sign of Ms. Mallory. At this point I'd think she's either dead or doesn't want to be found."

Speculating the worst wasn't something Donovan needed help with. "Has the wolf turned up?"

The possum shook his head. "The telephone was installed at his home as directed. Evidence from his car confirms he's turned. Clothes were torn and..." The possum wrinkled his nose, "the car was urinated on."

"And you didn't go after him? Seeing as the mess we had to clean up nearly cost us his services before we secured them it's something you should have taken the initiative on, Edmond. I can't find out what he discovered at the warehouse if he's shot dead by a farmer or frightened citizen, can I?"

The possum's tail tried to hide itself even as his eyes narrowed.

"Cain's nose has answers to all the lies we've no doubt been told. I checked Keller's bindings myself after Mallory confined him. That raccoon did not *escape* Sandy's cottage. Even if he did then how did the Countess find out before any of us?" Donovan lifted his cane. "If she felt the raccoon through my snares around town then so would I."

The possum didn't know.

"I want Sandy found. I want the Countess found. I've been privy to none of her messages back East to the council. That I haven't had a cable yet is frankly maddening."

"That's because they are still deliberating," came a tired voice from the hallway. "And the council works on its own time, not yours."

Donovan leapt to his feet as the lioness pushed his study doors wide. Countess Von Haften was clearly perturbed, clearly harried. She had a smell drifting off her that he couldn't pick out.

Donovan's heart started pounding. "Leave us, Edmond." The possum complied, closing both doors. Donovan began pacing, unconcerned with how his fidgeting looked. "So many messages back to Europe. Why are any discussions being had without me, much less decisions made, Evelyn?"

She stalked past him and shuffled bottles around on the small bar before pouring a brandy. She seemed anxious, on the verge of exhaustion.

"Well?"

She swallowed, gazing at the rabbit as though he were a meal to follow. "The council approves your use of the steel for Nosfur detection. Congratulations. We'll of course be taking the formula back home to duplicate your results in Dublin, Rome, Barcelona, and any mill where we have a controlling interest. More than I thought when we actually got to counting them." She swallowed again. Glass empty, she poured another. "You are to be commended as a pioneer in advancing the cause and as a thanks I just might fuck you once more since you're clearly more pent up than I am." She said it flatly, as though her heart wasn't in it. "Right now, I'm tired. I'm going to bed."

"No! I need answers, Evelyn. What happened in that warehouse?"

Her groan was that of fool's being suffered. "I killed a monster. Did you forget why you needed your carpet replaced?" She lapped her brandy like water, closing her eyes while the last swallow went down. "This project of yours, to somehow tame the Nosfur as some form of docile citizen, will be recognized among the council of the Martyres of the Black Well as a heretical fool's errand doomed to failure."

"You're wrong, Evelyn. Ms. Mallory is loyal to a fault."

"The raccoon fed on a vagrant youth I had to kill to spare from further agony."

Had Crawford found evidence of that? The information Donovan lacked was maddening. "Even if Keller failed, Sandy wouldn't—"

"Sandy can do *nothing else, Donovan!*" Von Haften snapped. "I'm sick to death of reminding you."

"Mallory gave herself to my cause and abstained from the vein for years, Countess, endured pains you can't conceive of to prove her devotion."

The Countess set the empty glass down loudly, tail lashing, and hissed in disgust. "Devotion? Damn you Donovan, I'm sore, I'm tired and if you won't do what we sent you here to do then I'll see to it personally. The first ties have already been cut and the press will be making their discoveries very shortly."

Donovan felt cold "What discoveries? The steel? Damn you cat, what are you talking about?"

The Countess's rage fled at once. She took a deep breath having clearly said more than intended. "I'm going up to rest and don't want to be disturbed. Not at present, anyway."

"What have you done, Evelyn?" Donovan asked.

Countess Von Haften didn't answer and took the brandy with her when she stalked out.

***

Dick Leicester emptied his office desk by lamplight, visions of marble in mind. Marble floor for his claws to click on, marble arches to pass under, marble stairs to descend at day's end. He'd made it to city hall.

Fondness for teaching had atrophied over the years to the point where he'd grown sick of the enterprise. As he'd personally told teachers who'd washed out over the years, get out of anything you've lost passion for and fast. His wife had balked at his interest in politics, but the excitement of seeing a burgeoning city expand into something grander grew more exciting with each passing day. He had found purpose again.

Bad enough that building youth up from the dirt butted pedagogical heads up against hoodlums who wanted to cuss and slander. When the herbies started rolling in with voting initiatives things had gone to Hell. Kids that needed protection from bullying, kits that started fights amongst their own, lower-class imbeciles who wouldn't amount to anything now had the vote and would ruin the world for upstanding folk.

Dick took a drag off his cigarette, remembered that he'd packed his ashtray and stubbed it out on the worn wooden desk. Noah's Plank was a wreck of hand-me-down supplies and slip-shod facilities. Someday he'd sign the papers to spruce up this school or dynamite it and to the Devil's wet hell if he cared which. He'd be running for higher office in a year or two at most and wouldn't even remember this place.

DC was a day's drive away, marble halls and offices for miles. Dick's future was all marble. He'd cool his feet on the steps of Olympus itself soon enough.

Someone scrabbled at the door.

"Yes?" Night staff were few this late, only the sleepy hare custodian and himself. The presence at his door spoke no words, only scraped again.

"Come in." He closed his briefcase. No answer. "For Noah's sake, what is it?" He crossed and opened the office door and a body fell inward.

It was one of the students, the goat kid the staff had spent an entire day searching for. He gagged and wretched, shivering as he tried to push himself up. "Help," he managed to bleat. "Superintendent Leices…" the goat trailed off as he tried to push himself up. "Help me."

Drunk. Of course. The little shit had been truant for the day and was drunk as a saloon spittoon rat. Goddam typical herbie miscreant. Dick was late for his first round of drinks with two new aldermen colleagues he'd be sharing committee duties with, and he was going to have to pump this little bastard's stomach just to keep him alive.

"What did you get into son?" He made no move to touch the kid, wearing a new suit and refusing to get any stink on it. "Somebody sell you turpentine they claimed was top shelf 'shine? Probably cost a quarter you stole from your former squirrel-sitter."

"It hurts," The goat kid shuddered, rocked on his elbows and wretched. A spackle of mucous popped from his mouth and struck the Alderman's clawed foot, spittle running between his toes.

Disgust coiled Leicester's tail in a shudder as he danced on one foot, shaking the defiled one. "You stupid shit." He kicked out his wet claw and wiped it roughly on the kid's soiled shirt, shoving the runt on his side in the process. "I can't get out of this damn place without having to deal with your sub-mammalian nonsense. God give me patience."

"She said you could help…" the kid moaned, jaws opening and closing around his flat thick teeth.

"Who said such nonsense? Has Mallory turned up? Why didn't you just go to the janitor. I'm no longer superintendent, you stupid kid."

"She told me to see *you*," the kid coughed as he got his hooves under him, stammering through sobs. "She brought me...after the raccoon hurt me."

Spittle still slid between Dick's toes. He'd need to go to the lavatory to clean it and be twenty minutes late at least. His new colleagues would make note of that. "You did drink, didn't you? Ungulate little moron, if I never have to deal with you ever again..."

The kid teetered to his feet. Blood had dried on his blue school uniform shirt, speckling one shoulder. "I'm so hungry," he said, confused.

Dick growled as he stared the kid down "You goats eat any goddam thing. Why not ask your lady friend to—"

Leicester's voice froze in his throat. The ungulates eyes were wide open, but not open. They weren't there. Black wells of darkness gaped up at the basset hound that spoke of something the canine knew from pure instinct.

Ravening hunger.

The kid's mouth fell open. Slick white fangs slid into the gap.

And the kid was on him.

Pain erupted at the basset hound's right shoulder and ear, a fang puncturing the thin membrane to the collarbone underneath Dick's jacket. Fire filled his chest. The superintendent let out a reedy scream, clutching the boy's head and stubby horns as he stumbled back. Collision with the desk sent them both to the floor, blood welling hot. Dick Leicester smelled his life, copper as a ferryman's coin, slicking his fur as it erupted in the kid's throat. He cried weakly, head beating the old planks, senses reeling then muddling.

There was no cool marble beneath him, only panic's heat. Leicester slipped into cold as the goat kid's grip became iron, heat only at the point of the sup. All his dreams of a bountiful future slipped away with him.

***

Scents of revelry were bleeding out on mid-town from the middle floor of the south-side bawdy house, another den of prostitution under Torrio's control. Mike "Lefty" Carstairs smoked to disperse the brothel's invasive stink, his wolverine's nose being very sensitive, and waited for Torrio's men.

Two would be popping by for cash collection in an hour if the schedule passed through Dan O'Bannion's circle was accurate. There'd shortly be a cool fifty percent in his pocket and two dead dogs to send the message to Torrio that he wasn't the only game in town.

The violin case rested on the secretary desk by the locked door. Its steel and walnut contents could easily be assembled before Johnny's boys made it to the fourth floor. Lefty's record for prepping the tommy gun was forty seconds and the marks would be a minute on those stairs at least. Maybe more if they hit one of the sitting rooms to cop a feel on company time. Easy money.

Night wind rustled at the fur on Lefty's chest, whiskers shivering as he listened. The car he waited for would be noisy for the hurry they had to pretend to be in. With about an hour to wait giving him plenty of room to play with, he wasn't waiting alone.

Reddish furred arms wrapped around his tan abdomen from behind and slid the leather belt free before working the buttons of his pleated trousers. "You're well-dressed," the Irish squirrel said in a breezy Dublin lilt.

Mike reluctantly wondered in that moment if he'd wind up having to ace her. "Not for long."

She made an amused noise and kept going.

Lefty never drank before operating, preferring to get his blood pumping. Fortunately, this job put him somewhere he'd not run afoul of anybody's family this time. Last week's errand had been unpleasant. A husband walking in on his wife's dispatch—she'd worked for Dean O'Bannion and stepped way out of line—all that pointless running, the extra knife work O'Bannion wouldn't pay Mike for. Such a mess.

The cub hadn't seen much. Mike wondered for days after if he would have finished the child off in that case. He'd all but forgotten that overturned house and its anguished yowls. The cub would make it. Neighbors had to have heard.

He was glad for the chance to clear his head. His pants were now on the floor and his toes curled.

The squirrel's claws furrowed his back. "What's so funny?" she asked.

"Just mullin' what a funny thing life is."

"I'll give you something else to mull," the squirrel whispered, running hands round his shoulders, up his neck scruff. He wanted things to go faster But he didn't make her rush. One needed to take time with the finer things. A fuck now. A whiskey and cigar after Torrio's dogs were cold.

His claw reached behind him, found her flank and slipped digits under the lace. Strangely her pelt was cool, like she'd come out from an ice box. He found the deep crevice inside her unmentionables and—

And one set of fingers intercepted his. "You need the magic word, Lefty," she whispered in his ear and somehow that was cold too. "Wolverines know their manners."

If she held off too long, she'd be here to see him assemble his Thompson, not a good idea. If the climbing rodent wanted to fuck around… "Does a man who pays need manners? It's my nut you're getting." He turned, regarding her at last, imagining everything hidden in that slim dress. She probably had pink tits to go with that red fur, raw as steak tips.

She fingered at the dress strap, eying him up and down as she slipped it off. Damn, coy was sexy when done right. "You don't know what you're buying, but we can show you."

The door to the room opened, and a well-dressed fox slipped in. "We certainly can."

Mike's claws covered his bare tackle so rapidly he all but clawed himself. "Who the hell are you?"

The fox tipped the straw boater's cap tween his ears as he closed the door behind him. "Just a friend coming to see how you're faring?"

"Anybody knows better than to barge in while…" Mike studied the manic gaze in the fox's eye and realized he'd seen him before. "Wait, aren't you that Bucky guy? Word was Torrio…"

"Had me whacked?" A red eyebrow bobbed. "Why Mike, that's obviously not true. Better Angels of Johnny's nature took flight."

Mike realized that if he was made, it was red handed and red-cocked. Even with the vulpine fella looking him over naked, he still didn't feel his hard on-flagging.

The squirrel stepped gingerly away, and he saw her lean naked over the bed where Mike's jacket lay. Her tail was all the way up and he saw everything she had underneath. She'd been fully dressed just seconds ago, and now bent as though awaiting a gynecological exam.

"Well!" Bucky grinned. Something seemed wrong with his teeth. "It's warm in here isn't it, Sandy?"

"Hot as hell," she answered amiably as she rummaged and drew Lefty's small automatic from his inner pocket. Lefty tried to swallow but his throat was dry.

Bucky Cavali slipped his necktie loose and hastily doffed his jacket, tossing it into a corner.

"I hate messes, don't you, Mike?"

The wolverine's ears dropped. "What are you doing?"

Sandy massaged his shoulders again a blink later, impossibly, as though she'd always been behind him. "Look in the closet, Mike. We have a surprise in there, just for you." Cold wind on his neck, no breath, just air disturbed. His hackles rose with his rebellious cock.

The closet was next to the case that had his Thompson. He couldn't assemble the thing in time, but if he got the walnut stock out, he'd have a club that would out-fare claws. "Okay," he muttered and teetered from the pile of his pants past the open window with its breeze blown drapes.

The door was ajar and one hand fumbled for the catch on the violin case. Inside the closet, filling the whole bottom, was a large oaken barrel, top open, dark and deep.

"The thing about better angels," Bucky said into his ear, breathless breeze even colder than the squirrel's, "is that they need their better demons. But you know all about that, don't you Lefty?"

Lefty turned, hackles like ice and the fox was already naked, the squirrel and he shoulder to shoulder. Fangs large as coffin nails thrust below black wells that should have been eyes.

A red furred finger brushed the light-switch and darkness became intimate.

Much later consciousness stirred back from the syrup of confusion. Smells dug in, clammy wet brick and leather. Numb limbs complained in throbs.

Cold cement pushed away as Lefty was borne, no hoisted, up into a thread of greyish light that illuminated nothing.

The words he picked out made no sense. "Careful. What's leaked is lost."

Flesh broke and pain lanced out from his side under the ribs, but Mike could only moan. Pressure tightened around his neck. Steel fingers scraped shut.

Feet shuffled, claws clicking as forms without warmth crowded, varied scents of fur and skin had not a breath among them. "Put your feet up on the rail boys and girls. Any friend of Sandy's is a friend of mine," a familiar ghoul told the others.

The site of Mike's pain twisted, and the stink of copper rose. The shapes of hunched creatures resolved in outlines, queuing, salivating.

Mike turned once more as the steel pressed against him, no, he realized in a growing panic, within him. He blinked through the waking pain as a small glass was set on the bar and slid across to a waiting set of claws under dry but ravening fangs, copper essence to its brim.

A shape writhed close by, sharing the dark with him. Within the naked mass a mammalian eye blinked open, rolling aimlessly, finding Mike's.

Stark misery told him what he'd never wish to know.

"Sorry about the noise. New keg tonight." A rag stuffed Mike's whining mouth as life escaped, twist after twist.

***

Moonlight washed well-gnawed bones and hide. Pooled but stagnant water sated him.

There was more prey on the wind, but distant. Paws were cool as they dug the mud and the grass whipped his nose as he loped. He knew where the den was with its familiar scents. He wanted to rub and mark and curl into sleep. Stone underfoot was rough and a creature bundled in wool screamed as it dived for the dark. The wolf was already full.

Down ravines in the night, bright pockets of fire shone above and hoots echoed from hidden dens. He marked rot in the dark spaces he darted through and found the sheer summit that smelled of himself before scrabbling upward towards the hole he knew. He nosed his way in and found the soft space that creaked.

He smelled stinks of his pack mate and wanted to play for dominance. Instead, he fell asleep dreaming of muddy pits that smelled of death and strange relief. Desire touched fear that had no root, sense memories of roars from the skies and barks across bloody ground and warmth stolen from bodies against the cold. Darkness settled on the nightmare.

Crawford woke to ringing and fell off his bed. His eyes blurred open to the muddied carpet on his floor. He was back in his apartment.

Up too fast, he teetered and fell on his bed, smelling the deep soiled stink of his own pelt. He'd need another shower. In a panic he checked himself for blood. A few drops on his chest and his tongue caught the taste on his muzzle. Had he…?

He stumbled out of the room, indifferent to his nakedness. The ringing resumed. It was the bell of a telephone. It was still dark outside and Crawford realized that he was alone. The door was open to Charlie's empty room. The ringing resumed.

A thud below brought Crawford to gaze at his splayed toes, tracking mud across the main room where a candlestick telephone rested on the side table by the ashtray.

The thud came from the floor below. A gruff voice shouted up about tryin' a' sleep.

Crawford tucked tail and sat naked in the chair, eyes wandering to the scrawled note under the phone atop a proud new Ma Bell user's manual. On the note Charlie had scrawled, "When were you going to tell me?"

Crawford fumbled the ear receiver off the hook and lifted the phone in front of him. "Uh. Yes?"

"Did you kill anyone?" Donovan Calvert asked.

Crawford concentrated. "I don't think so."

"Did you find Sandy?"

"No. I didn't smell her at the warehouse. Just…" Crawford struggled to put sense memories back together. "A raccoon, wounded. Lion too. Female, in heat I think. Don't ask how I know, I just…also an ungulate. A ram or goat. There was blood spilled there."

"The first ties have already been cut…the press will be making their discoveries… she chose those words with such zeal."

"Who chose what?"

"I need you to go to Noah's Plank school. It's near the warehouse where you parked two hours ago. That's where Sandy Mallory taught evening classes."

Crawford glanced at the small clock ticking in the dark and realized he'd been changed for only a short time. That was good news, wasn't it? "How do I get back there? My car and clothes—"

"Are in front of your apartment. You may not have been in a state to notice. You always know the way back to your den."

"It was only a couple hours—"

"The moon was only out for a couple hours then was hidden by clouds. Likely with that and exhaustion you completed a cycle prematurely. We'll discuss all this later. Have a drink to stave off another change and get. To. That. School. Find Superintendent Dick Leicester. He's been sworn in as the new Aldermen for ward forty-three and is packing up his old office. I've rung him several times but can't get a connection so something's kept him there on the line. Bring him to me. Tell him I sent you."

Crawford looked down at his naked self and his muddy feet. "Why don't you have a guy there already?"

"Because if the Alderman is in danger, then you are the only one besides myself who can protect him. I am unavailable."

"Course you aren't. What about your squirrel?"

"We'll find Sandy Mallory in due time. Your automobile key is in your mailbox." Donovan hung up.

Getting his clothes up from the car was not a good bet while naked so Crawford threw on another shirt and slacks and got the key, taking the time for a quick couple swigs from the bottle Charlie had put back. He felt disgusting under clean clothes but there wasn't time for anything else.

It did occur to Crawford that continuously drinking to block the change might make it difficult to drive, but he felt better, as though changing and the short nap that followed had relieved him in some way. Fortunately, neither drinking nor changing into a feral cannibal before driving were strictly against the law. Currently.

The tiny marker gauge in his Chevy showed that whoever recovered his car had topped off the gasoline and his gun was in the glovebox. "Membership in the rich rabbit brigade has privileges," Crawford muttered, idly wondering where Charlie had been out to, tonight. He did remember him mentioning finding release of one sort or another and hoped he was having a good time.

The drive back to the school was fast in the dead of night, the city devoid of traffic. He counted only two cars in its lot. One Model T was on low springs and likely belonged to whoever kept the place up at night.

The other was a cream-colored Packard Twin six belonging to somebody higher up the chain. Cases in the rear seating were stuffed with office knick-knacks. He smelled dog around it, meaning it was likely Leicester's.

The school itself was two buildings joined by a short bricked in connection, one the classrooms, the other likely boarding for youth as Crawford had heard of the place before. It was a dumping ground for orphaned cubs and kits who weren't delinquent enough for juvenile workhouses but too difficult for regular public or religious schools to handle.

The main entrance was unlocked. Broom bristle scratches echoed down a deep hall from the custodian hard at work restoring the place for the morning rush of spitball throwers and bookworms.

Smells mixed, chalk-dust, lye soap and stray cub fur. Memories of his own scholastics prior to meeting Kamila floated back. He'd been one of the invisible cubs, doing well enough to keep grades from landing him a hiding, but never exceeding expectations.

He wondered if his son saw school the same way he had, just a cobble on the path to neither better nor worse. With a broken family, he had to think Lucas would strive to be a better mammal than his father.

Crawford put his musings to rest.

The Superintendent's office had to be above the tail-pulling rabble. He followed stale scents on his way up the stairs and Crawford kept the smells collected from that warehouse in mind, seeking just a hint.

Vegetation gave a particular class away, rot clutching a trash pail. Nose poked in, he detected the faint remains of several species, including a goat.

And a squirrel, he was sure of that. Days old scents faintly layered.

Back in the hall, two steps more caught something strong and rank.

Blood, and its worst companion, the sweat of fear.

He drew his '08, curled his toes to keep his claws from clicking as he crept past open doors demarking the school's administrative offices. Chalk dust gave way to ink and stray perfumes. The blood scent became a stench, speeding his heartbeat.

The door past the teacher's lounge had a tarnished superintendent placard and Crawford saw the telephone on an empty desk through the open door, receiver hissing free.

Crawford heard the whisper of a sob as he crept forward, gun slick in his grip.

Shoulder on the door, he pressed in, gun following the space that expanded, senses open wide.

A basset hound was on the office floor, sightless eyes skyward and surprised lips parted. Across the office, a small body shivered in a fetal position, horns and hooves nearly together. The goat cried; head hidden in hands clutching the pelt on his scalp.

He checked empty corners, as did his nose and ears. There was just the canine body and a kid.

"Are you okay?" Crawford lowered the gun and crept forward. The hound's body smelled warm. "Are they still here? The one who did this?"

An eye peered through fingers, terror stricken. He bleated in terror before closing the sight of the dead dog away.

Time was short, but Crawford didn't want the poor kid dying of shock. He covered the door while he made the same soothing noise he'd made for his own son after a bad tumble down a hill as an energetic toddler, sobbing whines and nursed knees. "It's okay. You're okay. I'm an officer of the law and I'm going to help you."

"He's dead," the goat kid groaned in a Scottish brogue. "He's dead. I'm sorry."

Fortunately, there was a telephone. The police would have to get out here and start combing the place. A murderer on the premises wouldn't spare the janitor if confronted. Crawford wondered after the children in the next building, all slumbering, all unaware of danger.

Donovan would want to know his crony was dead but the bastard could wait. "I'm getting you out of here," Crawford leaned back to the hall. Ghostly stillness stretched in both directions. Back in. "Calling friends, then we're getting you with your classmates and waiting with them."

"I don't want to hurt you."

Crawford froze. "What?"

"I didn't mean it. I was hungry. I didn't know why…"

Crawford glanced at Leicester's body, confused. Blood pooled round the head in speckles. Blunt trauma could have his head or neck broke, the surprise on his face lent to something rapid. Crawford glanced round for the culprit, a pipe, a knife, something to indicate whatever kind of wound was on the hound that Crawford couldn't see.

What didn't register properly were the substance of the goat's words. He couldn't have done this. He was a runt, barely belly high on the wolf and terrified.

I was hungry, he'd said.

"What's your name kid? I'm Crawford."

"Samson."

"Okay Samson. Did you hurt this dog?" The terror in the kid's shiver didn't add up to that. "Did he try to hurt you?"

The hands parted enough for the stubby kid's dry nose to poke upward. "He did. But I hurt him worse because they made me thirsty." His voice was thick.

"What made you thirsty, Samson?"

The kid's mouth opened as he sobbed again. His lips, no longer pressed together were crimson with blood. "I just...was." The fangs in his mouth shivered with him.

Crawford nearly fell over the hound's body pushing himself back against the desk. His heart pounded as the gun rose, then dropped again. "You're Nos..."

"What?"

"How long have you been like that?" It put ice around Crawford's heart to realize that the kid was more terrified of himself than he was.

The body of the basset hound easily outsized the kid five times over. But like a doe in her own raided domain...

The gun was warm in Crawford's grip. His gaze found the kid's eyes, met them, held them. "You didn't mean to do this, right?"

A sobbing headshake. The fangs were out like cutlery and wouldn't retreat, easily larger than Crawford's own. His natural ones, specifically.

"Look, I'm going to call someone who can help us, alright kid? It's somebody who knows what's been done to you."

"It was a raccoon. She watched him...drink. I went to sleep and I was in the dark. It was cold..."

Crawford felt his stomach churn. "A raccoon hurt you. That's okay, I can handle them. They still here?"

"She killed it." The boy closed his eyes, swallowed like he himself was going to wretch.

"Who did, Samson?"

"The lion."

Time to call the rabbit.

The phone toned in wait. He holstered his gun. Ma Bell picked up after a short spell. Crawford gave the exchange and virtually no time passed at all before Calvert answered, "Leicester?"

Crawford sighed. "He's dead."

The line crackled as Crawford watched the body cool and the kid cower. Calvert's voice became steel-beam heavy. "How did it happen?"

The kid gazed at something out the schoolmaster's window, starting to dissociate from where he was. Crawford had felt that very impulse to disconnect, long before coming to Chicago. Nobody ever wanted to shoot you for feeling that unless it prevented you from going over the trench into no-man's land at next whistle. Crawford realized where the lead soldier he'd found had come from.

"He was bit, by…A Nos—, look a kid got attacked too."

"Kid?"

"A goat boy, one of the students here. He has fangs now. He got scared…"

The kid listened but kept staring out the window. He had to know, somehow that his life as it had been was over. Killing did that, and realizing he'd been turned into something made for taking lives would be terrifying when it came.

"The goat kid has been turned and bit Leicester, drank his blood?" The question sounded clinical yet pained.

The outside brightened. Crawford hastily crossed to the window overlooking the parking lot and peered round the curtain's edge. Cars were arriving, lots of them, pulling in across the lot from his own Chevy and braking hard with headlamps blazing. Police spilled out of some cars and ran smack dab into press hats with cameras spilling out of others. Tails flashed as they moved to the building, squawking at each other.

Somebody had called them all at the same damn time. "Press just showed up, Chicago's finest too. Lots and lots of brass."

"No."

"What?" The kid had approached the basset hound corpse, was touching its brow, sobbing louder, coming to the then and there. The newly fanged killer faced his first meal.

"That dirty *cunt!*" Glass broke on Donovan's end.

"I've gotta get the kid out of here."

"No!" Donovan shouted then took his voice icy low. "You need to kill him."

Crawford watched mammalian shapes in trench-coats and brass mingle on the front steps below him. Muzzles angled up and he ducked back out of sight. "What?"

"Two in the head, then get the body out of there by whatever means available. He can't be found by the general public any more than you can." There was whispering from the possum. Donovan made a noise of assent. "Wrap your gun in a coat to muffle the sound."

Crawford watched the goat cry. The kid was now a weapon, unable to stop himself and with even fewer resources to fight his nature than Crawford had.

And he was in pain. Even with eyes growing as dark as coal, just like Celeste's had, Crawford could feel his misery.

The kid would do this again. It was inevitable.

Feet hammered on the stairs below, snarls from shoving came with it.

"Mister Cain."

"I know," Crawford was hollow as the gun cocked almost on its own. Back in the trenches again and again only one choice to make. Misery gripped him as reason left. "I know." He hung up.

Chapter 16

The Bargain

Celeste bound shadows through Chicago's core moving enclave to enclave. The sisters were nowhere to be found and she needed answers, fast.

Bucky was planning something reckless and something had brought Sandy to the brink of insanity. So many years care-free and loving, then five spent a willing, penitent slave, and now...what was she?

So many mysteries to unravel and too little time.

Slipping free from shadow for a moment, Celeste got her bearings at the end of a row of shops. She glanced at the dimly illuminated contents of a closed toy store window, festooned in curiosities. A range of dolls rested with glass eyes above painted fur and stubby limbs. One figure in a miniature wood-doweled chair caught Celeste's eye.

The tiny doe was serene, flat teeth carved in a smile. Memories stirred, misted by time. She'd had family once, prospects of a life planned for her by doting parents. She'd been expected to be a good wife, obey a husband, birth many fawns.

That hadn't come to pass. Bucky Cavali was her progeny now, her unintended legacy. Celeste had to know how Bucky had happened before seeing the fox and squirrel again. She had to confirm if the suspicion slowly forming was right.

And she knew what that truth would cost her.

Few places had what she needed, just a few enclaves the Sisters had touched, markers left by which they could be contacted by the desperate who knew of their power. Or those who sought to bargain.

The speak Celeste found, the second visited that night, was one of Chicago's oldest, deep underground, unmolested by Prohee pickaxes or police truncheons due to deep connections and payouts. "Sacristy," she said to the weasel through the slit, who politely blew pipe smoke upward when the door opened.

"You looking to pray?" He was wearing a non-descript dark coat, almost clerical.

"Loudly," Celeste said. A tiny chapel built in the disused church's basement had two supplicants in pews before an alter representing the eponymous Ark of Noah.

Behind it, confessional spaces for priest and sinner waited empty.

In the priest's booth, voices bled through cracks. A well-oiled door parted and prayers got louder down a short passage. Celeste entered Sacristy. The speakeasy was packed, booths cacophonous with sound. The ferret at the bar concocted gimlets, Manhattans, and even alcoholic egg creams, which the mustelids were all the rage for. Weasels comprised the better part of the boisterous business down here, smattered with felines and canines.

"What can I pour for you madam," the tender asked.

Delays stole nerve away. She slid a folded fifty. "The Sister's bonded. A double if you please."

He unfolded the smug leonine face of Ulysses Grant and his eyes met hers with trepidation. "If you're requesting what you appear to be, there would be no change returned."

"I know. I am."

He turned without another word and crouched, moving a few bottles to expose a lockbox he picked at. The bottle he extricated was unlabeled and dark as night. He worked the cork carefully.

"Am I the first?" Celeste was nervous but genuinely curious.

The ferret's eyes stayed down as hints of sugarcane and molasses rose with other less discernible scents. "I was told by my supplier that is the most confidential of questions."

"I see."

Celeste's money disappeared and two fingers of the dark concoction slid oily in a highballer before her. "You must not carry it away. You must drink it yourself on this spot. House rules." The weasel didn't blink.

"You mean their rules," Celeste said as she gingerly lifted the spirits high. There was little light in the basement to play off it but something stirred in the liquid's recesses.

The weasel backed away but did not take his eyes off the doe, even as money was waved by a cream-lipped mink growing impatient down the bar.

To delay was to draw attention. The last moment to pour the thing out passed in a flash as Celeste tipped her throat back and sweet velvet fire clung to tongue, then throat and was gone in four swallows. The aftertaste was a ghost of syrup and cinder, a hint of things to come.

She'd signed their contract now.

"I'm told that you'll...

"Not want to be here. I know." Celeste pushed away from the bar. Through the confessional she felt the first whispers in her mind, memories crept and scratched.

Chandeliers, mirrors, silver.

Too fast. She hurried through smoke and the night was still pregnant with distant, near feral hollers. The speaks were open wide, swallowing the thirsty.

"You can hear me." Celeste spoke aloud as she scaled a building's shadows to cloud-broken moonlight. Her new home was west of here but she doubted she'd make it. "I signed the contract. For what I give, you have to tell me where to find you tonight. There will be questions."

Restrained laughter was heard, here but not here. Guarded emotions bound the secrecy of a lost world in exile.

Two rooftops later, her sense of the present failed her. Celeste fell to her knees, gasping at the fire inside her, igniting all she'd buried away.

"That's the bargain," Celeste told the Chicago night sky.

"C'est le marché," the white-powdered stag said to the trim nervous elk, both standing in the Parisian parlour with its blinds drawn from the Revolution's prying eyes. Celeste held her breath in anticipation, her ears back as she watched her father and her husband-to-be transact. This moment, mere days after her twentieth birthday, had been long in coming.

The elk's eyes darted from Celeste's gaze to the window, then returned to hers, steady with yearning that he couldn't disguise. "You've registered me as Captain?" Pierre asked.

Jean Marc Val de Mot, doting father of two daughters and a cautious optimist in dark times, nodded succinctly as he raised his brandy in its simple cup. "Our last ship will be sold to the war effort against the British and Prussians at a patriotic discount to impress the Revolutionary council. Though the holdings in nobility of the Val de Mot family may find themselves appropriated by those who'd condemned our class, monies collected by this agreement ensure we have a foothold in what society is to come as…merchants." The word was awkward on his tongue, but Celeste's father had acquiesced to pragmatism at last. The purge could be escaped, their family name an acceptable sacrifice.

Celeste, growing impatient for the next matter at hand, felt excitement flower within her.

There was a commotion outside, and Celeste's younger sister Lavert rose from her mother's lap by the window, her porcelain doll waving in her tiny fingers. She'd been taught to speak in hushes. "I see fire, Mama."

All in the parlour froze and the elk swallowed, meeting Celeste's eyes once more. Only Celeste kept her eyes on Pierre rather than that window. Such a long dark road had followed them both from the gardens of Versailles where kisses and promises had been traded in earnest, through to the long stint in exile after the Bastille fell, the peasants revolted, and the blades fell on their feline King Louis and his Austrian bride, Antoinette.

Jean Marc set his glass down, crept to the window. "Jacobin sans culottes," he muttered evenly. "They are moving on."

Breath returned to every set of lungs, Celeste's included. Excited as she was, she'd learned well to fear the dangers that lurked outside. The Place de Revolution was a mere mile away and the scent of butchery stalked any open window.

Pierre, Celeste's hopeful husband to be, took a deep breath. "Have you decided upon our other business?" The elk cocked his head towards Celeste.

Jean Marc looked to his elder daughter and then the elk in waiting. A smile broke his lips and Celeste's heart melted. "My daughter's affections have been for none but you. I would be foolish to deny her a singular joy in these times. You both have my blessing."

Celeste gasped as joy descended like a jewel. Through the brambles of this Revolution's misery, happiness had found her at last.

"May I speak with my bride to be, Messiers de Mot? En prive,'" Pierre begged.

Father and mother traded telling looks. Madame Val de Mot smiled reluctantly. Her husband nodded his rack in assent. "You shall have your privacy."

They decamped to Celestes' private room in the cramped apartment, her hand clasping Pierre's warmly as they sealed the world away. Their lips found one another's in seconds, the young doe feeling his giddy joy like a storm's current.

There was something more in the air. "Such nerves, Pierre. I've not seen you thus since the hornbeams shaded us at Versailles." Her body tingled with giddy desire as she remembered Pierre's hands seeking her secrets out.

A thud from the apartment below started them both, and Pierre laughed nervously. He took her hands in his, turning them over in study. "I've long wished for this moment," he said with a flutter of joy.

And sadness. Celeste felt his warmth. "We've many moments to come."

Another thud, a shout. Commotion on the stairs.

"And not without cost," Pierre said, his voice catching as he raised her fingers to kiss them, overwhelmed with emotion. "I was compelled to make sacrifices."

The commotion beyond their walls thundered the floor. Something was wrong. "We all made sacrifices, Pierre. Whatever you have done to…" she trailed off as the outer apartment's door was struck. She heard her mother gasp and her sister cry out.

Pierre seized her, drawing her tight enough to steal her breath. "Celeste please forgive me," Pierre gasped, heart pounding. "The sans culottes took me! I negotiated…"

Wood splintered. Her mother screamed. Growls of denouncement filled the apartment. Celeste tried to pull herself away but Pierre held her fast. "I negotiated for your life! You are all that matters!"

Their door burst open. Cursing, blade-wielding mustelids, canines and raccoons flooded the room, seizing and dragging them apart.

"She is to be spared!" Pierre shrieked. "That's our arrangement!"

A club descended and broke Pierre's muzzle. He fell as claws clutched and tore at Celeste's dress. She was borne against kicking hooves through the destroyed parlour, past flashes of blood and cries of pain, down the stairs and into the dark of night.

She was fed to a fetid horse-drawn cart, the surrounding street filled with jeering creatures. Whips cracked and she was hauled by torchlight to a hovel where a dark cellar awaited.

A long night of aches surrendered to slats of light by cruel morning. Cries bled from the unseen plaza where denouncements went unintelligible. Screams were met by thundering cheers. Celeste's heart gained stone-like weight as moldering onions came as solidary sustenance. A day passed. Another.

Pleas for information of her family were rebuffed, her desperation increasing the baseness of her offerings. She offered the guard her bracelet and was compelled under rough hands to give it for nothing. Mangy dogs or raccoons came and she offered blessings, then a kiss for their favors. At the absolute depths of a week's despair, she offered one mutt a fondle. Under his cold touch and stinking tongue, she learned that her mother was nowhere to be found while her father was in the Place de la Revolution for the display of all. Nothing more was given.

Despair took hold, any dreams trampled.

And then the lynx came.

Night had her cell a moon's lick from darkness. Celeste did not sleep, merely existed. One blink saw emptiness beyond her cell and the next placed him there.

"Do you know how long you've been here?" His voice was evenly affected, the French of a minor aristocrat or a well-connected merchant. His dark attire and non-descript cap betwixt erect ear tufts left him classless in appearance. There was no scent, no specks of Parisian filth, no trace of the world upon him. He sat upon a chest amongst the flotsam beyond her bars, legs crossed in indifference.

Celeste's voice cracked, days unused. "No."

"Fourteen nights I have watched. And you have waited for me."

"Who are you?" If he were playing a game she did not care of its outcome.

"I am deliverance from pain by the means you will choose."

Celeste studied him. The lynx' pelt was cream above his dark vestments and she could make out a slivery face and hands. "The Jacobins have chosen the guillotine no doubt."

"They will choose nothing." Spoken with mild indifference.

Celeste sat up, wincing through an ache in her shoulder. "I don't understand."

The lynx's head was only partly occluded by shadow, but impossibly she could not discern his eyes. "You have but two fates precisely and will choose amongst them yourself," the lynx's raised fingers were devoid of callouses, pads thick as a bull tender's. "Hundreds languish in jails throughout Paris but none other have warranted this offer from me. Tomorrow night you will die, or tomorrow night you will live. Forever."

Celeste hobbled to her hooves, ears brushing the cell's damp ceiling. "You resemble an Egyptian Sphinx to bring such cruel riddles here. There is no way to live forever outside of God's grace. Are you a man of the cloth?"

The wan smile was so devoid of emotion it could have meant anything at all. "God's grace, as you would call it, helps one imagine eternal life. I supposed that's something for the thirty-five dragged to under the blade tomorrow." The lynx tilted his head in consideration. "If the rain holds back, it may be forty."

"Such cruel indifference. Doubtless the Jacobins keep water so scarce as to keep spit off their faces."

"I am not one of Robespierre's lot."

"Then who claims to give eternal life? Is this more revolutionary mythical grandstanding?"

"Answers will come in time. Concern yourself with the question as one resigned to fate. Die tomorrow or live eternally. The desperate cling to the latter, but you are not desperate, you are not in love, not in hate. Your only care is for the family you've lost."

"I have not yet lost them."

"You know you have. You feel it. Your mother went to the guillotine two days after you were taken. Your father went last Tuesday."

Celeste registered the words and realized that despair's pit was ever deeper. Never another warm embrace, doting advice on manners, no scents of lavender on pelt as they read letters in silence. All gone. Celeste was one with the stone beneath her. "I was told my father was stocked at the Place de la Revolution."

"His head is, for now. Time sent its birds." The veneer of pity was so thin as to be insulting.

"You're a cold bird aren't you, seeking misery for carrion."

"No." The lynx uncrossed his legs. "Were I so, there are cells to haunt where they wring with more misery than you."

"I've nothing to offer," Celeste muttered to the floor. "And only one thing left to negotiate for. My sister." She didn't dare make it a question, but her eyes rose to search out the lynx's. She didn't know if he had knowledge, or if he was simply lying to gain her favors. *Some villains traffic in the flesh...*

"She lives. But this Revolution is hungry. Every day, commoners by the dozens suspected of treason or sedition lose their lives. Last before dusk are the nobles, treats for the patient and bloodthirsty."

The lynx rose. As the moon was permitted to peer further under his cap, she saw his eyes were pools of night itself. Strangely, Celeste felt no fear.

The lynx smiled, and fangs glinted in his jaws. "While I can certainly appreciate thirsts for blood, one should be more discerning and far less cruel. That's what separates me from them, Celeste. I don't seek your misery. I'm no villain who traffics in flesh. I wish to bring you deliverance."

Celeste hadn't realized she'd stopped breathing until she failed in her attempt to speak. "You're no creature of God."

With a smile the fangs grew. "Nor of Satan. I'm no creature of class or creed or any fetter of modern craft. I simply am, and I seek to offer deliverance from this world's vainglorious struggles. The animals screeching out there all day seek one another's suffering for nourishment. Would but the act of their consumptions be a gift for those who are deserving...Imagine being fed upon and yet in doing so be fed. What a glorious upending of the natural order that would be."

"I don't understand."

"You will. If you choose it. The falling blade need not be your final intimacy. Think carefully on the possibilities of persisting far beyond all you know."

His fangs nearly touched the bars between them and Celeste realized that she'd been wholly unaware of his approach to the limits of her prison and her approach to his in kind. Her nose sorted his essence and the lynx had only one scent to offer, the faint aroma of fresh blood.

And no breath at all.

He closed his grey-flecked muzzle over the fangs which seemed to recede beneath his lips. "In anticipation of your decision, I will leave you with a gift."

He produced a white kerchief, wrapped loosely around something fitting neatly within his palm. Celeste accepted it and when his thick feline fingers touched hers, they were silky and cool. She unwrapped it slowly. A dark chunk of bread, enough to feed one for as much as a day, rested on the cloth. The scent off its crust was strong and slightly bitter.

"Hungry as you may be, do not eat this now. For this morsel represents me, a form of Eucharist in a way that will connect you to me when I return for you tomorrow night."

"If I don't eat it then?"

"Then you will die with far more dignity than they intend to allow you, a mercy I've bestowed to many."

Celeste pondered his words. What mercy even meant was a mystery in this pit of mortar and iron…Only one thing still mattered. "How do I rescue my sister?"

"I can help you find her. If you don't accept my offer, it won't matter for you to know where she is."

"Is she kept in a place like this?"

"Yes. And guarded."

"But not always. This place is not guarded if you are here."

The lynx's dark eyes widened over the smiling fence of fangs. "The dog who lied for your stolen favors won't see you again. They'll presume he deserted." He turned and the dark aspect of his clothes hid him entirely from sight. When Celeste saw his face again, he was at the cellar's solitary door. "I cannot save Lavert myself. Make your decision for yourself, not for her."

Celeste glanced down at the coal-dark lump of bread. She had no desire to die, and none to live either. Only her sister's fate concerned her and she did not press the point. "Two last questions before you go."

"Be quick," said a diminishing shadow with tufted ears.

"Pierre?" Even in saying the name she realized it was bitter on her tongue. His betrayal had drowned any faith in true love.

"He served his purpose to their Revolution. I suppose informants can't be trusted."

Celeste nodded, still feeling nothing. Years of yearning and hope, all gone to dust. "Why have you chosen me?"

The lynx had already vanished. The voice was like a breath, almost imagined. "Because you have surrendered desperation and released all pretentions. Life and death are but abstractions, a lesson I can't teach the most willing student. That makes you pure to me."

And he was gone.

Celeste wrapped up the bread, ignored the sighing of her empty belly. The lynx was wrong. Her sister Lavert was no abstraction, even in despair that disdained grief.

She wondered if Lavert still had her doll, or if they'd taken it from her in cruelty.

Celeste didn't sleep, didn't need to. Later in the day a guard brought her moldy oats and putrid water. Later still, claws echoed on stone as three brass-buckled Sans Culotte arrayed before her cell. The marmot between two partisan cats unfolded the scroll with slow ceremony and cleared her throat. "The Committee of Public safety has found you, Celeste Val de Mot, guilty of crimes against liberty and the inviolate rights of mammals under the Supreme Being. In three days hence you shall be taken from this place…"

Celeste's attention wandered. Mention was made of decapitation, the glory of the revolution and the wish that the Supreme Being, whatever that was, would spare her from removal from his brilliance for her many seditions.

They asked if she had any statement to make in her defence.

Celeste sighed and replied from honesty. "Que l'enfer dans lequel tu te noies soit la propre pisse du diable."

The marmot's whiskers drooped and his escorts merely blinked. The scroll flapped unrolled as they left her.

Dusk was an hour away. The revolution had countless more scrolls to unroll. Cubs, kits, and fawns were killed indiscriminately. She knew this.

The bread was appropriately bitter. Cold disdain for all she could imagine would be sinful if her expression of resistance were in any way sweet.

She was no fool. The lynx's promise could be nothing more than the cruel gambit of a sadist who sought to quash her last spark, laughing at the foot of her guillotine as the blade fell. 'See,' he would jeer, 'you yet had hope to crush.'

Celeste didn't care. Even a failed gambit to free her sister was better than none at all. If it failed, she'd barely feel fate's cruel design unfold.

So, she finished every crumb, chasing some on the cobbles like a voracious bird. Celeste waited for the dark.

He arrived with it, a presence at the cellar's window, then the lynx stood before her, the cell's door having never once opened. He wore the same clothes as the prior night and his eyes were black as the silk of his doublet. "You chose."

Celeste only waited.

There was a flutter at her shoulder, her fur at the neck disturbed by the brush of a feline nose as he was behind her in a blink. No breath from the nostrils, nor from the opening mouth. Something sharper caressed her shoulder. "There will be only the briefest pain. Time will slow before it stops for you."

Celeste felt her heart fluttering at his touch, hands wrapped possessively around her waist. One of her long ears brushed his.

"Are you afraid?" he asked.

She responded with her hand over his. If this was to be an end, she would embrace it.

Twin lances of fire kissed her throat and she gasped as his arms crossed her chest, gripping her tight. Light speckled her vision as every nerve danced within.

Warmth trickled on her shoulder blade making her realize. The lynx had sunk his fangs into her and was drawing her blood, drinking it as Bordeaux from a pricked wineskin.

Celeste tried to cry out but couldn't. She tried to push his hands away but found his grip solid as marble.

As she bled into the lynx' mouth she heard him swallow, mewling in appreciation. Dread shivered through her as the nectar of her life was consumed in greedy gulps, the pins and needles of sensation's flight already receding, slipping her beneath the lapping waves of sleep's pull. She was going to die after all. He'd lied.

But, oh, such gentle passage. Pain had fled along with the rudest language of the nerves, leaving only the glow that accompanied the aftermath of peaceful sleep or rigorous coitus. Was that what this was? A carnal ending to existence? So many worse ways to exit this world to whatever suffering or succor awaited beyond. Celeste felt she could count the swallows between her and the black veil of death. Her shallow breaths slowed in tempo.

Her ruined dress acquiesced to the lynx's fondling and her breast slipped free. A velvet paw cupped her, fingered her areola, finding a spark of final excitement as his fangs receded. Celeste slipped away with a stir from lips to loins and realized that death itself could love her.

Oblivion folded round. A voice found Celeste's last breath. "A world in darkness will be your sweet thicket of repose."

And it was.

The stones were the first new thing she felt, cool and glinting back moonlight. Squeaks in the fresh dark attested to vermin about her and Celeste could almost count the whiskers the tiny creatures tugged and groomed.

She rose effortlessly from the darkest corner. No aches troubled her limbs. Her eyes opened and night's details put day's to shame. A guard slept beyond the cell; a Jacobin hare's body buzzed with life. His breath was a bellows, his shifting a cacophony, the rushing circulation of his heart a babbling fountain pushing in and out of his center.

"You know what to do," a familiar voice coaxed. "He wants to give himself to you. Under the right circumstances they all do."

Celeste was hungry. Her teeth felt nothing until they hurt for the briefest moment, then cool air made her wince.

Instinctively, she forced her lips closed before calling out. "Wake up. I've something to give you."

The hare cracked open an eye and regarded her balefully, half aware. "What?"

"I have a treasure, one that will release you from obligation forever. You'll be a hero to the revolution. The key is on my person." How easy a lie comes when another yearns for its truth.

One of the hare's feet scratched the other leg as he shuffled off a trunk to the cellar floor. He crawled tiredly on his knees to the bars that Celeste sat back from. "Give me this key and I can give you a draught for when they cut your bourgeois head off. It'll hurt a lot less."

"I'd like that," Celeste replied and leaned out with her palm closed. The grasping hand that came her way was clumsy, fur mangy over the river of life underneath.

Hunger granted her speed. In a mere second the hare's arm, shoulder, and whole head had been pulled through the bars with meagre resistance. The flesh of his elbow was like cake, the current underneath erupting under virgin fangs that washed her lips, throat and breasts. Her decrepit dress soaked, her first meal messy as a newborn fawn.

The hare was long limp when she stood again, a mere twitch in one leg his last glint of life. The whole of her dark world came truly alive.

"Bon soir, Celeste," said the Lynx as he worked key in lock and dragged the door open. "Forever it is."

Light of hoof, she escaped with him neither losing nor missing a single breath. Faster than wind they ascended to the roof and with quick tears at her nourished frame Celeste shed herself of the last skin of the rotted nobility she'd been bred from, watched the dress carried in the spring breeze across scabrous Parisian shingles, down into the night.

She stood proudly naked and bathed in the pale blessing of the moon. Blood flowing through her veins made every strand of fur invigorated, every bared aspect of sense and sex alive. She felt the earth turn, teeming with life of the world beneath. The lynx in his demure vestments vicariously watched her drink in the fullness of it all, proud and patient.

At long last, the Lynx was at her side and whispered within her ear. "I have long sought one who could see the world anew for me, show me joy again. We will dine on that joy together."

"Dine?" Celeste didn't breathe her now useless lungs but felt herself taken away when trying to speak.

"You will see. Come, I'll show you all the ways in which to dance."

With light hooves and engorged heart Celeste fled Paris with the lynx and lit for the forests around Le Roule to the North. Feral animals spoke in dialects lost, trees groaned secrets and insects hissed symphonies. The Lynx at last gave his name as Ferrault.

He showed her the binding of shadows, explained the bending of wills, and the defiance of gravity's sluggish grip. As dawn's lid approached Ferrault imparted the cost of their wager. "The sun will harm us and the night will nourish us. We must go to ground at caves I've prepared."

Celeste, at the tailing of her blood drunken revelry, realized that she'd spent the whole of her first night as a child of the dark stark naked as a feral beast. "We can't be in the sun? I need to find clothes if we're to sleep."

"I'll keep you in comfort," promised Ferrault, and brought her to the cave he'd bedded down in purest darkness. There were stolen linens that Celeste wrapped around herself as though she were a newborn to be swaddled. Something tickled Celeste's mind as she settled into her first oblivion but failed to resolve its import before her eyes closed.

Consciousness stirred her with the scent of blood, dried in speckles on her own chest. She was hungry again, but with less urgency. The lynx was pressed behind her, body cold but comforting in proximity. "Shall I show you more of your new world?"

He'd obtained clothes for her that fit more loosely than any of the garments she'd partaken as a noble woman. She felt free of limb as they darted through small hamlets, sampling the scents of sleeping villagers. They fell across a tavern on the outskirts of Charrone, leaping to a gable where mutterings around drink could be heard from the groaning, farting creatures within. Celeste listened with piqued interest. News had reached the town of a noblewoman's escape, having employed demonic means to slay her guard. Celeste knew that she was being spoken of and was amused.

Yet also confused. Something weighed upon her mind, a need subdued in memory. The transition of flesh from decaying cage to resilient vessel had shed so many inhibitions, brought so many possibilities to the fore, but some tug of mortal concern nudged at her. The spell of her abandoned cares confounded it.

Hunger was the root of that fog. She needed to assuage it.

"Remember what I told you," Ferrault whispered from the shadow adjacent hers. "We tread lightest when we tread fast."

A weasel bustled out to a ditch designated by stink as a place for relief and fumbled at trousers soiled at the knee, muttering fragments of song about Marie Antoinette and Austrian brothels.

Ferrault was beneficent. "We'll let him depart this world in exquisite peace."

They snatched him away and held him through the short ordeal, struggles fading with the drum of his heart. They left him on a high roof for the crows to greet.

With senses freshly attuned, Celeste listened to the tavern's rabble, now one voice short. "They've decided," said one to another. "No ending the days with nobles after the deer escaped. They're sending them all to perdition within the week. They'll be down to just thieves by month's end." The reply came obligatorily. "Supreme Being bless the Revolution." This was repeated, loudly by rote, lest the softest voice draw suspicion.

With blood's intoxication at its peak, the hoots of partisans became mere noise once again.

Yet some concern persisted. Out in the dark, with the moon hidden and trees bowing under autumn's weight, Celeste gave voice to it. "Something just beyond reach calls to me. I can't put word to it, but I feel something essential escapes my notice."

Ferrault chuckled. "My dear, the doors to the farthest paradise are open wide. Nothing important escapes you. I have done my best to ease you into this higher plane of existence by cleansing your fears away. I want as much joy for you as for myself."

Celeste could read reluctance drip from his words. "What fears have you taken?"

Her slender hands disappeared in his thick furred digits. "Trifling pains and regrets you needn't carry any longer. So long I've waited for a spark against which to flint hundreds of years of wondrous joys." His fangs crept and receded. "You and I will know them intimately." He crept forth on the tree's branch, the world a bed of black below. His lips hovered around hers. "Forget all that came before rebirth, Celeste. You had no one who didn't betray you and are due so much more."

Betrayed. She'd been betrayed. She closed her eyes a moment, delving inward. The cell, the streets, the jeers.

"Celeste, come now."

The filth caked floor, the bitter bread, and before her terrors…

"Do not ruminate. I've striven so hard to save you from pain. Heaven bears no foul memories, and this is heaven. With me. Don't you see?"

But memories tumbled down through the haze of her blood flush. The elk who loved her until he betrayed her, the elderly nobles doting on her, the only legacy that mattered. Pikes in the air, clubs down on her mother's shoulders, her father's back.

"I can only take the pain away once, Celeste."

The apartment in Paris was crammed with fragments of life, worn from too many hurried flights.

Pleas from Ferrault became a growl. "Don't start this life with regrets. *Listen* to me."

The fine bone china, bolts of cloth cut for marriage. The tiny equine doll crammed in the tiny hands of a shivering, anxious fawn.

"Lavert!"

Balance left as though drawn like a rug and Celeste tumbled, twisting. Her shoulder struck a lower branch sending cold fire through her body and the ground met her back in a sickening rending of flesh. Pain flared like a burning lance.

Celeste cried out in desperation, unable to move.

The lynx settled to the ground as a dry leaf and kneeled before her, brimming with disappointment. "Look what you've done. I'd literally taken the knowledge of the world's evils back out of your belly and returned it to the garden's serpent. So few like us can bestow the gift you've scorned."

Celeste couldn't feel her legs, her airless gasps sending echoes through her body. "I am dying again."

"No. It will cause you pain, but your frame will be rapidly restored. Sadly, your essence, oh Celeste, tainted again with the worst of knowledge for all your days." Ferrault pouted as though a grand masterpiece been spoiled.

"You promised you would help me find her." Celeste hissed as she tried to roll over. "Where is she?"

"I told you that you could if you put your will to it. But that was another doe's blood, another life's toil. I freed you of that world's pains. Or I tried to."

"No. No!" The shout's affect was a bayonet stirring her ruined guts. Fingers of cold worked through her back and hips and shoulder, ministering mercilessly at tendons and bones. "I need to find her."

"You cannot move, Celeste. You will take hours to fully heal and you will be perfect again but you cannot find her. You haven't the skill of persuasion that I have to coax an honest answer. And it is already too late."

The forest floor itself held Celeste with shackles of despair. "You don't know that."

"Didn't we both hear that your escape prompted the moving of nobles to the front of the charnel line?"

"She is but a child!"

"Revolutions themselves are children, self-assured, hungry, violent. You know this. I told you plainly and openly that I could save only you, that only you were fit for this choice because you had the strength to let go of all that came before. That is why I chose you. Oh, what are you doing?"

Celeste's spine snapped when she forced herself up with all her remaining strength, agony spreading hoof to fingertip. She screamed.

The lynx made no move, cocking his head. "You're making it hurt worse. You can't hurry this, Celeste. Mind this lesson."

"I want no more lessons. I want my sister, here, alive. You must recover her." Each word was chewed from agony.

"That is what you want?"

Celeste met his gaze with hope and fury and threat in one glance.

"Very well. I must get you to our place of rest first. You've lifted the ears of ferals for miles. Being devoured over days while eternally conscious is a most undesirable fate."

"There's no time." She screamed again as Ferrault bodily raised her without effort.

"We have nothing but time."

Celeste had no strength to object and bade him hurry with hisses. They were at Ferrault's cave in mere minutes, and he lay her prone upon their blankets before departing. Celeste could only stare at the stone ceiling, conjuring horrors in its shadows. Guilt was the most relentless pain as an hour passed in misery.

She had to act. Rising from the stone floor was a lance of punitive agony but Celeste felt sensation returning to her fingers and toes, her pains resounding. She stumbled and fell many times in the dark as she hobbled, steps becoming steadier as agony settled to dull fire.

Paris was miles away. Binding shadows as Ferrault had taught her was difficult while injured but she made her way through the pain, past the gates, past taverns where huddled masses feared Austrian or English spies, or monarchists rotting the country from within. Fear stank potently.

On two occasions her control slipped, and she found herself in the corner of a nocturnal Parisian's vision. She realized she could literally search for her sister forever, a fleeting ghost haunting shadows night after night, keening after the last branch of a family tree cut to the stump.

Her dread could only be confronted in one place. The lists would be posted in the Place de la Revolution in the dark heart of Paris. The Sienne blew its stink east and with it the faint but potent traces of coagulated blood, an open-air abattoir for revenge against decrepit nobility.

The guillotine stood at its center, bare against the elements. The monolith cast a dark shadow across the cobbles and within that shadow, a stirring.

"I told you to wait." Ferrault slipped free and stood in the guillotine's wake.

"Have you found her?"

"I found them all. All dead but one, kept in stocks. I warned you Celeste. You could have left that life behind you. You've done this to yourself."

Celeste's heart was still but she felt it catch regardless, the numbness of her wounds receded. "One alive. Lavert was last. She was last. Show me!"

Under the clear moon there were few shadows to bind and Ferrault's tufted ears parted in consternation as he raised a hand, indicating a long plinth at the square's distant edge. Pikes erected fell back into shadow, each one topped by horrors.

Limping, Celeste crossed the plaza, terrified by that which resolved in shadow. The plinths bore periodic stakes bearing lists and behind them pikes bore severed heads in various states of corruption, some gaping as though alive, some eyeless and ears fallen, the oldest russet stained skulls with patches of pelt. Insects buzzed around the gore sloughed below them. From plinth to plinth, she passed the anonymous expressions of death. Beyond them, in the dark shadow of the wall, prone live figures in stocks writhed, muzzles twisting and fingers clutching, forced to reside in the midst of the gore's relentless stink. "Lavert. *Lavert.*"

"Keep your voice down. La Place has guards." The voice at her shoulder scolded. "They are there," Ferrault indicated reluctantly.

And Celeste found what remained of her father and mother.

Her father was recognized by the rack that had crowned him, or the half that still remained. The pelt-flayed skull twisted to the side on the remaining branch's weight. Mere inches away, Celeste's mother grinned liplessly, eyes sunken as though in disappointment.

And next to her…

The voice at her shoulder was slight. "I tried to warn you." The whiskers of Ferrault flitted in her peripheral vision.

The severed head of Lavert was a doll's visage, blank and thoughtless. Her eyes were mercifully closed but her tongue lolled from a gaping mouth. A cry, a plea, her last uttered sound was lost to history.

Celeste had no power to scream, her voice a frail keen as her heart was pierced by ice. She tried to remember what Lavert's laughter sounded like, but grief buried it. "You said one was left alive," she finally managed to stammer.

The voice that replied came from the dark behind the stakes, a shape awoke and writhed, pilloried in the stink. "Celeste. God in heaven, Celeste."

Behind the arrayed heads of her family, the muzzle of Pierre rose, nose clenched against the stink, eyes gritted from dried tears. "My love, please. Free me. The guards have moved on and they beat me, my love, they beat me." He cried anew, clenching his teeth.

"I warned you," Ferrault said again. "But here you came, and here he is. Your last tie to a life best left behind you. I tried to save you this pain. I tried so hard."

"Who is…" Pierre winced at unseen bruises. "Please. We've little time."

"Yes," Ferrault growled. "That's indeed true, Celeste. It's up to you to save him."

Celeste stood still, hollow as a burned husk awaiting the final gust of wind. Pierre writhed in his stocks, the elk she'd promised her heart.

And his legacy between them.

She stepped upon the plinth, her hoof setting into the dried ichor of her family's spent life. "You negotiated for me, Pierre. You knew they were coming for us and you bartered for me."

Pierre broke down in tears, the wood creaking as his whole body shook, in shock's wake, relief of a lost lover found once again. "I did, Celeste. I begged and cajoled them. For you, all for you."

Celeste could smell his bitter breath as her muzzle came to his. In his eyes, she saw the hot morsel of love's hope.

Her lips brushed his, and then past them. "And all you had to trade away for that which was precious to you was my infant sister's sweet life."

Her fangs sprouted with a speed that hurt and she dug savagely, pitilessly. A gasp escaped Pierre's throat, then another as the elk bucked in his bonds, hooves scrabbling uselessly. She twisted and they came eye to eye, his white and bulging, her's inky as night. He saw just enough. Pierre left his disgusting stolen existence in terror and Celeste drank until he shivered to stillness.

Stepping back, teetering on a fresh rush of mortal life, her own heartbeat in living pain once more. She was still unable to weep as she kissed the cold forehead of her sister and closed her mother's eyes.

A long time later, she stepped away. A goodbye was impossible, as was any indifferent God's grace. She turned back to the lynx.

Sympathy painted him like a doll, disdainful in its falsity. "The guards will be round soon. May we go?"

She struck Ferrault as hard as she could and the lynx flew back as though a rag discarded, skidding on the cobbles.

"You did this," Celeste hissed, fangs erupted. "You killed my sister."

The lynx sat up, fangs bared. "I told you that you could only save yourself and you did. You ascended! You didn't *need* them anymore." He all but screamed as though scolding a fool.

"Damn you!"

"Damn yourself. I gave you something better than life."

"I didn't want this. I wanted my family free, my sister free!"

The lynx leapt to his feet at preternatural speed and his thick tail lashed. "I don't care what you want, you stupid fawn. You arrogant, noble-born ungrateful slut! There is no freedom in *this* world, not for nobles, not for peasants, only wants of the heart and flesh and their due satisfaction. Even those who presume themselves free are bound like slaves to spectacles like *this* in order to stave off stockades and execution. There is only death through pain or what I offer, *no other way.*"

She hissed with Pierre's blood on her lips, and the taste of something else, sweet and familiar. "I didn't want this."

"You were ready to see the world with me and drink its finest veins and live uninhibited as gods through one another's joy. *That's* what you should have wanted."

"Lavert was everything to me."

The square behind Ferrault was like a night's sky, stars weak from unseen light. "Then why was she so easy to forget? This was always her fate as it was always your father's and mother's fate. Letting them go took the barest whisper. It was your strength to recognize that."

"I never want to see you again." Celeste cried and the blood that stained her cheeks were hot rivers of hate. "I'll kill you if I do."

A smile touched the lips of the lynx, who was already slipping into the guillotine's shadow. "A few dozen years roaming this world alone will help you see differently, perhaps longer. I've patience enough."

The stink of something rank and foreign, not of the body but of industry, filled Celeste's nostrils as the Place de la Revolution drifted away. "A hundred won't make you any less than hateful to me."

She rolled over.

The stink of tar drifted across a roof in Chicago, Illinois.

She regained awareness of place and time.

Her family had died a hundred and thirty years ago, dust long distributed. But the Sisters, they were here now.

"Tell me where to find you. You have what you wanted, you infernal water rat and decrepit bitches. Now!"

Senses congealed. Celeste smelled filthy water rolling under low docks in her mind, glimpsed a statue of Abraham Lincoln she'd passed many a time standing within a thin copse of wind-tipped trees. For a moment her mind lost focus and she remembered the woods outside Paris, the naked dance of first drink, the horrible power of newborn thirst and regrets weighing a century.

The Sisters now had those experience as their own and the wounds were raw again as on the day she'd fled. Betraying lovers, betrayed Kin, chasms of grief without depth.

Celeste rose and hurried to Grant Park by the lake, binding shadows at ground level, passing clocks in the display window at Marshall Field and Company. A mere few dozen minutes had passed in which she'd relived weeks.

She was lucky for the time's passage within the dream, or she'd have woken up screaming in Chicago's flaming daylight. It infuriated her to know that in the grand scheme of bargains accepted, that would have been her problem.

With the fog of strong drink and the ghostly memory of all she'd sought to forget, Celeste arrived at the designated place. They were waiting.

"Payment accepted."

"Honesty elected."

"The truth's guess makes ruthless the fox you've rejected."

Celeste stamped a hoof. "I've no time for your stupid limericks. I didn't turn Bucky Cavali. I tried to kill him as Johnny Torrio wanted. Now I'm out of a job and the fox is going to wreak havoc of some sort, I can feel it. How did he come about?"

The sisters traded knowing looks. "The black bread was bitter," Baliosi smiled.

"The drink ain't no quitter," Leguna raised a brow.

"Sandy 'ready told you that rabbit's a hitter."

Celeste flicked her ears in irritation. Even having taken her memory in coin they had to play with her. "Sandy told me that the rabbit steel manufacturer tried to make her create one of us and she said that one needed herbs to help the process. I remember the black bread Ferrault gave me a hundred and thirty years ago and thought that was symbolic-The bastard had a Christ complex if anyone did. Now I see that it was for a purpose, substances in the blood prevent death and bring about the change but I never baked Bucky anything before I bit him!"

Celeste tried desperately to unscramble the night she'd killed Bucky in memory. They hadn't eaten at the speak, nor after when they'd taken their detour to see the sisters together.

Other than Bucky's blood, Celeste had only sampled one thing that night. The bathtub Gin she'd feared was the very elixir she'd elected to take tonight, but clearly hadn't been.

And it had been absolutely cloying with Juniper. "Soak a couple boards or somethin' makes em think it's whiskey. Isn't that what you usually make?" Bucky had said.

The Sisters were still.

"You did this." Celeste said. "You gave me the balance of herbs to start the change. You knew I was supposed to kill Bucky, and you drugged him with the herbs to make him like me instead." The city's noise was a white rush behind her. She'd been too full to drink all of him, only to the half. "Why would you do that? How *dare* you do that?"

Grisand smiled, the otter's teeth crooked and unsympathetic. "There are bigger wheels turning than you, mon Cher, bigger than all of us. You only see where one spoke meets the rubber."

"What is that supposed to mean?"

Leguna took a step forward and the old coyote raised her hand in supplication. "A dead dog won the election."

Grisland nodded. "And these shores will soon need protection."

Baliosi took a long thoughtful moment before providing her coda. "So you gather together, with another who weathers threats of the old world's selection."

"The more you talk the less sense you make and I'm sick of this idiocy. You had no right to force me to bring a Nosfur unto the world, especially a vicious bastard like Bucky Cavali. What plans do you have for him and how does anything from the old-world matter? Are you referring to Europe? France?"

Grisland closed her eyes and opened them again. For the first time Celeste truly noticed that the Sisters looked through her rather than upon her when they tapped whatever the source of their prophecy was.

"A doe's time alone turns the page,"

"To one whose lost love shapes his rage."

"The magnate depraves the steel-pouring slaves who make this world your cage."

Celeste crossed the space from herself to Baliosi in an instant. The young lupine bitch was in her hands and hoisted off the ground in an eyeblink, putting them nose to nose and fang to fang. The cigarette fell out of Leguna's mouth and Grisland made a rattling gasp.

Smells sweet and corrupt seeped from the young wolf's clothes and her blue eyes met Celeste's with maddening serenity.

"Why shouldn't I just kill you?" Celeste hissed. "Show you what a violated life looks like. I had an arrangement here with Torrio's Chicago Outfit. I was comfortable. It was good."

Baliosi smiled sweetly. "It was never good. It was just familiar. It's the trap Pierre would have set for you in that world or Ferrault in this one, tying you down either way. You'll find out soon how dearly you needed us."

Celeste let the wolf go and she skipped back to stand with the others. Leguna bent and recovered her cigarette. "We've a schedule to keep. You've a place to be," Leguna said around her smoke.

"It's going to be a busy night," Grisland added with a wide otterish smile and Celeste didn't know if she was referring to her or themselves.

"If you interfere with my life again I'll kill you all," Celeste said.

"Careful about promises made," Baliosi said with amusement. She brandished a bottle from nowhere, its contents catching the pale light.

Celeste immediately recognized it and it was gone again in an instant. She had to ask. "Where do those spirits you capture go? Where do you cellar our pain?"

Leguna's one eye creased sadly. "It's not all pain, dear."

Celeste watched them wander away, turning over every cryptic word.

Leaving in another direction, she wondered how many steps she took back to midtown were known in advance by the three sisters bickering over smokes as they exited the park. Or how many of her actions could be guided by higher forces they were attuned to. Bucky and Sandy waited at Madison and Lasalle. They'd regret inviting her soon enough.

Chapter 17

The Gift

The light on the stoop was weak. Only the keenest night vision would catch the soiled plaid fabric, tied to appear as though binding an eaves trough in danger of falling above a rickety door at the corner of Madison and Lasalle.

Celeste perched on the opposite roof and opened her senses, waiting. At twenty minutes past midnight a feline sidled up to the door, trench-coated, high collared with reluctant glances of a butterscotch muzzle under a wide brimmed hat. A cigarette winked and was ground out under a toe. Being carnivore, her trolling the night alone wasn't half as suspicious as Celeste would be in her position but the cat seemed nervous. A small hatch yawned, and a dog's muzzle poked, sniffed, retracted. The door opened inward, and the cat slipped in without another word before being sealed away.

Celeste spied further, unable to hear the faintest mutter from other patrons. Speaks had spoken codes or flags alerting patrons to either be silent or clear out. Being a first night explained any slow traffic.

Time to see what the fuss was about.

Binding high shadows, Celeste crossed the street without touching hoof to pavement and found herself on their rooftop.

The scent of blood was faint but close.

Down the building's opposite side an alley bore meager light tinted by a maroon shade, and Celeste could detect traces of life's elixir dabbed against the bulb, burning like incense above a second door hidden from the street.

Her eye followed the alley, coming to a brick wall, messily mortared and still smelling wet. Of course. Mortal mammals would never expect to scale a wall to reach libation, though many mammals' claws could.

For one like Celeste, crossing that barrier to reach the source of that scent took less effort than a single step.

Reaching the concrete soundlessly, she realized they hadn't bothered with a lock. One push and rose-petal light spilled out. Through a small vestibule, coats and shawls hung. Past that, mammals devoid of breath hunkered in small groups, conversations low but amiable, blood drunk.

She made out Bucky's voice right away; "What's with the hissing thing? I'm a fox for fuck's sake. I growl, I don't hiss. That's cat shit."

"So's you think," A New England-affected voice chided. "The fangs make it hahd when they go straight down like that, locking the jaw when ya grimace. Try a growl while yah grown. Do it with me."

"Graughauugh."

"Gruhgguggg."

"See. Mouth changes shape, tongue rises. Ya hiss or gahgle." Celeste saw an old wolf talking to Bucky with one immense fang and one shorter one, grown-in after a pulling. A fly buzzed the fragrant contents of the cups between them.

"That's news to me. Sandy, did you know we couldn't growl?"

Sandy didn't answer. She was behind the black-oak bar, tail twitching lower as she met Celeste's gaze with trepidation.

Celeste for her part stared balefully back. It wasn't as though she was going to accept this invite and start trouble right away.

"Celeste," Bucky set his mug down and drops of blood flecked the table's varnish. He was smartly attired in a black suit, pinstriped white to convey a grey ensemble with starched shirt and matching white tie to mimic a bare fluffed chest. "How's life treat a doe on the go? You're not still sore about me making friends with Johnny again, right?"

Well, then. So much for that. Celeste took four strides, and a closed fist took the fox off the stool, jaw spinning hard enough to snap his neck. Scandalized gasps lit all at once from the half dozen patrons, easily most of all the turned in Chicago, as Bucky flopped and squirmed. His spine started to work itself back into shape with groans and snaps. Facing the ceiling on his back, he didn't get up. "You broke my neck."

"And we're still not even," Celeste told him. "I could pull that head off and stuff it into a decanter, see if anything worthwhile malts out of it."

The wolf now alone at the table hissed his fang and a half. "Missy, that's no way to treat ah host. It's a tough sunny world out theah and you could learn some manners if you don't want yah invite cancelled."

Celeste lowered her ears. "I crossed this stupid vulpine over the brink just a few days ago and he ruined my crèche as a thank you, so I owe him some grief." Her gaze returned to Sandy Mallory, still unused to seeing her young again. "You escaped the rabbit to tend bar," Celeste said. "All those years a mindless slave and all it took was a bit of fox cock to set you off."

Sandy hissed, fangs at length. "I made a mistake with Calvert, obviously. I tried to take another path out of guilt, Celeste. You know guilt, don't you dear? You shared enough of it after the steamer from Dublin."

Celeste had enough of her wounds opened up for one night. "Say another word to me about France and I'll end your existence," her fangs came in slow.

"You two wanna take this outside?" came a sigh from the floor. Bucky was testing his fingers and toes. "I just wanna run a business, show my lady a good time. Best you both have a drink and forget bygones, right?"

Muttered assent came from each table. A few bloody mugs raised and wiggled. The blooded and sated didn't care about decades of other's drama.

Sandy came round the bar and Celeste noted that she was now resplendent in a grey dress, cut at flapper length and showing plenty of leg.

Sandy's tail twitched and she clenched her jaw. "I want to be friends again, Celeste, but you hold on to far too much. I made a mistake with the rabbit, and I've apologized to everyone here tonight who the Martyres chased at one time or another. I wasn't the only one who fell under the rabbit's sway. I do accept I was the most gullible."

"And what happened to those others," Celeste stalked over and stood before the squirrel who set a mug upon the bar. "Where are those who fell under the steel magnate's *sway?*"

"I don't know," Sandy fidgeted her hands and her tail crossed round. "I'm sorry that I don't."

Celeste knew that Sandy was holding something back, and wondered if she should press her.

Bucky cleared his throat, pulling himself off the floor with care. "Does it matter? We're here now, all of us. Cozy, flush and happy. That's why I invited you, Celeste. I wanted to make up for my…well…I guess I messed up your plans a bit."

The bar was definitely oak. The fox's skull could go right through and take a day's rest to stitch back together. She had no doubts where that would leave her with the other patrons. "Why did you want me through another entrance, Bucky? That wasn't a trap, was it?"

The fox laughed, one yip that clearly hurt. "Celeste, c'mon. I was letting you through the delivery door to see the vintages and pick the best for yourself! A mutual friend had them sent here."

Celeste's gaze roved around. The speak was wood paneled, darted with cheap art interspaced by weak lamplight, oiled bouquets here, President Harding Playing Poker with other dogs there. Burgundy curtains obscured corners and a phonograph had run off the needle some time ago. Bucky's gin joint was a salute to every swank-on-the-cheap speak that Celeste had ever stalked.

Behind it was a curtain parted into darkness.

Stronger scents of blood drifted from that direction.

"Oh I know what you're thinking," Bucky wagged a dark finger, amused. His head had straightened, wagging tail brushing the bar. "Goods *were* on display, but the noise got to me, so we moved them to the cellar."

Celeste was hungry and anxious in equal measures. "Couldn't be satisfied with the Sister's hooch, could you Bucky?"

The fox shrugged and bones cracked when he did. He worked his jaw carefully, wincing. "Whiskey don't do much for me no more. You think I'd start up a joint just to watch others enjoy the goods? The Sisters did put up great 'shine." He circled the bar woozily. "Great last sip for our new stock, calms 'em right down."

Celeste studied tables at the other side of the room where a beaver with fangs flanking block teeth and an ewe sipped silently. Money under glasses confirmed Bucky was running no charity.

Celeste turned to Sandy who'd remained stock still. "Show me."

Sandy cleared her throat. "Care for a glass? I know you'll be thirsty."

Celeste stalked around the bar, eyes on Bucky who tottered out of her way when she didn't slow her pace. They had some understanding at least, though his carnivore sensitivities were as bruised as his snap-wrung neck.

Just maybe he'd think his affront to her with Torrio was settled with that injury. He'd be wrong.

Before Sandy's hand reached the curtain, Celeste grabbed one and threw it back. Blood filled her nostrils, making her heady. A strip of fly-paper hanging beyond the drapes had fat, engorged insects beating wings uselessly. The room beyond was cool, filled with suspended shapes, twisting in the dark.

The shapes had tails. One of them moaned piteously.

"Go on," Bucky put his hand on the wall, claws furrowing the wood. "Pick one out. Freshest is at the back."

Bucky and Sandy followed Celeste in. The curtain closed out the light and revelry and with the pull of a rope Bucky turned on one dangling electric bulb.

What Bucky called his vintages were naked, varied species suspended by four hogtied limbs and muzzles hanging limp, gagged in leather. Blood dripped from spigots driven into their buttocks or sides and tied in place. The assortment of species were almost all carnivores, mixed sexes plainly exposed. A rabbit looked on the verge of death, one wolverine squirmed as he turned. The one furthest from the curtain struggled more vigorously than the others.

From the dappled cream and butterscotch fur color Celeste recognized the cat who'd slipped in the street-side entrance. Her clothes topped a messy pile against a far wall, the bottom layers of which were wet and mouldering.

Celeste's fangs were out. She smelled their suffering. She was hungry.

And unabashedly disgusted. One hundred and thirty years turned, and she truly hadn't seen everything. "What did you do, Bucky?"

"What did *we* do? Couldn't have gotten this far without my Irish lily." Celeste heard the wet smack of a kiss behind her and Bucky slipped round the doe, hand twisting each captive on one side of the cellar. Some groaned in pain, one tried to scream but only mewled. "Marks of our mutual friend Johnny Torrio. Some are from O'Bannion's gang, others small time wiseguys and gals who've made moves on his turf. Woulda taken Al or Frankie a week to put them in ditches full of lead. Lookit me! I'm making better use of 'em then plains coyotes did with the Buffalo. Nothing gets wasted."

The fox came to the end where the female cat blinked in the pale light, eyes registering all about her. Her pulse quickened as she started panting and Celeste felt it like a quake in her bones.

"I've got a dog in the other bar, catching the stock led in. Usually, he gets first sips after tapping but I had this one saved for you, a little peace offering."

Bucky traced a finger down the cat's flank. "Nice huh? Now, I don't take liberties with the stock back here. It's just not sanitary and I don't run *that* kind of outfit. They can go down the street for that." He snickered and beckoned back past the curtain.

Tears were streaming down the feline's cheeks against bound thighs. Celeste had to look away. "How could you do this Bucky?"

The fox frowned, his own fangs jutted from his pouting lip. "Aren't you sick of rats? Or waiting for your old boss to throw you scraps one at a time? Here you get to try the best vintages, figure out which species is best. First one's even free."

"You...moron," Celeste hissed, and the cat began struggling in terror as her eyes went from the other dangling souls back to the doe before her. Celeste knew right away her own eyes had blackened to hunger pools. "Do you know how badly you've exposed all of us with this sick game?"

Bucky's ears dropped. "Game? Celeste, you're wounding us. Isn't she wounding us, Sandy?"

Celeste felt the squirrel's presence at her shoulder and turned when she didn't respond. Sandy's eyes were roving over the hanging prisoners, seemingly noticing something for the first time. At last, the squirrel's tail twitched. "Bucky, we need a word in private."

Celeste rounded on her. "No, Sandy. Why don't you tell us what's wrong? Two days ago, just *two days* ago you were years into swearing off the vein forever. I learned you were teaching letters to orphan children. Now you do *this*? There was a mercy in the worst of what we were forced to do. What is this?"

"You don't know what I've had to do to survive..." Sandy took a step back as though finding herself in an unfamiliar place, grey dress rubbing up against a suspended hare who was more than likely dead.

Bucky growled, eyes narrowing to black slits as they darted from doe to squirrel and back again. "I don't believe this. Dammit Celeste, I give you a seat at the biggest table for our kind this town has ever seen, a club you *made me* join, and you start on how *mean* the whole thing is?"

"Nothing I've ever done in this life has been close to this cruel, Bucky. You need to understand that."

The fox stared daggers at her. "Oh really? How many dead bodies you think you step over to get to any of the speaks in this town? How much blood was just washing down the gutters when you started killing for Johnny and the crooked cops and these fuckers—" He shoved the cat who swung like a pendulum in her harness, "who were as much in the game. Some of these were muscle, some were thieves. This cat was a bag runner for the purple triangle. She's counted money right over broken bodies who held out, paid short, or had just nothin'. Don't be a sap."

He'd been a mistake. He was supposed to die. The words were right on Celeste's lips but she held back. "I made you what you are but I didn't torture you, Bucky. That's the difference. You weren't writhing in my closet for days on end while…" Celeste was immediately conscious of the fact that most of the ears around her belonged to people suffering at that moment. "This crosses a line."

"Really?" Bucky shivered nervous energy out through his tail. "We've crossed lots of lines already, and would'ja look at that, another line."

The fox turned and went to the door at the far end of the room, opening it slightly to whisper a question through. When he closed it again, he had a bottle in his hand, dark green tinted and sloshing. "The sisters gave us two cases of this stuff, last drinks before the send-off." He spun the cat and pulled her gag, slipping the bottle between her lips before she could draw a breath to scream. Whiskey poured out her lips and down through her fur to drip on the floor. "So let's be merciful," Bucky said, pulling the bottle back before grabbing her throat and yanking it back. Fast as a blink, he buried his fangs in her throat.

The cat gasped and renewed her struggles. Celeste didn't stop him, knowing the results would be far worse if she dared tear him away. Blood escaped the fox's slurping lips, ran down the cream and scotch fur, following the rivulets of booze past her sex to the stone floor.

Bucky pulled back and the cat gasped. "Was a last drink the favor you gave me, Celeste? Did you wanna turn me right there on the Sister's cellar floor? Probably woulda hurt less, *'specially* right after a drink." Bucky forced the bottle between the cat's lips again as Celeste regained the control she didn't know she'd lost and shoved the fox away. He hit the wall flat-backed and didn't make a sound without any breath to knock out, only a fang-fenced hiss.

The bottle fell to the floor and shattered. Celeste had one clear look at its color. It wasn't the special stock that the Sisters had planted in the speaks which meant that Bucky wasn't gathering memories for them. She hoped there was nothing in there to turn any of the wretches before her. That would be beyond cruel.

"Well, that was a waste," Bucky drew a handkerchief from his vest, dabbing at the blood on his lips. "Finish your gift, Celeste. Don't let it suffer. You hate suffering so much, don't you?"

"Stop it!" Sandy shouted, stamping a foot. "You should go Celeste. I need to talk to Bucky alone. I'm sorry this didn't work out for you or us."

"She doesn't go," Bucky cut her off, "until she finishes the gift I gave her. Because if she doesn't, I'm gonna leave that cat to twist until she starves." He stood straight and showed all his teeth. "Go ahead. Show me what you think mercy is."

Celeste looked into the cat's eyes and saw the same pleading she'd seen in stocks in Paris so long ago. Had this cat done evil things? Had she bartered with others' lives? Celeste didn't know. She didn't hesitate.

Tipping the cat's head back, she bit again and drank. And drank. Blood spiking, she felt the wriggle of the cat in her grasp invigorating her senses. Such a splendid gift, Ferrault would say. Fuck him and fuck Bucky Cavali too.

She felt the weightlessness of stolen life with the same headiness as always, and despite the circumstances, she wasn't sickened by it while in its throes. Such was impossible when the blood was singing.

"Feel better?" Bucky's question was smug and self-satisfied after the cat went limp and she drew away.

The one morsel of information she'd gained from the sisters tonight hung before Celeste. Anything to take the smile off his face. "I didn't make you," Celeste said as she let the dead cat's head go.

"What?"

"I," she licked her lips clean, "didn't make you."

"What do you mean you didn't make me?" Bucky said. "You told me you were lonely."

"It was an accident. You were an accident. I was paid by Torrio to kill you for stepping out of line and after your clumsy attempt to rape me back at your place I was happy to do it. I was looking forward to shovelling dirt over you."

Bucky's grin fell away completely and his muzzle went slack. "That's not what you…how?"

"Doesn't matter how, Bucky. I had a ditch ready that the wolf you killed went into instead. Insects should be opening a speak of their own in that stupid mouth of yours."

Bucky chewed for words, a quip, a taunt, any kind of rejoinder. His voice was thin when it came out. "You told me you liked me. You said that you didn't want to be alone."

Celeste closed the dead cat's eyes. The stink of suffering was still heavy in the cellar, but she fought her urge to feed again down and kept herself to a detached, serene buzz. She was in control of herself.

Sandy for her part went to put her arm around Bucky, clearly disturbed by something she couldn't give voice to. "You need to leave Celeste."

"I do," Celeste went to the far end of the room and pulled open the door there. A second room full of barrels awaited, most open and empty, the few sealed with crimson fingerprints about their lids and bearing the faintest scents of death.

Beyond that was the false speak. The wolfhound cleaning a glass there looked up with a question in his eyes. Celeste could see the strain of controlling his appetite in order to hide the fangs and the dark shine that would terrify any mark coming through the 'delivery' door of the fake speak.

"He's not cutting you in enough, whatever it is." She walked past him to the street level door, knowing that whatever rage or self-pitying misery seeped into Bucky now, he couldn't make a scene with so many 'friends' in earshot. She turned back to see him standing at the door to the cellar, Sandy's arm around him. He was shuddering with the things he wanted to say.

"I lied, Bucky. I do want to be very much alone. You both reminded me why."

Celeste went out.

It took her three blocks to find a public phone.

***

Crawford left the window of the Chevy open and let the night blow through his fur. He wanted to be as numb outside as in. It didn't work.

He'd done the unthinkable and now had to figure out how to handle things. He couldn't formulate a plan on the window ledge, nor within the ruined hedge where he'd landed while shouts rang through the school, police and press bickering on their way up.

Crawford had gotten to his car, bundled his unfortunate package in the back seat and started the engine when he first saw lightening up above. Press flashbulbs were flooding the Superintendent's office and a play of shadows represented the cop's poor attempts to keep the scene uncontaminated.

Crawford drove south, passing rickety homes before winding east to put himself parallel to the river. He slowed just enough to draw his still warm weapon and fling out at hard as he could. Traces of moonlight caught the nickel-plated spin, but he didn't see or hear the splash. He drove on, lighting a cigarette at a stop. "What the hell did I do?"

An old ghost in the back seat in olive greens could answer no questions but Crawford could hear the rejoinder. Crawford asked himself that a lot, didn't he? After the fact it was always his favorite question.

"Don't you start. I had as little time tonight as I did in France."

"Start what?" The voice under the blanket behind him was confused as he stirred.

Crawford put a hand back. "Don't. Somebody's going to see you."

The kid's stubbed horns popped into sight for an instant and huddled again. "Where are we going?" He sounded more numb than afraid.

Great question. Far as Donovan Calvert knew the kid was dead, which in a sense was true. Crawford couldn't bring him home as Charlie would have even more questions he'd have to stall on. The kid needed to be somewhere before the sun came up, secure and safe. Crawford didn't know precisely what daylight would do to him but could assume it wasn't good.

He couldn't put him with other mammals. Convents, shelters, and churches were out. So where was a dark place where one could be alone? Speaks were crowded...

Unless they'd been made otherwise. An idea came together, and Crawford took a bridge east of the river to get him back to the office, which would be staffed at best by one nighthawk taking tips and any officer who might pop in who forgot something. He finished another two smokes on the way over and gave the kid the skinny when he parked. "You stay out of sight while I go into my office. We've got places we've raided and shuttered that stay empty for weeks pending investigation. I'll find one that's good and get you set up there."

"Set up?" He sounded worried.

"You may need to stay for a few days while we figure things out."

"Alone?"

Crawford heard the fear in that voice, and it hurt. "Not for long, I promise."

Crawford hurried into the building and ran smack dab into Cirreli exiting. The fox was surprised to see him. "You weren't here for the assignment pass-down. We've got three pre-dawn speak raids."

Crawford didn't remember any announcement. "I wasn't told."

"Word went round right after you left early. Agent Rothscub took your assignments. Come with me."

Crawford followed Cirreli back to his desk and the silver fox jotted some addresses down. "Two are speaks we've been keeping an eye on for a few days, one's a tip-off."

"Dissatisfied customer?"

Cirreli shrugged and passed the slip over to Crawford. "We're passing round the hat for Lockley and Tooley again. Both have young ones and widows trying to fend. I'm sure their dads looking down from heaven would appreciate it—"

Crawford dug into his wallet, peeled away five for each one.

"Thanks Crawford. You're a pal."

Crawford stuffed the list in his pocket, noting that Cirreli had circled the one he was expected to show up at. Great. Running on a mere two hours of stolen sleep and already on a timer to work again.

He found the right records, choosing three recent cases, vacant basements close to here. He could smuggle the kid in, snatch some winks and be at his raid point in time.

The office phone rang. Cirreli answered it as Crawford scribbled destinations down.

"It's for you," the fox called across the office.

There was nobody else here. Crawford sniffed. "Is it Charlie?"

"No." Cirreli held out the phone and receiver. Crawford took it and sat down. It had to be Calvert. "Hi."

"It's me," Celeste said.

"How'd you know I'd be here?"

"Where else could I check?"

Crawford's head hurt. "I've got a situation."

"So do I."

"We need to meet," they both said at once.

***

Back at Daley's where she'd met Crawford previously Celeste stared at the kid and the kid stared back and the wolf watched them warily. The kid had blood on his breath, his first feed, Celeste assumed. "Is he dead?" she asked.

"Who?" The kid asked in a voice so tiny it could have barely been heard by anyone at the table, much less the beaver who brought tea and coffee orders and one steak pie. Anxious wolves, especially weres, were hungry as water was wet.

"You bit somebody. Is he…?"

The kid went ashen-eared, and Crawford leaned forward. "Kid can't be blamed. This was done to him against his will."

"By whom?"

"Some lion gave him to a raccoon who, well, that racc's dead."

"And the lion?"

"I haven't met her. Donovan Calvert knows her, but they aren't friends. He called her a," he glanced at the kid, "he doesn't like her."

"That might be useful." Celeste studied the goat as he looked down. "How do you feel, kid?"

"My name is Samson," he answered, and Celeste caught the Scottish. First generation immigrant. If he had people, he'd be a threat to them now. It was only because his body was a child's that he'd not drank enough on his first feed to be bouncing off the walls. Smaller Nosfurs became full much faster and paradoxically didn't lose as much control in the euphoria.

And this kid smelled of fear. Celeste realized he had no chaperone, brought into this world as a disposable tool. She didn't know who the lion was, but if they couldn't turn a kid themselves, they were either not a Nosfur, or were a coward. They'd earned Celeste's disgust all the same. "Does anything hurt?"

"No. I mean, after I…I felt really good when I… drank, but also bad for feeling that. I didn't want to hurt him." He stared into the diner table-top's dull shine past the coffee he'd never enjoy.

Celeste felt a cold pit within. Ferrault had been a selfish, opportunistic bastard, but he had at least brought her into the world with the intent to prepare her for it. "Don't be sad. You did what was natural and that's not your fault. You could not resist."

Her glance met Crawford's and she could register the anger he was holding onto himself, guarded in that instinctive way of his. They two needed to talk.

With his heightened senses they would literally have to leave the place for the kid not to hear them so she laid it on the table. "The lion who did this wanted to kill somebody well connected, yes?"

"And then phoned the press and the police to arrive and find both of them." Crawford added.

"Donovan sent you to save the kid?"

"He sent me." Crawford gave a flinty enough gaze to confirm what she suspected. Donovan might want the kid as a specimen for his grand plan, or not at all.

"We needed to get out of there." he added. "I've ensured nobody will know the Superintendent was…drank."

"He made me turn around while he shot him," the kid whispered, then ducked his head in worry that somebody might have heard. Nobody seemed to.

Celeste took stock. "Have you called Donovan yet?"

"No. I'm figuring out my angle on that. Also, there's a squirrel he's looking for."

"Sandy Mallory."

"You didn't say if she was a friend of yours?"

"She is not. As far as I'm concerned, the rabbit can have her back. She's making a new set of mistakes."

"Do I want to know about the old set?"

The kid looked up. "I know Ms. Mallory. She's my evening studies tutor at school. Mr. Leicester was angry about her not being at lessons." He trailed off at mention of the Superintendent again and went to a quiet place inside himself.

Celeste watched him sort guilt and grief, knowing that reconciling them would take a long time. "Where are you taking him?" she asked Crawford. It chilled her to realize the goat kid had no real inkling of what his life would be like from this point on. Had anyone even told him that he could never see daylight again? She doubted it. If he was expendable, then the monster who did this would be indifferent to having sunlight burn him to madness. What creature could do that and claim to have a soul?

"I need you to protect him," Crawford said earnestly.

Celeste was pulled out of her anger with a start. "Mister Cain, what makes you think that he'd be safe with me? If I told you half of what I've been through in just the last few hours…"

Crawford clenched his muzzle, looking exasperated. "He's a Nosfur, you're a Nosfur. He's a vegetarian, or was— "

"You should stop there before you put your foot in something fragrant. I have enemies, Crawford. He's not safe with me."

The kid looked at her with worried eyes and she refused to meet them. Her own worst sins had been too recently exhumed. She wasn't going to fail this kid like she'd failed her own sister.

Crawford scratched his muzzle. "The only hideouts I have are emptied speaks still covered in broken glass and we both know I can't tell Donovan I didn't finish his…instructions. I need you."

Celeste shook her head.

Crawford snorted. "You damn well know he can't be safe with me. I lost an hour or two tonight. Next time it could be a day. Or a week. I don't know if this," he hooked fingers into feral claws and waved them at himself, "Is going to take me forever at some point."

"It won't." Celeste said with certainty.

"Grateful for that."

"I don't know if you will be." She regretted saying that as soon as it left her lips.

Crawford looked at the crumbs of his steak pie and swallowed. "The problem still stands."

The three of them were silent and the kid poked at his coffee, watching ripples form and abate.

"What did you call me for, anyway?" Crawford growled. "Plainly you needed something from me."

Celeste was grateful for the momentary subject change. "I needed to give you a warning. You and your Federal friends."

"All ears," the wolf muttered.

"A new speak opened, well-hidden but somebody might find it eventually. It's at Madison and LaSalle and whatever you hear, whoever you hear it from, you need to stay away from it, far away."

"Why?"

"It's… a trap. Any Prohees or cops go in there, or whatever spies you stake out joints with are dead if they set foot through that door…and in the worst way possible."

"You can't be serious."

"I am. I'm figuring out what to do about it, but you have to stay clear while I—what are you doing?"

Crawford's hands dove into the pockets of his coat and bailed their contents around his plate and coffee. His badge, a dinged packet of Luckies and a worn lighter hit the table before he fished out crumpled paper. There were three addresses on it. The bottom one was LaSalle.

"What happened?" The kid stared at the tarnished shine on the wolf's badge, then watched the doe and wolf trade gazes.

Celeste had no blood in her to go cold. "Crawford, why is the address I just gave you already in your pocket?"

The wolf swallowed. "Two stakeouts turned up taps and one anonymous tip came in."

"When are you…?"

"Soon. There are raids at all three at a coordinated time in case the Outfit puts out calls to warn the others. I'm supposed to be at one of the other speaks for three a.m. My section head is at the one I've been assigned to."

"Would he have the ability to call the raid off?"

"Yes."

"Then have an excuse for why when you find him. Say it's another anonymous tip."

"Okay, can you take Samson then?"

"No, I must get to Sandy. She's the only means of turning Bucky around before he exposes us to the city and creates a bloodbath. You have to get the kid to the address I'm going to give you. He'll be safe there. You also need to call Donovan and give him whatever good news will stall him."

"Did you get a new telephone?"

"Forget my telephone. Call *no one* from my telephone, ever. You already know why."

Crawford rubbed his eyes. "Right. I need to stop at my place to get ready for the raid anyway. Donovan would expect me to call him from there."

"Good wolf. When I get Sandy and her former student together, we can have a heart to heart, make her figure out what's important."

"I don't want to hurt her." The goat kid pressed his lips together and Celeste watched fear cloud his troubled brow. She swallowed. "You won't hurt Sandy, Samson. What you don't know is that she's like us."

The kid sat back, startled. "She never tried to bite Mr. Leicester though. She didn't try to hurt anybody." Hope sprang in the boy and Celeste knew she'd break a heart to quash it. She instead reached across the table and put her hand over the kid's. He was giddy and scared and confused and would take a long time to come to terms with the life ahead. Was it a good or bad thing for him, being an orphan? There was nobody living to yearn for, or to lose.

Celeste picked her words carefully. "She'll be different, Samson. But in many ways still the same. I want you to know that when you do see her."

"I'm gonna go on a limb and guess that I shouldn't say anything to Donovan about knowing where Sandy is," Crawford said dryly.

Celeste nodded. "We all have places we need to be rather quickly."

"I need a goddam nap," Crawford muttered.

Celeste was already up. "All this tea and coffee should handle that."

***

Bucky sipped his blood and said nothing, watching the still city night outside the second-floor refuge above his speak. Downstairs the blood was warm and the guests had started to lose their inhibitions, secluded corners finding familiarity between acquaintances going back decades, in a couple cases centuries. Bucky left them be, keeping mum about what had happened in the cellar.

"Bucky there are seven…taps downstairs now," Sandy said.

Bucky sipped, looked out, made an indifferent noise.

"We were given five tip offs, I counted. Torrio made sure we had the right names."

"Yeah."

"So, who are the other…suppliers."

Bucky's ears dipped as he finished his glass, giving the world a withering stare. "Who cares?"

Sandy blinked and crossed into his field of vision, clearly worried. "Bucky, we opened this speak with the express purpose of removing bad people from the world."

"So? Bucky turned her way. "I explained it all to that stupid doe downstairs, didn't I? That's meat dangling below us. They'd kill us to line their pockets so what's to be concerned about?"

"But…who are the other two?"

Bucky rolled his eyes and shrugged, annoyed that he needed to remember this. "Meals who saw too much or were in the wrong place? I don't even remember which of them are which." Bucky sampled bright coppery notes rolling back on his tongue. "I only know that I like fox less than I thought I would, and ermine seems to have the best aftertaste. For now, anyway."

"We're not supposed to kill innocent people. You promised." Sandy was becoming incensed, her fangs slipping halfway out.

Bucky set the glass down loudly, taking a moment to feel the sensations of revelry below them. His new brothers and sisters of the night were raising glasses and dining on the spoils of Chicago's long war.

He took a step and reached out, amused by Sandy's recoil as he touched her jawline. His other hand went to her shoulder, daintily slipping down her dress strap. She put a hand up to resist and he made cooing noises with his own fangs slipping low. His hand quested round her fur to find her breast. Blood made her flush, innocent blood or guilty blood, what did it matter? She perked under his exploration. "So much older than me yet so innocent. Goddamn I don't know why I love that about you."

"Bucky I've seen the worst that we're capable of..."

"So, see the best in it. Aren't you happy with me, Sandy?" Bucky felt a faint tinge of desperation, that same emptiness that touched him when Celeste confirmed what he'd long suspected. "Tell me you're happy with me."

Sandy looked into his eyes, sympathy tinged with doubt. "I want to be happy with you Bucky, but I can't if you break promises." She stepped back, hand guiding the black fingered paw away, but he pressed forward, hands moving possessively behind her back.

His mouth pressed to hers and their fangs clicked as they connected. Stupid as she was being, Bucky loved her, he absolutely knew he did. And he needed her to love him.

She told his hungry mouth no as her back met a wall and his chest met hers. "No", she said again as his tongue pressed against hers. He didn't want to hear it. He wanted her to drink with him and understand how things needed to be and let him love her the way she needed to be loved. He closed his eyes and angrily hunted for the return of her kiss and was surprised to find himself against the opposite wall, his own back pressed hard enough to bruise and hand hard on his throat.

"You must listen to me, Bucky," she insisted in that Irish ire of hers and Bucky found himself both intoxicated and afraid of her power. Her fangs were fully extended when she put her nose to his. "If I'm to be your partner then you need to agree to how we're going to run this place. We don't kidnap and kill those who do not warrant violent fates."

Bucky was hard. All at once he forgot about Celeste's inflicted wounds and the stupid squabble about stock downstairs. His cock positively throbbed and he was sure Sandy's anger was helping it along.

"Are you listening to me?"

Bucky grinned. "I want to get you out of that dress and lick you clean, just show you how devoted I am."

He fell to his knees and buried his nose in the navel of her dress, wondering how fast he could hike it up without tearing it. Get her mind elsewhere and they could talk shop later.

"Bucky, you need to get up."

"I *already am*, doll."

"No," she grabbed his muzzle and pointed it up at hers. Something not in the room illuminated her wide eyes. "You need to look out into the street. Right now."

***

Crawford felt like a heel dropping the kid off alone. He didn't need to be by himself after what he'd been through but If Charlie was back at home there'd be no way to explain. Were it his own cub this had happened to, could he even entertain the possibility of leaving him alone? That question took him to a dark place he couldn't explore so he forced the question south.

"You aren't like me," the kid said as they drove.

"No," Crawford answered. "I got bit like you did but it did something different to me."

"Do you know who bit you?"

"Yes."

"Did they mean it?"

"I don't think so."

"Do you know them?"

Crawford felt uncomfortable. "I can't really talk about it."

The kid was quiet for a while. "When the raccoon had me it was scary too." The kid shuddered and Crawford let the wheel go a moment to squeeze his shoulder.

They were quiet the rest of the way to Celeste's new place. She was now residing on the city's outskirts. Doe was toeing out of town bit by bit and he couldn't blame her.

Crawford let Samson in with the key Celeste had provided. The place was empty except for a table and two chairs. A staircase rose to a darkened second floor. "I promise one of us will be here soon. Turn on a light if you'd like but don't go outside or go near windows. You can trust Celeste. She's one of the good ones and she'll be quick."

The good ones? Asked the ghost in the back seat of his mind as Crawford hustled out with muttered apologies.

The divorce papers remained where he left them back home, near the phone. He stared at them while he called Donovan's exchange. The rabbit was not pleased. "Why the hell did you make me wait so long?"

Crawford let his tiredness sell itself as detachment, told the rabbit he'd heard the unfortunate rumor that the Superintendent was shot in the neck by an intruder. Donovan asked if anyone saw more.

"No. Hope you're happy."

"You acquitted yourself well. And you did what you had to do."

"That what you tell everybody who does the unthinkable for you?" Crawford growled and hung up. Hopefully that sold his guilt, and the rabbit would give him breathing room. He needed a short nap before reporting to the scene of his assigned raid but realized that being late meant four more cops would be dead.

It was then that he noticed the slip of paper that had fallen off the table. It was the same pad on which Charlie had asked when Crawford was going to tell him about the phone. Except that was gone and a different message was scrawled; *One raid cancelled, speak moved. Two sites left, teams split, schedule moved forward. You're at Wacker drive at 2 am. I'm at LaSalle. Don't be late.*

"Oh shit." The clock on the wall said it was now well after one in the morning. Crawford rang the office. Whatever night clerk replaced Cirelli answered with a yawn.

"Have the teams moved out?"

"For what? Who is this?"

"The raids. This is Agent Cain."

"Evening, Agent Cain. Can't say much about why, element of surprise? Yeah, they loaded up and drove out about half an hour ago. Beatie was upset that you weren't there and—"

Crawford hung up and clawed the floorboards hustling out.

Chapter 18

The Raid

Charlie waited as Leslie reconnoitred. Lights on, looked like nobody home. They established their pattern; two cars rolling in fast, one blocking the alley. They'd get the door down, in within five seconds, get everybody corralled and register secured. Then get everybody outside so bottles could be catalogued and poured down the nearest drain. Sewer water would get feral vermin drunk for days.

The party had two agents and four police officers, badges and buttons covered. Five, including Charlie had thirty-eight specials but Leslie Spettle, the ferret on point, hefted a Thompson Model 1921 with a fifty-round drum. That tool of the department saw little use and was rarely ever fired. Scofflaws most often pissed themselves and reached for sky when they saw it.

"That lip rouge on your cheek, Charlie?" Leslie asked as she slotted the drum and drew the bolt back. "If we met her, would she kiss and tell?"

The ferret smiled needled teeth at the wolf and his ears blushed. A mere three hours had passed since he'd fled the party that bastard Pederson had clamped down on and he'd never taken that bath as he couldn't get dry in time. "I don't suppose she would."

The car's engine started. Any moment now.

Leslie laughed. "You're alright for a wolf, even if that pansy routine of yours makes you look so genteel. Never any stories to tell."

Charlie tipped his pork pie as the car started rolling. "What can I say, Agent Spettle? In rumor lies legends."

"Good hunting everybody," Leslie said to the group and waved out a window to the second car. The driver gunned it for a block, then swerved and broke at the base of the stairs. Leslie leaped out, trench broom up and hungry. The officers rushing the ram didn't hesitate, taking the door off its hinges.

"This is a raid!" The door flattened into the vestibule of a tiny bar that two officers filled, and Leslie swept. There wasn't a soul in sight.

"They see us coming?" a cougar cop muttered.

Charlie felt guard hairs rise as he filled in behind them, turning his eyes back to the eerily empty street. "Smell that?"

One of the cops at his flank was a hound and his nose worked. He shivered. "Somebody bled in here. Several people."

Leslie took a deep breath. "I see two bottles behind the bar. Officer Minsk, secure the register. I'll cover while the rest of you find the cellar. The proprietor's somewhere."

They tapped the walls with their guns. The cougar cop, Charlie couldn't remember his name, called out. "Door here." Plaster frame in the wall swung into darkness.

The smell of death hit everyone.

"Flashlight," Agent Spettle said. The tommy gun jittered in her brown-furred hands. "Quick."

A canine cop hung up his gun and produced one. The weak beam lit indistinct shapes in the darkness. Large whiskey barrels, mostly. He joined the cougar, both pistols up, and they marched into the room, swinging the light around.

"What is that?" the dog shouted. "Oh my god in heaven! What the hell is that?"

There was a moan and rattle that chilled every bone behind a badge. The voice of the lead cop echoed as though in a cave. "Agent Spettle, you need to see this!"

Leslie stalked forward to the open door, glancing back to Charlie. "Agent Rothscub, leave one of the others to watch the street."

Charlie followed Agent Spettle into the dark, round barrels that smelled of bitter herbs burying something rancid. Over her shoulder, in the quivering cone of light from the dog's flashlight, he saw shapes dangling from the ceiling, naked, bound and bleeding.

When the light hit one of them, a naked weasel screamed through his gag. Next to him a wolverine shivered. Charlie recognized the wolverine from rap sheets back at the office "That's Lefty Carstairs, contracts out for O'Bannion." At hearing his name called, the wolverine moaned plaintively.

"Who did this?" the dog with the light shouted, his beam quivering across the brickwork of the room the wretched hung in.

A rush from the dark struck the hound dog and the flashlight left his grip, bouncing once before coming to illuminate a stack of rags. A blood-curdling scream filled the dank space and receded as he was dragged away in the speed of a breath.

The cougar fired his revolver twice, deafening reports that rang Charlie's ear drums. Shots illuminated suspended sufferers and slithering things at the periphery of the senses.

"Get another light!" Leslie hurried forward, tommy swinging. With most of the team having natural night vision, the two lights they'd brought seemed like over-preparedness. But the dark outside the spilled illumination from the tumbled flashlight was impenetrable, blacker than the deepest night.

The dark behind the dangling prisoners moved.

Another cop, a rookie cat not a week on the force, passed up the flashlight, shaking visibly. "Stay back with Minsk," Charlie told him before pointing the flashlight ahead and illuminating both Leslie and the bound rabbit she stood next to. The creature thrashed as the light struck him, an iron spigot jabbed into his side dripping red.

Dean, the taken officer, screamed somewhere. "They're killing him," the cougar officer shouted.

Charlie remembered his name. "Wait for us, Cagney! Stop!"

"I'm coming Dean!" Cagney raced ahead and threw himself at a thick curtain, crimson light bleeding through as it billowed. Charlie and Leslie hustled forward, bumping into hanging wretches. Charlie's paw pads met something warm and slick, and he slid, flashlight angling to chain-bolted rafters. He didn't drop light or gun as Leslie pushed the curtain barrier aside before her, tommy up to fire.

Charlie was numbed with realization that his foot was covered in blood and other filth but put himself together to shout through panic. "Leslie! Stay out of there!"

Cagney disappeared without a sound, but Leslie was pulled down in the flashlight's glare, screeching. The tommy clattered back out of her grip as she tried to bat away whatever clutched her legs. A strike had rent her muzzle. Blood and bone shone through the part in her pelt from cheek to eye. Wide eyes glazed and claws scrabbled the cobblestone as she was slowly, almost playfully dragged through the curtain. Another scream pealed the nightmare behind her, the dog, the cougar, Charlie wouldn't ever know.

On the back of that scream came tinkles of laughter, joyful and cruel. Something liquid made it gurgle.

Charlie's heart was bound in ice, but his gun raised, and he fired through the curtain, six pops emptying the special.

The tommy gun lay where Leslie dropped it, a mere foot from the curtain. Charlie took deep, racking breaths, fighting the urge in his limbs to push away, turn tail, run for his life.

Crawford had been in the war. Would Crawford run for it? Would Chief Beatie?

"Where are they?" The rookie cat shivered back behind the barrels, looking to the Prohibition agent wolf for authority.

Charlie dropped the thirty-eight and dived for the Thompson. He spun it at the barrel and the shiver of the curtain just beyond, like a living thing breathing, made him cry out as he grabbed the stock, dragged it, wrapped his finger around the grip. He leaped back and to his feet, holding the submachine gun with one hand and the stock under his armpit while the other held the flashlight.

Going through the curtain was death, so he ran the light across where it met the wall and saw the cord that would draw it.

Two fast steps, snatched it, dropped the flashlight. It bounced, painting the horrors dangling behind him.

The curtain fell away to show the server-side of a larger bar, glasses neatly arrayed. Tables beyond were dimly illuminated by crimson-shaded oil lamps. Cornflower wallpaper had indistinct shapes.

Not a soul in sight.

"Bureau of Internal Revenue! Come out with your hands up! Leslie? Dean! Cagney!"

Nothing.

He hefted the tommy gun and took slow deliberate steps. Beyond empty lamp lit tables, corners receded into darkness.

Peering around the bar he saw the cougar, Cagney, staring at the ceiling with blood welling at his lips, chest dancing for breath. Charlie hurried around. "Did they scram by another exit? Can you speak?" Charlie panned the gun around, tracking every spot of darkness.

Then the impossible happened. A shadow beyond the light grew in size and then shrunk. Then another, tricks of vision that made the dark corners of the room appear to sigh. He turned slowly as he dropped to a crouch and put a hand on the cougar's neck, his own pelt crawling as the cougar's life flowed forth.

Shadows under the scattered tables shifted at the corners of his eye. As he turned to a formerly dark corner that a lamp illuminated better, he realized the shadows had moved.

"Charlie," Leslie's voice came from his left and Charlie span on his claws to see the ferret's faint shape in the dark. Her face was a toothy ruin, and her hand held to her chest had two fingers and two slick bones.

The wall behind her slithered.

Charlie grasped at an oil lamp on the nearest table and hurled it into the darkest corner where it broke and burst. The wall behind Leslie became limbs, tails, teeth and black oily orbs atop muzzles of various species climbing the wall itself, fangs like rail spikes in rictus smiles.

One of the creatures within the clutch held out a glass that dripped ichor on the floorboards. "Put a foot on the rail, son," it coaxed. "Your heart's beatin' soooo fast."

Charlie screamed and fired. The tommy gun spat fire and things on the wall shivered, leapt or fell. A wolf landed on a table next to him and Charlie sawed its shoulder with lead. A beaver bled from a shadow under another table and Charlie shot the buck teeth in between fangs. Leslie disappeared into the miasma, her skull opened by bullet or claw. Charlie stopped firing to tug Cagney's arm. He lay still, eyes sightless.

The fire spread. Monsters hissed and screamed. Charlie dived back around the bar and ran back into the cellar, spinning to fire behind him through dangling mammals. He took another glance at the sufferers, silhouetted by the curtains beyond that were already starting to smoke. He couldn't leave them to burn alive.

Charlie closed his eyes as he swept and fired, sending them to judgement in blossoms of flesh.

Back past the blood bar a breeze beckoned from outside. Screeches cut the night, creatures fleeing the hell-speak. "We've gotta go!" Charlie shouted to the rookie right as he came across the cat's corpse. His uniform was slick with blood and one of his arms had been twisted halfway off. His eyes were sad in surprise.

Shapes rustled back past the barrels. Charlie fired through one barrel and blood came out in a rivulet. He gave the stack a shove and the wobbling toppled two of them as he retreated back into the false speak they'd broken in through. Warm spring night was just feet away. "Minsk, we have to leave! Now!"

Officer Minsk was prostrate atop the smaller bar, blood running down its wooden front. A shadow behind the tableau broke and a wolfhound with twisted fangs and eyes black as death slipped forth, tapping a bottle of booze on its palm. "The cash isn't yours Prohee shit-heel!"

There was a small explosion from back through the cellar and fire illuminated the hound's flank.

"Go to hell you bastard," Charlie raised the Thompson.

It clicked. The drum was empty.

The wolf hound gingerly set the bottle down next to Minsk's corpse.

Charlie began backing for the exit.

Hunching, tail shaking, the hound followed. "This was the first job I managed to get in thirty-five fuckin years," it growled against the rising roar of flames two chambers away. "Do you know how important this was to me? Bucky and his squirrel put faith in me and in one night, just one night, you ruined it all."

Charlie's mind went blank. He couldn't go claw to claw with this monster shaped like a mammal.

The hound smiled. "I'm going to stick that gun all the way inside you. Throat down, ass up, doesn't matter. It's going through your job thieving hide."

Charlie backed over the threshold and under the pale light of a distant streetlamp, a whole other world. The cars were still there.

"The undertaker will wonder if you actually enjoyed it. I smell it on you, wolfie. I know what you were up to tonight."

"Fuck you."

Its claws dug splinters out of the door frame as it advanced. "You ain't getting so lucky. In fact, faggot, you'll go out worse than…" The wolfhound's vision was dragged upward by something behind Charlie that wiped the glee from his muzzle. The black eyes narrowed.

Charlie heard a low, guttural growl and ducked as he turned.

It was on top of the car, a grey wolf but…not. It crouched naked, a massive feral bulging with sinew. Claws like kitchen knives clutched the window frame and the long neck jutting from its torso presented a vast head and muzzle with ravening jaws. Teeth in a slavering fence easily out-sized the wolfhound's fangs.

The beast glanced down at Charlie, eyes cool flint that took him in. Then it leapt.

Over Charlie's head, to the speak's short staircase. The banister kept the mangy hound from a straight dodge and that was enough. Claws caught pelt and the creatures twisted together as they went down in a crack of wooden planks. They thrashed in each other's clutches as they rolled around the landing, movements too fast to see.

Charlie didn't watch.

He scrabbled around and got in the car, dropped the gun in the passenger floorboards. His hand was on the key before he froze.

He had to get to a phone and call for help. The building was on fire and someone in his crew might still be alive.

Right away he knew he was wrong about that. Realization dragged claws through the gut. He could only run now that the Thompson was empty.

Then he remembered.

Fragments of exploding banister showered the car as the fight carried out into the street, bare grey hulk on dark-attired streak. Charlie gave them the barest glance before diving into the back seat and rummaging through the kit. Flares, white gloves for directing traffic, extra cuffs.

And the slender tommy gun backup magazine, twenty more forty-five caliber rounds waiting to fly.

He grabbed the gun, spilling out the far side of the car from the scuffle that rattled a streetlamp. Charlie slid off the drum, drove home the maga-zine and drew the bolt back. Forward and over the Ford's hood Charlie braced himself.

The hound was a flash of black from one side of the street to the other and scaled the wall at a speed that Charlie's eyes simply rejected. He didn't bother to aim. The tommy was a hose, not a needle. He pulled the trigger and peppered brick, stamped window glass, and stitched at least one in the hound.

It slipped and he tracked it down, gravity the only reliable ally in the moment. Emptying the whole magazine Charlie was lucky to count two or three hits. His clipped target struck the concrete before darting into the short, bricked alley. The grey lupine feral was on him, claws and jaws wide.

They disappeared from view and unholy howls drifted back.

Charlie was alone. Lights down the street winked on, then off. The whole quarter of Chicago kept under cover as howls turned to screams and gurgles.

Charlie was so numb he didn't even know if he'd wet himself. He rounded the vehicle, its hull glinting with the fire spreading through the damned speak, spilling smoke out through the upper floor windows into the night sky and out the false front's ruined door frame.

The stink of burning flesh was something he'd never forget, and it took all his effort not to retch as he got behind the wheel. He knew full well that anybody left alive would have escaped by now. Tears filled his eyes as he fumbled again for the ignition key. Wiping them away to see better, he caught movement out the corner of his eye by the alley and caught his breath.

The enormous feral lupine exited the alley like a nightmare on all fours, bloody fur glinting by firelight. Shakily, limbs flexed, jerkily receding to modern mammalian proportions, the head's thick neck losing its distention. The mammal gingerly picked itself up on two feet. Gazing around, it saw the car and Charlie realized he was looking at Crawford Cain.

The grey wolf was unsteady as he approached the car, filthy, naked, and dazed. Charlie's claws gripped the wheel tight enough to tear it off as Crawford stumbled around to the passenger side. He opened the door and spat something disquieting out onto the pavement before taking a seat next to Charlie.

"Is this really happening?" was all Charlie could say, his teeth chattering. Sirens wailed as flames leapt before them.

Crawford blinked, seeming equally surprised. "Yeah."

A burning curtain blew out past the windshield. "Look, we need to go a block or two east to find my clothes. I kinda remember where I left them this time." Crawford looked ready to pass out, bracing his paws, no, hands, on the dash.

"Then we'll talk," he said.

***

Bucky realized as he watched the speak burn that he'd not even had a chance to name the place. That was as upsetting as the gunshot graze he nursed on one arm, yet another wound to lick. His supply was gone and much clientele with it. Goddam Prohee bastards.

Only two patrons to escape stuck around, one mink still hefting a half-empty glass of life, fast cooling. Sandy stood further apart, not looking at the distant conflagration, nor at him. That annoyed him. He'd done this for her as much as for himself. Gave them a future, secured them a piece.

Johnny would think him an idiot when word got back. The disdain of that would almost be worse than having Celeste off him.

"All I wanted was to make people happy," Bucky muttered, ears low. "And get some nicer suits."

The old wolf with the one short fang and the mink with the pint glass just stared at him. The mink had a reluctant sip, as though wondering if she'd be expected to pay.

Bucky hissed. "What I don't get, and I mean, what really pisses me off to ponder, is why Celeste would rat us out."

Nobody said anything.

"I mean who else could it be? Fine, Celeste is upset with *me*, but to ruin this for all of us!" Bucky shouted over the sound of timber collapsing. The scent of burning blood, his very best stock, would be diluted soon under fire department lake-water. Disgusting.

"I guess I have to start again. We'll have more friends come by when we do, right?"

But for the sound of fire raging, the rooftop was dead silent. "What, nobody here's ever experienced a little adversity?"

The mink found her voice. "I saw Felingdra burn after being shot. She's nearly three hundred years old, never came this close to the end. I know she's not coming back."

Bucky scuffed the roof with a claw. "So, when I open again everybody gets one on the house!"

The wolf sighed. "Bucky, this was a riot and the bees' knees, but who we auh remains protected in…discretion. You haud a brilliant idea, it's just that you might need a different one."

Bucky fumed, wondering if he should go down and see if there were any straggling cops to kill. He'd worked *so hard*. "I'm nothing but careful," Bucky growled. "Nobody's gonna stop me from taking a piece of this town, 'specially some French doe slut who can't appreciate ambition." He fought for composure and smoothed his hackles back. "You're all invited to the reopening just as soon's I find a new space. Sandy and me'll build this up in no time, right Sandy?"

No answer.

Sandy was gone.

***

"All I wanted to do was make people happy," Bucky said. Sandy watched the speak burn and wondered how many of Bucky's own words he believed.

A finger brushed her shoulder from a bound shadow behind her. The voice that emanated was familiar. "We need to talk." Celeste muttered.

Sandy started. "Why are you here?"

"Too much to say here. Step away with me."

With decades of practice at her claw tips, Sandy effortlessly sunk back into a shadow in the lee of a rooftop chimney. In the dark she smelled the doe's pelt with clarity. It had been years since they'd been this close.

"You won't believe this, Sandy. But I can help you," Celeste said. "You don't need to be lied to again by anyone, Bucky, or Donovan. You just need to come with me.

Bucky paced back and forth, tail flicking angrily. "What really pisses me off to ponder, is why Celeste would rat us out."

"I didn't do that," Celeste retorted so low that only Sandy could hear. "I knew how badly that would go."

"Why should I believe you?" Sandy hissed under her breath, warring with her desire to turn the doe in to all present. "You wanted Bucky laid low, didn't you?"

"Not like this. So many died and Bucky doesn't understand it's finished. Look, come with me and I'll show you something important. We won't be long. You can follow at a distance, so I won't be leading you to any trap."

The way you did to me, Sandy heard Celeste refrain from saying. The squirrel watched Bucky stalk and curse, turning over implications of the path she'd walked with him. She silently reached back to meet Celeste's offered hand and felt its coolness. So much time had kept them apart, so much vanity disguised as grace. Somehow, she knew that Celeste had no traps waiting. "If we won't be long, I'll go with you…"

She slipped away to follow. Bucky's tirade and approaching sirens fell behind.

***

Donovan hated using the telegraph to communicate, even with overseas parties lacking other means. It was simply impossible to know what the other party was thinking. Only the length of delay gave indication as to whether impulse or deliberation formed each reply. He needed to know so much more. "The Countess hasn't told you everything. She has endangered a sensitive operation that weakens our foothold here in America. Stop."

Edmond, working out of the booth behind Donovan's study wall, translated and sent with diligence. It was nine in the morning in England which made it three in the morning in Chicago, but sleep was impossible anyway.

The reply translated a minute later humored him at best "We are satisfied that your work in America was exemplary. Stop. Your metallurgy advances have aided the cause. Stop. Your solution to the vermin problem is insufficient." Edmond took a deep breath.

"Keep reading," Donovan said.

Edmond swallowed. "Eradication is not a feature of the Martyres of the Black Well. It is our very calling before God. Stop."

"Till the next flood fill the well," Donovan made the sign of the supplicant's descent from nose to navel with his one free hand without even thinking about it. "I do hope to speak to you all in person soon, Herr Wilheim. I have much to show you that may correct, no scratch that. Say… *expand* your perspective in beneficial ways. Stop."

The long silence that followed told Donovan he'd oversold himself. Edmond fidgeted.

Well, if one shoe had to drop. "One final question before I let you back to your business. Stop."

Edmond sent. They waited. The buzzes that came back sounded impatient. A single word. "Ask. Stop."

Donovan gritted his teeth, "Was the decision to displace an elected city official by means of a…vermin attack the Countess's idea or the Council's? If hers, were you consulted? Exposure to the world could put this whole country in a panic." Edmond stopped to write it all down and then sent hastily.

The reply buzzed in had been prepared, he was sure of it. "Exposure of vermin to public awareness is the risk taken when we suffer their existence. Stop." Edmond bristled for them both at the chastening in those words.

Donovan felt heavier than an anchor. "I will contact you again in a day's time. No doubt the Countess will have you appraised of progress. Stop." The disdain he dripped on the last word wouldn't cross the ocean.

Edmond turned to his master when they signed off. "Now?"

"Yes. Disconnect all the lines. No calls, no wires."

The possum vanished and returned in minutes. "Done sir. Our man just returned from Noah's Plank. The wolf was successful. The Alderman's death looks like a rather conventional murder."

Donovan crossed the room and poured a drink for poor Dick. "Are you certain?"

"Two reporters and one officer confirm Richard Leicester was shot at close range through the throat. They have no leads."

Donovan nodded. "Cain is a resourceful dog. Is the Countess aware?"

Edmond rubbed his still swollen jaw. "She didn't see our man arrive. She's not attempted to either call out or accept any calls. No telegrams have come."

"She's opened a whole separate line of communication with the Martyres that circumvents any means obtained here. Somebody will have to tell her that her plan to expose Nosfurs in America failed, a small joy I'll savor. What is she doing now?"

"She's in your bed."

Donovan met Edmond's gaze with incredulity. "Doing what?"

The possum searched for the right word. "Waiting."

Such cheek. Just because their tousles lit a fire in the rabbit didn't mean a simple bare flank and a come-hither stare would draw him back to her bosom after tearing his plans asunder. She presumed him a mindless toy.

"I'm glad she's rested. Preserving our contracts with Leicester's committee is now our top priority. I'll need everything signed thus far collected and his colleagues brought to speed. City Hall will have to be reminded that regardless of who takes his position on the newly convened labor board, many jobs and projects are at stake that Mayor Deever needs to shore up support. I'll ruin the career of anyone who tries to circumvent that."

It would be incredibly suspicious that contracts had been signed for a committee that hadn't convened yet by a man who had only just taken the oath of office before being murdered. Donovan would have to play his card as another victim who lost a friend. He'd have to finesse which levers to pull at the right speed with the new mayor, and his immediate circle.

"Send a courier to the forge with the instructions I prepared and have the foreman authorize overtime for anyone who wants it."

"Sir."

"I have to visit the Countess."

Whatever questions Edmond had were put away and he set to his tasks.

Up Donovan went. He found Evelyn in bed, naked as the day, blueprints of one of the projects on his desk stretched out on the bed before her.

She ran a claw up a building's skeletal angles. "Did whomever you reach on the Council make you see reason, or did you offer enough Nosfur suffrage nonsense to demonstrate that such was not possible?" She rolled on her side and indifferently let him see all of her. Donovan's body tried to betray him immediately.

Strength. She was toying with him, and they both knew it. "What would have been the result had you succeeded?"

"Had I succeeded? In what, Donovan?"

"You did manage to cause a hiccup in my plans." Donovan crossed to the bed and snatched the blueprint for the Wrigley Building's North tower. "Leicester is dead."

"That's quite sad," she said, gaze distant. For someone who'd played her hand so well she didn't seem pleased with herself.

"Pity that the man should be shot by an intruder in such awful fashion. He was in such a state when the police and press simultaneously found him. Him and no one else."

Her slender golden brows raised, and Donovan waited for a curse, a hiss, anything.

Instead, infuriatingly, she nodded. "My condolences. Did he sign all your papers?"

Donovan met her gaze and said nothing for a spell. "Enough of them."

"You must be relieved."

The rabbit took a deep breath feeling his arousal gratefully abating. Disgust burgeoned. "The Council didn't answer my question when I asked if killing my primary contact in America was your idea or theirs, nor the absolutely disgusting means you went about it. Really Evelyn, a *child?*"

The Countess sat up, folding her legs, and straightening her back in a posture that was aloof and dominating. She showed teeth. "You want to draw shame from *me*, Donovan? Do you think it was easy?" Her voice wavered. "Do you have any idea how personal this battle is for me? I was eight years old when my family was taken, one by one in our country home in Graz. Drained, discarded in stables, in parlours, and in the case of my youngest sister, a budding flower of life merely old enough to walk, in her own open doll house, slumped over miniature furniture like a sleeping giant. Can you imagine how that is burnt into my soul, rabbit?"

Donovan said nothing as the lion rose and slipped off the bed. "This house, this stone edifice for your vanity, it resembled that dollhouse, which was why I wanted to see it burn when I first saw it."

She stalked past him to the window, indifferent to her own state of undress. "My pain was born in Graz, pain without hope. And it grew, Donovan. When a swordsman from the Martyres of the Black Well finally found the ghoul that had plagued us, cut it open and burned it, I was shocked to learn that we'd invited this monster in. A sheep, Donovan, who'd allegedly run away from home was taken in by my father in a gesture of kindness on a night of bitter cold, given a place in the servant's quarters and food the wretch claimed he was too unwell to eat." She gazed out into the night, her tail a lash.

"The Von Haften family was powerful, feared in so many circles. But my father was a benevolent soul, no claws on the necks of God's unclean. We let an affront to the natural order into our home and the lowly creature nearly ended my family's line in a single hellish week. I held just two of them as they died, Donovan. Most of them, my younger brother and sister included, were taken unseen."

She turned back, her arms folded with resolve. "I am not alone in my grief, thanks to an order that took me in and trained me to face my family's mistakes, never to disrupt God's hierarchy through follies of suffrage or wasted sympathies."

Donovan felt her anger as something palpable but couldn't abide her reasoning. "And so, you felt entitled to destroy the life of a child who wasn't even alive when your tragedy happened."

She sneered at him. "Don't presume to moralize with me. I don't have to like the sacrifices that are necessary, but they *are* necessary."

"And which sacrifices were yours?"

She stiffened at a distasteful memory. "I'd have managed with the raccoon, but you damaged him to an extent that he could barely remember what he'd been made to do. That's why I had to…" She broke off, anger gathering lips back from teeth. "They are tools of death, and I thought you understood that until this foolish dream of yours tricked you into thinking you could circumvent our very purpose. That was the most offensive thing of all Donovan. We opened our door to you and in return you've used your ingenuity to thwart us. I suspect your next meeting with the Council may be a short one."

Donovan took a deep breath. Of course, destroying a goat kid's future would never register as harm on par with her own. He knew well of the Von Haften family's tragedy. He also had information on its history that he'd never had cause to raise, leaving her pains to her. "Tell me, Evelyn. Since you feel that what you've done is just, do you presume that the one who turned that sheep that caused your family so much pain was like its protégé?"

"What do you mean?"

"The sheep. The murderer. If it was just a lowly creature that stepped out of place as you'd have it, who made it that way? Who drained its blood, fed it the balance of herbs and brought it through the dark? I'm certain you would have pursued that truth."

She was growing uncomfortable, perhaps intuiting what Donovan knew. "That's irrelevant. What matters is that beast took everyone I ever loved from me. Yesterday evening I returned the favor, used another like it to prevent your mistake."

"Wrong Evelyn." Donovan took a step closer, eyes locked with hers as she towered over him. "You still haven't faced the fact that this disruption of order as you call it started long before the Martyre's first specist diatribe that sought so long to block my membership. I had access to the records, Evelyn. They did trace the progenitor of several turned over the past three centuries, all based in the same circuit in Europe, all sired directly or as second, third or even fourth generations. Were you blissfully unaware that a lynx turned your sheep to thirst, Countess? Or did you willfully forget because putting down vegetarian commoners and Nosfurs both made satisfactory symmetry for all your revenge fantasies?"

He saw her hand move but wasn't fast enough to stop her from knocking him off his feet, stars exploding behind his eyes as his cheek found the carpet, one ear bent.

She was atop him, feral as a demon. Claws pierced the fabric of his vest through white pelt to flesh. Donovan moved his head to extricate one trapped ear and grinned at her. "I wondered how you got the kid's blood to drain when the raccoon had no fangs. How'd you do that, Evelyn? You bit the boy yourself and handed him over, didn't you?"

She cuffed him again and his nose cracked. A warm flow of blood trickled forth and he realized it might be broken. But she was the one crying.

Now they were getting to truth. "Be honest, Evelyn. You're offended by the Nosfur deep down because they take something that you thought was only yours by birth, the will to kill and consume. It's the most offensive thing about them to you. Tell me I'm wrong by making me bleed some more, lion. A goat kid can't have scratched that itch."

She struck him again, harder, weeping. Blood speckled the carpet. Donovan shook his head to splatter her mouth, tongue, and chest with it. She spat blood out, making the rabbit laugh through cracked lips. "You tried to steal the fire back when you bit that child and made Keller turn him into a killer you intended to dispose of. *You* were the goat kid's progenitor, Evelyn, not that raccoon I was trying to save from himself. You were the goat kid's lynx. Proud of yourself?"

She screamed and hauled the rabbit bodily off the floor, throwing him across the corner desk. Stationary scattered and Donovan caught himself on the desk's edge to ensure he struck the floor feet first. Training asserted itself and he remembered both the small automatic and slender blade he kept under the desk.

He sniffed. More blood trickled forth. "Revenge is difficult with your quarry gone, isn't it Countess? The ship collision that killed my father sent an idiot captain and shoddy frigate to the bottom of River Mersey, so I had to forge my revenge in steel that built the sturdiest ships in Liverpool. I *knew* where to place *my* fury."

"You killed the Nosfur who wounded your mother," Evelyn hissed, tears in her eyes. "She lived another ten years. I had only an empty house and quiet crypts. They had to know their place, Donovan, the Nosfur in hell, the unclean vegetarians under heel."

"And so, you stand against history," Donovan shouted back. "Despite all I have to offer the order you stand against *me.*" He met her gaze steadily.

She took deep breaths reigning herself in. Naked, her sinew and muscle stood out under her golden fur and Donovan wasn't afraid to admit to himself that he might die equally frightened and aroused.

"I'd have you know your place. That would be enough." For the first time in their long painful battle of wills she looked away. "I'd kill a goat to dispel evil to the world. I'd kill your City Hall stooge, I'd kill..." She stood tall and glared hard at him with resolve, blinking her tears away. "It was poison in the offered veins of the first Martyre that killed the first plague of Nosfur, down in that well. If my hate is a poison Donovan, then I'll become whatever I need to in order to stop them. And you if you get in my way. Gladly."

Donovan crossed around the desk, dizzy and bruised, and came to stand toe to toe with her. He sighed as the truth settled in. The Countess and the council that sent her had no imagination, no concept of a better world in the making. All she allowed herself to have was the same ancient, handed-down grievances and an urgency to bolster old hierarchies half-dead.

Blood dripped down his chin as he decided the time had come. "Alright then, Evelyn. Let's play this out. I'll lay the last stages of my plan out for you, all of it. You don't know what I've already set in motion. Once you see it all before you, I suspect that you will feel quite differently about how to proceed. If not, well, then I will acquiesce and complete the original mission as directed. I'll even kill Sandy Mallory myself if it will make you happy."

Her fury was coming under control, but her hatred hadn't abated. "I'm already out of patience, Donovan. I've seen your grand plan and I've seen your forge."

"But not what lies underneath. In the base of that mill lay the results of all I've striven to create, all I have accomplished. Sandy Mallory was but a gatekeeper, proof the plan could work. Once you see what lies there, once you understand, you will see a whole new world. And you can decide for yourself if you wish to destroy it." He took a deep breath. "I won't stop you if you do."

His eyes fell to the space between her breasts, and he saw, flattened within the fur and held on by the thinnest golden chain, the pendant he'd given her. He stepped forward, ready to be struck again and prepared. When she didn't resist, he touched his broken nose to it and to her, spreading his blood upon them both. He held his hands behind himself like a prisoner. "I'm tired of fighting you. I'll give myself to the Council and answer for any perceived crimes. Give me one day to settle some of the fallout your interference caused and tomorrow night my little kingdom is at your golden feet."

Above his brow her nostrils flared as she smelled his blood mingle with her own fur. Her breathing settled as she regained control. She laughed and it was pained. "Then give yourself to me now as it may be the last time I have you alive."

Was this lion predictable? Or was Donovan even more so? "Of course, Countess."

She showed teeth again. "One more thing." Her hands came up to undo his shirt, one button at a time. "Drop the knife."

Donovan didn't mind doing that.

Détente established, the Countess tried to coax Donovan's nose downward where heat was already rising, but with claws out and a defiant grin the rabbit scaled her frame instead. Their fury at one another took carnal shape.

***

Crawford watched Charlie drop into the chair by the phone and stare at nothing. They'd both driven in silence and carried the tension inside.

Crawford let the blanket he'd thrown around himself fall to the floor. His limbs ached, but with an assortment of small pains associated with the fight he could just barely remember, rather than another onset of change. He was getting reasonably good at discerning the difference. "Are you hurt?" he asked.

Charlie shook his head and looked around, registering that they were actually back home. "I need…" he blinked. "Do you still have…"

"We both need one." Crawford fetched the bottle and two glasses, pouring generously. Charlie held his like a drenched sailor pulled from a stormy sea, shivering now and again. Crawford thought he should go throw clothes on but didn't want to leave him alone. "Take your time. I don't smell wounds on you."

"The others…"

Silence hung heavy while Crawford figured out what to say. "They're not in any more pain."

Charlie's shoulders shook and he wept. Crawford leaned forward and took a hand. It was warm and clenched his like a lifeline. "Charlie, nothing could have prepared any of you for that. Don't think for a second there was anything different that you could have done, you get me?"

"You fought them."

"I fought *one* of them, and it didn't expect me." The memory formed of two jaws parting wider, wider until the split spilled whatever blood had filled the wolfhound out into the alley. The murky memory was sickening, but he'd carried more back from this change. He'd controlled it, he'd done it. It had been him. Mostly.

Charlie glanced up, cheeks wet. He drank the whiskey in two gulps. "What...happened to you? You weren't *you*."

"Simon Govic did. Whatever he had, he gave to me. I lost some time a few nights ago."

Charlie put recent misadventures together. "That bite made you one of those things?"

"No. Something else. They're called Nosfurs. Blood drinkers that can only come out at night."

Charlie blinked. "So, like Dracula?"

Crawford frowned. "What's a Dracula?"

"Exactly what you said, but in a gothic horror novel from...Europe. It's written as a series of letters."

Crawford chuffed. "Does everybody know about these things before I do?"

"These things aren't real though." Charlie blinked. "Weren't."

Charlie eye's traced him up and down and Crawford felt strangely fine with his own nakedness.

"You saved me," Charlie said.

Crawford finished his drink and set it by the telephone. He didn't want another. "It was the first time I brought this around on purpose. Still not sure how. I'd been fighting it for days, seeing..." how to explain this, "looking for people who knew what was happening to me. I think it comes when the moon's full and takes over no matter how hard I fight it, but if I deliberately bring it forth, this were thing—"

"Were?"

"That's what it's called. If I *invite* it in, I think I can control it. I can be...me when I'm *it* because it's a part of me. Does that make sense?"

"Does it make sense to you?" Charlie dried his tears with a hand. There would be ample time to mourn Leslie and the others, Crawford knew. Charlie had too much to come to grips with in the moment.

Charlie swallowed. "I should be dead. If it weren't for you, I would be."

"Likewise, Charlie. I heard the Thompson. You injured it." Crawford squeezed Charlie's hand tighter, rough palms pressing, trading warmth.

His friend was going to be alright, and Crawford felt gratitude knowing that.

That certainty, combined with the contact made Crawford feel a comfort deep within that he'd not felt in a long time. So many doubts, buried truths, self-hatred at the reasons for his failed marriage and his under-table drinking were finding cause, melting way. Crawford sat naked before his friend in every way that truly mattered and it felt…fine.

Charlie's eyes held his and he took a deep breath. The stillness brought a moment of clarity. "I'd never have been able to tell you the truth Crawford," Charlie's tail wagged once and then went still, anxiety still guiding him. "I've long known that…I've suspected that you…"

"That I'm like this?" Crawford became conscious of his own nakedness but didn't care. He realized he stank of death but that didn't matter either.

"No." Charlie gritted his teeth. "Not…that. I have to say this, Crawford. I've been holding it for so long. If I'd died tonight, I would never have said a word. I've long suspected that you're like *me* and you don't know it."

Crawford couldn't put word to truth, so he waited.

Charlie sighed. "Crawford, I go alone to certain parts of town because I take my comfort with other men. Pansies, fruits, all the spitting, cutting things you've ever heard about *those* people? Well, I am incurably, and unapologetically, one of those people."

The apartment got quiet as Crawford turned over Charlie's words, his own gaze leaving his to fix pointlessly on the bony ebony of the telephone in the meager lamplight.

Like *me*. Charlie only needed the green fatigues of a British corporal splashed with French trench mud and he could be a certain badger's twin. *Fear made men honest with each other, didn't they?* his old ghost asked. That question followed Crawford home from France, dug through every silence between himself and Kamila in Virginia.

He took a job for a cause he didn't believe in, folded within himself like a puzzle to be forever unsolved, and vanished from his own life.

His breath was catching, so Charlie leaned forward and kissed him. Lips pressed, parted, breath traded. They held that connection for a moment and Crawford's hand went to Charlie's shoulder. Charlie breathed something.

Crawford parted reluctantly. "Yes?"

"We can't. Not now. We need to call the office, figure out what to say now that the speak is burnt down, that we've lost…everybody."

Of course. Crawford felt the cusp of something he needed to unravel at last, but the timing couldn't be worse. "We'll tell them we came back here, we were both wrecks and we needed to put ourselves together. I'll need to make a quick call right after. Then we go in."

Charlie clearly had so much to say, grief, release, a bouquet of emotions. But he sat up straight. "You get cleaned up and dressed. I'll call the office, tell them we're coming. We'll work out the particulars on the way. Thank you for coming to my rescue."

Crawford could weep at that, but grinned weakly, no hat to tip. "Any time, Charlie."

CHAPTER 19

WINDOWS INTO HELL

"What is this place?" Sandy asked from the shadow of an adjacent rooftop, nearly two miles from where they'd left Bucky cursing the world at large. Dawn was mere hours away.

"It's where I live for now. I'm putting considerable trust that you will guard that secret," responded the shadow next to Sandy's.

"And why should you do that? I'm still not convinced you didn't get your revenge on Bucky and me by informing the Prohibition police on us. How else should they have found us on our first night?"

"I already told you I didn't do that and why. I've kept to myself, but I've known many in that speak whose existence was threatened tonight, not to mention that police will comb that place for evidence that endangers us. Bucky will hopefully pull anything incriminating out while he can."

Sandy doubted that. Living long on the vein didn't elevate Bucky's presence of mind. So much had happened in so little time since Donovan's lion assassin attacked her on her return from school and tried to end her existence. With time and space taken from the venture they'd dived into, Sandy felt compelled to reconsider her recent choices. Again.

And ruminating with her was the very doe she'd shared time with on that most dangerous of voyages, whose trust she'd betrayed under the very best of intentions so long after. Sandy would learn quite soon if they were here to make amends or if Celeste had other plans.

"Bucky is in a complicated state of mind," Sandy said, herself unconvinced. "He'll need time to put himself together."

"Bucky has too little mind to assemble, Sandy," Celeste replied. "He lost money and face. Nothing else is important to him."

Sandy wanted to point out that she herself was, but the words died on her lips. All those dead in that fire, two of them innocent. As had been the landlord. And she'd gone right along.

"Are you alright?"

Sandy unbound from the shadow and faced the distant horizon where morning would soon rise. She wondered what it would look like. "I honestly don't know how to live without hurting someone close to me. Or helping others hurt them."

Celeste revealed herself and stepped close. "You didn't ask for life taken from the vein, Sandy. I only accepted it as the better of two horrible alternatives. The perfect path for either of us doesn't exist. I tried to go this alone, well most of it, and you've always tried to find someone to share the years with."

"To bitter effect," the squirrel squinted at that distant lid of light where night tinted the darkest blue.

"It doesn't have to be." Celeste worked a shingle with her hoof. "I brought you here to meet someone you can help and who can help you in return." With a leap light as a skipped stone over water, Celeste was on the roof of her own abode next to a thick-framed dormer window that she opened with one hand and whispered a word.

Stubby goat horns on a small ungulate head poked out into the night. "Ms. Mallory?" The kid blinked.

Sandy was momentarily terror stricken at the realization that one of her students from Noah's Plank had been lured here. Her eyes met Celeste's in a silent demand for answers. This was a trap after all.

Celeste shook her head. "I didn't do this to him Sandy."

"Do what?"

"Ms. Mallory, why do you look so much younger?" Samson's stubby fingers were on the window's ledge, and he hopped up on it with both hooves, displaying the nimble, robust grace common for his species.

"Don't fall," Sandy said. "I'll come to you." Fury beat like a drum. What kind of trap would Celeste lay with a former student, that she would betray her true nature? She could only pick her way down using the natural talents of her species to maintain the frail mortality she'd cultivated so long with the students.

She had the claws of her feet on one of the building's drainpipes when she realized that Samson stood on the roof next to her. "I learned to jump," he said. "I've never been able to jump this far or this fast, and I practiced on the stairs inside."

Sandy looked up into the emerging pools of black above the fangs on the verge of sprouting and felt panic that skipped her heart in place. The boy skipped back into the dark, not yet bound to any shadow. "It's okay, Ms. Mallory, I know you're like me."

Celeste sat next to the dormer and gave Sandy a baleful stare as the squirrel glared at her. "I didn't turn him. But someone who knows Donovan Calvert did. Come inside." The doe was through the window in a blink and Samson leapt to follow. After a moment's hesitation so did Sandy.

The top floor of Celeste's new residence was barren, not one stick of furniture. Formalities were short, voices echoing through the house. The kid had been frightened and only remembered traces of his ordeal. "Her mouth smelled like something bitter when she bit me, and it hurt. Then the raccoon...," he swallowed. "I became weak."

The fear in that recollection tore Sandy's heart in two. Of all the cruelties she'd witnessed or partaken in, this was beyond the pale. This innocent child's life was over, another existence trapped in this frame had begun. "Why would they do this?"

Celeste spoke for him. "Crawford, he's a new...acquaintance I've made, told me that an enemy of Donovan's wanted his contact at City Hall dead. The Superintendent at your school won an election, and what happened tonight wasn't Samson's fault."

"He wasn't happy to see me when I was sent to him." Samson studied a wall, lost. "I was sick and hungry. I killed him." His voice became thick as he shivered.

Leicester had been reluctant to take Sandy on, doing it only for Donovan's patronage, always distracted, feeling the school's mission and its needful children below him, a steppingstone. She'd not miss him, and his death wasn't important now.

"Samson," Sandy stepped forward and wrapped the kid in an embrace. "I know you feel guilty about what you did." Her own guilt dangled naked before her, gagged from speaking, a demon that would return. "But you had no choice. The hunger you feel, It's the hardest thing to resist if you're not trained to."

Samson was working hard to bury his emotions, express the child's image of a brave man. His eyes didn't moisten enough anymore, and he blinked over and over, his face scrunching up with unrequited pain. "I don't ever want to hurt anyone again. Please tell me I don't have to do that again." His eyes went from Celeste's to Sandy's and back. Celeste kept her expression blank, fighting to appear detached. Only Sandy could tell how much anguish Celeste was sharing with him.

Sandy hugged Samson more tightly and all at once the little kid let himself go. The sobs were desperate, bordering on terror. Sandy buried her nose in his forehead and let her eyes rise to Celeste's. "I'll help you Samson. You won't be alone. Celeste, I need to use your phone."

Celeste fought an emotional battle without words. At last, she said, "Please tell me you're not calling Bucky. You couldn't put him in worse hands."

"I'll deal with Bucky later." Sandy ran fingers through Samson's fur on his shuddering head. He was crying silently now. "I can help Samson, but I'll need to call…"

"No." Celeste darkened. "You are not seriously considering calling Donovan Calvert."

"He has resources…"

"You remember what you were forced to do by him? I saw you without your fangs, Sandy. He taught you to literally torture yourself. He *can't* know this child is alive." Celeste wanted to say more but trailed off.

"I wouldn't turn the child in to him. That's a mistake that will never be made again."

"Then why in all hell would you call him? If he even sees you, he'll know you partook."

"What did you take?" Samson asked.

Before either Sandy or Celeste could say another word, the phone rang downstairs. Then again. Samson broke away and was on the hoof and leapt to the bottom of the stairs by the time both Sandy and Celeste collided at its top, his anxiety distilled into a burst of energy. They entered the small main parlour, and the goat was holding the phone, his trauma buried under nervous action. "Yes?"

Celeste snatched the phone from his small hand before Sandy could ask for it. With senses attuned all three of them could hear the gruff voice at the other end. "Kid's okay?"

Celeste traded glances with Sandy. "Samson's fine, Crawford. I saw the end of the raid and the fire that came after. I thought that was supposed to happen about now?"

There was an uncomfortable lupine cough. "They moved it up."

"I take it that was you who rescued the other wolf with the machine gun?"

"You were there *watching?*"

"I wasn't watching, I happened to notice the conflagration while trying to get my friend away from Bucky Cavali. I did warn you to not raid that place but obviously they went in without you and I was too late to intervene. Your friend is lucky that half the Nosfurs in that speak took flight."

Somebody away from the phone asked a question that Sandy couldn't hear.

Celeste heard just fine. "Yes," she said dryly. "I suppose you'll have to tell your hopefully discreet friend that there were indeed more of *those bastards* and still are."

"More Draculas," The lupine sighed. "Are you all there?"

Sandy had heard that word before but didn't interrupt and turned with Celeste to the faint glow from beyond the window shutters.

"The sun is rising soon, Crawford," Celeste said.

Sandy took the cryptic answer's meaning. They were all going to have to rest here and didn't want it announced aloud that they were trapped in place.

"Okay, I have to get my partner into work and report in. You all rest, I'll come tomorrow night. We'll figure out next moves then."

Celeste set the earpiece back on its cradle and stood next to the phone. "We'll all have to stay here for the day. There are two closets that can hold out the light until I manage to get better drapes and furniture from the Sears-Roebuck's catalogue.

Sandy eyed the phone. "May I please make a call?"

"Sandy, you may *not* call Donovan Calvert from here and if you're smart you won't call him at all." She may as well say it. "That bastard thinks

Samson is dead care of the Prohee I was just talking to. I didn't bring you and this kid together in order to risk his safety again."

"Who's Donovan Calvin?" The kid looked back at Sandy. "Isn't he some rich rabbit who helped you get that job at the school? Some of my friends think he's a hero for being a vegetarian and so rich but another of the teachers said he's a capital pig. They didn't explain that in civics."

First light was bleeding through one window's shades and Sandy guided Samson away from it, back towards the stairs. "You don't need to worry. I won't let anyone hurt you. I had other reasons to call him, other plans entirely. Celeste and I can discuss it later. Come."

Sandy led the child up, looking back to see Celeste standing by the phone, staring off into space and thinking. One thin ray of morning sun pierced dangerously close on the wooden floor, but the doe was ignoring it.

"Are you two good friends?" Samson asked when they lay together in a closet, the young Nosfur seeming comfortable in the dark while in his night-studies teacher's protective arms.

"We've known each other a long time." Sandy Mallory pondered the way forward, thoughts fading to fuzz as the dark took them both into dreamless peace.

***

Bleary dawn followed Crawford's Chevrolet to the office, both wolves reflecting on all they'd had to sort through. Tiredness notwithstanding, they had a story to get straight, half at best that could be true. Crawford had a peculiar raw sensation as they entered the somber office like he'd been tenderized. No doubt that came from the undefinable experience of changing to feral twice in one night, covering up a murder, battling a Nosfur to the death and confessing both his true natures to Charlie, all in the space of seven hours. He was a sordid mess of aches and emotions.

Four more cops and a fellow agent were dead and the fact that he felt completely outside himself, as though he'd stolen another pelt and skin to walk around in, didn't reduce the urgent need to stay focused.

"Cain. Rothscub." Beatie looked like death itself. "In here."

The two wolves trudged into the bear's smoke-filled den, Charlie checking corners as they entered. It had been hard to reconcile themselves to obscuring the reasons for five dead colleagues, but they had kept the story simple as possible, lest they both wind up in armless white coats with buckles on the back.

Beatie made them wait while he stepped out and Charlie made a low noise and pointed his muzzle at a tableau outside the office. A weasel in a dark suit embraced the chief, disappearing into his massive frame, sobbing. Charlie stared. "My God, that's Leslie's husband."

Crawford looked away. "You didn't kill Agent Spettle, Charlie."

"I could have been faster…" Tears welled in Charlie's eyes once again as he turned back and met Crawford's level gaze.

"I couldn't stop it either. Charlie. If you tell them what really happened, they won't believe you and you'll anger everybody who lost someone. Beatie's coming."

Beatie closed his small door behind him before sitting down heavily behind his desk, hollow eyed. His voice was ice. "Where the hell have you both been?"

Charlie was sniffling, burying tears. Crawford put an arm out and around him. "We were both a mess when we shot our way out, sir. I took him home."

"What, not to a hospital?"

"We…I was in a state sir. I'm…I'm sorry." Charlie sat upright, swallowing.

Crawford fought to avoid sounding defiant. "We needed some time before coming in. We couldn't get the others out and…"

Charlie cried and Crawford broke off, fighting his own tears back at the enormity of it all. Greif held its own schedule, Crawford knew. He shut up and kept holding his partner.

Beatie removed a handkerchief from his suit jacket and passed it over. "We'll need statements. Agents are racing in from Washington right now. To be sure, did anybody make it out of there alive?"

Charlie put himself together. "No sir. There were so many bullets fired, so many…the things they were doing in there…"

Beatie leaned back and Crawford saw that Leslie's husband's tears had soaked his tie. "The LaSalle speak is gone, part of the top floor collapsed down onto it." He looked between them. "The medical examiner is still working…many bodies were picked out, just one with a badge so far, officer Minsk.

Charlie frowned to concentrate. "We had him on the register when he was shot. No wait, he was stabbed in the neck."

Beatie held up a meaty brown hand and gritted his teeth. "Stop there, Agent Rothscub. Agents will debrief you on what the bastards did, may they rot in hell. All I need to know is if any other of ours were out in the wind…" He gave them hard Kodiak eyes, "like you two were for so many hours."

Here it came. Crawford fidgeted the buttons on his suit jacket and straightened his tie. "That would be my fault sir. Charlie can handle himself, but I decided to take him home."

"Was that your call to make, agent Cain?"

"No sir. I did anyway."

Silence was a hard object.

"Step outside, Agent Rothscub. Take a walk. Cirelli is here, he'd like to be with you while you wait for our pals from DC."

"Go ahead Charlie, we're all here for you friend." If the squeeze on his packmate's shoulder looked like anything at all beyond brotherly support, then Crawford could care less.

Charlie stepped past him and out.

Beatie and him were alone.

"Where the hell were you last night?" the bear rumbled, eyes narrowing to specks in his great head. "You were supposed to be with the other team raiding a place uptown. You never showed and they were a dog short when they went in."

"Sir, I know you're upset, but I got the instructions earlier in the day and we were supposed to have three sites we were raiding at three AM."

"If you were at muster right here like you were supposed to be you would have known that we cut one off and split the teams."

"I was tied up with a family matter, went to my assigned locale directly. Then I found out on a call to the office that the assignments had been reshuffled."

"I know that. I talked to the desk clerk." Beatie leaned forward and folded great clawed hands. "So why when he told you that you were supposed to go to the Wacker site did you instead go to LaSalle?"

"I got mixed up, sir."

"You got mixed up."

"Both raids were underway and I didn't think I'd get to Wacker in time so I headed over to LaSalle to help corral and hand out the tickets."

"You left the Wacker group with five agents to do a speak raid two days after the mob literally *ate* a cop like the feral animals they are and decided for whatever reason to make the Lasalle group a seven-agent team. Was there something that you knew that we didn't?"

Crawford felt like his clothes were shrinking around him, along with the office. Only the mammal who held his job by the reins got bigger. Sweat got cold. He really hadn't thought this all through. Charlie's account had the heat of battle in its favor. His imbecilic partner, however, did not.

"Like I said Beatie…"

"Yes?"

"LaSalle was closer. I'd already missed the door-down. If I'd gone to Wacker, well, the whole thing would be over completely. I made it to LaSalle in time to help Charlie survive a shoot-out with the last mook in the speak. Everybody else was dead." Crawford swallowed. "That's the important thing. I'd die for that wolf sir, I love him…" What the fuck was he *doing*? "…like my own brother."

His heart hammered in his ears, senses heightening to the point where he thought he heard the bear's as well. Conservative elements on the force aggressively pursued homosexual relations of any kind. Getting even attraction known could be career-ending.

"So," Beatie betrayed no emotion at all. "Did you yourself hit anybody on your return fire?"

"I can't say for sure sir. If the fire burned all the bodies inside the place we'll likely never know."

"Except for one body in the alley next to the speak. A wolfhound was torn to pieces."

Crawford buried a groan.

"Injuries were consistent with the killing of officer Tooley. So now we have a torn-up cop and a torn-up mobster."

Crawford didn't know what else to say so he nodded.

"There will be considerable mention of this infernal killer at the State's Attorney General's conference this afternoon."

"Are the police expected to start a taskforce to find this, this killer? Are we?"

"I don't know what's to come of this. Mayor Deever is already demanding more Federal funds for Prohibition enforcement. For you it's an idle question anyway. I was already mulling over what to do when word was slipped to me that you deliberately avoided your duties at a rent party you broke up a few nights ago."

How the fuck had Beatie found out about that? "Sir…uh, Beatie, there were circumstances there,"

"Dammit agent Cain do you know how hard it is when the very same silent-wet government officials who think this whole enforcement of the Volstead act is a joke demand that those appointed to put on a show for the public take it as seriously as possible? Everybody in Washington has two faces and no shoulders."

"No shoulders?" Crawford cocked his head.

"To cry on, you moron. When fines aren't collected, and offenders reoffend demands for results go *up*. Even in the midst of gang wars and massacres it goes up. If we can't perform the simpler tasks, how could we be charged with the complicated parts of the Temperance forces' moral crusade?"

The simpler moral tasks of chasing a poor musician out of his home. Crawford could have laughed bitterly in Beatie's face if he wanted to lose his job then and there.

"You're suspended as of now. Three days. No pay."

That should have stung, but in the moment it hit numbly and Crawford looked away. Behind Beatie's desk he noticed a weak glint of crystal and saw the decanter his boss took from the Chevy's back seat yesterday, evidence-tag blank.

Had the fill line dropped an inch? Crawford couldn't be mad. In Beatie's place, Crawford would be in the good stuff too.

Beatie was waiting for Crawford to say something, and Crawford couldn't think of a thing. The wolf sighed. "I suppose that's warranted."

Beatie leaned forward and showed all his teeth. "You *suppose*, do you? You stupid son of a bitch I've lost two good agents and the police force is now down six officers in three days. And in the middle of the worst single loss of life since Prohibition enforcement started you two fuck off back to your apartment to lick your goddam wounds? I thought Rothscub was dead! And as for you, I have no goddam idea what's wrong with you, but if obligations of the badge are too much to handle with your impending divorce, then maybe you shouldn't hold one."

Crawford's ears flattened tight as a trench bomb drill and his muzzle dipped lower and lower as the words rained down. But in the shame, there was anger stirring like embers. "How do you know I'm getting divorced?"

"Your ex-wife's lawyer called this office to find out where her papers are, see if you scrammed. Dammit Crawford I'm sorry that things aren't working out for you, but do you think for one second that the rest of the bureau doesn't need your support as badly as your partner does? I don't care what kind of wolf-pack hokum pulled you to Charlie's side. We *all* need you. And it's only because you helped keep him alive that you aren't in cuffs and facing dereliction. Do you understand?"

Crawford felt his limbs and jaws ache. The change was on tap. What a way to end the conversation that would be. "I do."

"Get out of my office and await instructions at home. I'll send them with Charlie. Dismissed."

Crawford went out and saw Charlie's back to him, Cirelli's silver-furred hand on the wolf's hunched shoulder. Well enough, Crawford decided. He left his car key on Charlie's desk and walked out. If eyes were on him his dignity wasn't affected. He wasn't sure he belonged here and felt as much a ghost now as when he steamed back from France.

He walked round the building to take a side-alley to the next street from the parking lot and stopped short when he saw a trio of mammals sitting in his car.

"One plan defeated, one pushed along," said the young wolf in the passenger seat.

"The iron sings a warning song," added the middle-aged otter behind her.

"For the blood forced to mind a right that's wrong." promised the old coyote filling out the space behind the driver, dirty feet up on Crawford's seat.

Crawford and the Sisters traded stares.

"What the hell are you doing in my car?" Crawford asked.

"We corrected a mistake," suggested the young wolf. "Took a phone call but the speak did burn."

"The fox did yearn."

"And the squirrel has spurned...."

They all traded glances and the old coyote wiggled her toes. "Well, she's spurned somebody anyway. We're not clear on that part yet. Irish squirrels are skittish, you know?"

Crawford glanced around the lot to see if somebody else was watching this. "I don't need your bunk but do need my car empty of vagrants when my partner leaves to go home."

"Ah, him," the young wolf said sadly. "Cute one in that bow tie of his, but he's no Brit badger, is he?" She grinned toothily and Crawford felt a chill as her words settled over him.

"Who are you people?" he growled.

The otter smiled. "There's a gift for you back here that'll help you still those nerves." She pointed down and out of sight. "It'll have its price, just like everything does." She smiled grimy teeth.

Crawford couldn't see it to but didn't want to approach. "What price?"

"To reconcile with an old ghost," the Otter suggestively patted the seat beside her. "The price is paid to him no less than us."

Crawford turned away, heart hammering, and hurried past the car to the alley adjacent. He didn't stop for two blocks.

***

Edmond was more agitated then usual when delivering his report. "Word came in that Crawford has been suspended from his position. Something about a speak raid gone wrong."

Donovan nodded and smoked. "That could be useful. Much as his access to the bureau's resources are valuable, his agitated state of mind may be more so."

Edmond's tail curled subconsciously around Donovan's chair-side cigar stand. "You intend to have him...solve another problem sir?"

"Do I detect an edge in your voice?"

The possum's whiskers twitched. "Apologies sir, but with all respect, why such familiarity with someone who would try to dispense with you as soon as..."

"The wolf?"

"No sir. He didn't sleep with you after trying to cripple you."

Donovan's ears rose in surprise and sniffed his bruised nose. Edmond usually avoided candor like the plague. "Is that something you feel should concern you, Edmond?"

"Again, I meant no disrespect..."

"However?"

The possum's tail released the cigar stand with a wobble. It was prehensile enough for Donovan's man to suspend himself from a chandelier but even at his angriest the possum had never surrendered propriety. "Von Haften has no respect for you, and I know it's been so long since you've had any serious relations—"

Donovan leaped and stood nose to nose with the possum. "My level of familiarity with the Countess is my concern. As would it be with anyone else. I've raised no qualms about your dark proclivities, have I, Edmond?"

The possum shrank at that, chastened. "Sir I only seek to warn you that—"

Donovan took a deep breath. "Be very careful Edmond."

"—She's trying to purchase Calvert Steel. In between her...visitations here."

"What?"

"I've tracked her twice in the vicinity of LaSalle and Washington near the Chicago stock exchange before losing her again. A series of trades today put shares with some holding companies overseas, nearly two percent acquired."

Donovan threw has hands up and began pacing. "That could be anyone. Five to ten percent of my company changes hands every few months. The Martyres member families own literally hundreds of transnational interests. They could already own a third of me and I'd never truly know."

"And if she's helping secure more of your company to oust you?"

Donovan moved to the window and peered outside to see the Duesenberg was still missing. She'd gone out with the dawn.

"I pay you to worry so I suppose I should have expected this. Understand, Edmond that I assumed from her arrival that the Countess would be meddling with my affairs. I have been preparing for the worst, especially in light of tonight, which brings me back to our distraught, endangered lupine friend?"

"Sir?"

"I'll need you to oversee certain preparations at the steel mill before I bring Evelyn. An evacuation drill needs to be scheduled and we'll need some extra ventilation. Summer is coming and I really think we should test the steam shutters in advance of the foundry becoming too hot to work in. In particular the Countess should be comfortable when she returns for her visit."

"And, if she does reject your final appeal when she…sees?"

Donovan smiled. "Then we make a second introduction."

***

Crawford wandered several blocks with the realization that he didn't want to go home with only a swallow or two in the bottle to settle his nerves. The three hags had rattled him with what they couldn't know, and he didn't want to see them again.

He had divorce papers to send off. He accepted that now and the sheer realization of that surrender left him, not relieved but empty.

The spark lit last night with Charlie put something in front of him that was an oasis in the desert of dread, a window into truths long avoided. He'd loved the woman he was losing, he knew that much, but it was now openly apparent that every male's walk and tail swish now had a more in-depth language he wanted, no needed, to understand.

Hope returned with him to his car, now empty of otters, coyotes, and wolves. Their scent remained, cinder and copper tang and dank clay from half-kept hides lingered. "They leave me something?"

No answer as he reached to the back seat, felt around and found the steel of his battered flask where the crystal of Donovan's decanter had been stowed. Thank God Beatie didn't wander back here to see Crawford's car restocked.

Pulling it forward, the flask was tightly screwed shut and sloshing with something he himself hadn't poured. He remembered the first time he'd seen the trio pushing their carts of detritus, bits of an obvious bathtub still.

Could it be poisoned? Crawford doubted that. He'd have time to mull things over on the trip back home, hopefully keep his condition in check tonight in order to visit Celeste again and figure out his next moves in regards to Calvert. The direction his allegiances were leaning wasn't much of a surprise. Celeste provided the information that helped him save the man who might be more than his pack-mate while Donovan had urged him to murder a kid.

He transferred the flask to the inside of his coat and left to take the elevated train before anyone at the office saw him skulking around. With luck, the press conference would just be more hot air blown about work to be done by Chicago's Prohibition bureau. Charlie would hopefully be able to skip out. God knew he'd dealt with too much.

***

Beatie was good enough to keep Charlie's name out of the papers. Regardless, the wolf was on the knife's edge of anxiety after a night of learning about a whole other world of creatures who wanted him dead. Only knowing that a friend with a big foot in that world might well and truly care for him kept him going.

The wolf stood apart from other agents as they filed into the warehouse where the haul from the raid at Wacker had been taken. Charlie had given his account of bullets flying and butchered bodies burning, leaving the teeming walls of blood sucking demons for later nightmares. Crawford had been right, a word about any of that would have him jacketed in Chicago Reed hospital already.

The warehouse was well lit and for that he was grateful. He wouldn't sleep at home now, so he reduced the number of unspoken questions about his sanity and fitness for duty by coming here instead to listen to Illinois Attorney General Brundage spout for the press.

Charlie took well-wishes from other officers and agents who mourned lost colleagues with him before leaving him to collect his thoughts.

Cameras flashed as the stage was set. A barrel Charlie presumed had been recovered from the Wacker drive raid was rolled onto the dais by two officers who took sniffs and gave each other suspicious glances before stepping away.

Attorney General Brundage's self-aggrandizing howl echoed under the rafters. "Accept this promise. When the scourge of intoxicating liquors has been poured from every den of ill repute, from the wet boardwalks of Jersey to San Francisco, only then will God's creatures know the tranquility intended for us." He brandished his teeth. "Until that day, the men and women of this city must be resolute in virtue."

The dog raised his clawed hand as if in benediction, immortalized in a camera flash. The raccoon beside the photographer scrawled notes furiously and chewed tobacco that Charlie smelled from the back of the small warehouse along with the embers of a half dozen cigarettes.

Under that was something...wrong.

Brundage kept on. "Last night's violence will see every last one of the mob's feral scofflaws cuffed and caged. Through the hard work of our officers of the law, supported by agents of the Bureau of Internal Revenue assigned to Prohibition enforcement, the good people of Chicago will see justice done, and a better world for our cubs."

Beatie stood by next to a vulpine reverend whose sermons had been printed in many anti-saloon league pamphlets. Only the Mayor wasn't here, which was fine with Charlie. The fanfare of the law's battle call was becoming obscene.

Charlie was grateful for late afternoon sunbeams that pierced the windows and painted the rafters. He was alive, luck he didn't deserve. He tried desperately not to think of Leslie's exposed skull and the way her feet kicked on that speak's floor.

A hand on his shoulder startled him. Cirelli grinned his easy silvery grin and whispered. "You gonna be okay?"

Charlie nodded, trying to still his anxiety with focus on the here and now.

The Attorney General placed an ivory-spatted foot atop the barrel, holding the illegal liquor barrel in place with his claws and orated for the news-mammals who took additional photos of his faux heroic pose. Was there a singe mark on that barrel?

The great kodiac nodded, glancing briefly into the throng of officers at Charlie with a wan smile that Charlie acknowledged with a curt nod. The honor to come next had already been offered him and Charlie had flatly declined it, papers be damned. Beatie puffed his pipe and hefted the fire-axe at his side. "Henderson was first through the door at Wacker and was nearly shot, so I'm gonna pass it to her."

The mountain lion accepted the axe, and Beatie muttered something to the cop about not hitting the AG's foot accidentally.

Seeing some whiskey dump might be therapeutic in some way. "I'm glad they had a good haul at Wacker last night," Charlie whispered. "They get many barrels like that?"

A weasel taking photos for the Tribune was down low as the mountain lion set foot to barrel and Brundage stepped back, adjusting his starched lapels. There was a moment while the photographer fiddled with his camera.

Cirelli looked to the stage then back. "I was told they dumped everything at Wacker down a sewer drain on site," he pursed his lips. "Beatie told me there was just one barrel taken from LaSalle. I think that's it up there."

Charlie glanced back at the barrel, saw the scorch marks, sampled the faintest drifting scent and felt his heart seize. His next words froze in his throat.

"Now?" Officer Henderson asked and got enthusiastic nods.

Camera flashes caught the axe splintering the barrel's lid but not the moment after it broke and came loose.

Blood fountained out onto the pavement, it's stink choking the air. Then came screams from the throng. A shape tumbled slimily from the barrel's opened mouth and rode the crimson wake, sinewy limbs unfolding within the morass. The weasel photographer scrambled, slipped on the blood and dropped his camera in the muck as he bolted away. The Attorney General frantically patted his necktie at his own mouth and nose before noisily throwing up all over it. He slipped to his knees in the spreading mire and crawled towards where Charlie stood. Seasoned cops hollered, a rookie pissed, and Charlie saw the world narrow to a tunnel of crimson as he and Cirelli put backs to the wooden wall of the warehouse turned abattoir. Beatie gasped as rivulets of blood reached for his thick clawed toes. "It's like a window into hell," he said as though his very breath was a stolen thing.

Charlie closed his eyes against the vision and heard a thud on the pavement before him. He opened them again to see it was the Attorney General, the top dog of law and order himself. He'd fainted dead away.

CHAPTER 20

MASKS TO STEAL

Crawford sat alone in the apartment, phone's earpiece off its rocker to grant him peace. He'd slept for a few hours. The papers for Kamila were signed.

He still loved her, still lamented all that time that he'd failed to show it, thinking his heart could only love only one person one way. That was the matrimonial promise, and the promise of a father.

To find oneself is to surrender the illusion of oneself so long carried and he'd been terrified to do just that. The war was behind him and so should have been all that happened there, all that he'd experienced. Truth not faced; he'd come back a husk.

He sealed the envelope and set it aside. The post office was just down the corner. For now, his career and relationships were both dashed on the rocks, so he hefted the flask the Sisters had refilled for him, set down a glass and unscrewed the cap.

The notes his nose caught were complex, sugarcane and malted corn. He poured an ounce, and it was dark gold, taking the light without much shine and warming his sinuses as he tried to discern its makeup. It was obviously home-stilled, but whiskey? Bourbon?

A whisper deep within himself told him the three weird hags meant him no harm. The smallest taste would confirm what they'd given him. What had the otter said? "To quiet an old ghost."

Crawford sipped. It rolled warmly forward and back on his tongue before going down like a small blaze. The trailing taste was vaguely sweet yet imbued with smoke.

This was damn good, like something he'd want to share with the doughboys back in the old world before the rain and the pounding. *The price is paid to him no less than us*, said nobody at all.

But Crawford heard it. "Who said that?"

The walls were blank witnesses. The phone's dead mouth hissed. The engine of a Rolls Royce chittered under olive-painted steel.

The glass was heavy. Crawford set it down and screwed the flask, feeling the first stir of heat that came with a really strong dram. A foghorn sounded, too close to be coming from the distant mouth of Chicago harbour but close enough to be from the disembarkation point in Saint-Nazaire at the mouth of the Loire River after muster.

The apartment where Crawford stared at sparse furniture was too cramped to fit in the driver's cabin of the Royce puttering under his khaki-uniformed rear.

"Where the hell am I?" Crawford asked.

"Not in the mud my good man," said the voice over his shoulder. A puff of English tobacco tickled Crawford's ear. "But not in the public either."

The comment was confusing. "This is a muster and training camp. No civilians anywhere near here."

The badger's thick muzzle grinningly crossed his shoulder. "Public. House. I think in America, you call them saloons."

"Oh. Right."

A pothole shook the car, gravel crunched under the armoured carriage.

The badger smoked and sighed. "France has a few charming watering holes in which we can get to business on our way to the front, providing the Huns haven't shelled them out. You know the way?"

Crawford thought so. He'd studied many maps. The metal of the steering wheel shuddered under his fingers. "I didn't get your name."

"Reginald Fenwick, Corporal for His Majesty's Infantry."

"Crawford Cain, Private in Second Division, United States Army."

Two soft pats on the shoulder acquainted them.

"My orders said we had dispatches for the front," Crawford said.

A fresh cigarette slid into view in the badger's fingers. Crawford accepted gratefully. The snap of a lit match bobbed by the wolf's cheek, and he kept eyes forward as he puffed.

"I can confirm the papers I'm carrying are just important enough to get there in two days' time," the badger said with an air of indifference.

Crawford nodded. "I can do it in one."

"No need. The orders with this mail bag essentially say that five Rolls Royce armoured vehicles just offloaded are on their way up to support the push and should arrive shortly after we do. Cable was cut around Soissons so telegraphy can't pass that up."

"So, they gave you an American driver and one of the cars to send that?" The checkpoint loomed as Crawford slowed.

Corporal Fenwick coughed. "Not quite. They'd have likely granted me one of those Triumph motorcycles. In this weather I'd have mud up my arse by Nantes. I feel that you and I should do the war effort a favor and get at least one of these fine beasts to the front sooner, don't you?"

Crawford stopped, rolling down the window as the guard approached. "Are you serious?"

Fenwick didn't answer.

"Destination papers," the cat shouldering a Lee Enfield rifle said in tired cockney.

Badger fingers passed up to wolf over to cat. The cat ascended steps into a booth and something was shouted from inside before the guard hurried down. "They say you're listed as a cycle dispatch rather than an armoured escort."

Crawford looked back at the badger, seeing him for the first time. His olive-drab uniform was askew, and his cigarette waggled between pursed lips. His eyes laughed within the black bars over white topping his wide nose and tufts on his ears were cocked with indifference.

Crawford immediately affected the most disinterested sigh he could muster. "Requisitions messed up the paperwork again. This was a smarter decision than two motorcycles I suspect, and I don't know what's in half those envelopes in his bag. They send us up with the armour I would guess it's important. They want us there quick enough."

If the guard wondered why they would need two couriers, he didn't feel like asking. "Wait a tick." Up the hill he went. Then back down again. A bulldog leaned out of the booth above, squinting. "Who's in there?" Also British. Crawford hadn't heard a single American voice since being pulled from his unit. He felt very far from home.

Fenwick leaned out the rear window, kept shallow by the cumbersome gun turret above them both. "Corporal Fenwick, despatch to Reims, getting armour to the front while we're at it."

"Speak up," the Bulldog demanded.

"Speak up," the cat repeated. "A shell cocked his right ear up."

Fenwick rose his voice only the slightest bit. "We're getting this car to the front along with communiques and knickers for the brass to try on for one another to photograph."

Crawford looked straight ahead and the cat fought a hard campaign for a straight face.

"Wot?" said the Bulldog. "Something about knickers?"

"No, Vickers sir. Manuals or some-such." Fenwick kept his tone straight as a ruler. "The French don't know what end to point I suspect."

The bulldog thought past a frown that screwed his blunt face. "Alright. You can move along then. Fight the good fight."

The cat nodded and waved them by.

Crawford got the Rolls Royce rolling.

"You can fuck right off sir," Fenwick called behind him.

"Wot?"

"Said we'll lop the Hun's heads off sir! On to victory!"

"That's the spirit!" came the shout behind the cat in Crawford's rear view. The feline sentry's heart was clearly lodged in his throat.

They rounded the bend, picking up speed and Crawford shuddered with equal parts hemorrhaging roadwork and laughter that split his sides.

He liked Reginald Fenwick immensely. It was possible this war might not be so bad after all.

Nearly six hundred miles to go, and Crawford figured quickly that the badger had made his numbers up. There was no way they'd arrive ahead of the train car hauling the other armour.

The badger coughed. "Forget rank going forward my friend, I'll take you for Crawford and I'll be Reggie. Alright?"

It was and Crawford nodded.

"Bringing this armour up allows us to avoid fueling bivouacs necessary for motorcycles, thus making stops preferable to our schedule. Tonight, we'll rest our heads in Le Mans after we take respite for a drink at a café I know there."

Crawford knew he could press to the front by mid-day tomorrow but the tight, dirty squalor of transport over the Atlantic had gotten to him. He knew a few men from his separated unit had made plans to get away for a bit of fun among the locals before marching to the front. A soldier's luck was often made and rarely found.

Reggie's hand rested on his shoulder again, its warmth settled in as a freshly lit cigarette's smoke teased his ear anew. It made him tingle temple to throat. "Trust me. I've run this route many times."

Crawford grinned. "They friends of yours at this café, Reggie?"

The liquid roll of his accent smoothed over any doubts. "They'll be our friends when we meet them."

Two hours later they sat on a French terrace on rickety chairs with glasses of wine before them. The dusk of the golden country rolled away into sun dripped mist. They toasted joy through adversity, scarfed down mutton and peas, drank and drank again.

Crawford couldn't remember when sweethearts had come up, but he knew that he did most of the talking. Kamila had been brave on the dock, their cub a nervous bundle in her arms. Conscription ruled one of them had to go, both being of carnivorous stock and in fighting health. He'd volunteered immediately. They hadn't argued long. "She was proud of me," Crawford sighed.

"Mates always are," Reggie agreed.

"I've got to write to her."

Fenwick puffed his smoke and watched its spirit depart. "Write when you have something sincere to say. Otherwise, you're just worried about silences. True love tolerates absences."

That gave Crawford something to think about, but in the fog of his wine he couldn't quite do that. "You've someone back home waiting for you?"

"No," said with a carefree smile.

Dark settled and they got to know different worlds through each other. Crawford learned of sturdy public houses, misty cobbles and Styx-like rivers rolling under bridges hundreds of years old. And those goddam rotten Tories.

"Sleep well mate," Crawford heard through alcohol's fog as his friend nestled down. The badger was a beacon of warmth just beyond Crawford's broad back in the small stone hovel they shared. Kamila's shape in Crawford's mind was a Grecian ideal, combed curves, and cryptic smile. He held that as smells of tobacco and badger musk bled into his dreams.

War touched them both next morning. Dawn was glassy eyed as they passed a lorry outside Paris. Low pounding rolled in the distance.

Bags being moved were long and unwieldy. One of them lost its flap to reveal the wilted limpness of muddy mammalian feet. Flies gathered. Downcast muzzles toiled as the dead were moved with nought a word.

They drove past and Crawford didn't think about the people in those bags. In his task-focused mind they were already an abstraction.

Another checkpoint. The fighting was *that* way. Crawford felt falling shells rumble deep in his stomach and wondered if there'd be a drink to have where he and his new friend were going.

It was a strange attractive quality that Reggie had, that sense that you've known a person you've just met your whole life. Crawford felt the urge to get the badger talking more about himself, find more affinity in the war that threw them together.

"I define myself by the company I keep my good man," Reggie said to the back of Crawford's head, and he imagined breath tickling his ear again. Crawford now wondered why the badger sat alone in the back seat like a chauffeured socialite rather than up front with him. Tactful observance of rank perhaps. Reggie sighed. "I'm short on good company where I'm from. You sir fit that bill." That peculiar lament bore a compliment that made the wolf glow.

Crawford found it hard to accept that Reggie had few friends, but when one spoke their mind… "I live far from the people I grew up with," Crawford supplied. "Everyone went to the cities."

"You'll meet new people." Reggie said confidently. "I'm glad to be one of them."

The terrain outside the car grew scars, scattered village structures chipped like dropped bricks. The war was closer.

"We'll decamp at a place a few miles ahead," Reggie breathed. "I left a bottle of Speyside here last time." The smile in his voice suggested the scarred world around them was more charming for its abuse. "We'll get ourselves cozy."

They soon came upon another hamlet throwing darker smoke than typical chimney fires. Charred skeletons of lost structures rubbed shoulders with strewn stone. Shell craters gouged deep enough to hobble the car if hit, one bearing the ruin of unlucky feral livestock, only it's hooves recognizable.

Reggie stood and opened the turret hatch to gaze at the devastation. Within the driver's seat, Crawford slowed, gazing at the charred foundations of a destroyed farmhouse. Within the ruin a tin chimneyed pot stove had a shape splayed up against it, burned black as night save the ivory glint of mammalian teeth.

The smell making its way in nearly made Crawford heave bile on the steering wheel. "We have to get out of here. This shelling was hours ago at best. My God, we felt it happening. When the ground rumbled…"

"Stop." The car shifted as Reggie stepped out into the mud and got in again next to Crawford. He put his hands in his olive-khakied lap and stared out the front slit. "We have to reconnoiter for survivors."

They drove slowly, stopping rarely, stepping out into ruin to put ears to the wind. Every switch of stale air carried horrors. The wolf felt death itself beneath his toes.

"We have a place to bivouac just short of the line, it's our rally point." Crawford got back behind the wheel, and they drove. Shelled out homes had details he didn't want to pick out. "I can have us there in three hours."

"I know the place. Not there."

"What?"

"The captain in charge of my unit, he'll be expecting me. I'd rather not…" Reggie closed his eyes and folded his hands into each other. "We can sleep in the car tonight. There's room enough back there. I know where to stow it and remain safe."

Safe. A word taken for granted for so long. "Are you sure?"

"Do you trust me?"

Crawford's eyes found a bastion of calm in the badger's reluctant smile and knew.

Past the town Reggie directed him down wagon furrows through a copse of trees, putting the vehicle under cover off the main road. With fuel topped off from the rear jerry can and tires checked for wear, they found time to relax as the sun slipped away.

"Where are we?" Crawford asked.

Echoes of rumbling that wasn't thunder touched their senses. "Close," Reggie answered. "Always close."

They arranged sleep rolls in the back seat and ate biscuits from a tin, resting close with the steel shell tight around them. That was fine. Finer was the bottle of wine that Reggie slipped from his pack. "Goodbye gift from our hosts in Le Mans."

It made sense now. "Your Captain would have found that."

"My Captain knows more than what I drink." he muttered so softly that Crawford had to lean in to hear even though the badger's whiskers were close enough to touch his own.

"What does he—?" Crawford asked.

Reggie kissed him. The contact was brief, lips dry and the badger's tongue a velvet brush that dipped against his own. The spark startled Crawford and the wolf drew back.

Silence was a held breath. Crawford felt the whole world shift underneath him and was frozen as Reggie met his gaze.

"What? What the hell?"

"It was something in the manner you carried yourself," Reggie said.

"Carried myself?"

"You were comfortable with every touch and leaned into some of them."

"I'm..." Crawford sputtered. "I'm goddam married!"

Reggie leaned away, suddenly clinical. "And out here miles from the shelling you still are."

Crawford said nothing. Lightning had struck the wolf's bones.

Reggie blinked slowly. "What's important is, how do you feel?"

Crawford couldn't respond. There was no anger, no sense of violation. With the thunder beckoning far off and desperate to break the silence Crawford decided to kiss Reggie back.

The contact was fuller and lingered through a complex assortment of emotions, a giddy uncertainty and a fear that...exhilarated. Reggie's lips were warm smoke.

Crawford broke away, thoughts trying to coalesce that couldn't. There was a space inside his soul the shape of a person at table back in Pennsylvania. He immediately tried to imagine what Kamila's pelt felt like under his fingers, her lips on his own and instinctively explored the silver wedding ring on his finger. Was it her he was feeling this sensation for?

The badger smiled as he watched the wolf play with his ring and there was sad humor there. "Times like these help one find themselves. I know you love her. No simple kiss changes that. Your heart has more room than you think."

Without another word, Crawford turned and rummaged through his pack for stationary. Reggie let him be.

The letter he tried to write was perfunctory and sloppy, the sensation of Reggie's kiss trailing his mess of sensations as he imagined Kamila in his arms and tried to pin down memories of their last embrace, their last coitus. The memory was fractured, sequestered. Crawford resolved himself to write in the morning and fell asleep in the badger's presence, dreams warm and indistinct.

Morning brought a buzz of uncertainty. He couldn't remember if he'd drank any of Reggie's wine. Nothing was spoken of the prior night.

They were at the front by mid-morning, the armoured car surrendered with the mail. They marched through mud-walled trenches on bowing boards just a half mile from Lucy de Bocage, and the nearby Belleau Wood. For good reason every step in the trenches was cautious. Only officers were requisitioned boots for their clawed feet. Soldiers who slipped needed to clean their toes of muck quickly to stave off trench rot.

The mixed American and British units spread wide out of sight, various species and sexes. While most of the bunkees on Crawford's oceanic crawl were anonymous tobacco-spittin' city boys n' girls, two familiar muzzles turned up. A cat named Merrit and a weasel named Liddel were both from Ohio. They'd been good company on the steamer, trading cigarettes and playing poker on hammock-dangled mess kits. Right away the wolf knew he'd missed an engagement. Their demeanor was fitfully restrained as Crawford introduced Corporal Fenwick.

"First wave went over yesterday," Liddel said. "We were still mustering, and they wanted to hold reserves. It was two Brit teams and one of ours, forty-four souls total." Liddel glanced at the silent Merrit and back again.

"Did anybody make it back?" Reggie was loathe to ask, already knowing the answer.

"No. Every now and again we peer over, but if the fog clears the snipers can see. We lost Teddy to one late in the evening."

A tarp shaped like a mammal lay further down the trench apart from all else.

"The brass is thinking of moving us down the line. They're digging more trench with hopes we can flank. We're at the shovels in shifts." Liddel sighed and sucked at a blister. "Everybody's miserable and wet."

Merrit said nothing, watching another private down the boards drag mud off a foot in slow drags of a comb. "Did you find your brother?" Crawford asked. "He was in a unit assigned here wasn't—"

Liddel grimaced and Merrit said nothing, gazing up and over the trench's sagging lip with empty green eyes. Crawford understood.

Huddled under the rain over creeping mud, the war became wet, sucking despair. Deluges came and went as the trenches dug east. Crawford realized that Kamila and his son still had no letter to read. All awaited the whistle, and he had no place to cleanly put pen to paper.

Silence broke in occasional echoes of gunfire down the line. Word flickered round that set hearts hammering at an insubstantial phantom stalking no-mammal's land. The Germans had gas.

"It burns your lungs, sets fire inside you that bleeds your insides out through your mouth, your nose, your bloody ears," Reggie said to the burning ember of his smoke, their moment in the car falling into memory. "Pray that anything else gets you, anything at all."

Prayer did little. Liddel was always hungry and Merrit morose. Her loss sent her inward. She could have requested leave to mourn but didn't. Time contemplating the emptiness awaiting in Ohio was unfathomable.

By the fourth night, Crawford felt an overwhelming urge to go home, slip back along the lines, out of the trenches and back to Paris. The checkpoints they'd cleared behind the lines now made sense. "Why are we out here," he asked Reggie as the badger squatted next to him, spreading apple and plum from a tin onto a thin bread crust.

The badger was intent of preventing spillage into the muck. "King and Country. And for home fires in America to keep burning."

Shells thudded somewhere. "So, what are the Huns here for, Kaiser and Fatherland?"

"Nothing at all," Reggie answered after a bite. "They should walk into no-man's land and hold still while we end their misery." He made it sound like the most gracious of favors and Crawford managed a smile.

Binoculars on stalks were passed around, ways to peer over the ledge without catching a sniper's gift. Liddel had stopped complaining about his groaning stomach and was having a shot at the binoculars as the sun peeked through the fog on the fifth day of ditch digging. He roved the glasses around while other men and women crowded round him, and he froze. "I see one of ours on the line."

Everyone froze. "What?" Crawford asked.

"It's Victor! Jennie, it's your brother, Victor." Merrit was through the crowd in two bounds.

"Is he moving? Is he..." The cat's voice cracked from days of disuse, her whiskers dancing upward in giddy nervousness.

"I can't...He's hunched over the barb lines." Liddel squinted. "He's dropped what looks like food."

"What do you mean food?" Crawford looked at Reggie, also confused.

"He's far off and I can't see properly. It looks like..."

Merrit snatched the periscoping lenses from him, hands shivering as she roved and focussed.

"Sausages," Liddel muttered. "Uncooked sausages. He must have been sneaking them back from the German line somehow. He's got an armful of them that he's dropped on the wire. They're all over."

Crawford's mind's eye connected the imagery with sense and he realized the unseen truth as Jennie Merritt got her brother into focus and vomited against the trench's mud wall.

The binoculars slipped from her grasp into the mud as she turned and sunk claws into Liddel's face with a yowl of anguish. Liddel wailed as she kicked and slashed. It took five soldiers to haul her off the ruin she made of the mustelid's muzzle. He fell back in the mud, crying to heaven in confusion in pain as the cat wailed in the grasp of the rest of the unit hauling her back. Reggie saw to the weasel. Crawford got the screaming cat by her clawed feet and held her as she emptied anguish out into the world.

Merrit went back from the front under guard that night and didn't return. What charges she was damned with, or mercies bestowed were never known.

Crawford prayed God would damn this war, it's worthless inches of French mud, its insult to fraternity amongst God's creatures. And for what? Come another flood no Ark would come to collect any here.

He tried to imagine Kamila's arms open for him back in America where she and Lucas were safe, and that gave him morsels of peace. But her warmth was a wraith. Reggie sat with him and smoked with him and misery kept them close.

Rarely were they apart, save when Reggie went to sniff out rumors. Reggie heard the news on the sixth night. "The ground is dry enough for armour now. It's official, we're going over tomorrow, second of four waves to the Marne crossing on the other side of the Belleau Wood. We must stop the German army from advancing past the river or we fall back to God knows where."

Everybody set to building more trench ladders in order to double the speed at which they could go over. The entire Second Infantry division had collected for the push. Reggie's British compatriots found themselves overwhelmed by boisterous Americans of both sexes and as time grew short, cordons were set off in order for soldiers who wished for a last opportunity at earthly familiarities to steal away for a few minutes at a time. "Don't let General Pershing walk in on you or you'll be riding his horse crop all the way to latrine duty," was a chide bringing nervous laughs.

The army being the army, Crawford and Reggie kept close but demure. For his own part, the wolf wasn't sure how he'd handle another kiss, much less the rest of the unit who stole calls to lust with desperate caution. Letters home would have omissions aplenty.

By the time the first armour rolled up and seventy-five-millimetre guns were fixed behind them, a heightened sense of urgency kept tails straight. The Huns were close enough to smell. Crawford could imagine the pickelhaube points of their helmets poking into view any second.

Soberly, he realized that American and British helmets would be poking into theirs instead.

As night came and precious breeze rushed through their fur, Reggie settled down. "I'm on the line with you," he said simply. "I volunteered along with several other mates in my unit. My Captain thought I was pulling the wool over on him."

Crawford felt the badger's warmth next to him and felt a stir he'd not felt since a week back in the car. "You could die."

The badger smiled and put a familiar hand on the wolf's shoulder. Crawford wanted it to stay. "I could live."

For the second time Crawford tried to write a letter back to Kamila and Lucas, but it seemed empty, devoid of real meaning and the depth it needed to convey. How to tell them about mud and flies and death and misery was so tenuous. The letter became perfunctory as a confidential dispatch. He almost wanted to throw it away. He gazed into a soupy night sky that didn't give a single star to see by and waited dawn's judgement.

Morning bled sun through clouds and tightened stomachs. They ate lightly, their constitutions allowing little else. Liddel was a sullen breakfast mate to one side and Reggie on the other.

The briefing came, directions terse yet somehow cheerful, as though an oasis of wonder awaited the inevitable routing of the Germans over the muddy hill. Were great commanders determined by saving their men from peril or by ensuring that those who went to God were cheerful and determined to the last minute? Was morale itself the only soldier they feared to lose?

Shelling began, whistling and thundering as morning settled into afternoon, the day dragging through eternity. Just past supper time they held the ladders, waiting for the all-go. The clock ticked down with the approaching thunder and Crawford only wanted the chance to sort out his many confusions later. God could give him that, couldn't he?

"It's going to happen now," Reggie whispered at Crawford's back, tone flat as a whetstone.

And just like that, the flag went up and the whistle blew. Feet shook the ladder as the soldier ahead of Crawford went over, then he himself was right behind. Mud gripped his foot and by moving fast he kept from being tripped. Distant gun muzzles flashed. Lead split the air in cracks and fenceposts and thin-limbed trees splintered. Scattered stones and a fly-buzzed carcass of a feral horse passed left and right.

Shells screamed down. A close hillock exploded, dirt and vegetation peppering them with hot earth and a sizzle of pain Crawford flicked from one ear. In the ringing echo he thought he heard a scream.

Reggie was at his hip, shaking the dirt out of his fur.

"Smear it!" Crawford shouted, grabbing cover.

"Wot?"

"Smear it on your face Reggie. Your stripes will have the Huns potting you if this smoke clears!" Crawford grabbed mud and clutched the badger's cheek with it. "We need to keep moving."

An explosion followed by a rain of dirt ensured he was as filthy as his comrade. Crawford confirmed his rifle's action was still clean and scrambled onward. A hot hole was their next refuge and a weasel's tail sprouted from the uniform splayed for cover within. "We've got to move, Liddel!" Crawford nudged the shivering weasel.

The soldier turned as though dazed and looked at Crawford with nothing. Red ruin dangled eyelessly under the fractured helmet. A muzzle moaned wordless questions. Liddel collapsed.

A Hun's bullet broke rock next to Reggie's skull. Badger and wolf clutched each other to roll away. Reggie fired back. Armour hissed slugs overhead. The Mercedes armoured cars couldn't make it far through the mud but the massive creak of something almost primordial was at their back. A rhomboid shape to their right chugged through the mist, iron hide stamped by rounds. The Lewis machine gun on its flank opened up.

"Mark four landship!" Reggie shouted. "Thank God!"

Crawford knew there would be force in kind and they needed to move to avoid being ground to death by lead or tread.

Under the zinging of bullets, they slipped under barbed snares, eventually coming within range of the Marne river where Germans mustered. Armour going either way needed the crossing at Chateau Thierry but the troops could swim if they could keep their guns dry. Crawford spotted the distant shelter of buildings in the murk, but they were too far southwest to be Thierry. Anyone heading that way would let the enemy slip by.

He saw more land-ships, "tanks" as the engineers called them, rolling north-westward toward the river's chokepoint and its solitary bridge.

"This way." Crawford shouted. They followed the direction of fire, passing a body they couldn't place for the country it came from. Gunfire intensified further along, and the banks of the river were now visible.

"I see artillery," Reggie said thickly.

A sandbagged bunker reinforced the other side of the Marne, wide bore belching fire into the sky.

"Too far to shoot," Crawford growled. "Can't wade across. We'll be shot halfway."

"The bridge will be full of Germans running into our armour. We're dead if we go that way," Reggie countered miserably.

A Whippet anti-soldier car rolled into view, guns dangling, flames spouting from the open hatch. Screams echoed inside the aimless shell as it rolled to the lake and in.

"We can't stay here," Flicked dirt from a close bullet agreed. The muddied pair slipped back into a patch of molested grass for meager cover, neither saying what they both knew. No infantry would cross that bridge in either direction in one piece. "We have to choke the Germans off. That's what we went over the wall for."

Reggie's face was a crag of misery behind the mud and his eyes said enough. "We did."

Hornet snips of bullets sought them out. They replied in kind as they scrambled over a patch of long grass into a henge of stone. Only the remains of a window frame betrayed it as a building long blown into oblivion by a fallen shell.

War's fog had reduced sight to mere yards as they went to cover amongst the walls, under the whistling of rounds and the blasting of shells and death making the air reek of blood and cordite.

"Which way?" Crawford shouted, confused and battling terror at every whistle through the air.

"I don't know." Reggie crouched like a lost soul in the lee of a stone wall. Time passed, then more. They had scant ammunition left and didn't know where to even point as dusk settled in, then the faint lip of last light. Then night. The fighting finally abated.

Eternity passed as they huddled. "Fighting's stopped," Reggie muttered.

"Maybe we pushed them back." Crawford muttered.

"Or they pressed on and we're behind enemy lines," Reggie said without emotion. "We'll find out at sunrise I suppose."

"So, what do we do now?" Waiting just felt absurd.

Distant echoes of the river and all that lay beyond it drifted by, undefinable.

Time passed, silence falling like a blanket.

"I watched you try to write your letter before the whistle, saw you frustrated." Reggie said.

Crawford turned. Somewhere an insect reluctantly creaked. "What?"

"The heart is the hardest thing to lay bare in times like these."

Crawford could only see Reggie's eyes glinting wetly in the thinnest of moonlight. "I'm not someone who writes letters. I know I love her, and she loves me."

"But there's more for you, isn't there." That wasn't a question. "Was I your first kiss outside of your marriage?"

Crawford should be angry at that, but instead felt weary. The war was all around them and nowhere at once, waiting. "Don't talk like that. I'm just...confused."

Silence took over for a while longer.

"Confused because you've been taught to believe that you can give your affection to one person only?"

Crawford sighed. "It was just a goddamn kiss, Reggie. What's it to you?"

The badger's outline in the dark was a fuzz of cocking ear, the mud still obscuring his features. "You know I've no one to write a letter to, none who knows how I really am," he whispered. "I just want to know what it's like for you to discover...this."

"This?" The air was painfully still. "We only just met a week ago." It was a long week ago, that carefree ride through France, that sun setting on wine flush ears. Crawford wanted that back more badly than anything.

Crawford saw the glint of a smile when Reggie spoke again. "But you've been curious for longer than that. I told you I could tell."

Absurdly, that was true. Crawford couldn't deny it, not to Reggie.

"And of course, you still love her," Reggie added. "Nothing else you feel has to draw that away. I wouldn't dare try."

Crawford turned that over in his head. "I do love her, yes."

"And I loved others too. There's enough room in my heart for so many. You're the same, you were just taught otherwise. We all were."

Countless soldiers huddled in their own terrified worlds, in ditches, in armour, in war's loneliness. Crawford somehow felt them all. "What are you even saying?"

"If tomorrow comes and there's Germans on all sides of us, how fully have you lived?"

Crawford tried to line up what his life had been like before the war, before Kamila and Lucas. Diligent son, reliable in the family pack. So much lived and not lived. "Doesn't matter. Nobody is ever ready to go."

"Are they?" The badger carefully slid his arm around the wolf and Crawford didn't push away. He didn't want to.

Reggie took a deep breath. "I'm ready to live right now. *Always* right now. Until my last moment…I'm going to live."

The arm around him tightened and Crawford found himself leaning into it.

A bullet. A shell, the peek of dawn and an artillery crack. They all lurked to bring about his last conscious moment. He shivered at that fresh realization.

Yet it wasn't fear that quivered through him. It was something akin to desperation that didn't have a name, a need to understand something that had long drawn him. Doors had closed because he'd been raised to never open them, mysteries of the self to avoid exploring at all costs.

He could go home in a pine box or be claimed by the forest. But while he was here in the mud, there was the need to rebel against death. To know.

Crawford settled back and fumbled back to the khakied thigh of the badger next to him, coaxed along by a welcome hand to where Reggie was unbuttoned. He found his warmth, hot and alive in the cool air. The badger's breath was restrained, a sigh settling over everything, and Reggie's fingers found Crawford's own breeches, loosening his belt, slipping through, careful claws exploring.

No shame. Of all the heat, none was that. Wolf and badger side by side, hands teasing one another through the darkness, slicker workings bringing the wolf past arousal into hot rasping thrill. Sliding palms brought him to the edge. Reggie's other hand slid down the back of Crawford's wide-spread khakis, thick fingers squeezing one buttock before a single digit, teasing its way around, slipped within the wolf and then back out with a wiggle that sent a lightning bolt through the wolf's core. Crawford came into the dark and his own hand came free warm with Reggie's own spending.

The electricity settled as Crawford picked out a star above that winked. They quietly cleaned themselves up, senses cast out to the distance where a thin thread of dawn would soon gather. With uniforms closed the mammals crouched.

"Love is in absence," Kamila said in Crawford's dreams to an empty chair dotted with ejaculate.

Thunder brought him awake to dawn. A shell whistled, then another.

They both startled in cover. Through the remains of the building, a barrel slipped into view not ten yards away, masonry and gravel cracking. Crawford blinked as he recognized the muzzle of a cannon pointing east. Shapes moved around behind the wall that was giving it cover and neither mammal spoke. Crawford's hand gripped his rifle as a feline under an American helmet poked over the sill. "Got live ones," she said in a Georgian lilt. A bear peered over with her. "What unit you with?"

It was as though they'd woken in another country. "Second infantry," Crawford responded. "You have anything to eat?"

"Sorry," the bear rumbled, eyes roving high. "Germany brought all the breakfast we're eating. We've orders to serve them back."

A shell rained dirt fifty feet away and it dawned on Crawford that they were neither behind nor past enemy lines. They were right on the doorstep.

"Brace and load!" Shouted a third unseen voice and the artillery's long neck rose higher. Crawford and Reggie turned and scrambled on their knees, peering past their night's shelter to see, in the clearer break of morning, the lake and all that teemed it.

German guns had crept forward to fortify in the dark and were now letting loose at the space further down the opposite shore. The bridge was dimly visible, topped with smoking debris that was clearly a choke point of death. Beyond it was the shell of a town whose name Crawford had forgotten loaded with forces mustering. Crawford's gun was up along with Reggie's and it was clear the Germans were too far for rifles.

Reggie was all business. "I can't see any soldiers on our side, just armour. Either they've grabbed cover or we're what's left."

Crawford's ears rang as a shell from the gun behind them fired at its counterparts across the distant lake. The scrub to the shore offered no cover for an advance. "We have to guard this gun if the Huns cross," Crawford realized.

A shell hammered the other side of the low wall with an explosion of masonry that would have torn pelt and flesh. At the bridge shapes swarmed west. Some fell, most didn't. The Germans were taking it, still too far to shoot.

Their cannon fired again, backed up by unseen others. Armour rolled past. Familiar fatigues covered a mammal who was limping behind it. Under the pound of the earth, the sound of a whistle drifted over.

"Advance, retreat? What the hell is happening?" Crawford's teeth ground. The pounding buried any trace as Germans were now spilling over the bridge. "We should be there goddammit."

Over the chatter of disparate gunfire, the sound of a rattle drifted like a large gear failing. A shell came down close to the wall again and air through the dust seemed to be changing color as the rattle became more apparent. The cannon behind them fired again and the bear bellowed into the echo left behind. "Gas! Mustard gas!"

The crew fumbled for their packs. Crawford did the same. Frantically, the wolf ran through the kit at his hip, then at the catches on his own pack. Sinking terror descended as he threw the rucksack off onto the ground. "My mask is gone."

Reggie stared blankly at him through goggle-obscured eyes. His muffled reply was cut by the explosion of mortar next to his head as bullets struck. To the west the air took on a jaundiced haze. Crawford dumped all his field possessions on the ground, the mess kit, rolled field dressings, the meager letter home that an eastward wind tugged and stole.

The hand on Crawford's shoulder was firm. "You'll have to retreat. Back south to the trenches, get another mask. I'll help guard the gun." The last statement was an afterthought, as though Reggie had suggested something silly. Lead slapped the wall again. The cannon fired.

The earth next to them both exploded, hurling both of them on their side. They scrambled from the smoking hole back around to where the gun crew hastily dumped a shell, seated another, anonymous in their masks and khakis.

"They're advancing! Fire and retreat!" The bear bellowed and the cat pulled the cord. The cannon fired one last time. Gunfire pocked the covering wall creating clouds of dust. Shaken ground had loosened the blocks under the cannon's tow wheels and the wolf nearly tripped as they grabbed cover under its bulk. The cannon crew were already scrambling away.

As the fire came down from the resurgent German line the wolf and badger traded glances, just an instant in which Crawford sought his friend in the dark circles of glass above the charcoal-glycerin pack hose.

Then the earth heaved once more as a shell burst a mere dozen feet away. The remains of the wall shielding the cannon fell upon it, shoving the cannon like a cub's toy. Its massive wheel skipped backwards as badger and wolf tried to roll away. Crawford came to a stop with his mouth full of dust.

Reggie wasn't with him.

Crawford scrambled back to the skewed gun, dust in his eyes.

Limp legs splayed under the gun's steel wheel.

The top half of Reggie squirmed on the wheel's other side, arms feebly digging, masked muzzle tilted back. He writhed as German bullets pinged off the cannon's barrel. The smoke in Crawford's vision was now the color of rot. He threw his weight against the wheel, shoulder numbed by the immovable surface. Again, pain lanced his side, but the cannon was still. He'd no strength to shout Reggie's name and the badger under the artillery's wheel pin-wheeled limbs in agony, the mask's glass clouded by frantic breath.

Gas crept along the ground. When it clung to the fur and settled to the pelt…that didn't matter. Crawford flung himself low and tried to squeeze Reggie's hand in reassurance. Reggie didn't squeeze back. His struggles slowed, bullets pinged and ricocheted. Clods of dirt from another close shell rained on them both.

Crawford's vision was greying. He couldn't draw the breath to say goodbye. He'd long wonder if instinct allowed him a choice. Kamila held Lucas in his mind's eye.

Fingers clutched at his friend's mask, and he pulled it away from the dying badger. Reggie's dark eyes rolled back, not heavenward but to him. Judging, forgiving, Crawford couldn't know. He fitted it on himself, smelling the badger's desperation. Another shell, another shudder of the abandoned gun.

Crawford Cain had one last glance at the wordless open mouth and clouding eyes before he turned and fled.

And lived.

Much later he found others, regrouped for a counter-offensive that he fought without feeling. The Germans were pushed back. Dead were driftwood upon the water, dotted the scrub for miles. Abandoned machines smoldered, but he never found the cannon again.

Crawford melted into the Third Division that retook Chateau Thierry across that bridge. Countless nights passed, tins of food eaten that he could barely keep down. When silence came it hurt his eardrums. He joined no group, made no more friends. He went into dark with contraband wine from liberated French cellars and vanished it down his gullet with cold pork. In the morning he could stand, throw up, march, shoot. At nights he'd mutely seek out the perfect blue bands of sky that dusk bruised and stole from him.

He took army orders, nerves obeying the command of people he'd never respect. He found wine again in the next town. He finally sent that letter to Kamila, boilerplate and perfunctory. Shells fell, none for him.

The war ended in a train car in Versailles. A signature closed hell's mouth. A steamer slogged him home.

He played with his son but didn't know him because he no longer knew himself. He helped his wife cook and excused himself when sausages slopped off the stove edge and hung listlessly down its side. Staring at a blank wall in the bedroom kept him from getting sick.

Of his time away there was no conversation. No recollections shared. Only deflections, muttered or sharp.

Crawford and Kamilla had sex in the dark, listless, rushed. He said he loved her but the words were postcards. She felt him retreat, tried to open the doors he closed but like a coward Crawford retreated further and further, stealing mask after mask, always stepping out to go look at the dusk alone. He'd let his son quietly watch it with him, blue as a French sky but never perfect, that foreign land within himself.

Then he'd drink.

"Why couldn't you find somebody else to drive that Mercedes? There were better men."

"What Mercedes?" Charlie asked worriedly. He stood over Crawford, sniffing at the flask he'd picked up, nose pale as a ghost's.

"Charlie?" The apartment was cut with afternoon light from the single kitchen window. Charlie teetered, looking frail.

"Charlie, what happened?"

The brown wolf swallowed, removed his hat. "Crawford, we're at war."

Crawford didn't know what that meant. He only knew that Charlie was disturbed by something inexplicable. He rose from the floor and the smaller wolf stepped into his embrace.

The here and now resolved itself. "No more masks," Crawford said.

"What do you mean?" Charlie asked.

Crawford tipped his muzzle back and kissed him.

Charlie gasped, then traded a breath with Crawford as he embraced him tightly. Crawford's roving hands around his hips asked a question and the brown wolf answered with a press of his body into the grey's.

They tumbled into Charlie's tidy room, Charlie turning on the hanging light as they entered, and they fell on the bed together. Crawford's heart raced, wounds numbed and his loins singing. Desperate arousal tented his slacks as he kicked them away. Charlie's hands kneaded Crawford's flank and one found his testicles, coaxing while his own belt was fumbled open. Tie. Shirt. Buttons came undone or popped and the brown wolf sloughed his clothes away to reveal darker flanks and hips that ruffled under Crawford's claws.

Cocks touched and Charlie gasped into Crawford's mouth.

"Yes?"

"Fuck me," Charlie breathed. "Please."

Twisting with a grunt of carnal urgency, Charlie got on his knees on his bed, tail high as he lowered his muzzle, faced Crawford and cold-nosed his cock. Crawford groaned, feeling the world shift as Charlie's tongue worked, dancing needily. Crawford nestled into Charlie's attention, rocking his own hips gently, letting the brown wolf lead.

Charlie rolled on his back as he licked Crawford's manhood, the brown wolf's own springing into lamplight. Crawford bent to nose it before lapping and tasting another male's essence for the first time, mimicking with his tongue what Charlie did with his, urgent licks, closed lips worshipping the shape of it, and when Crawford's tongue and open mouth slipped round Charlie down to the soft fuzz of his testicles Charlie sighed gratefully. Crawford drew that sound out again and again.

Through long groans Charlie disengaged, whispered into Crawford's thigh. "I'm ready now."

Crawford nodded, sliding off the bed and standing up while Charlie lay on his back, legs parted, guiding Crawford's maleness to tight heat in waiting.

He pushed, Charlie grunted, beckoning Crawford to push again. The larger wolf was warmed by the space inside and with small piston moves of the hips, slid further within. Loins burned and sweat built up in the thin points under his pelt, spreading his scent as his body whipped itself forth. Crawford buried his cock deeper, tongue lolling.

He saw traces of blood on Charlie's curling toes and smelled it too, carrion and crusted, but was beyond questions. "You okay?" Crawford whispered.

"Yes," Charlie replied earnestly, unaware of the slow distention of Crawford's limbs, the bunching of his muscles, only the increased throbbing of the other wolf's cock. Blood scent was calling on whatever lurked within Crawford, and he felt it's advance.

No. I'm doing this, Crawford almost whispered through swollen teeth. *This is for me. For us.*

As his feral self reared its head, the scents grew stronger; each pine floorboard, black crust of blood and golden swath of fur told their tales. Crawford grunted as climax approached and he growled as white-hot joy leapt forth unseen where the wolves connected. He started to slow his pace as the creature within demurred.

"Harder," Charlie commanded. "Just a little more."

As Crawford's feral essence receded, he doubled his thrusts, finding a natural roll to his hips made easier by his cock's slickness. Something in the way he moved tipped Charlie into fulfillment and he came on his own belly in short ivory lines. A long and satisfied moan escaped Charlie and Crawford slipped out with drops of pearl finding the floor.

They lay naked next to each other and Crawford felt the onset of clarity. There were ways to control the were within without drinking himself halfway to death. The realization gave him a measure of peace to sweeten the afterglow.

He reached out to the lamp on the table next to Charlie's bed to switch it off but Charlie's grip on his arm stopped him.

"Leave the lights on," Charlie said. "Please."

They lay and let their scents mingle.

CHAPTER 21

A NEW ANGLE

"Are you okay?" The question could apply to either of them, Crawford realized. So soon after his…rumination, he could see Reggie's eyes in Charlie's, someone he could love, and fail.

Regardless of how things turned out for himself, Crawford decided he'd protect him from bullet or tooth or all of goddamn Chicago if need be.

Charlie took deep breaths. Sex's escape had helped him center himself as he meandered through what happened at the conference. "Cops and press ran for it, some got sick right there. It's a full-on war when the papers hit the corners telling of…that barrel." Charlie teetered on the verge of shock but held Crawford's hand without shivering. He wouldn't be okay, but he'd persist.

"I'm so sorry you're a part of this," was all Crawford could say.

The sun was falling. Charlie gingerly slipped off the bed and steadied himself, collecting his thoughts. "What more can you tell me about all of this? Nobody else knows it wasn't just cannibals at that speak."

Crawford lived more than a double life now and to hide anything was unforgivable. "Tell me you can keep secrets for your own sake and I'll tell you the rest."

The blank stare under wide-flattened ears told Crawford how stupid that question was.

"Okay. There's a lot." Crawford stood and held him again. Warmth affirmed what words couldn't. "I'll need to drive us somewhere."

"We going to meet more like you?" Charlie asked.

"No. More like them." Charlie took a step away and Crawford put up a warding hand. "They're not all like that. I need to prove that to you."

"Enough *are* like *that*, aren't they?"

"I'm not sure."

***

"She left me, just like Celeste. I get Sandy out've a bad spot with some rabbit and just like that she's gone." Bucky tucked into his tagliatelle and sighed. Sighs of a broken heart were difficult when his hardly ever beat. "I'd've given this whole city to her and when the chips were down..."

His mother said nothing, just listening. Bucky's mother was an eternal fountain of patience, unlike his worthless father. He'd be back from the factory's night shift long after Bucky was gone.

"All I want is a way ahead I can profit by, Mamma, to get the respect I deserve. I'm owed that."

There was a knock at the window. Bucky had another helping of Tagliatelle, chewing thoughtfully before rising. At the window the mink clicked her fangs together looking sorry.

Bucky leaned out. "What? I don't want my mamma seeing you and having kittens."

"Bucky, the feds brought in the barrel they got from the speak and opened it. It's...ah, well you know you were malting a couple of the spent ones and—"

"Fuck." The cat was out of the barrel. "Thanks Fanny."

"My name's Felice."

Bucky slid the window shut and went back to Mamma. "With all I've cut my tail running from you'd think I'd be more careful." He had more pasta and laughed. The heavy sensation inside suggested he should probably stop eating but he didn't. Mamma made it so good.

"I need a new place, somethin' more...he turned his fork, "...portable. My vintages...they're too big, too heavy. And being strong don't get barrels that big in a Packard's trunk, you know? I need an operation I can move in minutes. Pigs knock and you've already skipped down the street." He looked up. "I'm sorry Mamma, this is boring and I'm talking your ear off."

Mamma wasn't bored.

He shoved the fork into the pasta, stirring his gripes around in it. If only Sandy hadn't skittered out on him in his hour of despair. How could he love and hate someone so much at the same time? Goddamn veggies. "I'm just lonely Ma. I've given my heart to people who've crushed it. I *saved* that rodent from some dreary school-teaching gig, watching snot-nosed kits she wouldn't take one sip from if she—"

He let the fork settle. "Too heavy to move fast," he muttered, feeling his useless stomach shifting. With that sensation came epiphany. Even in abandonment, Sandy had given him a way out. It was so simple.

And he was no longer hungry.

He pushed the bowl away. "Know what? I think its gonna come up roses after all."

He rose and walked to the head of the table, leaning to nuzzle his momma's cheek in a kiss. His lower lip brushed the dark spot where blood had sunk from the nape of her neck to the V of her house dress. The scent of her fur was something he'd miss. He closed her eyes gently to keep her head from rolling and spilling her from the chair. "Don't worry 'bout me ma," Bucky said. "I'll land on my feet."

At the window he told the waiting mink and the single-fanged wolf further down where he was going and when he told them why they shrank back into the dark.

Bucky had no time for this. "You'll be back. I'm the only game in town and you know it."

Given no answer, Bucky went his own way.

**

The day hustled along as Crawford and Charlie drove to see the Nosfurs. Shows and speaks and a thousand burnt dinners drifted scents over a city that looked alien when the shadows of the alleys got longer. They pulled up to the dark house near the edge of town with all its shades drawn and Crawford asked Charlie to wait a moment. "I have to introduce you. Be ready to leave quickly if I tell you."

Charlie's hand smoothed down the jacket over the hard shape under his arm. Crawford couldn't blame him.

"Look, Celeste, the doe, is a friend. I promise I wouldn't bring you here otherwise. Just don't pull a gun on anybody."

Charlie's expression was unreadable. "She's a goodie vampire. I trust you."

"Nosfur. And thanks." Crawford approached the door as dusk traced the building's shapes in pink. He knocked. Celeste opened, staying well out of the light with eyes on Crawford for the briefest instant before moving to Charlie. "Who is this?"

"Charlie Rothscub, this is Celeste. Celeste, Charlie. He's my partner. He knows about my situation. Ours too."

"Charmed," Charlie said flatly.

The doe's nose worked, eyes darting between them. "Will the whole Prohibition Bureau be coming by? I don't drink anything officially illegal."

"It's just Charlie and I. Look, can we come in? The kid is here, right?" Crawford saw nothing in the darkness over her shoulder.

Celeste didn't move. "He is. I need to talk to you first. Alone."

Charlie coughed. "Should I wait in the car?"

Crawford put a hand on his shoulder. "Don't go anywhere. You'll want to tell them all what you told me. I'll be right back."

Crawford stepped inside and closed the door. "Before you say anything..."

"Before *you* say anything. When I moved in two nights ago my new home was a secret. Now we already have enough people for a game of rummy. Not to mention we're dealing with a particularly sensitive situation now."

"Is the kid okay?"

"How okay would you be if you were told that the most frightening moment of your life took everything you had away forever?"

"It's been five days for me."

"You aren't an orphaned kid though, are you?"

"No," Crawford felt like a heel. "Regarding said kid, I have to get out from Donovan's thumb. He finds out that Samson is alive..."

"That's part of what I wanted to tell you. Sandy Mallory is here."

"Oh...You two making up?"

"In a manner of speaking. She's turning over past mistakes and I'm hoping she can take Samson under her wing. She has vastly more experience with youth than I do. I'd hoped to get her to drop Bucky, but she seems to have seen through his lies about the speak that burnt down."

"About that, Charlie, my partner outside, was the only one who made it out alive last night. He was at a press conference with other officers, the press and States Attorney. He, well, I should let him tell you."

"Crawford," her voice dropped. "If he's a government agent like you, and he knows anything that would provide definitive proof of what we are..."

Crawford heard the reluctant sympathy in her voice and read its implication. His teeth bared, and hackles went up. "Be careful, Celeste. I refused an order from Donovan Calvert to make the kid *problem* go away. Don't figure for a second that I'm going to let a hair be harmed on Charlie. He's more than a friend to me."

"How much more than a friend?"

Crawford said nothing and didn't give a damn what she guessed.

She smiled thinly. "His smell on you was suggestive."

"Things are complicated."

"Until they're simple. They used to be for Sandy and I."

"Really?" Crawford's brows went up but without amusement.

Celeste rolled hers in return. "I'm preoccupied with different scents on you. Something on your breath when you growled. What did you drink?"

"Some rum maybe? Why?"

"Where did you get it?"

The knock on the door startled Crawford. Charlie's voice was muffled. "Am I standing out here until you two fight again?"

"We'll talk more later," Celeste sighed and beckoned Crawford to let him in.

The three of them stood in the hallway.

"I was telling Charlie how decent a doe you were."

"Glad to know that some of you can be," Charlie said cautiously.

"That's fairly backhanded as compliments go," Celeste remarked.

"First impressions can't be too good when you see dying people hog-tied and dead ones skinned in barrels for later."

"Skinned..." Celeste's look hardened. Crawford was glad it didn't make her eyes go dark this time. Charlie would likely bolt or worse.

"Tell me what happened after the speak burned," Celeste insisted. "Please."

Charlie's eyes darted to the dark over her shoulder. "Before I do, is your electricity working? If so, I'd appreciate it if you turned the lights on." He breathed deeply. "All of them."

Celeste acquiesced, asking no questions before illuminating the main floor's three bulbs. Keeping his voice low, Charlie told her about the barrel, the conference, the opening for the cameras. He kept the description of what poured forth brief between dry-throated swallows. "Do you have any water?"

"Just the tap, no glasses yet. I'm sorry."

Charlie marched past her to the bright kitchen, checking left and right before entering.

Celeste stared into closed window drapes, her mood having darkened. "I'll have to end him."

"Celeste—"

"Not your friend, calm down. Bucky. All this is his doing and he'll only take things further. I have to find him, and I know who to ask." She glanced at Charlie, whose head was turned sideways under a rattling tap. "You did him no favors by telling all you know about us," she muttered.

"I disagree. I couldn't hide this Were thing from him and keeping him ignorant of what's going on nearly got him killed. I keep an eye out for mine, Celeste."

Celeste stepped closer, whispering, holding Crawford's gaze. "If you really care about him, you should leave him, get out of his life. You don't yet realize that what you are can't accommodate attachments. Don't learn the hard way as I have."

A cold well opened in Crawford as they traded glares. Charlie returned from the kitchen, water dripping from his lip. "You two look ready to fight again. I thought you were one of the good ones."

"She is," said a high Scottish accented voice from halfway up the stairs. "She brought me back to Ms. Mallory." The goat kid's hooves made the faintest sound as he descended, posture cautious. The kid glanced from wolf to wolf and Crawford suddenly had the image in his mind's-eye of Lucas glancing between alienated parents.

Samson looked to Crawford. "You're one of the good ones too. I know that I was supposed to die. You wouldn't let that happen."

Who the hell told him? "No Samson, I wouldn't."

"What more did Sandy tell you?" Celeste asked Samson in the silence that followed.

The goat's mouth curled in awe and fear in equal measures. "I'm gonna live nearly forever. And I'm going to want to drink. There's another way, yeah?" His voice wavered in a way that hurt Crawford to hear.

"Hey," Charlie took a hesitant step in the kid's direction and the kid looked his way in puzzlement. The goat and wolf were mirrors of frightened uncertainty. "Look," Charlie said. "I'm as scared by all of this as you are, and I don't know what to make of the world or what I'm supposed to do in it but everybody's going to help you." The brown wolf made to reach out, thought better of it and didn't know what to do with his hands. "You're not gonna go through whatever this is alone."

Crawford watched his partner recognize another pitched ship trying to right itself in a merciless storm and his own heart swelled. "No, you won't."

Samson gazed at Charlie and managed to smile thinly.

It was Celeste who spoke next. "There are ways to live without harming anyone...innocent. They won't be easy, and take discipline, but Sandy and I can show you." The doe looked up the staircase. "Where is she?"

Samson grimaced and shook his head. "She left when you went to answer the door."

"What?" Celeste rushed to the second floor at a speed the wolves would have missed with a blink. She returned moments later. "Where did she go?"

"I told her that I was worried about hurting people and that I needed to meet others like myself to know what to do and what not to do. She looked like something really bothered her and said she promised to be back. Said she had to fix a mistake."

Celeste closed her eyes and swore in French. "Which mistake? God *damn* do I have to nail that fat tail to the floor?"

Crawford scratched the front hall linoleum with a toe claw. "Guess I don't need to lie to Donovan about knowing where she is."

"If she contacts him and reveals that you didn't follow his instructions..."

Crawford needed a moment to ponder that. "Oh. That will be bad."

"I mentioned I had clothes at the school that I wanted to get before they threw them away." Samson muttered. "Maybe she went there to get them."

Crawford sifted his trench coat pocket for the trinket he remembered was there. "Investigators are all over that school. It's not the best place to turn up. Here." He held out the painted soldier in Union blues and Samson accepted, turning the bent soldier at attention over in his hands, lost in thought.

Celeste wrinkled her nose. "She wouldn't go back to Bucky. She has to know by now the vicious cur really loves only himself. I don't see her going back to Donovan now that she knows he means Samson harm. Noah's Plank is the most likely place for her to go."

"I'm suspended from duty," Crawford said. "Can't go there in official capacity."

"And I'm supposed to be watching him." Charlie added, "till they bring him back anyway."

"Fucking Prohee bureaucratic nonsense." Celeste paced. "I'll go get her then."

"Can we not swear in front of the kid?" Charlie asked uncomfortably.

"I know all the words." Samson muttered, still lost in himself. "Shit. Damn. Piss."

"Those are good ones," Crawford nodded. "I'll figure out Donovan's next move. He's likely calling me at home after that news conference. if I'm scarce he'll be suspicious."

Charlie coughed. "If you have to go out, I can stay at the apartment. The office will be calling to check on me since they want another raid debriefing after that barrel was opened." He glanced up to the dark of the second floor and stepped back towards the hall light. "I don't really want to go out right now anyway."

Crawford noticed the way Charlie's eyes darted for corners resembled the way ears on the steamer back from France flicked at every conceivable sound. "If I have to visit the rabbit, what will you say if I'm not around when the office checks in?" Crawford realized that both the Bureau and the rabbit were on him.

"You're washing up, or out getting a paper. You're not a prisoner. Call me when you can, and I'll let you know if you're needed."

Samson stood straight. "Can I go with you, Celeste? Maybe say good-bye to my classmates?"

Celeste emerged from an empty side room she'd paced through. "I'm sorry Samson. You can't be seen there again for you and your friend's protection. Sandy should be avoiding them also now that she's been restored so I'll bring her back fast. There will be plenty of time to learn new things."

"But I can help," Samson fingered the blue tin soldier anxiously.

"No. For your own good you must stay here." Celeste sought the boy's eyes. "Promise me you won't go anywhere Samson. There are dangers out there that we have to deal with first."

"She's right, kid. Trust her. I know I do." Crawford traded one quick glance with the doe that affirmed that. "You'll be all right."

***

Donovan drank scotch and watched steel pour, sniffling through his healing nose.

He'd spoken the incantations, dropped another shard into the vats and gave curt nods to the curious glances of workers in passing on his way back to his office.

Flags half-staff at city hall, no leads yet as to Alderman Leicester's murderer, nor a speakeasy raid gone horribly wrong, nor the grisly find in the recovered barrel that would shock the strongest hearts. Chicago was going to hell and Donovan knew the reason why was not in the glass he sipped.

Phone calls had been made and assurances given to the infrastructure board. Little did they know how many lives would be saved by the steel skeletons of structures being erected day by day.

This evening he had but one person left to convince. His contingency plan needed to be ready.

The moon was nearly full. Roof shutters opened throughout the mill let silvery light spill through the catwalks and hissing ladles to the floor.

He went to the phone. "Connect me to Cee-Ache-Ay, six, four, three, seven."

The phone rang several times before a voice squawked. "Cain. What is it?"

"It's Donovan. Word is that you're suspended from duty."

"Suspended people still catch sleep, Don."

"Stop being sore about the school, my lupine friend. I have news to help put that chapter behind us. I'll shortly know who was responsible for creating that problem you were forced to solve, and I'd like you to be here for that revelation."

There was a long thoughtful silence. "At your house uptown?"

"No. Come to my steel mill. Be here in an hour."

The wolf sighed. "Alright."

Donovan ended the call. The phone rang immediately. "Yes?"

"All is ready for the drill," Edmond said.

"Excellent. Carry on." He disconnected and crossed to the window overlooking the grounds outside the mill. A distant plume of dust rose behind a vehicle moving fast. He recognized his Duesenberg and knew Von Haften had arrived.

The shift bell sounded. It was time.

Donovan finished his drink and descended, passing lines of exhausted workers punching the clock one by one before they drifted to the lot where jalopies and Tee's were cranked to life.

The Countess entered, jaw pointed above the rabble drifting out, ignoring curious or appraising glances. Donovan stopped three steps above the floor in order to look her in the eye. "Stop right here. Concentrate."

"I know the steel is all around us. Am I to feel outward again?"

"No. This time you need to search and concentrate. Feel through your locket to all the reliquary steel present and sift carefully."

"Out there?" She glanced to the lot where automobiles chugged out.

"No," Donovan smiled. "Right here. There's a girder heading for a bridge downtown on that stack. You see the nail monogram?"

Turning, the lioness strode over to the girder. One hand touched her locket, the other rested upon the girder. "It's warm."

"It was forged this morning. Search, focus below you. Be patient."

She did as Donovan suggested, tail twitching under the short dress she wore. Then it froze.

She turned, jaw dropping. "How many?"

"You felt them."

"Yes. But so faint. How far down?" Her hand was over her blade already. Always the one overriding instinct.

"A few stairs. They'll expect me."

"Mallory was your only successful subject you said. Why can I barely feel them?"

"I never said she was the only one. Just the first." Donovan indicated a lone storage shed on the factory floor. "This way."

He worked the padlocked doors with quick practice. Pushing them inward revealed a wide descending stair dimly lit by caged bulbs along the wall. Donovan led her down.

Silently the lioness crouched, short sword now drawn, lips pressed over her teeth to hide their glint. Consummate hunter in her element. Donovan was amused.

At the stair's base, hammers clanged, and bellows blew behind tall doors. Donovan pushed them wide, exposing a great barrel vault of a room, receding into shadows. A dozen or so figures in miniscule firelight moved with purpose, pelts bare to the waist save females more modestly attired. They were of mostly vegetarian stock, ungulates, higher rodents and lapines of ages from young adult to greying elderly. They toiled between anvils, benches and oven-locked simmering flames, hammering red twists of metal into shapes that hissed as they were dunked into vats of water. The air was hot with exertion and the rank bite of beaten metal.

Wrought artifacts hung on walls interrupted by dark vestibules leading to other unseen chambers. Donovan stopped at a railing above a short drop onto the vault floor, short stairs to either side. There he waited.

One by one, the workers slowed and stopped hammering. Only the hiss of hot water and crackle of oven flames broke the silence.

"Et profectus est negotium!" His voice boomed under the vault's curve. His ears rose attentively.

"Impugnatio occurrit," came the reply.

The Countess stood behind Donovan. He knew she now felt the ebb through her blade and locket as he did.

"Donovan you bastard." She hissed.

Donovan laughed. "Smile for her, children."

They did, lips parting on teeth young and old, straight, and crooked, each with two gaps where Nosfur's fangs would otherwise be.

***

Pain was an old friend. Sandy felt almost comforting familiarity as it returned. The burning and the nausea were just physical, transitory things for her.

But not for innocent children.

Samson recounted the bite at Sandy's coaxing, the stink of Keller's raw burnt flesh, the terror that came with life leaving his veins. The kid didn't know those moments would revisit him for years, mold him, redefine every memory of his twelve short years in the sun. He'd watched the lioness watch him fade and saw the raccoon beheaded and fallen into his final breaths of sleep.

Hate seethed in Sandy Mallory, pure and furious as she'd let Samson recount his mortal end.

That anguish was pain that Sandy deserved, a betrayal worse than she'd committed upon Celeste. She'd not been there for Samson as she should have been, having sought violent delights with Bucky as a salve for Mr. Calvert's betrayal of her loyalty. The rabbit's love had never been hers to have, and the self-deception had been shameful and costly.

All that mattered happened in her absence from his plans. One of Donovan's vicious, rich circle of power players had spent Samson's mortal life to remove a single plank of the rabbit's power, discarding the kid like a game piece.

And so, Sandy offered Samson offered words of comfort and told him she'd return. The front door opened. Wolves came in. The window above opened, and the squirrel slipped out.

A short while later back in the Gold Coast of Chicago Sandy bore her pain proudly, leaping the wooden fence with its poison nails, breaking the window to her monastery-tidy study and forcing her way up oaken stairs borne by beams of penetrating fire, to the chamber where she herself had made supplicants of the dispossessed and lost, souls given to Donovan's stratagems. What once seemed noble in clouded judgement was now plain in its cruelty and vanity.

She took the vial and the packet she'd kept there and fled the tiny cottage that had been her willing prison for so long.

Vengeance would cleanse her and Samson both.

***

"How is this possible? They're working with reliquary steel forged from the nails of the ark. I can sense it. They should be in agony just to be near it." Von Haften demanded.

"It only tortures those who drink the blood of the living, remember? Sandy Mallory was sequestered in a cottage with this steel within its walls. Did you really think I was keeping her in a place that caused relentless suffering?"

Donovan took the steps down and approached a rabbit like himself, brown fur glistening in the firelight. She dipped her muzzle low as Donovan caressed her chin. "Blood coursing through veins brings the fire of the reliquary blade. Its complete absence over time gradually delivers them from any agonies in this place. They age far more slowly than mortals at the age of their turning, but with the speed and strength of the curse that afflicts them with their hunger. These supplicants have been cured, Countess."

The rabbit looked up, smiling a twin gapped smile.

Donovan kissed her cheek. "Like Ms. Mallory before them they have defeated that hunger."

The Countess remained where she was, sword still wielded, her other hand pointing at each in turn. "You never told me that there were others. You let me believe that Mallory was alone!"

"She indeed is my most disciplined fighter for the cause. These are innocent of violence, sequestered from a world that simply won't understand them."

"Innocent? They will lapse, Donovan. They will surrender to their urges. It's already happened with—"

"No, Evelyn!" Donovan spat. "And my friend here can tell you why."

The brown rabbit peacefully met the eyes of her benefactor, not looking to the lioness when she spoke. "We're building the instruments that will free us, tools to help us maintain our cleanliness in the eyes of the Martyres." The rabbit's eyes drifted down to the curve of the metal before her.

"Tell her where that is going, Mira."

The twisted metal was hot when the rabbit raised it with one right hand in blacksmith's tongs. "This is for Liberty Island. An explosion seven years ago damaged the Statue of Liberty and Mister Calvert volunteered to replace the bands on the torch she holds."

"Yes. A German bomb in the early stages of war damaged the grandest statue on the continent and became one of many opportunities as a wealthy benefactor. Such a pesky thing that war, it could have ground America in its tracks. So many small projects left unfunded, so many crumbling edifices of power and commerce that require investment. Chicago is the start, Evelyn. Trolley lines in San Francisco, boardwalks in New Orleans, a Terminal tower to rise in Cleveland, Ohio. My network will cover this nation in ten to twenty years' time."

"Built by near-immortal slaves trained to serve you," the Countess scoffed. "This is your grand plan, to save on labour costs while your company makes millions. You've used the Nosfur to defeat labor unions?"

Donovan sighed and his ears flattened as he rounded on the lion. "How can you be so blind to reduce it to that? My company will be making a new world! One in which those afflicted by this terrible curse will be aided in their vows of abstinence and a promise to refrain from harming the innocent at the educational price of cleansing pain. Imagine the works created here stretching to every city, every town, every corner of the world."

"Wrought by the hands of the damned," the Countess spat.

Donovan showed his flat teeth, exasperated. "You imagine you look at a room full of monsters, Evelyn. But truthfully, they are as blameless as God himself, bound by an oath to refrain from violence that no animal in this entire gangster-besieged city can be held to in a dry Anti-Saloon Leaguer's wildest dreams. At last, we can have a vice of unmeasurable harm defeated for all time. How can you not celebrate that? How can you not see the *genius* in that?"

A beaver with a girder against his back set it down on the stone floor and approached with hands in supplication "I beg your pardon, mam. I was forced into the life of blood-drinking by one who attacked me in the north while working for Hudson's Bay company. I have long sought to cure myself of this curse and Sandy Mallory found me on my passage through

Chicago four years ago. I passed the crucible of suffering and found a new path in life as a servant of the Martyres of the Black— "

The swipe of the Countess' sword cut his hand deep and the beaver recoiled without a sound.

"Stay back! I'll kill any that comes near me!" the lion snarled with a step back towards the stairs.

Donovan raised a hand as he approached the beaver. "See to the cut, Joachim. Back to the task everyone! I will straighten this out."

He leapt the rail with lapine finesse. The Countess backed slowly up the stairs towards the main forge floor, sword still drawn against the crowd before her.

"We need to resolve this, Evelyn," Donovan said ingratiatingly, wondering how soon his contingency plan would take to arrive.

***

Bucky's idea was simple enough, with rewards too great to hold back. He'd seen the light, as it were. They were just animals, all of them. Only wardrobe separated the creatures wandering into picture shows at the Biograph on Lincoln from the critters howling in the weeds past the city limits. Morality was a chain for the will to break.

He'd boosted a truck from a grocer's then broke a window at a druggist's a block over. Following the supply run where he obtained the drugs he needed, Bucky came across a cop car outside the place where he came to collect his stockpile. Bucky wanted to have some fun before the sergeant died, let him know just how upset Bucky was about his speak being burned to the ground, but he botched that. Life fleeing the dog's eyes was precious on the highest of highs and he restrained himself from literally rolling in his dead scent, rip roaring drunk on two veins in just three hours. He felt just pie in the sky now.

He threw up his pasta from before and pitied that his mother's last meal was wasted. But he was fed and she was free of this world's pains. Living forever would help Bucky forget in due time.

So much to contend with, people he loved who didn't love him back, bosses who tried to have him whacked and left him in the wind. The moochers who left him last were the worst, missing the elegance in his incredible plan. Fuck 'em all. The king needed no clowns.

Bucky dusted himself off, took the cop's badge and entered Noah's Plank School for Wayward Youth, meeting a raccoon janitor on the second floor.

"Need anything?" Bucky was asked around a toothpick.

"Naw. Feeling full." Bucky flashed the dead cop's badge at the raccoon. "Where are the kids? I was asked to check with 'em for more information."

"Several cops already did," the raccoon said, confused. "They didn't see nothin."

"Yeah well..." On a body-full of blood Bucky was hot and light of mind. "We do lots of checking. Was a scary thing that happened with that thing that has all of us cops here."

"Are you sure you're with— "

Bucky broke his neck. At last, some quiet. He opened his senses and listened carefully, sought out the smells. His natural vulpine senses were vastly amplified, and he picked out the direction quickly. There was a night-watchman who was easy to deal with. The open second-story window made it fun if a bit loud going down.

That woke a few of them, his real prize. Some rodent he couldn't figure out and a fawn rubbed sleep out of their eyes as they leaned out of the dormitory into the hall. "Who're you?" the fawn asked.

"I'm your jail-breaker," Bucky forced himself not to smile. Fangs would spook them. "I hated school when I was your age. Hated the rules, hated the hidings I got. Day I socked the principal and ran for it was the best ever."

A third head poked out, a ram girl with a bit of girth. Lots of wool on her but such a thick throat. "Who're you?"

"My name is Bucky. I want to be your friend. I've got a truck downstairs waiting to take us all away." His head spun, vision tinged in red. Three drinks in one night were obviously too much for him. He'd have to cut back. The kids huddled together, said nothing. He wasn't selling this.

"You ever want to see Coney Island? I did once. Merry go rounds and a Ferris wheel that shows you the whole city. Wanna come with me? I can take all of you." Bucky could smell the cotton candy in his mind's eye and had a teetering wistful moment as he realized he'd never enjoy the spun sugar on his own tongue again.

"Isn't that in New York? It's pretty far, isn't it?" the rodent asked.

"What are you girl? I never seen a smart hamster."

She blinked, "I'm a capybara."

"I'd love to show a capper bear and all her other friends all the best places. I know New York seems far, but I've got a really fast car."

No cotton candy for himself though. No sausage on a bun. It would have almost been better if he'd never have enjoyed those things, spared himself the heartbreaks of loss. He'd save these kids from life's slings, oh yes, he would. No tough going for them.

"Why do you look like you wanna cry?" The fawn boy asked.

He couldn't even do that right. Son of a bitch.

"Who's that?" called an even smaller voice in the room. "I thought I heard John shouting."

"He's our night monitor," The fawn informed Bucky.

"He took a break. So, you wanna go?"

Nobody moved. The ram girl fidgeted. "We don't know who you are, and we don't go anywhere with strangers."

Stubborn little shits. Bucky remembered the badge. "I'm a pig...I mean, a policeman. See?" He flashed it smartly and almost dropped it.

"You don't act like a policeman" the capper bear rodent said suspiciously.

"I am though."

"Where's your gun?" the fawn asked, very interested.

Bucky hadn't needed a gun in over a week. He couldn't even remember where he'd left it. Damn, he'd paid a lot for it too.

The cop had one. Why hadn't he taken it? Oh right, he didn't need it.

The blood had him hot and really bothered now. He'd drank too much and was being outsmarted by goddam kids. When he got his new place together and restocked, he was going to serve these three last.

"I'll got get my gun and show it to you, prove I'm a policeman. Heck when we go outside, I'll even let you fire it into the field. Won't that be fun?"

The kids didn't move, didn't answer. They looked ready to bolt.

"Right, I'll be right back. Just hang on."

A hop, skip and a jump had him back at the truck. He opened the back to grab the little rags with the ether bottle he'd picked up from the druggist's he'd broken into. This would be noisy, but he would be quick. The new speak would be packing light. "Never know what hit 'em," Bucky laughed as he slammed shut the truck's doors.

"Funny you'd say that," Celeste said. Bucky was thrown across the parking lot, muzzle and nose twisting in a long scrape of gravel.

CHAPTER 22

RECKONINGS OF FIRE, EARTH AND BLOOD

The aches returned. Crawford welcomed them. He didn't know why Donovan's summons made him suspicious, but he didn't want a drink to settle himself.

His hands were swollen on the wheel, early signs of the change. He'd felt it when kissing Charlie goodbye in their apartment. Drink kept it at bay for a while, but with a clear head he could take the change as it took him. He could keep himself and the power could be negotiated with.

He had to make peace with his other self.

A flashlight from the booth crossed his face for an instant before the gates to the steel mill were dragged open and shut in his wake. He didn't like that people working for Donovan knew his face. He'd end that association very soon.

The mill was a dark block against meager stars and the pale coin of the moon, lit at scant points by bulbs above doors large and small. Those doors were closed now, and Crawford idly wondered if that kept drafts from affecting the forging steel within. He tested the same door he left by last time and it was unlocked. Inside it was easily several degrees hotter than out. The ebb of his strained muscles made his clothes heavy.

"Not yet," he growled. Crawford looked up. The roof of the forge was opened in several places, casting beams of light down into dark patches of the immense space, backlit by glints of molten steel.

He ascended, keeping eyes peeled. He smelled faint mammalian traces from the day shift but didn't see a soul. His gaze trailed to the spot where he'd previously seen the singular figure bearing a length of steel too heavy for any mammal to carry into the darkness. That stretch was now partially illuminated, and he saw a small shed, its doors opened to descending stairs.

Something to investigate later. He needed to find Donovan.

The office was a flight up. Something didn't seem right. The room was lit in cold white haze emanating from nothing electric. When he got to the landing, he saw that the office's own roof had been folded back, probably to release heat when the forges made it uncomfortable for the rabbit's work.

Above that roof a pair of suspended mirrors reflected moonlight. The floor within the unlocked office was milky with pale white.

Inside, Calvert's desk was bare but for a handwritten note. "Completing a quick tour, will not keep you waiting."

Nothing left out to drink. Good, Crawford didn't want temptation. He sat in the guest chair and put his feet up on the desk, wondering what words they'd have and if the rabbit had any means of sniffing out lies about the kid.

The light itself tingled as it bathed him and a memory stirred, something Celeste had said about moonlight. A growing ache under his pelt was distracting, standing his pelt up under the clothes he'd hastily changed into.

Sense memory brought up the copper scent that flowed through a moon-washed alley and the field out by the school where Donovan had sent him.

And the heat of a speak on fire. His arms and legs felt cloth vices closing around them. His shoulder holster was tightening. He heard it strain. The moonlight was soothing fire. He hastily undid a few buttons on his distressed shirt. He had to breathe, focus. He could hold this off. He'd already proved it was his tool to use.

A growl escaped jaws that were raw from teeth seeking more room and as he looked straight into the redirected glint of the moon's silver smile Crawford realized Calvert had manipulated him. The moon's light penetrated him, unlocking the key to the primordial cage, unrelenting and beautiful enough for a song.

***

"There is no misunderstanding, Donovan." The Countess held her low sword ready. "You've abused the authority we were loath to give you in the first place and have collected more abominations than you've destroyed. As far as the council will be concerned the American experiment is over."

Donovan felt his heart sink. Even in lingering pessimism he'd dared hope that revelation of the grand endeavor would win her over. His cane was at his side, but he wouldn't draw it.

Her ending would be a disappointment. "Accept it Countess, you reject my proposal only because it keeps those in the gap who don't fit antiquated designations of predator or prey. My way forward corrects for a world view you refuse to see is flawed."

The Countess backed up the stairs up to the steel mill floor. "Oh, shut your *mouth*, Donovan. You don't care about fitting Nosfurs into society. You only want them for the endless labor they provide. You don't give any more of a damn about liberation for them than I do."

Donovan took a step closer, cane tapping the concrete under his feet. "I'm living proof that your presumptions are holdovers from a dying age, Evelyn. I've saved you and those other decrepit carnie idiots from yourselves. You just don't see it yet."

The Countess stopped her ascent halfway. She'd be loath to retreat from him.

"Children, let her see you again." Even just above a whisper Donovan was heard and heeded. They flowed in behind him like water and were shoulder to shoulder a few steps behind.

The Countess darted back, shooting glances left and right as she regained the factory floor. "You've made a pact with Satan himself."

Donovan put a hand up to stop his children's advance. "No pacts were made with the devil by these before you. If any ever were, I've broken them."

He reached the inward doors and sighed. "I'm sorry that— "

A howl pierced the hiss of molten foundry steel, echoing between the gargantuan forges. Up high, something toppled, glass broke.

"I'm sorry that the world to come has no place in it for you, Evelyn." Donovan threw his weight into slamming the shed door shut. He slid the bolt and locked it.

"Did we cause offence?" Came a sheep's reluctant voice below.

"Not at all. A moment, please." Donovan went to the phone box suspended on the wall and cranked its magneto to buzz the security gate. "This is Mister Calvert. The lockdown drill is in effect. All personnel should be outside of the foundry, all entrances secured from outside. I'll tour to check shortly."

He disconnected the call and wondered if the Countess was on the move or waiting behind those doors. It saddened him that he'd never see her again in her present condition, but she'd made her choices. A flicker touched his senses and he realized he'd been distracted from the sensation emanating from his locket and cane. As he took a moment to focus, the contact took shape in his mind, and with it, familiarity.

"No," he whispered. "How could you?"

***

Bucky noisily snorted bloody gravel and teetered to his feet. Celeste didn't give him time to recover. She crossed the distance in five strides, drove a hoof into the back of his leg, dropping him to his knees. She then threw a closed fist to the side of the fox's head, knocking him down again.

Bucky hissed and lashed his foot out. Celeste tripped and tucked into a roll that she rose from by a parked Ford Model T.

"You came for children," she hissed. "After all that you've already done you came to take children!"

Bucky shook wasted blood off his nose and muzzle. He was so flushed that his dark eyes were bloodshot pink. "What's it to you, deadbeat fucking herbie? You made me as a toy and abandoned me! You stole the life I had!"

"You chose that life and it had consequences. And you expected others to suffer it." She rushed him and they collided, spraying gravel and dirt. They grappled breathlessly, sinewy limbs grabbing and deflecting.

Celeste kept herself closed and tight, mindful of each powerful strike the blood-flushed fox could deliver. His blows were furious and clumsy, borne of desperation and frustration. Snorts of wasted blood flecked his chin as he clawed at her. "I fucking hate you! You were just a pretty thing on the arm and a quick fuck and that's all you'll ever be to—"

Her next blow connected and broke his nose. Blood wet Celeste's knuckles and she remembered all the tricks she'd learned from watching drunken sailors settle disputes in Nice half a century ago, keep moving, give nothing to grab. They darted together at speeds mortal eyes could barely follow. Bucky's veins were flooded with stolen life while Celeste's were modestly stocked but the advantage it gave him was mostly the illusion of overconfidence made worse by the complete absence of discipline.

She made him bleed that which was precious with each connected blow, a kicked shin sprained, a tooth knocked free. The fox rolled and backed away, swinging sloppily, wounding her but less effective in his blows.

Celeste could see in his eyes, one swelling, that he was losing a battle for which he couldn't conceive of defeat. Bucky thought himself the hero, thought himself deserving, thought himself the heir of a city carved up to feed him. In the real world he was losing.

"Shtop!" he lisped, tongue bit by an uppercut that snapped his mouth shut. He backed behind the dead cop's Ford, slipping to the dirt to crab-scurry backwards. "Jush fucken leathe me alone!"

Celeste advanced, blood dripping from a cut on her muzzle. Her wounds would heal, and his faster. Unless she was quick enough.

She stepped behind the car where Bucky retreated from, grabbed the spare tire and braced one hoof on the bumper. With a hard lean leveraging the car's weight, she pushed down. The front end of the Model-T lifted on its springs for an instant before torque transferred to the spare and it snapped off the mount in a twist of spokes.

She raised the rimmed tire high and took running steps forward.

Bucky's eyes widened, hands raised to ward off what he couldn't stop and down the tire came, fracturing his arm, then his rib cage. Another strike and his muzzle's top jaw was broken. Again and again, the wheel came down until the fox was a pulped mess. Blood splashed up on Celeste's face and she caught drops of stolen life in her mouth.

A moment later the fox was a wriggling ruin.

Celeste forced the boot lid on the cop's Model T and found what she needed. She'd have to work fast.

**

Foundry stink crowded Crawford's nose and heat worked into his pelt. Discarded clothes and the oily stink of the gun in his snapped holster was a thing somehow important yet disgusting as all other scents in here.

The light bathed him in joy. Crawford sang to it, lungs aching with the pleasure.

He tried to stand but his gait was better suited to all fours, so he leaped upon the empty desk, wrapped a thumbed paw around the chair and hurled it. Glass broke.

He leaped, landing on metal planking with vantage over the steel kingdom. Sapient memories battled his instinct to run to flowing grass beyond the barriers demarking this place. Out there the moon was everywhere. He could run and hunt.

He bunched his muscles and descended the steep stairs, thuds bringing him to where the exit was impassible, his claws scrabbling uselessly. He sought other escape.

And picked up the scent.

Feline. Female. Nose to ground, he found a trail. Footpads left scent, feline and lapine traces. Instinct had him wary, but the consciousness residing within tapped a memory. He'd smelled this cat before.

With instincts confused he knew only to follow.

At a sealed den's entrance, he picked up traces of the familiar rabbit. It had drawn him here, he remembered.

He stood on his haunches, claws on the warm steel and drew it in.

Footfalls were fast, near silent. He spun, arm dropping from the space where the blade tried to sever it. A lance of pain flooded his abdomen on the backswing. Crawford howled as he ground toe claws to stone and leapt, jaws wide. The golden-furred, black-decked lion was fast, but not enough. His claws raked her shoulder. She screamed and sprang back. With a snap of clarity from the pain in his side Crawford recalled the origin of the scent. "You terrrnd the keed."

The lioness spun the steel in hand, switched the blade to her left arm, the right bleeding freely. "How many monsters does Donovan have?"

Crawford understood that as he tensed. He remembered Donovan, but not the rabbit's importance. His mind was a soup of unfocused fury.

The lion went low, fangs bared as Crawford leaped. She slid under, blade angling to disembowel him and his immense claw was bit as it knocked the blade away. The lion rolled to her feet and ran while he fell on his side, fire following a path through his elbow up to his shoulder and back down again.

Crawford looked at the monstrous shape of his right hand and saw that a finger was now missing to the last knuckle. The lost digit lay on the foundry floor in a constellation of speckled blood. He roared to shake the very rafters and leapt to his feet.

The cat was halfway up one of the stairwells to the catwalk when he loped after, right limb favored.

She could hurt me worse, the rational core of his mind realized, but the scent of his own blood and her fear woke something more powerful. The cat was a predator. So was the wolf. There had to be one less.

"I'm going to kill you," the hiss washed down from shadows between moonbeams above. "Along with all of Donovan's abominations, experiments, and sycophants. Then I'll drag him back to Cologne in a box."

Echoes carried the threat between dangling chains and rolling cauldrons of molten steel. They warmed the metal as Crawford shook his pelt out. Droplets of blood flicked off into darkness.

The lion was drawing him higher to tighter spaces and he chased warily. The cat was close.

In the recesses of awareness Crawford fought for control, memories struggling with instincts. He should run, escape to the joys of night.

But she'd hurt someone. He'd remembered, forgotten again. His mate? No. A goat kid, a wolf cub, he sifted for truth. Blue paint on a toy, blue sky touching a farm. Who was counting on him now? Who did Crawford fight for? Truth retreated. He stalked it and the lion both. The hiss of boiling air buried sound.

A badger's ghost from a million years ago asked him, "Whose love bore you bleeding up this way?" And it tore the wolf's mask away as memory solidified. He loved all of them. Crawford's wife, his partner, his son. And Samson the kid. Life found validation in love in multitudes, pack members important to him in wholly different ways from one another, but all vital parts of the soul behind the fangs.

Pain from the missing finger subsided as purpose sharpened him. They were all under threat. He had to act.

Hell's heat bubbled up from cauldrons underneath, his belly and throat hot. His senses were overwhelmed, but he clung to that last kernel of consciousness at all costs, as he had when he'd saved Charlie from things among the flames and the dark. This power was his.

Crawford found a moment of stillness and let his senses drink.

A split second's flex of a link of steel above him caught his ear as weight shifted for a leap.

Crawford pushed back with good hand and bad as twin feline feet met the warm steel he'd just vacated, and the lithe lioness landed, dark vestments making an inky outline above the orange mist. The blade she'd tried to bury in Crawford's back twisted in her grip and she smiled. "Nowhere to run to, animal." she licked her fangs. "I'll say a prayer for my family over your skinned hide."

She took one step with her blade drawn high and an Irish lilt from no discernible source froze her and Crawford in place. The diminutive voice cut the air with certitude. "I'll say one for young Samson you heartless cunt."

Reddish furred feet clipped the lion's jaw, rocking her backwards. A thick tail twitched as the squirrel mounted the rail, inches from a fall into perdition below.

It was Mallory, Crawford realized, consciousness returning with force. It had to be.

The lion stumbled back, sword nearly tumbling from her grasp. "Donovan's vermin!" she screamed. "Does he know yet you betrayed him? I so wanted to see his face when he finally learned!"

"You'll settle for mine as you snuff out," Sandy replied.

Crawford braced to lunge, and the lion glanced his way as he growled, claws spread for the briefest instant. The squirrel's jaws caught Crawford's eye as fangs erupted between the rodent's teeth. Her own leap was so fast that his eye could barely track her. One of the lioness hands hefted the sword while the other pushed out to deflect the squirrel's charge for the blow. Rather than knock that golden furred hand away the squirrel bit it through the palm, leaving herself completely open. The sword plunged into Sandy Mallory's chest and then slipped free of the lion's grasp, the squirrel collapsing onto the catwalk while the lioness fell against the railing, clutching her hand to stem the rush of blood.

Through wracking pain, the squirrel said something Crawford couldn't make out, his mind now in full possession and his body beginning to recede from the change.

"What did you say you tree rat *slut?*" The lioness spat as she dragged her sword free of the squirrel's torso, causing the squirrel to scream. The lioness raised the sword and hefted it with two hands, blood dripping free, ready to cleave the prone rodent in two.

To the wolf's and lioness' surprise the squirrel laughed through agony that gurgled every word. "Smell the wound, Countess. They say I have to drain you to the half, but that's not true, is it?" The Irish squirrel coughed blood black as a well that inked her chin. "If the mix is taken by you or I, it simply takes time. Welcome, sister!"

Bringing her double fisted sword back, the Countess relinquished the grip of her torn hand, sniffing at the point where blood soaked her knuckles. She froze, dead still, the sword wavering in her grip. "No." Tears began to well in her eyes. "No. No. No! Du hast mich verdammt!"

"I truly hope so!" Mallory spat.

"Fick dich!" The lioness swung the weapon high with a yowling hiss and Crawford found the opening at last to leap, closing several feet in seconds and grasping the lion's sword arm with both hands. They grappled, he applied pressure, twisting. A bone snapped and the sword dropped to the grate.

Both leaned dangerously against the precipice, the rail next to the ladle's supporting chains buckling. Crawford scrabbled for purchase, his change receding and yet fueled by desperation. The Countess yowled as she wriggled free her broken hand and her bit one.

And the squirrel leapt again with the scream of the dying.

Torn from Crawford's grasp both lion and squirrel went over, grappling for purchase on the slick steel rail.

The lioness lost her grip. She struck the lip of the steel ladle, her body a dark silhouette that rolled into a goblet of liquid sun. There was an ear-piercing scream as smoking hands scrabbled for purchase against the slide, her pelt aflame. It was over in an instant.

Crawford gazed into the roiling iris of steel, stunned as it slid away on a massive clicking conveyor chain, machinery indifferent to its victim. The squirrel had an arm locked round the rail, arm clearly dislocated and losing grip.

Crawford fell to his knees before her. The change had fully receded now, and his mortal bleeding hand extended under his full control. "Let me help! I'm Crawford. Donovan sent—my God you were stabbed right through."

Sandy glanced into the dark past her own wound and smiled a wan smile. "Cat missed my heart." Her eyes roved distantly, a dark sheen coming and waning in their depths. They tracked Crawford up and down. "You're naked. And a right mess. Mister Calvert won't approve."

"Let me pull you up."

"No. You can't help. When you see him, please tell Samson that I'm sorry. He deserved better." Her smiling eyes were sad and yet strangely content. "He'll need Celeste. Or perhaps you'll do. I'll not fail you all again."

She released her grip, plummeting into the dark between the ladles. Seconds passed with Crawford blinking, wounded hand withdrawn, no sound from the depths of the mill below.

***

Celeste finished quickly and waited.

Bucky came to, squirming and sputtering and rolling his head back and forth. When the one un-ruined eye cracked open, the sight of Celeste standing above a pit's lip with the shovel upright in the mound of dirt next to her clearly confused him. He made an unintelligible questioning noise.

Celeste was glad to answer. "Because you ruined everything. For me. For those of us trying to lay low in this city, all of it to serve your greed and vanity."

He sputtered another inquiry and shook off the sand sifting down toward his muzzle.

"I don't understand," Celeste sighed.

Bucky cleared his throat with a noisesome ejection of blood and effluvia onto the sand. "You can't judge me. You got no right. You did this to me. You're a killer."

"Of gangsters, Bucky. I'm a killer only of killers and I know where the limits have to be. No indiscriminate victims. No children. Not ever."

It had to hurt to growl but the fox did anyway. "Stupid naïve herbie. We had the same job! At least I had some vision, some idea of the potential for the hunting ground we live on. You never learned to think like the carnivore this made you. It's pathetic!"

Celeste set her shoulders back, preparing herself. "And you never learned to think beyond that Bucky. Had you stayed I'd have helped you, but you never could put yourself above your wants. You're just a feral animal in a suit without any sense of restraint. That's by your own choice."

Bucky bared his fangs and thrashed in anger, stuck fast in the hard packed earth that buried all below his cheeks. His voice was plaintive as the situation settled over him. "I thought of *everybody's wants*! That's what this city is, a place to get your throat and your dick wet and make money providing! We're all hungry Celeste! We want relief!" His struggles gradually subsided and his ears, one of which was at a broken cant settled low. "Let me out of here and I'll show you what I'm destined for. Last chance, for both of us. Sandy got cold feet and ran, but you had potential. You were already on the inside for fuck's sake." Bucky was panting now, a panic reflex for lungs that would never work, above ground or under. "Just stop caring about fucking stupid vermin marks who will grow old and die in no time at all, each one wasted. We're eternal, right? We don't need to be alone!" He wavered on the verge of a scream, but his voice was breaking.

Celeste felt only cold certainty. Whatever the Sister's original plan for Bucky, it had to end here. There wasn't a shred of remorse at the bottom of this pit.

Or within her either. "You aren't destined for anything more than I am. We have our actions and our consequences and nothing else. We are eternal, Bucky. But you don't understand what that means. Not yet."

The growl became a spitting hiss of fury and anguish. "You made me! You made me and I have a destiny! I'm gonna get out of this fucking hole and drain every miserable brat in that school!" The fox roared, his thrashing on the point of breaking his already fractured neck. "And when I'm done I'll come for you— "

Dirt landed on his head in a torrent, filling his mouth and making him spit. Celeste was startled at the movement to her left and turned to see Samson heft the shovel again, dumping another load of earth on the squirming vulpine head at the bottom of the hole.

"You came for my friends!" Samson shouted, hefted more dirt, sailed it down. "You were going to kill them!" Another shovel, a shake of a muzzle put a nose and fangs above dirt. A mouth opened that could not speak as more earth rained within it. "I hate you!" Samson was on the verge of weeping, his eyes darkest pools of anguish. "I hate what all you all made me!" His yelling had quieted to grunts that in turn became hisses as his fangs pushed forth. "You think we're toys!" He shoveled and threw, shoveled and threw. "You think we're *food*! And you made me a thing like you!"

Celeste felt the cut of that that anguish, that first moment of truly understanding what she'd faced long ago. No mortal family, no mortal friends. His school mates in the building beyond may as well be on a distant world, exhibits in lost possibilities that would slowly decay as they passed by.

Sandy wasn't here to guide the kid as Celeste had prayed she would be, and she hated her for that. Alone in the dark with Samson, Celeste couldn't find the right words. "Samson," she took a step towards him and the look he gave her promised violence as he held the filthy shovel aloft. "Samson, please."

He dumped its contents down onto the twitching layer of earth below and then dropped the shovel to the ground at his feet. "You don't care," his voice quavered but didn't break. "My Mother and Father are already gone, and Sandy is gone and you're just somebody who will forget about me and abandon me too, first chance you get. That's what it's always going to be."

Celeste reached out and embraced the goat kid, drawing his face into her shoulder and settling it there. His stubby fingers clutched her arms and his chest heaved and he was silent as a grave as she let him cry. Out on the derelict field scrub swayed in the dark awaiting a dawn without promises.

She held him against it and didn't let go.

***

Donovan heard the scream echo through the walls, as did his acolytes. The shriek terminated in an instant. He held his talisman close and weighed the wisdom of opening those doors.

Sandy was here, somewhere close. And she'd…fed.

The others didn't know, and he didn't tell them. Loyal as they were he didn't want to cause them additional stress. Or bring the burden of difficult questions.

The scream had to be Evelyn's. It was disappointing that she and the rest of the Martyres could only see one way forward to ending their millennia-long war with those whose curse gave them infinite potential. Pity. He'd miss her touch despite the cruel games that came with it.

Minutes passed as he pondered his next move. A hammering on the door a few feet from where he stood startled him.

The sheep standing nearest to him tested the air with her nostrils. "It's a lupine. A wolf."

"Open up Donovan. I can smell you," came a weary mutter.

The propensity of all the preternaturals around him to have stronger scent was somewhat frustrating but Donovan regained composure and cocked an ear. "Are you alone?"

"Yes."

Donovan fingered his cane in his left hand as he worked the bolt and swung the door inward. The grey timber-wolf standing there was bare-chested, blood seeping from a shallow wound at this abdomen. He wore his stretched-slack holster with gun and pressed black pants that were torn. In his left hand dangled the latest scotch decanter from the office upstairs, crystal stopper missing. He raised a mangled hand missing its smallest finger and poured scotch on it, wincing, then taking a slug. "I went upstairs to clean up, found this in a drawer that's not locked anymore." Crawford poured whiskey on his abdomen, soaking his already damp pants, and winced again, taking deep breaths. "Your note said you'd be along. You were lying, weren't you?"

Donovan looked past him, high and low, weaker nose testing for a scent he hoped he'd never catch. "I was preoccupied."

The wolf looked past him and wagged the bottle at the Nosfurs on the stairs. "Hello."

They didn't answer.

Crawford met Donovan's gaze and held it. "I know what those mirrors in your office were for. Was I supposed to finish her or was she supposed to finish me? I'll know if you lie."

Donovan's fingers were slick around his cane, and he fought to keep the flush out of his ears. "Everything happened as expected. She was the one who wounded the child you were forced to handle. In American parlance, she had it coming. Where is she?"

The wolf snorted. "Ruining the purity of the next few girders you pour. But that's your problem. I've come to tell you we're done."

Donovan's gaze narrowed. "The deal was that you were supposed to find Sandy Mallory. You know that was the arrangement."

"I did. She was just here."

Donovan realized he shouldn't have mentioned her. "We've all been worried sick about her. If you see her, could you ask her..."

"She's around. I think." The wolf poured more scotch on his hand, more on his wound, took one more swig and offered it to Donovan who waved a hand. Crawford turned away, tail high. "Lose my number, Calvert. I won't answer. Have your people open the goddamned doors." Crawford wagged the decanter behind him as he wandered into the darkness.

Donovan tested the air once again with his nose. "Ms. Mallory?" he called into the dark. "Are you out there?" He took a deep breath. "Your friend Ms. Mallory is..." Donovan turned to see his acolytes had receded, the darkness behind him having grown new shadows as a bulb had been extinguished.

One of those above spoke to him. "You sacrificed so much for us didn't you, put so much of yourself into making this new world for us to toil in."

"Sandy?" Turning in every direction, shadows below, shadows outside. "Are you alright?"

A form settled into Donovan's back, molding to his and reddish-furred hands wrapped round his chest, under his arm and teased the fur under his chin.

The voice that spoke was younger than he'd heard in five years. "Tell me you couldn't do it without me, Mister Donovan Calvert. The confinement, the tortures, the wearing down of resistance and planting of guilt. All that pain for a cause to light fires within us that forged all this. For you." Her lips teased his ear and Donovan felt strength in her limbs, the pained twitch of her body against his.

"Ms. Mallory, what have you done?"

She coughed and blood dotted his suit. "Suffered, felt pain, nothing you didn't expect. Nothing you didn't demand again and again."

Donovan felt a chill as the implications set in. His first perfect pupil, fallen and tainted. The others had to see it. "Sandy, you've disappointed me. Why would you betray us this way? You were so important to the plan."

A cough, and she slipped round, hands winding with her, sliding along his shoulders, caressing his clenching jaw. "Our plan? You mean your plan, your aims, *your* benefit. I helped you teach them to feel guilt, to embrace agony for shame. But what have you embraced?" A hole in her chest bled freely on her perfect frame, her visage above as vital and new as the first day her progenitor had bit her. The dress she wore emphasised every tempting stretch and curve. Even wounded, she was stunning, and her fangs were ivory blades of wicked delight.

Donovan blinked as he tried to meet her gaze and failed. Where were the others? Why had they left them alone? The hot world of his foundry was now quite cold. "I loved you as I loved you all, Sandy. The pains we took..."

She silenced him with a finger to his lips and he saw the anguish in her eyes. "I loved and respected you so much it was a wound of its own and you didn't care. The pain of progress would always be somebody else's to bear. I know that now." She took a step forward. The wall behind Donovan prevented a step back. Instinct worked his hand upon the cane's ram's head.

"I think it's time you understood the real cost of the world you want to make, to understand hungers that you can't easily sate." Sandy crept close and whispered in Donovan's ear. "It's time for the rabbit who owns the world to *want*."

Donovan flicked the cane free but far too late. Fangs sunk fire into his throat, and he gasped as he slid to the floor with her, Sandy's loving arms embracing him tight enough to crush. The blade and its hollow cane rolled down into the darkness past countless bound shadows that grew eyes and watched with fascination as their world was remade once again.

Hours later the acolytes of Donovan Calvert wandered through the forge, still locked away from the world. Several of them carried the corpse of Mister Calvert and the painfully gorged Ms. Mallory through the cavernous bowels to a secondary exit beyond the forge's gates. There they regarded stars that winked coldly out in the unknown.

High above, other straggling acolytes sifted through the ruined office, finding Donovan's car keys and a wolf's torn shirt. The beaver, Joachim, clicked his teeth as he answered the ringing telephone. "Yes? No, you are not to enter. You must wait."

They found Donovan's coat with his flush wallet and the phone rang again. With cultivated patience the beaver lifted the receiver. The voice of the new caller held him in rapture immediately. "Yes?" He listened. "Yes. When I lived up north my name was indeed Joachim Brunner." His brow furrowed in confusion as another voice joined the call, then a third. "Who are you three?"

CHAPTER 23

THE WORLDS JOIN

Celeste wrinkled her nose. "I was born in the eighteenth century and have sincerely not seen anyone looking this awful since then."

"That's touching," Crawford leaned against the doorjamb in Celeste's kitchen, breathing carefully against his stinging wounds. His bandaged hand and abdomen throbbed like hell.

Celeste's eyes wandered to the hand. "You lost a finger? Shouldn't you go to a hospital?"

Crawford lifted the bandaged digit. "Still have a knuckle, bleeding's stopped. I was changed when it happened, more infuriating then painful. Maybe that's why those like me don't stick around long." The wolf laughed meekly, then coughed. "I found Sandy. She went after Donovan."

Samson poked his head from behind her. "Is that the rabbit who's… lion friend…?"

"She can't hurt you anymore," Crawford said. "I can promise that." He sniffed. "Why do you both have dirt on your clothes?"

"Someone else can't hurt anyone either." Celeste put a hand round on Samson's shoulder. "We must go. The kid and I, away from Chicago. I can't move addresses fast enough now that I've signed this new lease and if Donovan finds us— "

"I know," Crawford said, taking a reluctant breath. "I have to go too. It's not just what Calvert has on me. My control over this affliction is still too weak. If I stay in the city, it's just a matter of time."

Celeste said her next words with reluctance. "Your friend?"

Crawford nodded, his gaze distant. "I'll ask him to come."

"You should just leave him, quietly." She hated the taste of those words even as she spoke them. "If you try to say goodbye it will be worse for you both."

Crawford glared at her. "I won't abandon him like that, not after what he's been through. You wouldn't understand."

Celeste sighed. "Where will you go?"

"I haven't figured that out yet. It won't be tonight, but it'll be far. I've one stop I'll need to make on the way out. In Virginia."

Celeste said nothing for a long time. "I've never been," She thought out her next question carefully. "Have you been to Virginia, Samson?"

The young goat glanced up. "No."

Celeste looked back to Crawford. "I think we three need to stay together. We need someone who can watch us during the day until we get situated somewhere and collect supplies to keep us safe. You need somebody to watch for you when your changes come who you can't kill accidentally, like your partner."

Crawford closed his injured hand tight as he weighed implications. "I love him. I can't just…"

"If you find a way to manage *it* you can come back to him. If you can't…" Celeste took ginger steps toward him and put a hand on the wolf's shoulder.

She knew the prospect of isolation hurt, and couldn't want that for Crawford, or Samson. Time and betrayals from all who'd held her heart had long scarred her to silent resentment, chosen loneliness an antidote that no longer worked. She had to face that.

Crawford gritted his teeth. "I've got to say goodbye to someone else. That's what Virginia's for. I…won't be long there." He looked out the front window at his Chevrolet. Dawn's break was feathering its dark bonnet. "Do you have money?"

"Some."

"Okay. Be ready for tomorrow night."

Crawford turned to go, and Samson stepped out from under Celeste's touch. "Take this with you," Samson said and put something in Crawford's hand. "I don't need it anymore."

***

Chicago woke, car horns outpaced birds singing as roads followed canals into the core. Train-cars slugged past concrete giants and sleepy mammals opened up shops, sweeping away the detritus of another hot and bothered night. Hot sheets dropped at street corners promised the morning's peace would be short-lived.

Crawford felt no need to say goodbye to the city. His apartment was his only destination and he found Charlie asleep in the chair by the phone, muzzle crooked up onto its corner and whistling softly through his nose. All the apartment's lights were on.

How many of Charlie's dreams were nightmares and how many were promises of better things to come?

All of it alone. Crawford sighed. Reggie, God bless him, had been wrong. Times like these didn't help one find themselves. It just taught them to run quicker.

If they were cowards.

"Say something," Charlie croaked, one eye cracking open. "Like what happened to you for starters."

"Charlie, I…"

Charlie raised his muzzle, dew-light from the low sun brushing his whiskers. Crawford looked into those softened brown eyes and knew right away that Charlie understood something was wrong.

"What is it?"

Crawford wanted to throw a mask on, keep himself calm. His emotions were quick to bury when he was afraid, when he felt guilty. His friend had lived through terrors that no mammal should have to carry and yet…

"I have to go, Charlie. I've got to leave Chicago and I'm the reason. Not the Nosfurs, not the rich rabbit or his sick friends. I'm dangerous. I can hurt you in ways I could never forgive myself for."

It came to him that he'd never confessed about Tooley, that he'd killed the cop and that he'd been crooked. But that wasn't just another weight he'd be transferring to someone already carrying all the weight in the world, even if it would help Charlie understand, help him let go.

Charlie sat up in the chair but didn't rise, blinking as his eyes roved the stark lit corners of the small apartment. He seemed lost. "You saved me," he said in a small voice. "I'd be dead if it wasn't for you."

Pain burgeoned up like an acid well as Crawford realized what he was doing, what his words really meant in this moment; leaving Charlie alone, in a city at war, turning the very heavy wheel that was threatening to crush his mate with a gangster's bullet or a puritan's snare. Crawford had shown him hope and now was tearing it away. "But I don't have enough control to not hurt you. I need that, Charlie. For your safety…"

Charlie's eyes darted down to the fresh bandage on Crawford's hand. "My God, what did they do to you?"

Crawford shook his head. "It doesn't matter, Charlie. I hurt them back. Calvert's out of my life."

Charlie was out of the chair and locking lips with Crawford in seconds. Crawford tasted desperation, hot life gasping. Crawford spoke into his mouth.

"What?" Charlie whispered.

"Come with me. Goddamit, I can't…I can't leave you here in this shit. We have to leave this city together or—"

Charlie's arms wrapped round him and all pain ceased. The brown wolf's muzzle turned down against his chest and Crawford's own buried into Charlie's shoulder. They could have held that moment to the end of time and the possibilities it bore would hold all Crawford wanted.

"No," Charlie said at last.

Crawford slowly released him, and Charlie did in turn.

Charlie reached down and took Crawford's bandaged hand, held it gingerly. "I took this job to find a better person in myself, even when I didn't know what that meant, or what kind of person that would be. And I found out that I was wrong about one thing. That better person won't be found within the Prohibition Bureau. In fact, the longer you do this, the more necks you step on, the uglier you find yourself becoming."

"But, Charlie, if you hate doing this, the way I do then why—"

"Because *they* want me gone, Crawford. My *predilections* make me the kind of undesirable that we'd be put onto chasing if we weren't rolling over drunks for spare change. It's only standing outside of it all that helped me see it. Nearly getting whacked forces you to look at things, you know?"

"Yeah," Crawford muttered through a swallow.

"I can't run. I just won't, not anymore. There are shadows everywhere I could go, and I was already afraid of what was in them before that speak. No more. I can do lots more with a badge then with a picket sign. I can work the inside, help those like us, maybe even bring about a change in how we're…seen."

Countless reasons burgeoned for how that could fail, how Charlie could literally have his life ruined if anyone in the bureau found out. The current bureau anyway.

Charlie kissed his bandaged fingers. "Don't soil this with goodbyes. I've got vacation saved up aplenty to step out. When this is done, when I've made what mark I'm going to make in months or years, I'll go to the ocean. New York, Atlantic City, hell maybe I'll go to San Francisco and smell the salt off the bay as every cute merchant marine reminds me of you." Charlie cleared his throat, tears kept at bay. "That's where we'll meet for good. I'm going to find you and I'm going to love all of what you are Crawford Cain. You just have to promise me you'll be safe until then."

"Charlie…"

"Just…let me handle Beatie and the office. I'll tell them that you're going through things and had to leave abruptly. He won't like it, but I knew the questions would mount and you'd give something up. Problem is Crawford…you're kind of a lousy liar."

It hurt to laugh but Crawford needed it. A promise was made and sealed with a kiss and they made slow love in the light. When Crawford finally left with one stuffed suitcase, he promised to call and Charlie promised to live.

Crawford Cain made one final stop in Chicago at the Holy Name Cathedral. He'd been here only once before for an agent's wedding and remembered the tranquility cutting it off from the bustle of a city on the boil.

Inside Crawford heard muttered prayers as he passed the stations of the flood that drowned the wicked and saved the penitent. At the altar's carved relief, the navigator of Christ prepared his body for consumption by waiting carnivores at stern and Noah held course at the bow. They'd been rendered as monkeys with sage, sad faces, a species long lost to fossils in museums. The mammals about them gathered threads about their naked forms, representations of the first seeds of moral knowledge taking root.

Crawford knelt down to the worn reliefs of the scattered four-legged creatures who succumbed gasping to tumultuous waters of vice and violence below the ark. In the cut marble crest of a still wave Crawford flexed his injured hand and set Samson's lead soldier, its blue uniform faded and bent gun ready for a march into a nameless fight. There were people in the waves worth saving.

With that he left Chicago.

***

"Bucky is dead. Took longer than expected but I delivered on my promise."

Al Capone growled into the telephone. "You think Johnny's gonna take you back on the roll? He and the fox were in business. That dried up in just one night cause of that raid. Was that you?"

"It was not. And dried up? Thanks to that fool you've got the Feds landing on your doorstep like buzzards, Al. He was into awful things the law will try to put on your head and Johnny should thank me for closing that book."

"Well, he won't. He ain't— "

"I don't want my job back, Al. Not your money or pity. This is a courtesy call to inform that you're wasting your time if you look for him or I. Bucky is gone. I'm gone. This business of yours is going to have a bad end if you don't get into a different racket. I see that now. Bon nuit."

Celeste hung up and stared at her phone. "Stop eavesdropping. I've made bad decisions that I'm leaving here for good. We both are. Get some rest."

"Okay," Samson said from his bound shadow. "Do we know yet where we're going?"

"We have more ideas than time to decide." Celeste stared at the tiny bleed of light through the join in the curtains that kept the pain of day at bay. "I've been alone for too long making the same mistakes and I'm not leaving you behind. Wherever we wind up, it will be a better place than this. I'm promising that to both of us Samson." When she smiled it came easily, the tension lifting away to a strange relief that she couldn't place, a sense that a page had truly turned.

Samson slipped from cover and went upstairs, hooves clicking quiet as a ticking watch.

***

Donovan regained consciousness in pain. And hunger, the depthless, ravenous want of the starving. A voice at once angelic and demonic coaxed him with an Irish lilt as the Rolls came to a stop, and the door opened. "Come," she said. "Time to see the world anew."

Floating on nausea, he fell to cobbles, rose and drifted up steps under wide tree's boughs before collapsing against the great oak door. It thudded as he collided. He was heavy as the world.

The door opened and he fell inward onto the marble. A possum's nose twitched closely. "Mister Calvert!" Edmond was agitated. "What happened sir? Calls from mill security came in and the city and the police!"

The musky, anxious life above him had a pulsating ebb that drew him to seat himself, senses overwhelmed. That flowing vessel pressed hot against him.

"Representatives from Cologne wired, demanding answers regarding the Countess. We need to get our story straight sir."

The words were senseless, context irrelevant. Donovan writhed within relentless need. A twist of his head and the parting of virgin fangs brought him to relief in the form of pliant flesh. He closed his jaw around Edmond's throat.

Blessed nourishment flooded his mouth, over his lips and down his white fur, ruining his suit. The struggles were punctuated by futile beats on his chest that brought him to embrace the lifeline vein like a lover. Edmond and his master collapsed, Calvert suckling as the struggles weakened.

Pain fled. In its place, bliss heralded euphoria. How had he learned so much yet failed to understand until now?

Sandy slipped round the open door behind them both as she drew her hood back and her tail twitched high. "Have your fill. It's not like Donovan Calvert could have any less, is it?"

He made childish noises and drank.

"I thought not. That's what I've always loved about you, Donovan. You know what the world can give, and you just take it. From any of us."

He didn't care. Ambrosia flowed more slowly from the still frame beneath him. Heightened senses caught distant, anxious scurries of life within his mansion. So many meals ahead. His heartbeat for the first time since the mill like a drum, invigorated by the flood of sensations. "I want more."

"That's a surprise," Sandy laughed sarcastically. "But you don't want to overfill yourself on the first night, do you? Come, let me help you up."

She helped raise him off the floor, bibbed in blood. Donovan gazed at the world in new eyes that saw the essence of all things. "What did you make of me?" He asked, fearful and ecstatic in equal measures. Every shadow had a whisper he could hear.

"I told you," Sandy said, slipping off her coat and flicking her thick tail. "I showed you what real hunger is. You need to understand suffering if you intend to use it, Donovan. You, your good friends in Europe, you all need to learn." She smiled coquettishly as she reached out, holding Donovan's cane by its black lacquered shaft. She grimaced a forced smile as she did. "Take it, Donovan," she hissed beckoningly to the naked steel Ram's head at its crown.

Thoughtlessly, in the throes of his first blood drunk, he did.

Invisible knives stabbed his palms, hot coals gnawing his sinews and he hissed as he fell to the marble floor.

They came in from the night, his pupils, his children, fangless and patient, surrounding him. "Your father is now our brother, children," Sandy said proudly. "Help him up."

Donovan let the cane fall as he was bodily raised high, his hand still clutched in agony. "What are you doing?" he pleaded.

"You're now reborn in sin, Donovan. We'll help you learn restraint as we have," Sandy said gleefully, as she beckoned the children through the great hall of Donovan's house. "You and I are going to spend a night in the Garden of Eden I've tended for so long. And there you'll see the dawn at last."

Gibbering mutters of pain and confusion, Donovan's new family bore him forth.

***

The Chevrolet rumbled past the city limits, meager possessions tarped. Through the long dark, road winds funneled through Crawford's fur and the doe that sat on the passenger seat next to him. He could smell her concern. "The moon's waning. I can hold it off tonight. It's getting easier I think."

Celeste looked him up and down and cryptically nodded.

They found a hotel in Columbus and Crawford foraged a dump for a catch to feed on. Samson found the meal awkward, but Celeste killed the feral rodent for him, drinking just a little. Necessity took over and Celeste kept close, minding the young Nosfur as he fed.

Setting out at sunset, they were in Virginia by the following morning. Crawford got the two situated at another hotel before promising he'd return.

Hours later, the road map drifted to the back seat on a thin spring wind as he pulled into the homestead that had been kept in his wife's family for two generations.

Kamila knew. She stood tall on the farm-house stoop, tail drifting with patience and black-furred arms folded. Crawford noticed the Ford truck slumping by the small barn and smelled drifting scents of spring chick and feline. Kamila had help now.

Maybe just help.

He killed the engine and heard the music of poultry in congress. Kamila was still, silvery whiskers twitching and nose testing scents as Crawford left his hat in the car and approached, injured hand in his coat.

"You know a doe?" she asked indifferently.

"A friend. The cat?"

She was amused. "Hired help for the chicks."

Awkwardness made his hands heavy. "I signed and mailed it all," Crawford said. "The papers will be here in a couple days."

Her eyes narrowed and she looked away with a deep breath. "Come in," she let the door swing in its hinge at her tail.

The house hadn't changed much, a little cleaner. She'd bought a wireless at some point that drifted out an ad for pelt cream. Fanny Brice began crooning after.

"Cigarette?" she offered. Crawford took it with thanks with his good hand.

"Lucas is playing over at the neighbors. He may come back soon, I don't know." She kept her eyes on his as his own darted around. No toys anywhere, not Lucas' ball or his wooden farm livestock. He was getting older unseen.

Lit, they sat in same room where Crawford had methodically bounced Lucas on his knee and clinically watched for the signs of delight, only seeing confusion at a father both there and not there. They smoked in quiet, and Crawford felt time crawling as she waited for him to say his peace. "I asked for no conditions. When the papers come, I'll be out of your life for good if you want that."

Kamila said nothing, merely waited.

"I just want, I need Lucas to know that I wasn't the father he needed, any more than I was the husband you needed. I still love both of you."

"But."

Crawford forced his ears to stay level. "But nothing. I came back from France with doubts about myself and the world and didn't know how to talk about them."

She turned that over for a while and he saw tinctures of pain that she'd all but papered over. "You could have said anything, and I would have listened. I would have helped you figure it out. It hurt in ways I can't describe when you wouldn't."

Crawford steepled his hands as he tried to find the next words and was surprised when she gasped.

"Crawford, what happened to your hand?"

Dammit. He went to hide the wound away but realized that was useless. "War wound. Chicago was...I've left that behind."

"What happened?" The concern he'd become so familiar with was back, sympathetic without judgement. If flowed like a cool lake over him and he felt sorrow for what he'd foolishly relinquished with her.

"It's fine, Kamila. I came here to talk about what I've done to you. And Lucas. That's what matters. I came to come clean."

Silence fell like silk between them.

"Kamila, I had a...discovery over there, during the war. I figured out recently what I'd long denied. It was something that you or our conservative parents wouldn't have found acceptable."

"Something blasphemous? You were never that religious."

"No. Not to me anyway. Not when I figured it out."

She took a deep breath, her smoke rising, ever rising. "Something sexual?" She wasn't angry, just curious.

Crawford opened his mouth and closed it.

Kamila cocked her head and took another draw. "You were in a war Crawford. You think it never crossed my mind that you found a French wolf over there with the right scent or curl to remind you that a gunshot could end it all and cauda carpe?" Kamila's love of the classics, rearing its head again. "If I'd gone over, it could have happened to me," she added dryly.

"What if it was a badger?"

"Then it was a badger. It's the modern world now. What was her name?"

"His name was Reggie."

Ash fell off her cigarette and onto a folded knee. She was still again. "How long have you…"

"I'm not fully…queer. Or maybe I am. I like women too."

She stubbed her dying smoke out and hastily went into the pack on the small table between them for another. "So, it was guilt and not disinterest…our last time."

"Confusion mostly. Fear too. I couldn't write to you when it first happened. I didn't know what to say. Letting you think it was somehow you over all those months…that was just cruel, I see it now. And cowardly. It's my fault and nobody else's that you stopped loving me. You couldn't do otherwise."

A flame sparked light in Kamila's eyes. "I didn't ask you to leave because I didn't love you. I asked to leave you because I did love you. Both Lucas and I did, too much." She puffed her cigarette and sent its spirit up. "Loving someone can hurt more than not loving them can, Craw. And I wanted to love you. I couldn't just keep you here and be indifferent to what separated us. That was torture. Better to have a lost love hurt for a while than hang on to what might be nothing." She looked outside. "Do you get it?"

"I do." He wished he didn't.

"I'd have been mad. Confused too. But telling me could have helped us help you." She sighed reluctantly. "And love would be there. It's never in just one place or just one way." Kamila stubbed out her cigarette and her eyes were wet. "That's the hardest thing to understand. You could have loved this badger for a while and loved me hence and I'd have accepted that. You'd have just needed to give me time."

"Our parents…."

"Would learn to understand. Get me on your side I can make them understand. Religion doesn't even care that much if you read the bible front to back." She leaned back and thought. "Well, your late father was too into the blood of Christ chapters of the Ark parable. Now…if this Reggie was a vegetable eater instead of an omnivore, he would have had a shit, let's face it."

Crawford laughed. It came so sudden and surprising that he choked on the drag going down and had to fumble to keep the stub off the floorboards. Tears were in his eyes when he was finished. "It woulda killed him."

Kamila smiled and closed her eyes for a moment, letting relief wash over them both. "So much pain from so simple a doubt."

Crawford got himself under control. "But it didn't feel like a simple doubt. The pain it could have caused you, and Lucas…I'm so sorry that I made it worse, for him especially." Crawford remembered the note he'd quickly scrawled that morning in his pocket and fished it out. "I wanted to give you this, for him, just in case I didn't see him."

She reached out and took the folded stationary from his hand. "Is this confidential?"

"No. You can read it before you give it to him. It's as much honesty as he can handle. I never stopped loving him for a second. Or you. If you read it and don't think he should have it, then I understand. I won't hurt him again."

Kamila set it aside and said nothing for a time. The tension that cut the air when they had sat down had all but fled. "So, is this goodbye?" she said simply.

If it has to be. If it must be. He saw the pain in the eyes of one whose wound was closed but so ready to open once again. "The papers will be here soon."

She blinked. "Tell me before you go if there is someone else. Are you moving on?" There was hope in the question.

Crawford nodded and Charlie was in his mind's eye. "There is."

"And do they know what you have inside?" She was even more hopeful in that question.

Crawford didn't want to lie anymore, so he swallowed. "They do."

"Good." Kamila smiled a smile he'd seen reveal a thousand things in nine precious years. "I've met someone too."

They parted warmly, sun passing the zenith into early afternoon, clouds anonymous wisps in the blue sky he'd long stared into with his son.

404

Crawford drank in familiar details and turned one last time to smile at the wolf at her stoop, chickens singing, tail moving with the wind about her.

Crawford drove west towards the hotel, the homestead receding in his mirror and came upon a copse of trees on his left where youths were swinging from low branches, shaking apples loose. A half dozen cubs of every species, ruminant and carnivore played together, and their laughter chimed over the field. Among them a stubby grey wolf cub in denim, suspenders trailing off his hips with his tail, gave chase to a loping weasel in play. He was in Crawford's sight for just a moment, then gone in a flick of juvenile glee.

He could stop the car. He could get out and say goodbye to Lucas, but it would only serve himself to do so and wound the cub when he had to leave. Crawford's promise to save his son from further pain would be kept.

Crawford drove on, laughter fading behind him and felt a fullness in his heart that he couldn't contain. He pulled off the road a little further on where the Ohio River wound past, cutting a glassy ribbon to the center of the country. Crawford cut the engine and stared down its visible stretch, his focus blurring the deep blue of the water's crystal surface and the pale sky above where the clouds had fled. Both worlds he sought came together into a singular clarity and at last he cried.

Epilogue

Other Windows

Children from the forge found their way to the cellar, miles and days away.

Fangs grew back slowly, but they caused no harm. The call that led many of them to the hallowed place promised purpose, a future.

Far from cities where wants and warrants tangled, far from townships and territories where stills boiled new stakes, the forgotten and the free tended the cellar's precious manifest.

Within countless bottles swam distillations of spirit, shed morsels of tortured, hopeful lives. Some were the solitary fragments of souls departed but many tenuously held to creatures still rolling and squabbling through the world. All were equally precious to the Sisters.

Regret found a dying sibling and pressed the pillow down. Hope turned cards over and found fate unkind. Ambition saw the bend in weakened steel that killed a patriarch over roiling waters and fear broke budding love on a battlefield's mud under destiny's cruel wheel.

Lovingly the bottles were turned and polished, the burning embers of a thousand thirsty, desperate lives.

The sisters welcomed the new curators warmly and nestled them safe in the dark where the march of the world could not harm them. Safe from the daylight sun they were nevertheless gifted with countless ghosts to aquaint with.

Hands lovingly drew a bottle off the rack and the life inside was studied for all its pain and beauty. "It's like a window into heaven," the beaver said, whistling through the gaps of his missing fangs.

Over his shoulder, one of the sisters sighed with the weight of knowledge. "For some," Baliosi said, eyes drinking in the same light. "For some."

Acknowledgments

The Dry Spell was a five-year project from its initial conception to final readthrough and depended on the help of several dedicated readers and editors who helped perfect the brew you've just consumed.

Special thanks to my writing and reading group, NightEyes DaySpring, Utunu and Domus, who provided insights, grammatical chiselling and candid feedback regarding these characters and their messy, sordid, yearning lives. Thanks also to K.C. Alpinus whose valuable historical and characterization suggestions imbibed even more magical properties to Chicago's steel bones.

Thanks very much to Teiran and Fuzz at FurPlanet for taking this novel on, with Zia McMarten also offering helpful suggestions. And I can't forget Kyell Gold's invaluable advice in navigating the furry publishing sphere. You can get access to those insights yourself by signing up for his dispatches on his website.

Finally, very special thanks goes to my mate, Kim, who has been supportive throughout the whole project and forgave me many a night with my face buried in lore or historical analysis as talking animals dragged me through their many tortured calamities.

Dry Spell wouldn't be in your hands without any of these players, and I'm forever grateful for their help.

About the Author

Ryan Loup-Glissant, (AKA Slip-Wolf) has been writing and publishing furry science-fiction, horror and fantasy for 15 years from various haunts in the West Greater Toronto Area and Niagara Wine Region. The Dry Spell is his first novel after a long affair with short fiction.

He's travelled extensively, loves reading history and fiction of all types and is obsessed with crashing genres into each other at unsafe speeds. When not doing this, he does relatively safer things on motorcycles.

Also by Ryan Loup-Glissant

Novels (as **Ryan Loup-Glissant**)

With **FurPlanet**

The Dry Spell

Short Fiction (as **Slip-Wolf**)

In Print with **FurPlanet** and in e-book form with Bad Dog Books:

Relics, Rabbits and Tuscan Reds – *ROAR Volume 6*
Kypris' Kiss – *ROAR Volume 8*
Ashes – *FANG Volume 6*
His Palace – *FANG Volume 7*
Heavenly Flesh – *FANG Volume 8*
I Went Back 50 years and killed the Vicious Tyrant Adon Howlitz and All of You are Welcome – *FANG Volume 9*
Waters – *FANG Volume 10*
Smokey and The Jay bird – *CLAW Volume 1*
Every Breath Closer – *Inhuman Acts: a Collection of Noir*
Sighs for the Labyrinth – *Dungeon Grind*
Chain Link – *Will of the Alpha 2*
Mustard Mulato – *Will of the Alpha 3*
A Melody in Seduction's Arsenal – *Gods with Fur*
Lime Tiger – *Dogs of War 2*
The Oroborous Plate – *Bleak Horizons*
Vanilupus and Other People's Wits Take on the Inhospitable World – *Tales From The Guild: World Tour*

In Print with **SofaWolf Press:**

Jewels of Remorse – *Heat Issue 11*
Unfading – *Heat Issue 12*
Skyleaper – *Heat Issue 13*
West – *Heat Issue 14*
American Heat – *Heat Issue 16*

In print with **Weasel Press:**

Due – *Knotted Volume 1* (Also available as an e-book with Bad Dog Books)
Paint the Square Cut Sky – *Fragments of Life's Heart Anthology* (available as an e-book with Bad Dog Books)

www.ingramcontent.com/pod-product-compliance
Lightning Source LLC
Chambersburg PA
CBHW071146020726
47502CB00002B/289